Occupied

Andy Luke

Copyright © Andy Luke 2021
Amazon Edition

Cover Illustration Copyright © Katarina N. 2021

Edited by Claire Burn.

All rights reserved.

ISBN: 9798475199923

The right of Andy Luke to be identified as the Author of this work has been asserted by him in accordance with the Copyright Designs and Patent Act of 1988.

This may be a work of fiction. Names, characters, businesses, places, events and incidents could be either the products of the author's imagination or used in a fictitious manner. Any resemblance to actual persons, living or dead, or actual events may seem purely coincidental. Occasionally seeming typesetting errors may represent Belfast's uncontested windy climate.

ALSO BY THE SAME AUTHOR

Gran: A 24 Hour Comic, https://archive.org/details/GranA24HourComicByAndrewLuke

Absence: A Comic About Epilepsy, https://absencecomic.com

Bottomley – Brand Of Britain, To End All Wars, Soaring Penguin Press

Axel America and the US Election Race, AG Publishings

Spide: The Lost Tribes, A Vanguard

Chaos Magic: Collected Poems 2011-2020, A Vanguard

For more information, please visit
https://andy-luke.com
https://patreon.com/andyluke

GLOSSARY

Ach – exclamatory phrase expressing light regret or disdain
Away ta fuck – do be on your bike, dear fellow or milady
Aye – yes, that is correct
Babbie – a baby human infant, oft loud
Black bastards – vulgarity in reference to the police, used in anger
Blue Peter badge – a valued prize for national service
Boke – the occasion or item of foul vomit
Bollocking – a severe reprimand
Bollocks – 1. nonsense, 2. general exclamation, 3. satisfactory result, i.e. 'the (dog's) bollocks'
Boutye – 1. hello, 2. how are you?
Catch a grip – a call to be sensible and re-orientate
Craic – 1. an enjoyable social time, 2. banter, exchanged witty remarks
Cheers - general expression of gratitude or celebration
Chinned – to connect one's chin with an oncoming fist ('you're lookin' chinned)
Chip in – to contribute
Dander – a relaxed walk with no particular purpose
Dole – 1. social security benefit, 2. social security benefit offices
DUP – Democratic Unionist Party, ruling Ultraconservative group in NI
Eejit – a sensible person who performs idiotic action
Fag – cigarette
Fruitloop – one who does not possess the insight of an eejit
Gaff – home, the place where one lives
Game – willing ('I'm game')
Gander – to make visual inquiry ('have a gander')
Greasy spoon – a low budget cafe restaurant
Gub – 1. mouth, as in the noun gob, 2. to punch
Gulder – a loud shout expressing anger
Gurning – crying or complaining

Halfers – a transaction involving 50%
Hallions – a worthless or contemptible person ('bunch of hallions')
Hole – 1. bottom, 2. anus, 3. vagina, 4. over-research
Lavvy – lavatory, where you take a piss or shit
Lost the biccies – 'they lost their temper' (commonly), or 'biscuits'
Melter – annoying person (e.g. 'you're melting my head')
Minging – stinky, unpleasant
MP – a minging fruitloop, eejit or hallion given to gurning
No dozer – someone not easily fooled, not a heavy sleeper
Orange Order – male Edwardian cosplayers, comprised of Orangemen
Pigs – plural form vulgarity for police officers
Pished/pissed – drunk, also 'pish' as in 'piss', to urinate
Pissing down – raining heavily
Quid – a pound sterling
Roadkill burgers – microwaveable patty w. dubious ingredients
Roll-up / rollie – hand-rolled tobacco cigarette
Scally – a confidently disruptive or irresponsible youngster
Shag – vulgarity for the act of sex, as in screw, bang, poke, hump or shaft
Shinners – short for Sinn Fein, ruling party in NI for re-unification
Slabber – n. one who shows off or talks excrement, v. slabbering
Slag off – to share negative or malicious personal opinions clandestinely (slegging)
So it is – expressing agreement with one's own preceding statement
Spide – a young lower class loutish male usually in sports clothes (fem. millie)
Sunshine – condescending address to a subordinate; corrupted endearment
The Troubles – N. Ireland's 1969-1998 low-intensity conflict
Themmuns – collective term for an othered, perceived opposition

To lamp (someone) – to strike, punch or gub
Toe-rag – despicable person
Wee – 1. small, 2. intimate, 3. piss ('our wee country')
Your ma / your da - insult, vulgarity to imply sexual relations
Yous – collective form of you ('yous uns')

EOGHAN

Where the tents rattle off their frames
And we, the people, needed this space
Brother, what they built will be our bay
No coffee shop, Beaujolais or B.K.
In the absent moment Britain built to bring us in
Where we grow a small patch of green

Politics, no, I'm not interested mate.
There's children in Effrica. Do that if you want to do something.
I think its very important, this sort of community work.
It was seeing those thousands march across the Brooklyn Bridge...

Azrael West. 9 to 5. Gales. Squally depression.
Bible weather becoming Cerberus and bipolar.
Morning Star. 24 shower. Fog to bleak to Blake
Rough wind east I'm slouching towards B & M.

WE ARE THE BOYS OF NORTHERN IRELAND LIBRARIES
WE CAN READ BOOKS AND WE'RE PROUD DICTIONARIES
THERE'S ONLY ONE JAMES JOYCE, ONE BERNARD MACLAVERTY
COME ON YOU CAMUS; COME ON YOU NOAM CHOMSKEEEEY!

Day after day when sleep is full-head
Kettled time, unemploying consent
I raise my thumb and my plectrum and stand
and make clear my squat pen protest.

No walls to trap us, hell, no roof
The art of empathy, a just space

Well, just one art and there they gathered
For thy art I wore on my sleeve, here where
Time concreted over and grew a small patch of green
Where the tents rattle off their frames.

1

Leon's fingers tangled themselves in the pit of black cables as the TV headlines blared at the back of her head. The lead news story was a dog who could drink water. As she fidgeted with the leads the image of the newscaster drifted like an electronic ghost, adding to the extra-terrestrial quality of the subtitles. Leon's black clothes and long hair sparred with the glow and her nose twitched in the flickering. She gave up and got up, showing the knotted cables in her hand.

'Give me my tobacco,' she said.

'We're out,' said Padraig.

'WHAT?'

Padraig was mid-twenties, with an unusually large head, especially his ears which sprung out of a baseball cap over a grey hoodie. He shrugged. Fred crouched beside Padraig on the sofa, a small mess of a lad with disjointed teeth and a weaselly face.

'The tobacco I asked you to keep for me?' snapped Leon.

'Sponsor's tax,' said Fred.

Padraig laughed and laughed and laughed. 'Mwah-ha-hahaha! Mwah-ha-hahaha!'

'We're a pair of human filters,' pleaded Fred.

'Yis are a pair of oppressing patriarchal melters,' yelled Leon. She stormed past them and whipped her coat off the chair, slammed the door behind her.

'Yeeee-ohhhh!' roared Padraig.

Eoghan McBride was watching Amy Goodman, presenting the news through *Democracy Now*, on his computer screen.

'*Monsoons in Thailand killed hundreds and caused millions of dollars in damages. The Chinese and US governments have given aid with Japan and New Zealand promising to follow.*'

'Jesus,' said Eoghan.

Eoghan McBride, twenty-nine years old, sighed and ran a hand through his brown tufts. He adjusted his glasses and reached across the computer desk for his pouch, papers and filters.

'*...four hundred and seventy-seven Israeli prisoners in exchange for defence forces soldier, Gilad Shalit. Another five hundred and fifty are to be released...*'

He liked that Amy Goodman balanced the bad news with the good. Democracy Now, rather than Democracy Ka-Pow.

'*It is thought the new Libyan government will declare the official end of the war soon.*'

Eoghan felt a hand on his shoulder. Josie leaned in, and he felt her black locks warm the back of his neck. They covered his skinny head and drooped down on his grey thermal pullover.

'Honey, Gary's here.'

'Oh! Already?'

He shuffled the half-rollie back into the pouch. They hugged.

'Don't be bringing the flu home with you. Wrap up.'

'*Basque separatist militants announced the end of a forty-three year campaign of political violence...*'

He put on his beanie cap and reached for his coat. I'll be back for tea. I promise not to fraternise with the pigeons.

'It's pissing down,' said Josie. 'Cats, dogs, hamsters, gerbils.'

'*...Tunisian Constituent Assembly, the first free election since independence in 1956...*'

Gary Carell didn't enter the hallway. He had a rucksack, taller than him, taller than the door. He'd broad shoulders and his face was a picture of health: square chin and nurturing smile. Running in a by-election as a *People Before Profit* candidate years before, he was unsuccessful only so far as reaching the Stormont government. Everybody around there liked Gary Carell.

'Austerity measures and the financial crisis continue with rising unemployment. The doors of St. Paul's Cathedral in London remain closed for the first time since Word War Two...'

'You ready to go?' said Gary.

'You've a filled rucksack,' noted Eoghan.

'Rucksacks.'

Eoghan looked down to another, slanted against the wall. He stepped out, and closed the door over. It was spitting rain as Eoghan and Gary made their way downhill to the city. The over-filled rucksacks wobbled about above their heads.

'There's a gazebo on your back. Artisan protest, with a hint of Baden Powell,' said Gary.

'Hopefully without the young boys. Are you going to --'

'I think so,' Gary said. 'Listen. John can't make it. Would you speak in his place?'

'Me?'

The police drove by, close to the pavement, scrutinising the pair. Eoghan and Gary passed the art college and arrived on Donegall Street. Under the needle of St. Anne's Cathedral was a hairdressers, a sandwich shop, a printer's, and Writer's Square. The Square, more like a convex hexagon, was a nexus of streets and alleys, with the police ombudsman on one corner and the electoral office on a corner at William Street. Literary quotes were engraved on some tiles and small stone arch at one entry off the empty pavilion. Outside William Street an old man in a wax jacket and coal hat approached.

'Are yous the communists?' he asked.

'Ah... no,' laughed Gary.

'I hereby swear I am not,' said Eoghan. 'Nor have I ever been at any time, so help me God.'

'Aye. Ye'll be laughing on the other side of your face. This here is an illegal protest.'

The old fella wandered off and they carried on across the pavilion. At the far end was a steep set of twenty steps. A lanky woman in her early twenties sat there, with green hair falling out onto a pink jacket. She'd too much make-up on, accentuating her other-worldly quality, and her thin twitching face shimmered as she spoke.

'You're here to do the talk,' she said.

'Sorry,' said Gary. He shook her hand. 'Have we met?'

'We talked on Facebook. I was at your rally last week. About the 1932 strike. I asked if I could photocopy your poster.'

'Catriona Kennedy,' said Gary.

'Yeah. Cat.'

Eoghan smiled. 'Those flyers are all over the place. Thanks for that,' he said, trying his best not to sound sarcastic.

Cat helped as they unwrapped the gazebo and fitted poles, slotting it into the ground-posts as the winds battered them.

Windows opened from the *Shac* housing accommodation block. Residents looked down from the seven storeys of twelve glass panes built into flat red brick resembling a hive. Below there were nearly two hundred people on the square's pavilion, its circular style and tall steps giving it a colosseum-like appearance. Among the crowd Leon watched the speaker, Deirdre, a frizzy blonde haired woman in her forties. Deirdre was covered in hi-vis. She held a pushbike with her on the steps, the megaphone in her other hand. Eoghan and Cat stood left, keeping the gazebo from blowing over the knee-high fence into the shrubbery that lined one side of the pavilion.

'Sorry, I'm a bit out of breath,' Deirdre said, though showing few signs of it. 'Dame Street camp send their regards. People are unhappy... about the banks, the IMF, the Irish and European parliaments. But we, we are in the first stages of a global movement. Gathered, for equal rights. Let's make that happen!'

The crowd applauded and Deirdre rolled her bike down

the steps. Gary took up the position.

'Thank you, Deirdre. Cycling a hundred miles from Dublin to be here! Now, I think we can take another speaker. Give a warm welcome to a good friend, from the Socialist Workers, Eoghan McBride.'

Eoghan stepped out of the crowd and got slaps on the back from Gary and Michael. A tubby grey pigeon flapped its wings on the step beside him and paid close attention.

'Thank you all for coming. So here we are. Across the world there's a new optimism in the Arab Spring. Uprisings in Bahrain, Yemen, Egypt and Syria. Yet we're stuck with the same old liars. Governments and the opposition working, not for us, working with bankers and multi-billion dollar companies. I'm sick of it. Sick of choosing sides from the no-choices they give us.'

'YEAH!'

Though she was far back, Leon could see Eoghan spitting with the anger.

'Those old oligarchs,' he shouted. 'Their Titanic has sunk! Winter is coming!'

'The King of the North!' someone shouted.

'Mwah-ha-hahaha!'

'The fuck?' Leon murmured. She looked around, annoyed Padraig was there.

'People are waking up,' said Eoghan. 'People affected by the cuts, by the austerity drive. Seventeen trillion in bail-outs, thirty billion to end world hunger. Do the maths. How about we don't wait? Until another hospital is privatised? Another school closed? Let's draw a line!'

'Right on!'

'They need to understand we are not going along with this. We control our own fates. Let's pitch tents, here, tonight. We have nothing to lose. Let's occupy this spot and show them, we control our own fates! Their time is up!'

'G'wan son!'

'YEAH!'

The crowd was bouncing. Eoghan stepped down amid applause, screams and hugs.

'Jasus, where did that come from?' said Gary

'You were gonna do it anyways, sure.'

Gary got back up the steps, and waited for them to settle.

'Well I can't top that. You heard the man. Bring tents, bring your friends and their tents. Bring tea and food and say we're not moving!'

They'd make their stand to the front of the Square, starting in a half-secluded grassy nook. On the path Leon and Kiera – rain-coated and seventeen with red curls and all excited - tied the striped gazebo to a shrubbery fence. Beside them was a triangular grass patch against the wall of Shac's block of sheltered accommodation. The main patch in front of them was shaped like a trapezium with room for sixteen tents before the pavement. They'd pitch round two strong trees and Anto Brennan's Spanish Civil War memorial, a bronze sculpture of an International volunteer. Leon read the engraved inscription: *'Dedicated to the people of Belfast, the Island of Ireland and beyond who joined the XV International Brigade to fight Fascism in the Spanish Civil War 1936 – 39, and to those men and women from all traditions who supported the Spanish working people and their Republic. No Pasarán!'*

Path and grass already muddy, Fred joined the poles by their elastic innards. In his hands they came together to look something like a Wicker Man, animated by a drunken Ray Harryhausen. Padraig unfurled Gary's bright red tent, and Daniel held one end of it which flapped against his black bowl cut and dark thermals. Cat and Kiera sat on the wall and laughed at their efforts.

'Aren't you in my art class?' asked Kiera.

'Thought you looked familiar, said Cat. 'Fuck's sake. Are boys not supposed to be good at putting tents up?'

'That wind,' shouted Fred. 'A devourer of worlds!'

'We're overthrowing capitalism,' said Padraig.

'We are?' Fred asked.

Gary read aloud the note sewn-in to the tent bag. *'Take the pins and join them to form extending structure.'*

Cat took that as her cue to get up and assist. Meanwhile, Leon pushed through the twenty or so activists and reached Padraig and Fred.

'This is my thing,' she shouted. 'It isn't your thing!'

Fred burst into laughter.

'Away ta fuck. We've every right to be here,' said Padraig.

'You can help,' said Cat.

'You two are only here to cause trouble. They're no help!' yelled Leon.

'Awk! Sheet's all caked in soil,' said Cat.

'I follow the news,' insisted Padraig.

'You didn't hear them to the saleswoman in *Castlecourt*,' complained Leon. *'Why are the female plugs on your PS2 not shaped like vaginas?'*

'See I told you it'd be like this,' said Fred. 'Come on. Kebab shop's two doors up.'

Padraig let go off the sheet. Daniel tried to catch it and it struck him on the cheek. Kiera joined them to pick up the slack.

'Where's the flysheet?' she asked.

'What about the poles? Where do they go?' said Leon.

'You fold the poles inside it so it stands on its own. Like a Wendy house,' said Kiera.

'I don't recognise your binary gender-coded artefacts,' spat Leon.

'It's supposed to be a dome,' said Gary.

'Aye. Designed by Salvador Dali by the looks of it,' said Cat.

An hour later Eoghan returned by taxi with his guitar, an overnight bag, and a second tent. Padraig and Fred migrated from the kebab shop with a more pro-active outlook, yet they weren't help enough to keep up with Eoghan's canvas as it soared over the pavilion. It came down at the steps, scrubbing Padraig with wet dirt. Gary stopped it moving with a well placed foot on the trailing string.

'One way, then the fucking other,' said Padraig.

'That's climate change for you,' said Fred.

Eoghan said to Gary, 'If Josie asks, tell her I stayed at yours, will you?'

'Huh? Why?'

'No reason.'

'Let's mount it here and take it across. We want these poles through the lining again,' said Gary.

Gary rattled the poles as the others climbed over and cleared ropes to the sides. Fred unrolled the thick tarpaulin and Padraig fiddled with the cross-beams as the gales moved the half-tent around. A dollop of rain spurted off Eoghan's lenses and dribbled down.

'Ach! Right in my fucking eye!' he squealed.

Padraig said, 'Same thing happened Peter Robinson. His Iris got wet! Mwah-haha-haha!'

'Okay, this looks like what a tent should look like. Let's see if it pitches like one,' said Gary.

The rain splashed loudly pelting the top of the gazebo. Cat, Kiera and Daniel shivered underneath it with their hands stuffed in her pockets. Cat examined Daniel. He'd barely said two words the whole time.

'Was that a Spanish accent I heard earlier?'

Daniel's face said nothing.

'Pub over the road if you need a piss,' she said.

Kiera said, 'Think the kebab place will do us tea?'

The lads came around with the black two-man unloved ridge tent. They hooked the pegs and buried them in the soil: hammer slap, slap, and secured with a heel. Then came the guy-ropes: one anchored inside the drain gratings; one rope lashed around the taller of the two ash trees. As soon as the tent was mounted the shower and gales stopped altogether.

They brushed and shook out the rain from their hair.

'When you speak to Josie say this was your idea,' said Eoghan.

Gary laughed, and looked out at the two tents with pride. 'It's a global movement. Is Josie not to know you fired the starting pistol here?'

'Your speeches are up on YouTube already,' said Cat.

'Crap! You're kidding!'

'This needs a test run,' said Padraig, and he unzipped the black tent.

Cat wondered, 'Don't you need a ground sheet in there?'

With Fred at his back Padraig dived inside on his belly. Fred followed him, straight into a puddle. Padraig screamed.

'Fuuuuuck!'

2

A street-light beside them on the path turned out pockets of rain onto the October twilight. There were thirty people gathered around the small, striped gazebo. Some sat on the fold-out chairs or along the wall and a good few just stood. There was the guy always selling *Socialist Worker Party* newspapers; five visitors from the neighbouring *Shac* block of flats; a half dozen people hid their faces from the two news photographers; there were a couple of people wearing Anonymous masks and they made hip-hop hand gestures for the camera; there was Martine, who said she knew everything that had to be done, and Leon waited on her hand and foot. Martine was padded head to toe with combat patterns. Her hair was hazel, cropped, and her eyes were wide as if in a permanent state of shock. She stood over Deirdre, who sat with a pen and a pad at the ready.

'Okay! Ready to begin?' asked Eoghan. 'Okay! I nominate Gary to facilitate. All in favour?'

A few raised their hands and twinkled their fingers. Padraig mocked them. 'Is this a Quaker thing?'

'They don't all have epilepsy,' said Fred.

'Oh grow up,' spat Leon.

'Motion passed,' declared Eoghan.

Padraig put his tongue between his lips and let out fart noises. Gary demonstrated the system they would use for hand signalling during meetings. 'So disagree is hands down. Flat hands for not sure. Triangle for a point of order.'

'Heh! It looks stupid?' said Padraig.

Eoghan was becoming exasperated. 'It means everybody will get the chance to speak. One at a time would be easiest. And let's be respectful of other people's opinions, even if we don't agree with them.'

A boy racer with strobing rims sped down the street pumping out *Carnival Spide,* heavy on the bass. *Thunk thunk thunkthunkthunkthunk, thunk thunkthunk.*

'The first order of business is organising the camp,' said Gary. 'The shelter loaned us these chairs, but we'll need our own. Man there...' He pointed to a large fella, older with a greying beard, checked shirt and industrial blue trousers.

He spoke with soft Southern tones. 'My name's John. John Travis. I've chairs and other supplies at home. But I think the wisest course of action might be to draw up a wish-list.'

'Agreed,' said Gary. 'Has anyone got suggestions?'

'Just off the bat, water containers; a first-aid kit; dish-towels and cloths; and a washing line.'

'Sorry John, could you repeat all that?' said Deirdre.

Kiera struggled to free her rain-coat from under Eoghan's chair leg. Eoghan was watching the photographer who circled them with his tripod. 'Press?' he asked.

'No! Lift it up!' said Kiera.

'What are you going to need a washing line for in this weather?' Padraig scoffed.

Martine pushed out past them and made her way to the photographer with the tripod. 'Who are you? Where are you from?'

'Uh, Timothy, from the Telegraph. I just need to get a few —'

Martine raised her voice. 'I didn't give my permission!'

'Trying to stitch us up! Tory propaganda!' Leon tutted, brushing her hair inside her scarf.

'Mwah-haha-ha. Yous look like Al Qaeda,' said Padraig.

'What harm will it do? The demo is already on the BBC website,' explained Cat.

Eoghan groaned and drew a few stares.

'I just wanted to hear what you have to say,' said Timothy.

'Do you hear that, Leon?' snapped Martine.

'Oh yes! The women have been given permission to speak!'

'You'd rather he censor you,' quipped Padraig.

Gary put his fingers in the form of a triangle. 'Please. Respect goes both ways. Everyone should be welcome to contribute. Cat?'

'We'll need torches and gloves.'

'A can opener,' said Padraig.

'Towels,' said Kiera, a pitch higher.

'Camping supplies,' muttered Deirdre as she scribbled.

Cat shivered. The rain was off but remnants flapped from the slim corners of the gazebo's canvas. Cold was chopping through the open space. More passing drivers honked their horns, and a few random wanderers came by having had their curiosity piqued.

'A brush and shovel. Plastic bags for rubbish,' said Cat.

'We should buy things from the charity shops first, before we go to the High Street,' Leon told the group. 'And if we use their bags we should turn them all inside out. We shouldn't be seen endorsing any corporation.'

Martine shook her head. 'I'm not sure. If we leave the branding outside, we're making it clear these multinational patriarchies --'

Leon raised an eyebrow. 'That they're full of shit?'

'That they need to recycle,' snarked Martine.

'We'll need a dedicated dry area for toilet rolls and paper work,' said John.

'And a toilet!'

'There's the pub,' said Eoghan.

'We'll want a fire for boiling water and cooking food.' John raised his hand as he described it. A metal bin, about four foot high.'

'A bin on fire in Belfast, okay,' said Deirdre.

'I know fellas who could set a car on fire,' joked Padraig and he erupted into harsh cackling. 'Mwah-ha-ha-ha! Mwah-ha-ha-ha!'

There was an uncomfortable silence. Martine held up her arms and crossed them, signalling a block.

'Look out Padraig,' exclaimed Fred. 'This one's into karate!'

'Is this all just a joke?' barked Martine. 'Are we all just here to muck about?'

'Yeah. Are we going to be talking revolution? Or are we going to do something?' said Leon.

'Time is moving on,' said John.

From the street there was a long honk of a car horn and a little lad with a baseball cap, a spide boy, leaning out of the window as he screamed. 'Yeeee-Ohhhhh!'

'Who's going to watch the tents at night?' said Cat.

Eoghan finished rolling his cigarette and raised his arm. Leon and Gary put their hands up too.

'Great. Half shift, then I'll relieve you,' said Gary

'Mwah-ha-hahaha!'

'I'm willing to sit up through the night, but for now I've a tent to put up. Excuse me,' said John.

'Okay,' Eoghan said. 'Any other business?'

'Do we need any more? I'm freezing my balls off,' said Cat.

'We need to list our aims and objectives,' Leon instructed them. 'What are we protesting about?'

Eoghan sparked up his cigarette, inhaled, and came out with an American accent. 'What are we rebelling against? Whatta ya got?'

'Mwah-ha-hahaha!'

'We need a social contract to establish safe spaces,' declared Leon.

Gary solicited a list of goals for the group to accomplish: decreasing homelessness; opposing government cuts; turning back austerity; getting good media coverage; maintaining the camp and welcoming newcomers. People drifted in and out. Eoghan got away to help John, while Gary found himself caught up in the chatter around workshops and petitions and Leon's want for a march to City Hall that night.

Chill cut on the path as Cat and Mary walked around to the pavilion. Mary was in her mid-twenties with long blonde hair and a slight sadness about her mouth. Cat studied her outfit, a grunge shirt and sari, hipster acid-wash jeans. She said she had seen her at *Fresh Garbage*, an indy clothes shop. They walked up to John and Eoghan, unpacking a tent.

'Sorry, what did you say your name is?'

'John.'

'I'm Eoghan. Wait. Are you *that* John?'

'Well, I've been called many things, though mostly distinguished as John.'

'The John who messaged me? You set up the blog?'

'I saw that,' said Cat.

'No, not I,' said John, and he tossed a bundle of guy ropes to Eoghan.

'Well we can't refer to you as John,' Eoghan said casually.

'Why not?'

'Well the other John is around here somewhere.'

'Is that a Southern accent?' Mary enquired.

'Galway, my dear. Though many years have passed since I set out from the gusty port of Salthill.'

John bent down and tugged the tarpaulin. It wouldn't move and when he looked up he saw a new crew of reporters, sound-men and photographers stood along one end. He waved them away. 'Excuse me? Would you mind? Thank you, sir.'

'We'll call you Galway John,' said Eoghan. 'So we don't get you and the other John mixed up.'

Galway John's tent was a green tunnel model which would sleep three people. It had seen a few tours. John said he was was experienced camper and the group got it standing in no time.

'I'd love to stay the night,' said Cat.

Eoghan pointed to the red dome. 'That's Gary's. I can go in with him and you can have mine. There's no sense in the tents being empty while we watch over them.'

'If you like I can drive you home to pick up bedclothes and an overnight bag,' said Mary.

The assembly was breaking up then. Deirdre skipped off on her bike, passing the press. Gary settled into his dome tent and Eoghan pushed a rucksack in after him then went to his own tent and pulled out the black guitar case he'd brought with it.

Padraig sat on the little wall beside the gazebo. He told Fred he wanted to hang about for a while. Fred said he'd warm up the PlayStation. Eoghan, guitar case in hand, passed him leaving and joined Padraig.

A galoot called out at them from the road. 'What are yous protesting about anyway?'

'Incest!' yelled Padraig.

'It *is* the best,' said Eoghan.

He took his tobacco from his pocket. Padraig scrounged for one so Eoghan rested the pouch on his lap, and gave up the first rollie to him. Another young driver went by, with bass-thumping dance music: *thunk thunk thunk thunkthunkthunk-thunk, thunk thunk thunkthunk.*

'Boy ravers,' said Eoghan.

'Squatting out another load,' Padraig said.

'Circus freak music isn't it?'

'Saw them in Bangor there with it turned up to eleven in the car park,' said Padraig.

'If it was me I'd put on one of those *Teaching Company* lectures. Circle round them. Blast it out of sub woofers.'

'See yer man has his tent up.'

'Aye. That's Galway John. He's pitched it in the middle so we can put the others around them; to build up heat,' said Eoghan.

'Yous'll hear each other snoring,' said Padraig.

'Well, that's solidarity. Snore-idarity,' said Eoghan.

Over on the grass in front of them, Martine raised her voice to Galway John. 'We don't need your male charity!'

Galway John told her softly, 'If you two don't want it for tonight, it can go to someone else.'

'What the fuck?' murmured Eoghan.

'You can't be a gentleman nowadays. Those wee girls are mentalists,' said Padraig.

'Leon's alright.'

'I know Leon. She's a neighbour of mine. Total fruitloop. A bit psycho. Sorry. I'm Padraig.'

'Eoghan' pocketed his tobacco pouch and they shook hands.

Leon was yelling now. 'We are women, not freeloaders! We work for our accommodation!'

Padraig shook his head as his rollie burned black and dropped away. The argument faded. Galway John had said something to calm the women down and Padraig watched the three of them walk off to the kerb.

'Scuse me for asking, Eoghan, but what do you hope to accomplish?' His query was sincere. 'Not all that guff from earlier. I mean you personally?'

'Reasonable question. I want... a sustainable socialist revolution. Without catching pneumonia.'

'Mwah-haha-haha! I don't know about socialism,' admitted Padraig.

'Are you on the brew? Welfare?'

'Yeah.'

'Well that's socialism. Are you not political at all?'

Padraig nodded firmly. 'I watch Alex Jones. *Prison Planet. Truth Live.* You ever see him?'

'Fuck Alex Jones! *We're on the march, the empire's on the run.* Alex Jones is up his own arse. Wanker nutter with a gun,' said Eoghan.

'Aye, but he doesn't report anything without giving the source of it,' said Padraig.

'I don't think *Daily Mail Online* counts. But yeah, sourcing is important. Cite, don't shite, as they say.'

'I watch *The Kevin Trojan Show* sometimes, but something about him... I don't trust the guy.'

'Trojan's a mixed bag. Some good investigating, some tabloid slabbering,' said Eoghan.

'He'd find fag ash on your sleeve and tell everyone you're on sixty a day.'

Eoghan thought hard. 'Didn't he have Nick Griffin on?'

'He did. Fair and impartial, my arse.'

A car door slammed and they turned their heads to the kerb. Galway John held a cardboard box in his arms. Martine followed him up the path carrying a gas stove, and Leon, struggling with a portable generator and a folding table. The two women put it up and Galway John unpacked his box. There were pots, plates, mugs, spoons, tea and coffee.

'Fuckin 'ell, it's MacGuyver!' yelled Padraig.

'I had an idea this was going to kick off from the news. I won't be sitting up this bitter night without a hot Java beside me,' said Galway John as he set the box on the wall.

'Tell me there's whiskey in there,' Eoghan begged.

'Nothing would please me more than to share a bottle of Highland's Mountain Dew. Alas, no.'

'He's brought hot chocolate,' cried Padraig. 'You're the star, big man!'

Martine and Leon lay back watching the rain spread in bubbles down the side of the green canvas, lit by the orange street-lamp overhead. Slapping beads sprinkled canvas in spitter-spatter. Galway John had supplied them with two groundmats, a sleeping bag, a duvet, a pillow and an inflatable one. They lay with the covers wrapped around them and watched a floating daddy long-legs suddenly scramble from a gust which made it seem for a moment that the tent was caving in.

'I wish those lot would shut up out there,' said Leon. 'Still, John came through.'

'It's all about domination though,' said Martine.

'Probably. You hear him call us girls? Fuck. Off.'

'It's like Camille Paglia says. Not a shred of evidence supports the existence of a matriarchy anywhere in the world at any time. Look at their love of rugby. Essentially it's gladiatorial combat.'

Rain drops tapped hard, a few seconds apart, on the walls of the tent. Leon rolled over on her side. Martine continued to talk. The rain got heavier, and the walls were weeping.

'Mass propaganda for a nationwide militia. It's essentially military slavery,' sniped Martine.

They could hear Padraig laughing outside. 'Mwahahahahaha! Mwah-ha-hahaha!'

The belly of the tent fluctuated, sagging then pushing and the rain crackled and rapped, like a billion silica gel balls ricocheting.

'Sounds like a Gatling gun,' said Leon.

'Could be weather weapons,' said Martine. 'You know? The CIA?'

Leon rolled on her back and opened her eyes to study the pattern of the rain, alike some moving multi-cellular bacteria. The wind flapped inside the tent, punching the plastic walls and tearing the corners.

'This is what Hell sounds like,' she murmured.

That night Eoghan sat on the wall under the gazebo with his guitar and sang them a song made up on the spot.

'And what did you protest, my blue-eyed son?

And when will you sleep, Eoghan sang as he strummed.

Sparking the gas cooker, John joined him in proclamations.

Padraig knew few words but recognised great observations.

Cat licked up a cigarette like a mouth organ.

Rolled up and saw the heavens lay a barrage upon them.

The teapot was boiling and streets they were screaming.

Mary crooned while sky tumbled, her trousers stream-
ing.

They heard a voice cry out, *fuck up, I'm trying sleeping!
No good having tents if you're not gonna sleep in them!*
And it was long, it was long, bloody cold, so bloody long,
And it was a long night that did fall.'

More hours into morning's darkness, the gazebo shook in bitter cold wind. So too did the bones of the three men on wet chairs underneath. It swept through the raised planter of shrubs and pushed the limbs of two mighty trees. The three tents underneath folded and puffed in the spitting rain.

'Those branches will come down in a storm,' said Padraig.

'Nonsense,' said Galway John. 'They're too big. Those, my boy, are ash trees. See how they curve towards the ground, then turn upward at the tips?'

Eoghan's round glasses brushed against his brown beanie. A red bandana hung over his black denim jacket and stone-washed shirt. Though well-read and deeply cynical, his expression maintained an untarnished innocence. Padraig's glasses were strikingly similar to Eoghan's, hanging lopsidedly on his hook nose inside the grey hoodie and brown jacket. They could pass as siblings but Padraig's face was spotty, coloured by years abusing cheap tobacco, Buckfast tonic wine and microwave burgers.

'What do you make of all that shit with MPs' expenses: a fort, and a duck pond?' said Padraig. 'And Iraq?'

'The cunt Blair knew – he *KNEW* it was a lie – and no-one wanted that war,' said Eoghan.

'Except God, whispering in his ear about killing everyone.'

'Blood sacrifice for oil,' said Eoghan, wearily.

The rain played percussion on the little table, gas stove and iron kettle. Galway John looked out to Donegall Street: the parked cars, abandoned by who-knows-who; four street lights either side stressing drizzle; the broad steps and high columns in front of St. Anne's arched doors and forty feet above the spire, a light at its base like a near shackled star. The cathedral bordered on Talbot Street, its depths hiding upmarket restaurants. The intersection of hollow streets pushed the wind down the wall of the flats beside the tents, creating what Galway John called 'a wind trap.' Behind them, grit and packaging swirled at times with a whine to a rising moan. Industrial sized bins stood at the rear of the flats fenced off from intruders where a security light illuminated Eoghan's stream of piss.

'Galway' bent forward shouldering a sixty-two year burden. Eoghan noticed his bald spot among fraying brown hair with white flecks. His blue eyes burned with passion and pride. He began to talk through his overgrown beard about the old outside water taps. There was one to the rear of Writer's Square, past William Street, by the social club. Eoghan and Galway set off across the exposed pavilion with the kettle and a pot.

'You just have to know where to look for them. There's one on the other side of Royal Avenue. One by the art college. Ah, do you see it?'

The tap was stiff but when it flowed it was unleashed, hammering the kettle and spraying Eoghan's trousers. Back at the gazebo – where Padraig fixated on a slimy snail stretching between concrete tiles – Eoghan dried off with one of Galway's tea towels.

'What are yous actually gonna do out here?' asked Padraig as he rolled mucus from his eye.

Galway took a moment before firing up the cooker. 'Plenty, my boy. A shelter for the homeless. A food bank...'

'They run workshops and lectures at OSX,' said Eoghan.

Padraig looked confused. 'What's that?'

'OSX? The London camp,' said Eoghan.

'Sounds like a Windows upgrade. Mwah-ha-hahaha!'

'Shush!' warned Galway.

'Sorry John, sorry. Hey, it must be 3 a.m. now. Surely.'

Eoghan shrugged. 'My phone battery died.'

Galway sat down beside them and rolled up his four-layered sleeve to reveal a silver-strapped analogue wristwatch. 'Twenty past two,' he said, then took out a metal tobacco box.

Eoghan said, 'There's loads of things we can do here: live music, poetry, street theatre.'

John's brow wrinkled. 'That was the point of this square ten years ago when they built it. A place for community run arts and culture. Of course there's no funding for arts events unless they happen to be sponsored by Balfour Beatty.'

'Balfour Beatty sponsored arts?' asked Eoghan, and heading off Padraig's question he added, 'A major arms manufacturer.'

'Just speaking metaphorically,' said Galway John. 'You lads are too young to remember but there was a time we had some pride in our city.'

The younger men laughed.

'That's going back! Mwah-ha! Fuck all that 'our wee country' shite.'

Eoghan nodded and waved away a vexatious fly. 'Nothing's changed. Ruled by a bunch of Edwardian in-breds in London, and a bunch of kiddie-fiddling clergy at home.'

'Eoghan, tell us how you really feel,' scoffed Padraig.

'I will! The political divide here in Northern Ireland has got fuck all to do with religion. It's never been about that. It's all just smoke and mirrors to cover a load of extortion rackets.'

'Aye,' said Galway. 'Too many people too hypnotised by tribalism to see that. We're probably best not talking about religion at all. As a rule, I'd say.'

'So why are you here?' asked Padraig. 'Protest's fine, but I've got frostbite in my bollocks out here.'

'Drawing attention to the plight of those less fortunate? By voluntarily going through what they're forced to go through every night,' said Eoghan.

'It's captured the attention of the press already. As it

should,' said Galway.

'As a permanent presence the camp-site reminds them that our issues should be on the agenda. There's more than Unionist-Republican power plays. There's the rest of us caught in the middle.'

'Fucking cold,' said Padraig.

CAT

Open geodesic funnel by smoke's fires, by city exposed. Rain drips nights, peels pink the thighs.
Turrets on this castle from my heart down to my toes, shoulder's limbs, round my nose; wet, stink and cold.
Numbering nothing to say or do but sit wrapped by now, knees amorphous for subzero shift
address crystalline bodies and smoke moist ears, goosebumps crushed; I shiver, shudder, by torrent's tears
And billion taps, comets on the road; folding arms for relief up the sleeve; and atichoo cold.

Like the mass walk-out from school here they draw the line to hold the line. Fair trade and equality,
everybody! Sometimes the mucus on the edge of my diamond crusted eye, some days the fire
wants my cry. There's evening minutes I will not keep; a spreadsheet shakes me to pull the sleeping bag
lining close. Letter writer wonders what's the use. There are nights we bed down high on rebellion,
head vibrating, when our dug-in tunnel's pillows are our flags. In sleep a call to charms, to
City Hall, dream climb railings, everybody Occupy: this General Assembly for all.

And the wonders how we'll ever wear it out as an after-thought to teach-ins, homings, food drops,
counselling. Here's to banker's trials bridging elderly go free on shopping aisles. Scream for you.
Cars in shoals and clapping feet. 'Ole, ole, ole ole!' 'Oh lay!' Shifts over, rigid, hold onto
MPs in prison. The city needs another garden. Ex-prisoners to read and write,
a University entrance module as a light. Catriona's tired and it's

the wrong kind
of tired. Heavy red blusher on cheeks smeared on temple, scarlet pillow. Head sweating, feels so tired,
wavering in and out of mind, sick to loose an arm across her hip, rests on magic and drifts.

3

The wind changed direction every few minutes. It rose in speed and dropped and rose again. The temperature went back and forth. Mary slept on while Cat tried to escape the tent, pushing in on itself. A harmless tiny spider fell unnoticed onto her coral jacket. The bright daylight scrunched her brain. As she exited, she tripped over a rope and almost hit hard soil. She bent over and fixed the peg back in the ground, jacket hanging from her bony frame like a wing on a moth. Under drowned dyed green hair and colliding cosmetics, she recognised the three figures at the gazebo were pretending not to have noticed her near fall.

'We survived our first night!' announced Leon. 'This is the dawn of a new era. Isn't it a great feeling?'

'I feel like shite,' said Cat.

'Did you not sleep well?' asked Gary.

'Slept okay. I just don't like waking up to find I've dribbled on my shoulder. I'm only twenty-two. Here, what time is it?'

Daniel shrugged.

Leon straightened her beret and flicked her long black locks over her shoulder. 'It's time to bring the message of resistance to the people. No more! No more! El Pasarán!'

'I reckon that's half nine,' quipped Gary.

As if in response cathedral bells awakened in dull tolls. Cat raised her head. St. Anne's narrowed in span with its height, rising to the spire. She looked to the turrets and columns for the belfry. None was found.

Dong dong dong dong!

'Okay. Ten o'clock,' Gary conceded.

Leon held a lighter horizontally to the ring of the gas cooker. Before it lit she'd burned her thumb twice and evoked a trinity of fucks. There were a half dozen mugs and Cat found herself complaining about all of them being dirty. Gary apologised and said he'd clean them up. She sat by Daniel and rolled a cigarette. Daniel swept a hand slowly through his chestnut hair, shielding brown eyes from the sun's rays. Like Leon he dressed all in black but in stark contrast he said nothing at all.

'Mary will be up soon, the noise of them bells. Where's Martine?' enquired Cat.

'Left. Said she was having back problems. I thought you might have heard her,' said Gary.

'She was making a point about the male-built environment,' said Leon.

'I see,' said Cat, nodding her head in time with Daniel.

Gary called for someone to watch breakfast. He took the kettle to the wall and began scrubbing cups in a basin of shallow lukewarm water. In its place on the hob Cat found a pot of baked beans, and on the second ring, rounds of bread in a dry frying pan.

'Interesting way to do toast,' she said.

'You know in some parts of England they fry their bread in a puddle of oil,' said Gary.

Cat said that was disgusting, and the others agreed.

Teenager Kiera Shaw's frizzy ginger hair bobbed over the back of a pale blue raincoat and orange sweater, half-way to her denim jeans. Marching down the hill with sturdy boots to the camp that afternoon she found a dozen more curious visitors: lone activists; whole families; reporters. A pigeon that navigated a tent rope as it landed quickly took off again as a masked Anonymi tripped over it. A few feet away the pigeon hummed with laughter. People were painting signs. There were donations: cutlery, towels, blankets and pillows – more than they'd room for, said Mary. Kiera talked mercurially with complete strangers. The excitement was there in her sparkling eyes and spread over her freckled cheeks. Mary by contrast was overwhelmed with the attention. Weariness pressed down on her bushy blonde eyebrows. Her pale blue jacket stank. The phone battery was dead and it annoyed her more than it should have.

Gary was well known locally as a community leader and would-be independent politician. His likeability had women of all ages fawning over him. There were ladies with plastic Tupperware containers sealing in cold pasta and soup. They came in their numbers with metal tins full of chocolates and shortbreads. Someone brought them fire-lighters and a pink basin. Eoghan and Leon divided their time between helping sort donations and soap-boxing to all and sundry, loving the attention the cause had brought and keen to share their knowledge on everything from the *Reclaim the Night* movement to the Spanish Civil War.

All eyes turned to the sound of Galway's jeep, bumping as it mounted the pavement. He and Gary came with an olive green ridge tent and talked of using half of it to store supplies. They also brought a second gazebo, identical to the first. They were trying to figure out the best way to align the two to provide cover from the elements. Everyone had their take on it.

'So, we rope the new one at the corner, with its back to the wall to buttress against the wind,' said Leon.

'No, no, no. We don't want our remaining supplies blowing everywhere,' said Galway.

And visitors were full of enthusiasm for their efforts.

'I really respect what you're doing.'

'Do you have everything?'

'What are you protesting about anyway?'

Cat's face lit up when she saw Kiera, and she welcomed her back. Mary told them she needed a break from the mayhem. They offered to join her for a dander around the streets. So they passed the *Shac* flats and crossed over by *The John Hewitt* pub. Signs of the 2008 recession were evidenced in boarded up small shops and mighty office blocks, dust thick on windows and cracked paint on doors. They stopped by Exchange Place, a curved archway over a tight dark alley bordered by *Printer's Cafe*. Kiera put her nose against the glass of the tiny closed deli.

'I wonder if they have that bread with the crusts you can chew on. Practically a sandwich in themselves.'

'Somewhere around here, I think this one, used to be the *Rape Crisis Centre*,' said Cat. 'It was shut down a few years ago. Lack of funding.'

Mary's damp frayed scarf blew back in her face as she walked with them. She read the letters off the glass front of the spacious photo gallery.

'*Belfast Exposed*. I got enough exposure last night to do me.'

She read the sign above the door next to it. 'What's this, *Northern Visions?*'

'It's a television station,' said Kiera. 'You won't get reception unless you're in Greater Belfast.'

'They're one of those community initiatives. Online too,' said Cat. 'Maybe we can get them to run a feature on the protest. We're near enough we could have our own daily show.'

Mary laughed. Cat took out a flimsy pocket notepad, clutched it in her palm, and scribbled down.

'What are you writing?' asked Kiera.

'Details. If we're going to do this we need to reach out to groups across the city. People who can support what we're doing.'

They rounded the corner to the more opulent Merchant Street.

'*The Rainbow Network* are around here somewhere,' said Mary.

Cat paused again to scribble.

'If you're making a list, maybe we should go and sit somewhere. Like a cafe,' said Kiera.

'It's Sunday. There's nowhere open,' grumbled Mary.

They worked their way round to North Street, running parallel with Donegall Street. There were sole traders and small businesses which would have been selling groceries, tattoos, books and film memorabilia. Weeds grew around the grey shutters of the former *North Street Arcade*. Cat looked up to the red chip paint on the rusted arch and remembered the poetry cafe, record store and pet shop. She'd been fifteen when the arson attack gutted it and the feelings of the community that dearly loved the arcade. It had remained derelict since.

'Seven years ago. Bastards,' said Cat.

'My mammy says it was paramilitaries working for some developer,' said Kiera.

'Open secret,' said Mary. 'Someone wanted to bulldoze the whole thing and start again.'

A few doors down there was a greasy spoon cafe. The women looked to one another, and nodded. Cat led the way along white tiled walls to the hot glass shelf with a lone abandoned sausage. Yellow cardboard cut in star-shapes gave prices of some items. The waitress left her perch facing the mounted television. Cat asked for coffee, and Kiera and Mary for a pot of tea between them.

Cat bent her frame between the plastic table and chairs, bolted into place, and took out her pad and pen. 'We need to reach out to the unions some more. I think that's Gary and Eoghan?'

'Not Leon?' chided Kiera.

Cat laughed; didn't elaborate. They were all thinking it. The coffees arrived quickly.

'There's a local *Greenpeace* group. They'll be no bother tracking down,' said Mary. 'Greenpeace John was there yesterday. With the bike?'

'I met a woman with a bike,' said Cat.

Mary looked up from rubbing a napkin against a stain on her trousers. 'That's Greenpeace Deirdre. She's good too.'

'What about *Women's Aid*?' said Kiera.

'They're based on the Malone Road. Nearly three miles. *The Women's Resource Centre* at *Queen's* would be closer,' said Mary.

Cat noted the details. 'It'd be helpful to have contacts at both places. I think there's a women's shelter on Fountain Street?'

Coffee disappeared. Cat asked for more. The waitress let Mary out back to use the toilet.

'Do we have time for another cup?' asked Kiera.

'What time's the General Assembly?'

'Seven, I think.' Kiera checked her pocket for her phone and cursed, discovering she'd left it at home.

'Mary was talking about getting a wee solar charger,' said Cat, writing again.

Kiera put her finger over her lip. 'Shh.'

They listened, and heard the dull toll of cathedral bells.

'Six o' clock,' said Cat.

The waitress placed their coffees beside them.

The Monday morning traffic passed in roar and rumble over wet tarmac. There were five tents. The additions were a two-man olive ridge tent, for sharing with supplies, and Mary's blue tunnel two-man. The second matching gazebo was up, with green and white stripes, and strapped to the first. Gary's old electoral poster boards were reversed for use as signs with hand-written slogans placed around the square:

'No House. No Job. No Fear.'

'Join the revolution. Bring a tent. Join A Protest.'

'The Occupy Movement? The 99% bailed the 1% out. We are still loosing Hospital A + E Schools and Welfare!'

'99% don't get why the 1% just won't take responsibility.'

Eoghan, Cat and Gary were meeting and greeting. Cat happily received another tent and two empty ten litre bottles for water. The man promised chairs and bundles of blankets. One old woman took Eoghan's hands and pressed a pair of gloves into them. She'd also brought them *Fifteens*: coconut and marshmallow tray bakes, wrapped in foil. Cat and Mary had just set these on the trestle table when they saw Kiera. They walked the path to the kerb to meet her. Suddenly, unzipped orange tent folds cast Leon kicking into the world.

She'd just awoken. Her face was matted and she was dressed how she slept – in black from boots to beret. 'Morning sisters!'

'Oh. Still here?' chirped Kiera.

'In the new world of the Amazonian warrior women,' exclaimed Leon. She tugged on her own stained sleeve, smelled an armpit and wrinkled her nose.

'The Atlanteans you mean,' said Cat.

'Martine forgotten us again today?' Mary asked.

'She's very busy,' said Leon, zipping up the door.

'Good,' said Kiera cheerfully.

Mary feigned innocence. 'You don't like her?'

'Bitch was ignoring me. Not a word. Like I'm invisible.'

'Maybe she doesn't like gingers,' said Cat innocently.

Kiera laughed. 'Fuck you!'

They wandered over to the gazebos and sat looking out at the lads pitching the new tent.

'Maybe Martine's on the spectrum. Like that fella with the laugh,' said Cat.

'Fucking Padraig,' growled Leon.

'Do you two not get on?' wondered Cat.

'He's my downstairs neighbour.'

Cat raised a painted eyebrow. 'Are you two... are yis...?'

Kiera chimed in. 'She means are yis banging?'

'I don't have time for relationships. I'm too engaged in the struggle,' said Leon firmly.

'Does he ever laugh during sex?' asked Cat.

'Okay stop, I'm gonna wet meself,' said Kiera.

'Padraig Mahon is diametrically opposed to everything we hope to accomplish here. He's an agent of disinformation with no moral guidance.'

Mary pondered this. 'So, he's an anarchist.'

Eoghan wasn't much use pitching the tent. He hadn't slept in two days and yawned too hard. He'd already slid in the mud.

Gary and the quiet lad, Daniel, caught him before he fell. Eoghan rubbed his eyes and when he took his hands away the bitter old man from before the rally was stood on the path in front of him. He was dressed in the same dark flat cap and black wax jacket,.

'I warned you this is illegal,' he said. He took a deep breath. His face was stern, his brow creased. 'Well. As a diligent member of the local community, I've lodged a complaint with the cops who will be around shortly to have yous lot rounded up.'

Gary's smile dropped. Eoghan shook his head, and felt his temper rise.

The old man took his time to savour their reaction. Then, he let out a wicked laugh. 'Hahaha, had yous goin' there. Oh! Funny stuff! Oh… ha. Really I'm messing. Don't look so scared.'

'Right,' said Eoghan, still not sure what had happened.

The elderly man wandered off to the road, all the while laughing to himself.

Joe Duncan was twenty-seven: tall, with a red chequered shirt on broad shoulders and ripped blue jeans. He was clean shaven and handsome with a wise twinkle in his eyes. Eoghan found him pleasant and unassuming. Gary begged their pardon and went off to Galway's jeep for another supply run. Eoghan took Joe to meet the others.

'Hi.'

'Boutye.'

'Yo.'

'How yeh doing?'

'Alright. Where you at the assembly last night?' asked Cat.

'Wasn't me,' said Joe.

Eoghan hesitated. 'But you're thinking of joining us?'

'Maybe.'

'That's good.' Eoghan beamed.

'Why is it good?' asked Kiera. 'He might be a serial killer.'

Leon shuddered. 'Oh God.'

'I could be.' Joe smirked.

'Are you planning to murder us in our sleep?' Cat enquired.

Joe looked about to say something, and then pressed his lips tightly together. Daniel, the quiet Spaniard, gave the biggest grin. Kiera put her head down and took out a silver cigarette case.

'He could be a spy, you know. In the sixties a tenth of American SWP members were Feds,' said Leon.

Eoghan nodded. 'The London Met run deep undercover agents: Mark Kennedy, Jim Boyling. Piece in *The Guardian* last week. Kiera! You're much too young to be smoking!'

'Too late, grand-dad. What time is it?'

Joe checked his wristwatch. 'Quarter past eleven.'

'Shit!'

'Oh God,' said Cat.

'We've a class to get to,' said Kiera.

They pulled out their bags from Mary's tent and ran across the road to the cathedral and onto the art college.

Using Galway John's gas cooker, Eoghan and Leon enjoyed cups of tea in the midday breeze. Daniel was laying out his clothes in the new tent when he heard John's jeep bump back up onto the pavement. A trailer was attached, loaded with a large orange sofa. He helped them hoist it onto the kerb, before Galway drove off to free up the road. They hauled the three-seater to the gazebo.

'Why would anyone want to throw this out?' said Eoghan.

'You could sleep on it,' asserted Leon.

'Oh! I could!' said Eoghan.

On Botanic Avenue, Shay sat on a blanket beside the *Spar*'s cash machine. He had a patchwork quilted woollen coat on over a tracksuit. Just twenty-four Shay had the looks of a teenager: waves of dark hair mopped around a warm, freckled face. Now the sun had stood down from its midday assault he sat in the late afternoon grime and shade. He saw the passing trousers, skirts, city shoes, and heels. His own trainers were still wet with the last week's rain. His fingers were hard with the cold and he trembled. Everything hurt, but he'd gotten used to it.

Mick and his collie, Murdock, stopped to see how he was doing.

'Not so bad, Mick. Keepin' 'er lit. Got my *Tayto* crisps. My board. Here, you couldn't spare us a roll-up?'

'Sure. Would ya hold Murdock a moment?'

'There's a good boy, good dog,' said Shay. 'Aren't ya? Who loves ya?'

'He loves you. There's a smoke for yeh, Shay. Y'want another?'

'Too kind, sir. Too kind.'

A woman joined them, two women. A pair of arty trainers and drainpipe blue jeans, and cheaper, casual shoes with rounder darker jeans. The sun struck his eyes as he looked up.

'Alright Shay,' said arty trainers. 'How you doing?'

'Who's that? Awk, Cat, darlin'. And… sweet Kiera! Didn't know you two knew each other. Small world, aye?'

Shay took Cat's hand and pulled himself to his feet.

'Don't bother getting up when I call,' teased Mick.

'Have you dyed your hair again, Cat? Swear it was blue last month.'

'Yep. And here I am. Lean, green fighting machine.'

'Why the fuck are you out on the streets?' said Kiera.

'Nah, nah, Red. I've got a sofa… or, I'm between sofas. The hostel…'

'Forget that,' said Cat. 'Get your stuff. We've got somewhere.'

'Aye?'

'We're camping out as a protest. Spare tents, hot water,

food.'

'Here, sounds good Red.'

'I saw your set up by the Cathedral,' Mick told them. 'It's worth checking out, Shay.'

'Okay. I'll have a gander.'

They said goodbye to Mick and Murdock, and made for Shaftesbury Square junction. Shay took the decline on his board, casters riv-rivetting on the brick path as he glided.

The radio piped through the evening mist, moistening the sofa which Eoghan, Cat and Kiera were squeezed onto. Gary and Shay sat on either arm. The seven o'clock news played on the radio nearby.

'News International have agreed to pay two million pounds to the family of murdered schoolgirl Milly Dowler...'

There were twenty or so gathered around for the general assembly. Among those standing they couldn't help notice the stern old man in flat cap and coal jacket. He seemed unimpressed. His eyes burned holes through them.

'Labour MP Margaret Moran is to appear at Southwark Crown Court facing twenty-one charges. Three MPs have been imprisoned...'

'Okay!' said Eoghan. 'Galway, would you get the radio? Cheers. I'd just like to say well done; all of us: forty-eight hours, people!'

Some twinkled and vibrated their hands, as per the agreed signal, and others applauded.

'You may give another round of thanks to Cat and Kiera,' said Gary.

'We asked about the art college. It's not agreed yet – we've to speak to security – but they may be willing to let us use the toilets and showers,' said Cat.

'The building's open twenty-four hours. So, fingers crossed,' added Kiera.

The group twinkled their hands again, and moved onto talking about getting a marquee tent to provide better cover.

Eoghan had recycled a soup can on the Sunday for a donations jar. There was little in it, but it was a start. Cat wanted a tent for Shay: perhaps he could share with Daniel? Shay put his hand up and gave a friendly wave. Daniel smiled and nodded.

'Good, good,' said Gary. 'Right. We've gotten more press coverage: *The Irish Times; The Newsletter; Slugger O'Toole; The North Belfast Herald and Post Incorporating...* sorry, I can't read that bit. Oh, this is important. There was someone here from *Shac* complaining about the noise.'

Eoghan pointed to the wall ten metres from them where rows and columns of windows marked out self contained flats.

'So if we could just keep it low? Be respectful of our neighbours. Thanks,' said Gary. 'On the subject of our neighbours, the Dean of *St. Anne's* was here. He said we can possibly use a room for meeting if the weather is bad.'

'He said something about giving him some notice,' Eoghan clarified.

'God!' cried out someone.

'He's not going to close the cathedral anytime soon,' remarked Galway.

'Too bad,' moaned Leon. 'Religion is the weapon of the war on drugs.'

Mary strained to comprehend. 'What... does... what does that even mean?' She began to laugh.

Shay chirped up. 'Drugs are still drugs tho.'

Cat raised her hand. 'I haven't eaten. Does anyone wanna go halfers on a pizza?'

'I'll chip in a few quid,' said Kiera.

'I could do with a bite,' Mary admitted.

'Great! What do you like for your toppings?'

'For goodness sake,' said Galway. 'A bit of discomfort, and you run for the nearest shop. Have you never made use of nature's store?'

'Aye, John,' giggled Kiera. 'We should be picking wholesome city berries. Maybe catch a pigeon. Put it under the grill.'

'Don't be silly,' said Cat. 'It wouldn't fit. You'd have to pot boil it.'

Galway harrumphed. 'The good people have donated fresh foods, canned foods...'

'Then,' said Cat, 'when it's tender, slice it into strips.'

'You could grill the skins,' said Shay. 'Get them nice and crispy so as to use them as dishes.'

Kiera dry heaved. 'I'm gonna boke.'

'Will ya get a move on? It's bloody freezing out here,' someone said.

Gary asked who would watch the camp over-night. Eoghan declined. He said he was beat. Daniel said he would.

The suspicious old man stepped forward. 'I'd be willing to help out,' he said. His voice was rough, and short.

Eoghan poised his pen over the notepad. 'Okay. Name?'

The leather-faced pensioner had a scowl that never moved. 'What's yours?'

'Eoghan.'

'You don't have to tell him!' Leon protested.

Everyone looked at Leon.

'What's yours?' asked the old man.

'Leon,' she said timidly, and then confrontationally, 'Why?'

The man had a low, deep intonation. Plainly he said, 'That's a funny name for a girl. Are you a lesbian?'

Leon was furious. 'What if I was? Do you hate lesbians and gays?'

'No,' he said. 'I just wondered why the boy's name.'

Gary opened his mouth to speak but Cat beat him to it. 'I wondered about that too.'

'If I was a lesbian why would I want a boy's name? I'm named after Leon Trotsky, one of the greatest communists of all time.'

'I see,' said the old fella. 'So you're a tomboy?'

'Tom isn't really a girl's name either,' said Eoghan.

Gary clapped his hands together. 'Soooo... next up. Talk of a march on Saturday?'

'Yes,' said Leon. 'I want a visible opposition to the bombing of Palestine. A march focussed on human trafficking. A protest against Edwin Poots. We'll call it *Demo Against The Dickhead.*'

'We should focus on one thing at a time,' Eoghan cautioned.

'What about…' Cat thought for a moment. 'If we have a demo on Saturday and follow it with an afternoon bringing people into the camp. Like an open house.'

'A day of assembly,' said Kiera.

'A Carnival of Resistance,' declared Leon.

Most of the group twinkled their hands in agreement. The old man – who would later admit his name was Bob – let it be known the hand waving looked 'a bit too weird' for his liking. Gary and Eoghan explained the hand signals to him but he didn't seem interested.

4

Wiggling fingers quickly became euphoric applause, then excited screams and foot stomping.

Of the dozen or so there only the old fella, Bob, seemed unaffected by the big announcement. His jagged outline didn't move nor his steely green eyes.

Gary was chairing the Tuesday evening meeting. He waited for the applause to die down. 'So to get back to what we were talking about: Eoghan, Cat and myself will take point on press relations. That's a good way to start, isn't it?'

'I can't believe it. Best email ever,' said Leon.

Eoghan looked up through the darkness to the light of the cathedral. The news had put him in a contented dream state. Gary waved a hand in front of him.

'Sorry, oh yeah, yeah... maybe he'll come by the Carnival.'

'Luke Devlin, the *Red Barn* busker's up for it,' said Cat.

'I know this fella: brilliant rapper,' added Shay.

'Anyone feeling a might colder?' asked Galway John.

The sky churned and then the heavens thundered. The downpour was sudden: relentless; everything fell. Those at the edge of the gazebo were drenched. At the back, it soaked the people on the orange couch, now a great sponge. Mary and Joe and the half dozen others huddled, crammed together, watching the tents collapse. It was supernatural, even by Belfast's standards. Belfast's gods, throwing tantrums. A few folk ran through the wash over the road to the pub. The ash trees quaked. Placards were snatched up and chucked over the concourse. Eoghan and Daniel ran after the essentials, the basin and pans skittering across the splattered paths. The gales tore at the guy ropes, tugging hooks out of the soil. Cat's tent suffered the worst, three corners to the sky. Galway John and strange old Bob braved torrents and mud to secure it.

Ten minutes later they were tying it down all over again, their fingers raw and stinking with dirt. Gusts tore off Bob's cap, exposing his bald head and big ears. The sky lit up over the Cathedral's needle and sheets of rain shimmied off the cars.

Leon, during a lull, thought she'd be safer in her tent and squelched off down the path. She used both her towels to mop the ground-sheet. Over the next hour she trembled in a shaking bed of oozing sludge, the pages of Klein's *No Logo* turned to mush. Her clothes clung: a black wetsuit. Rain pushed through the sides, sliding like mercury. The hammering became drilling.

She'd learn later the flood hit hardest to the north and west of the city but it rolled down from those points to the camp. The Rivers Farset and Lagan met half a kilometre away and washed closer to them. The drains overflowed.

It plundered all belongings. The merest touch of the side of a tent and ice water streamed on the skin. They shivered in their hives, limbs in pools.

Mary thought of her birthplace, Dublin, a hundred miles away. The storm had hit there first, and killed two people. Cat was in with her in the tunnel tent, a damp coat under punches. Shaking and half afraid the tree might collapse onto them, she unzipped the flap and her green head of hair dangled outside. The men had cleared the sodden couch away, to make more room in the gazebo.

Most campers sat there on the fold-out chairs for hours: smoking, drinking, cursing their stupidity. Ducking the raindrops that followed where-ever they moved to, sliding down their necks and their bum-cracks. Catching bone chill, sniffs and sneezes, losing tobacco. The water-fall filled up the cutlery tray and every pot and bucket plonked. It went on all night. Everyone met the ghosts of the street, and died a little inside.

At eight the next morning it finally stopped. Birds picked worms rising from the wet mud. There were socks hanging off guy ropes and sleeping bags strung between trees in the sun. Shirts and trousers dried over shrubbery fences and towels were laid out on the concrete path. Galway John took home what he could to be washed. Most tents had to be remounted. Eoghan, Shay and Mary went for breakfast at *Blinker's*, a greasy spoon which resembled the cafe in *Seinfeld*. Cat, Leon and Daniel stayed at the camp sliding Gary's old electoral boards under tents for protection from the muddy soil. There were plenty of boards and they were inserted under the door of every tent too, so people could protect their knees from the mud.

'I can't see us lasting to an election,' said Cat.

'If I had my way there'd be an election every week,' said Leon.

Cat sighed. 'So how would that work?'

'Family fun day,' said Leon. 'Many polling stations use schools, yeah? So you get in a bouncy castle to make it easy for the mothers. An ice cream van, and the community meeting in the playground, actually talking to one another. Jugglers, clowns, live music...'

'Hmmm,' said Cat. 'Like what we have planned for Saturday?'

'That's it. Voters will have it rammed into them the importance of education and art. The ruling class that have governed us for centuries would be over-turned in months.'

Daniel and Cat lifted each end of a tent, and Leon slid a board underneath.

'That aul fella was a help last night,' said Cat. 'Pity no-one can get a word out of him.'

'Bob. He told me to shut up,' said Leon.

'Well you and Shay, yis were hardly quiet. Daniel, you've been on night watch with him. What's he like?'

Daniel nodded, slowly. A subtle smile.

'You don't say much either,' moaned Cat.

His eyebrow twitched.

Leon tried to rally them back into action. 'You've gotta really lift it.'

'Huh. Uh! It must be water-logged,' said Cat.

An old guttural groan came from within the tent.

'Ah... maybe leave this one,' she whispered.

Leon's beret was perched on the ridge of her tent. She felt it: still damp. When she turned around she was full of anger.

Padraig strolled up the silver path with a spring in his step. He called out from his animated moon-like face, 'Goooo-ooood morrr-rning, Vie-et-nam!'

'Well look what the sewer spewed up,' snapped Leon.

Padraig put on his best Geordie accent. 'Day Five in the Occupy encampment, and Leon has been sleeping in a damp patch.'

'You're an idiot, Mahon,' she said.

'How are you, Cat?' asked Padraig.

'Cold, wet, malnourished.'

'And... Daniel?'

The young man stopped rubbing the grass stains on his black jersey. He raised his eyebrows, bottom lip pushed out faking sadness.

'Hell. The state of this place,' said Padraig. 'I guess Dovid Vonce was right.'

'Who's he?' asked Cat.

'Fuck-nut blogger,' Leon informed her. 'Claims we defecate in the streets.'

'Scatologist. Mwah-ha-hahaha! Mwah-ha-hahaha!'

Leon said, 'He's obsessed with us to the point you think he wishes he was here.'

Padraig rubbed his wool cap. 'To be fair, it is a swamp. Like on *M.A.S.H.* The Swamp.'

'The internet thinks we're all funded by George Soros,' said Leon.

Daniel nodded affirmatively.

Hot sun and clear skies dried out the camp quicker than anyone thought it would. Workers, shoppers and wanderers called by to check on their needs. Placards were laid over the sofa, though Kiera chose the safer fold-out chair as she hurriedly compiled a new wish list. She ticked off the fresh towels, blankets and roll mats as they came in. They filled the gazebo with crisps and chocolates, two tubs of tuna pasta, and a pot of soup. Joe came back, and Mary paid close attention as he helped her and Shay with their tents. A stray brown Staffy was investigating everything, and ran off with one of Eoghan's wet socks. Martine and Michael, one of the Anonymous, took Leon off to the pub. They were going to stick it to 'The Man' with a sit-in.

Among the visitors that afternoon was Jacqueline Hughes. 'Jack' was in her late-twenties, wearing a long plush blue dress and lugging a blackboard, no sweat on her golden tanned skin. Eoghan tidied up his neck-tie and fixated on her cropped auburn hair and stylish painted eyebrows. Padraig adjusted his beanie, and followed her glossed lips. She spoke with an English accent, and a hint of elocution lessons. Eoghan stuttered as he introduced himself and took the blackboard from her. He widened the frame so it sat up free-standing.

'I retrieved this from a skip last week. Thought perhaps you could use it.'

Padraig circled in, putting himself between Eoghan and Jack. 'It's strong. Maybe not storm proof. Thanks very much, love. So, I'm Padraig, and this is Cat.'

'Hello. Were you here for the storm, Padraig?' Jack asked.

Padraig pinched his beanie cap. 'Naw, no. I missed it. Just came down to help them recover.'

Eoghan masked the stain on his jeans with his hand and lamented, 'It was nasty. But we knew what we were getting into. It won't be like that every night.'

'A lot of people went home afterwards,' said Cat.

'I'll be going home if it starts tonight,' said Eoghan. 'Forecast's good for Saturday, mind.'

'Yeah, I heard,' Jack chimed in. 'Your *Carnival of Resistance*. All being well, I'll pitch a tent with you then. Is that cool?'

'The more the merrier,' mused Cat.

'Have you been on a protest before?' enquired Eoghan.

'Oh loads. I was at an anti-G8 demo in Gleneagles, Edinburgh, when they brought in the riot police. Well, do you know, one of them grabbed me and pulled me away. I pulled up the visor of his police helmet, and I looked him in the eyes and spat in his face.'

'Mwah-ha-hahaha! Mwah-ha-hahaha!'

'Sure, I'll show you round and let you meet a few of the others,' said Eoghan, and they took a walk.

'Padraig, you're drooling,' said Cat.

Hours later and the visitors were petering out. Of note was a stocky gub of a man, late thirties but prematurely aged. He stood fixed like a tree trunk halfway down the path and yelled at people under the gazebos.

'What are yous protesting about? What is all this?'

'We're actually a millennial cult,' joked Cat.

'It's true. All these tents contain rocket ship parts,' said Kiera flatly.

'Don't be cheeky, wee girl. Sure this is pointless. Why do it?'

'No reason!' Padraig yelled back. 'We're only here cause we get turned on by self-flagellation!'

'YOU WHAT?' he growled.

'Nothing to worry about! Austerity! Billions in bonuses! All made up! Just pretend! Even *we're* not real!'

'Ya fuckin' freak!' he spat, and raged off down the street.

Eoghan and Daniel returned with water kegs refilled. Daniel picked up a lone empty ten litre bottle and walked off with it. Cat made a face.

Eoghan assumed command. 'The first order of business is tea,' he said.

'Here, do you think Jack was serious about pitching?'

Padraig wondered.

'Who?' asked Cat. She shook her head, confused, and looked to Kiera, also confused.

'The English girl. With the long dress,' said Padraig.

Kiera brushed back her red curls. 'You said Jack. I thought you meant a boy.'

'With the blackboard? Sure, it was only a few hours ago'

Cat spluttered. 'Eoghan, half the city's in and out of here! Am I supposed to remember everyone's name?'

'Get used to it. This sort of thing doesn't happen because of three or four people,' he replied.

'Every person makes a difference,' said Kiera.

Cat swatted a fly away from her and replied, vinegary with sarcasm. 'Right. Like the people on Facebook. The comments are already filling up with twats claiming we're communists. *Yeah, they're really important.*'

Kiera laughed. 'I don't know what I'd have done without my punctuation being corrected!'

'We're all equal,' asserted Eoghan, and with his tongue-in-cheek he told Padraig, 'History will remember you as a great man.'

'Fuzz,' muttered Padraig.

Eoghan stroked his stubble.

Through gritted teeth Padraig repeated himself. 'Cops.'

There were two of them: a burly man in black flack jacket as large as the night; the second, a rake in his shadow. The larger one had owlish eyebrows and an intense glare above a broad grey moustache.

'Oh shit,' muttered Eoghan. He turned around and put on his happiest game face. 'Afternoon, officers.'

'Hello. How are you all?' asked the big one, his voice rough and stern.

'Tired,' said Cat, no pretence about her.

'The floods were shit,' said Kiera.

Eoghan gave her a dirty look and returned with an all-innocent gaze at the police. 'Is there a problem, officers?'

'Oh no problem,' said the big one. 'Though we hear it's going to be breezy tonight.'

'Right, right. And how are you?' Padraig chirped.

Eoghan fixed him with a dirty look too.

'We've been fine,' said the thin one, trembling. His features were less pronounced, cheeks set back and wide-eyed. He seemed to be taking in everything around him. 'I saw my mum, and we had scones earlier.'

'Well… okay…' said Eoghan, not quite sure what was happening.

Suddenly Padraig took a step back. Leon stepped into the circle, with Martine and Michael flanking her.

'*Who do you lot think you are? What gives you the right to poke your noses in?*' Leon raged.

'Well, we're police officers,' said the large one, not rattled.

'*Names and badge numbers,*' demanded Martine.

'Sergeant Oliver Barker,' the big man said, extending a hand, 'and this is my partner, Constable Stanley Corbett.'

Corbett smiled helpfully. He took out his wallet with an identification badge and passed it to Leon. 'We just came over to say perhaps you should move your tents.'

Michael, who'd had more than a few pints, spoke up in anger. 'They have every right to be here, occifers.'

'*Who says we have to move?*' Martine yelled. 'I am so sick of this. You pigs with your fascist, authoritarian, *SHIT*.'

Michael oinked.

Leon fumed. 'There's real criminals running around and you're so blind. Walkin' in here, with your swinging batons: who can we bollocks up tonight?'

'Leon! Martine!'

They ignored Cat. Michael made sheep noises.

'*This world is changing,*' said Leon. 'Your time has come!'

'You peelers!' snapped Martine. She opened up the phone on her camera and began recording.

Corbett replied calmly. 'I just meant –'

Leon affected a high society air. 'Junior will be so pleased I beat up a peacenik!'

'Fuck's sake, that's enough,' said Eoghan.

Barker stressed, '*ALL* Constable Corbett was saying was you could move the tents back some to get them out of the wind; while you only have a few tents?'

Martine folded her arms and looked away. Leon looked to Michael, who was already walking it off.

'We're sorry, officers,' said Kiera.

Padraig explained, 'Everyone here thinks they're massive bell-ends.'

Gruffly, Barker said, 'We spotted a skip up the by *The Irish News* building with some palettes in it. If you wanted to use them you could make a stronger buttress between the tents and the ground.'

'Thanks. We'll look into that.'

Eoghan's words trailed off. He heard a sorrowful sniffing. It was Constable Corbett rubbing his red eyes with a tissue, tears streaming down his cheeks.

'I'm sorry, I'm so sorry,' he cried.

'Oh Stan. Come on now,' said Barker sympathetically.

'I try, I really try.'

'You do, and you have a perfect record,' said Barker. 'She didn't mean it. We're all under stress.'

'Didn't she?' Corbett said. 'And she's right. Lily's probably filing for divorce. I did my best.'

'And that's all you could do,' Barker assured him, putting his arm around his partner.

Barker turned to Martine and Leon. 'You've really upset him, you know. Stan. Stanley. What about those gifts you brought?'

Corbett reached into his pocket and took out two big bars of *Fairtrade* dark chocolate. He reached out with them slowly, and terrified.

'Thank you,' said Cat, embarrassed.

Daniel returned. After setting down the water keg down

he walked over to them.

'Hello Daniel,' said Barker, more chipper now.

'Oh hi,' said Daniel. 'Thank you for the yoghurt. And Bob wanted you to know he really appreciated the bananas.'

The sun crashed when it set, spilled light drizzle on the general assembly. Yet spirits were high. There was going to be a celebrity visit, maybe at their carnival. Cat teased Mary about the looks she and Joe were giving one another. The stray Staffy – whom they'd christened Shelby after the dog Occupy Denver had elected as their leader – stuck his brown snout in a half dozen crotches, before Daniel settled him. Padraig's friend, Fred, joined them, and he said the camp needed to make clear their policy on pets in tents.

Eoghan was checking his smart-phone when he interrupted them. 'God. Have any of you seen this? About Oakland?'

'Why? What happened?' asked Gary.

'The cops came in: threw their tents in the bin. *WHAT? NO!*'

Leon urged him to elaborate. 'What is it?'

'Fucking no. *Fuck*. FUCK!'

Cat took out her phone.

Eoghan's face was white. 'Tear gas. Rubber bullets.'

Daniel gasped. 'Jesus.'

'There's flames in this one.' Cat showed Kiera a photo of an older man under batons.

'Christ.'

Bob shook his head in disgust.

'We'll put out a statement; and send them a letter of solidarity,' said Gary.

'I can post something tonight,' said Cat, her voice hoarse with concern.

Eoghan was furious. 'Next interview we do I'm making sure they see this.'

'How are things looking for Saturday?' wondered Mary.

'We need more flyers,' Eoghan told her. 'And we've to

email Billy's –'

'*Fucking black bastards*,' said Padraig, Eoghan's phone shaking in his hands.

'It's not right,' growled Leon.

'Jesus God,' murmured Shay.

There was a sudden south-easterly wind and the rain began to fall heavier. Chairs were brought in from the lash. No sooner than they'd done so than the wind eased and the pressure dropped.

A consensus was called to end the meeting. Then the rain stopped completely. Eoghan, Gary and Mary decided to go back to their homes. Padraig asked for the use of their tent. Mary told him 'under no circumstances.' Gary relented, and mimed handing over keys.

It was raining again just after midnight. The second gazebo offered little cover. The generator Galway had left them powered an electric lamp which glared upon greasy paving. Old Bob and Daniel were on night shift. Leon, Kiera and Shay were in no hurry to get to their sleeping bags and sat out with them.

'That sofa's going out,' said Bob firmly.

'No!' exclaimed Leon. 'I like the colour. It's like the one on *The Wire*.'

'It's piss,' said Bob.

Leon studied Bob with contempt but his stern features made her think twice about challenging him.

Kiera chimed in. 'Perhaps the Orange Order will take it.'

'The streaks give it a reddish quality. It's a Socialist emblem,' declared Leon.

'John said he'd shift it,' said Bob resolutely.

Cat joined them, with a blue plastic bag in hand. She pulled out a can and set the bag underneath her chair. She cracked a beer open, and swallowed.

'Uh, uh,' said Bob. 'You can't drink that here.'

'Why not?' she said.

'It's against the law,' said Bob. 'And didn't yous agree no drink, no drugs?'

Shay cried out, 'No drugs?'

Kiera let out an almighty sneeze.

'Bless you,' said Cat, and she took another swig of beer.

'Hey! I'm fucking serious. If the cops come it looks bad on all of us.'

'Lighten up, Bob,' said Kiera.

'Listen. Any shit tonight falls on me and Daniel. If you want to drink, take it to your tent.'

Cat's tent was a two-person light green dome model, with two net windows at the front. Keira stepped over the guy rope and hunkered inside with her.

'God, he's a grumpy old sod,' said Kiera.

'I heard that!' yelled Bob.

'You were meant to!' she yelled back. She zipped up the tent behind her and whispered to Cat, 'He's here all of two days. Who put him in charge?'

Kiera's own bag, roll mat and pillow were already laid out there. The tent was humid and damp. She took off her boots and zipped up the door. The street traffic carried past them in waves. The drinkers were raucous.

Leaving closing pubs for late-night clubs – from *The Merchant* and *The John Hewitt* to *The Kremlin* and *The Shoe Factory* – Donegall Street was the route. The precipitation put its pat-pit-pot upon the tarpaulin, wind changing its points of impact every minute. Kiera took a shot from her inhaler and Cat passed her a can of beer.

'Thanks. Do you think we'll stay the course?'

'If that rain's like last night, I'm off home. Fuck it.'

'I guess this camp isn't supposed to be a pleasant experience. Anyway, these should help us sleep,' said Kiera. 'Cheers to the beers.'

'Cheers to the beers.' Cat took a long, deeper glug.

'What a day.'

'You missed the big debate: twenty minutes on the pros and cons of *Buckfast* tonic wine,' said Cat.

'Chav's choice! Lurgan Champagne!'

'Some randomer wanted to know if Buckfast Abbey was Protestant or Catholic.'

'God save us,' groaned Kiera.

'Eoghan told him it's cross-community piss for undiscriminating idiots.'

Shay's freckled face appeared at the mesh, long chestnut hair hanging down. 'Hey, can I join yous?'

Cat sighed. 'Come on then. But just one. I'm friggin' wrecked.'

He ducked inside, tramping and wriggling and twisting so as to take his shoes off.

'Wriggly worm,' joked Kiera.

'I'm *Earthworm Jim*,' he said.

'Your feet stink,' remarked Cat.

'Sorry, love. So what's the craic?'

'Kiera was asking what she missed.'

'Oh, that guy! *Agent Mulder*,' said Shay.

Cat smiled and shook her head. 'The fella was going on about the Bermuda Triangle and the CIA...'

'Apparently the triangle was built in World War Two to keep Nazis out,' explained Shay. He lifted a thumb-sized paper packet out of the fold of the tent. 'What's silica gel?'

'Don't open that!' Cat warned him. 'Manufacturers put them in things to keep them dry. It's like salt.'

'Can't smoke it though?' he wondered, fondling the beady packet.

'Or put it on chips,' said Kiera.

Shay mused, 'I wonder if could you make a suit out of them. Keep dry with hundreds of little packets taped to your arms and legs.'

Kiera exploded with laughter. 'Have you been smoking them already?'

The tent shook in the wind and then fiercer. Padraig's

face appeared at the netting. He pulled on the zip. 'I heard there was a party!'

'No, absolutely not,' said Cat.

Fred was behind him. 'It's raining!'

Kiera raised her voice. 'Guys, there's no room.'

'Aw c'mon,' said Fred.

'It's my pub and I make the rules,' said Cat.

'Health and safety,' added Kiera. 'What are you doing back anyway Fred? Thought this was a load of old hippy shit.'

Padraig cut him off, pleading with Cat. 'At least give us a few tins. We'll have our own pub.'

'Bloody hell. Fine!'

Cat gave Shay two tins which he slid through the opening of the zipper. They listened as Padraig unzipped Gary's tent, the next one over, and cracked open their beers.

'You shouldn't have,' whispered Kiera. 'They're a pair of greedy fuckers. Went through that six-pack of *Tayto* between them.'

'Got rid of them, didn't it.'

Then they heard Fred's voice, as loud as if he was in their tent. *'Oh look Padraig, there is a deck of cards here.'*

'What are you on about?' Padraig was heard to say.

'What shall we play? Jack Change It?' asked Fred.

'What cards? Any why are you talking so loud? I'm right here.'

'Padraig, shall we play Poker? Fred Poker?'

Kiera cast a glance out and looked back to Cat. 'You know he thinks that's funny 'cos that's his name.'

'Huh?'

'Fred Poke.'

'You're not serious?' Cat laughed. 'What sort of a name is that?'

Padraig called out. *'For fuck's sake!'*

Fred called out. *'Where's the towel?'*

'Jesus! I don't know! Move the sleeping bag!'

Cat growled. She thrust her hand behind Kiera, grabbed

the towel, and threw it to Shay.

'*It's sliding everywhere,*' Padraig screamed.

'Over here,' Cat yelled.

Shay unzipped the door, and the flysheet, and held out the towel.

'Morons,' said Cat.

PADRAIG

End of pizzeria and kebab shop
The leccy's out again, bee-bop-bee-bop.
Oh my PS3, why hast thou forsaken me?
Wherefore art thy Walking Dead torrents?

I was made to be a house-cat so
where was I last night? Bellowing morning
lorries bawling, like devils come after
me, and I'm blessed by the teas that bind

Lizard Cameron and Greedy Goblin,
coke fiend George Osborne: their conspiracy
austerity? We shall see, we shall see.
With dissenting tents and flag of fire.

We face this drizzle and grand theft auto
A shifting turner; squirrel motorbike
Our action plans, response of common sense
Movement not only camp, see winds on tents

5

With his guitar case in his hand Billy passed by *Shac*, the block of needs-housing, on his way into the camp. A large girl was at the door jabbing the keypad. A voice crackled through the failing electronics. The front hall was lit with a luminescent light stained cigarette yellow and the cathode tubing flickered. Billy heard the door swing shut and the glass shake as he passed. On the path behind the tents Cat spray-painted, '*NO TO AUSTERITY*'. The canvas was a twenty by five foot old duvet cover, one of nine donated. Eoghan, Padraig and Kiera – in muddied clothes – held the corners with Galway John, who had thick string for threading through cut holes.

Billy chose the secondary path in the middle of the site. At the gazebos Daniel knelt, coating the top of a flat block of wood with glue and fixing that to a piece of board. Mary was also occupied with re-using the old electoral boards, inking '*WE ARE THE 99%*' onto the reverse. Gary held it steady. The gazebo group were deeply occupied so Billy circled on around to the banner makers. Gary did a double-take as he walked past.

Cat's aerosol clanged and fizzed.

Eoghan watched to make sure the lettering fit, and that she didn't over-spray. 'Careful with that. We've been getting bother from the racists. We don't want to be getting blacked up. Oh hell, *there's marks on the concrete!*'

'Sure, people will put it down to alien crop circles,' said Mary.

Eoghan laughed. 'They'd believe that sooner than their

own government is defrauding them.'

Cat paused and erupted, 'ACHOOO!'

'Bless you,' said Billy.

'Thanks.'

'Holy God!' said Eoghan.

'Not quite,' said Billy. 'Need a hand?'

Billy Bragg, the internationally renowned English folk singer was stood there, in the mud, with them. Billy seemed ordinary, and iconic: spiked hair, grey but youthful; eyes tired but clear; an optimistic, honest smile. Eoghan and Galway were excited. Gary too, immediately there shaking his hand, with the others in tow. When Billy set down his cuppa to play twenty minutes later, *Shac's* residents had their heads out the windows or had come down to the camp to join them.

In the twilight the wind beat down upon the tents. The orange couch sat abandoned and stinking outside a gazebo. A bin bag shook, tied to the pavilion fence. Leon shoved the last pasta scraps into it. She'd missed Billy Bragg's appearance and was sulking because of that.

Eoghan – who was setting up the chairs for the General Assembly – couldn't help but gloat. 'We were jamming together: *Milkman of Human Kindness, Help Save the Youth of America...* what a rush!'

Kiera sneezed, and sneezed again, her three pocket tissues sodden. Daniel played with Shelby, the young black Staffy stray. Shelby weaved between the fifteen present, pausing to shove his nozzle in a sweaty armpit here and there. A few wore the masks of V and the Anonymous movement, protected from Shelby's French kisses.

'There were people drinking here last night,' said Gary. 'I'm not going to name names.'

Bob and Eoghan glared at Padraig who looked to Cat, Kiera and Shay.

Gary continued. 'Every Occupy camp has a no drink and no drugs rule for a reason. Let's forget last night happened and stick to the policy. Now, is everyone ready for the march tomorrow?'

Leon shook her head. 'Why aren't we doing something about the schools? Or the hospitals?'

Eoghan sighed. 'We discussed this already. Those things will take time to put in place. Austerity is a catch all.'

'It's inclusive,' said Deirdre.

Gary elaborated. 'It's a way in for people who might not otherwise be part of a group demonstration.'

'I'll just stay here,' said Bob.

Cat held her notepad down, stopping the breeze flapping the pages. 'So we have the Socialist Workers Party. And the Feminist Network are invited.'

'I saw that on Twitter,' said Joe.

'There's a Facebook event page,' confirmed Jack.

'And it's on the blog,' said Cat.

'There's a blog?' exclaimed Padraig.

'We are everywhere,' divulged Anonymous, apropos of nothing.

'Meet at twelve for the march then,' said Mary, 'and back here afterwards for the carnival.'

Eoghan cheered. 'Pièce de résistance! Now. Cat is on the face painting. We've got Luke busking. I've my guitar. Shay…'

Shay whistled a line on his tin-whistle.

'Maybe they'll let yous audition for *X-Factor*,' remarked Galway.

Kiera was shocked. 'How does someone your age know about X-Factor?'

Galway extended his arm. His breath followed in sturdy melody from his diaphragm. *'Oh Danny Boy, the pipes, the pipes are calling. From glen to glen, and down the mountain side. The summer's gone…'*

Though the cold air clamped on their bones everyone hooted and hollered. Shelby wagged his tail and danced around and round.

'You're ready for Broadway,' said Gary with a smile.

'Would you not have done a duet with Billy?' Shay asked.

'Ah. I am but a humble man.'

'I can't believe I missed that.'

Eoghan relented. 'Alright, alright Leon. We got you a comp ticket for *The Empire*. I'm sorry folks, that's the last one. What's next on the agenda?'

Cat took a folded sheet from her inside pocket. 'This came into our email. I've printed it out. It's from Dovid Vonce.'

'Who?'

Young Kiera shrugged.

'TUV member for East Belfast,' explained Gary.

Daniel, foreign to Northern Irish politics, asked again. 'TUV?'

Deirdre sighed. 'Traditional Unionist Voice.'

'Wankers. Them and the Unionist Traditional Voice!' exclaimed Eoghan.

Padraig waved his arm. 'And the People's Unionist Front!'

'Splitters!' yelled Leon.

Eoghan cried out, 'The only people we hate more than the Romans are the People's Unionist Front!'

Shelby barked three times.

'The TUV,' said Galway sternly, 'are Jim Allister's wild dogs and wife beaters. They prey upon the wounds of the bereaved.'

Gary motioned for them to bring it down a notch but Cat carried on, groaning, 'Aye and Vonce is the worst.'

'Racist, sectarian, homophobic over-emphatic diarrhoea keyboard. I've read his blog. The guy shits asshole.'

'Say what you feel Leon.'

Mary laughed. 'He shits asshole?'

'Vonce's provider threatened to close his site down over hate speech,' noted Joe.

'I think he said the *Gaelic Athletic League* is the sport of Sodom,' said Cat. 'And apparently we're all mates with the Ayatollah and Hezbollah.'

'We need to show reasonable debate doesn't need unreasonable views,' Gary informed them.

'Sounds like he's a pound short of a pound,' muttered Shay.

'John, would you like to read this?' asked Cat. She handed over the piece of paper.

Galway John fitted thin-rimmed spectacles under his grey bushy eyebrows. Shelby barked, and Shay stroked him quiet. John cleared his throat, and read, with theatrical flair.

'Occupy Belfast. I want to know what you think you'll achieve. Writer's Square is a public right of way and you are disrupting a vital recreational space.'

They laughed and groaned, heads shook and eyes rolled.

'Furthermore, your presence makes the property look decadent, and unattractive to tourists and investors.' Galway paused, pained to be reading it. *'Have you thought about the cost of policing your anarcho-communist demonstration?'*

'He's one of us,' Leon screamed with mirth. 'One of us! One of us!'

'Who IS in charge of this protest? My constituents are very interested. Please have your leaders contact me as soon as possible.'

'He sounds serious,' remarked Daniel.

'Taake mee to your leadersss!' hissed Shay.

'Send him Rick Astley's photo,' said Joe.

'Shelby's our leader,' said Eoghan, 'Isn't that right boy?'

Leon rubbed the Staffy's head. 'In Dog we trust.'

He barked and she let him go. She took out her phone and readied the camera. Shelby ran behind a chair.

'Send him a picture of my gonads!'

'Eww, minging, Padraig,' said Kiera.

'I don't want to see your balls. No one does,' said Cat.

'Sure, I'll let you paint them.'

'It *is* a load of bollocks,' Eoghan declared.

'I'm not having Padraig's balls represent us,' said Leon, quite seriously.

'He'd not know who's balls they are. They could be anyone's balls,' said Shay.

'Anoniballs,' said Eoghan.

'You could use a low resolution shot,' Jack suggested. 'And there's the angle of the photograph to think about.'

'Well yes. It *does* matter to consider the political message inherent in Mr. Mahon's ball-sack,' said Galway, thoughtfully.

'Mwah-ha-hahaha! No complaints so far!'

'Except from the clinic,' quipped Kiera.

When the laughter died down, Jack asked, 'Are the balls to be interpreted literally, as in do they evoke a social occasion?'

Eoghan wondered, 'Would the heaviness of the balls be interpreted as a provocative act?'

Leon blurted out, 'He'll call the fucking police!'

Gary, ever the rational voice, agreed. 'We'd have to send the photo as a general press release; in case Vonce thinks we're picking on him. *To political parties across the divide. Scrotum pledges to fight for equality. No longer shall workers dream of going to the ball. Now they will have two balls.*'

They were in stitches laughing again.

Bob put his head down. 'Dear God,' he muttered.

'Are the balls a symbol of male fertility?' Jack asked.

'No!' said a half dozen people.

'Are they balls, or are they something else?' Joe wanted to know. 'Are they like *Schrödinger's Balls*?'

'Or like that painting of a pipe where underneath's the caption: *this is not a pipe.*' Cat hand-signed a caption. '*These Are Not Balls.*'

'Fuck away off,' sneered Padraig.

'He grows bored with his balls being tossed about,' said one of the Anonymi.

'Aye, your ma had no complaints.'

Deirdre raised her hand. 'Do the balls open up a conversation about sexuality and permissiveness?'

'Well, see, that's what I meant by heaviness,' explained

Eoghan. 'Could be they're shrivelled up from the cold here.'

'Right, right,' said Joe. 'Then you're highlighting the emasculation felt by the *New Man*.'

'Two balls: duality,' said Kiera.

Padraig shrieked. 'I'm not emasculated!'

Bob sighed. 'Fuck's sake. Alright. What sort of lens are we talking about?'

'That's enough. I'm blocking this discussion,' snapped Leon, now quite irate.

'You're cock-blocking,' said Shay.

'The whole thing is anti-feminist. And misogynistic.'

'Would you feel better if we sent him bush?' asked Jack.

'Bush versus Bush all over again,' quipped Eoghan.

'I don't think we're any closer to solving this,' said Gary.

The moon shone. The blue sky rained. The sun shone. At midday on Saturday people assembled around the camp. A few times Eoghan had to recount the dozen folk in Anonymous masks who were constantly jumping about. He gave up counting heads at fifty.

'All set then?'

'Any-time,' said Cat.

She and Leon held the large banner by wooden poles, pasted and duct-taped to the looped fabric at the sides, through holes at the top and bottom. Padraig took up one of the sturdier placards. On the reverse a photograph of Gary's smiling face beamed down at him. Gary took the megaphone for the first stretch along Royal Avenue, the broad main street. It was ten minutes straight to City Hall. They passed the monumental disused *Bank of Ireland* building, and the junction with North Street. The banners and masked Anonymi drew stares as they advanced on *Castlecourt* shopping centre.

'Today we oppose the cuts to health and the emergency services, to those with disabilities and in the education sector. These decisions were taken by Westminster, and Stormont. They who let their friends in the financial market off the hook.

While tens of thousands lost their homes.'

No one had thought to factor in the traffic on Royal Avenue. The large banner curled in on itself as Leon and Cat sidled to the kerb. By contrast the Anonymi played with the cars until a few bold drivers scattered them.

'We are the 99%!'

'We are the 99%!'

Shoppers on the pavement froze. Kiera politely weaved through them with placard aloft. Padraig was unflinching, holding his sign like a saluting rifleman. Fred didn't carry one and generally kept his head down. Eoghan and Galway walked casually past the old bank buildings, the first converted to a *Tesco's* and the second to a *Primark*. Horns honked in support and some with blame for the sloth of the Castle Street junction lights. The citadel was in sight.

'They say cut back!'

'We say fight back!'

There was break-out chanting. 'We are Anonymous. We are legion!'

Belfast City Hall was a palatial Edwardian structure, styled like a fort with lanterns on each of its four corners. The main build was two levels of Portland Stone, two dome levels above and a third iconic green copper dome. Opposite, on Donegall Place, *Burger King* operated from another historic building. That's where Fred decided he'd rather be. The others crossed over and were met with waves from the taxi rank and more horn hooting. People leaving the grounds darted away from the crowd at the gate though some did linger. Placards rested against the fence.

Cat, who'd been holding the big banner, told Mary she could take it on the way back. Her arm was killing her. Daniel passed out flyers. Cat and Kiera each took a batch. Padraig even took a few. A boy racer passed yelling unintelligible blather out his window.

Gary passed the megaphone to Eoghan.

'Hello,' said Eoghan.

The megaphone was as hoarse as a forty-a-day smoker. He tried again, and it squealed.

'I don't like it. There's something very wrong here,' said Bob.

He sat under the gazebos looking at the skateboarders who flipped their boards off the wall and into the sun. On the pavilion kids bounced a ball around, echoing on concrete. People were talking. People he'd never seen before. Over a hundred folk were milling about: mothers with prams and wee tots; environmentalists, hackers and makers. On another wall sat Eoghan and Luke Devlin, side-by-side and strumming out tunes. The Anonymi danced the waltz and the twist. Padraig took on Leon in a political debate. At first it was a matter of Padraig's pride, until he saw there was more fun in making her lose her temper. Joe put up his tent single-handedly. Mary studied his muscular body, slurping her glass of orange as he bent over.

Daniel helped Jack pitch her small ridge tent. They turned away for a moment to Shay, strolling through the crowd playing his out-of-tune tin whistle. When Daniel looked back, Jack's tent was misshapen and lumpy. She opened the flap.

'Ah, come on! Out of there!' she yelled.

A journalist crawled out. Jack swatted the air waving him away. Then another came out, and the next one, and the next one.

Gary got up on the wall on the pavilion side of the square and raised the megaphone.

'Everyone! Everyone! If I could have your attention for a minute! Thank you for coming to our first ever Carnival of Resistance. There are, today, 2,300 occupations in 2,000 cities around the world!'

Sporadic applause broke out.

'What happened at Oakland was unacceptable. Tear gas. Nearly a hundred arrested. The whole world saw the heavy-handed barbarism of it. And in response more and more people are occupying spaces, telling privileged autocrats we've had enough. We're only a small camp. We've been here a week and we're not going anywhere. Not until economic measures are enacted to reverse the damage done by austerity and injustice!'

Most everyone clapped or cheered.

'Anyone is welcome to join us camping out. Thanks to Mary serving tea, Cat at the face painting tent, and the musicians, Eoghan and Luke. We have a wish list and a donation box doing the rounds. Thank you for all your support.'

There were placards tied to the fence from the pavilion to the gazebo. More tied to the lamp-posts and propped against the fronts of tents: *'Occupy Belfast to Wall Street'* in black, and underneath in red, *'We Will Fight'*. *'This is the Revolution. City by City!' 'Tax. The. Rich.'*

Emmett sat with them under the gazebo. He was in his twenties, friendly, and spoke with a cool Southern accent. 'D'yih hear Jimmy Saville's dead?'

'Dirty paedo,' said Bob.

'Tell the press that,' said Mary.

'A weird critter for sure,' Joe remarked.

Bob held a brush up to the roof of the gazebo and gave it a push ejecting a bank of built up rainwater. It slooshed onto the path, and Mary's shoes.

'Oh for fuck's sake!'

'So, Emmett, you came all the way from Galway City for this?' asked Joe.

Thirty-something Emmett wore a thinning scalp of blonde hair, a black tee and blue jeans. 'Me and the Missus were booked for a break. That's her there, and our little one with the bubble blower.'

He waved but the child's mind was elsewhere.

Mary spotted Deirdre Hoffman setting her bike against the lamp-post. She wondered how she could have missed her, padded in fluorescents with long frizzy hair trailing out from under her helmet. 'Hiya Deirdre!'

'Hello folks,' she sang. 'Is that... Emmett, isn't it? We met at the Galway camp last week.'

'Oh, yeah. Deirdre. You were cycling to Dublin. How was that?'

'Ah. It wasn't great. Flash floods. Thankfully the tents were raised up on palettes, away from those waves washing down Dame Street. We had the march to support legal rights for whistle-blowers. I'm surprised to see you here.'

Emmett beamed. 'I've come to steal your ideas.'

'What's it like there?' asked Joe.

'The Galway camp? Alright. We're surviving,' said Emmett.

'You're too modest,' said Deirdre. 'They've a permanent information booth, with flyers and petitions. The kitchen area is all neatly arranged too, so it is.'

'We try,' said Emmett.

Mary gasped. 'A kitchen area?'

The football soared over to the gazebo and was stopped by a worn man of about fifty, though he was muscular with the frame of a thirty year old. He kicked it back to Gary and then came cautiously to the gazebo. Mary patted a seat for him to sit. He'd the markers of a hard man for Bob's suspicion: black tee, black jeans and faded tattoos.

'...dish racks, little nets for the cutlery,' continued Deirdre. 'Tents in rows and clean – at least when I was there...'

Mary looked to the muddy puddles at the mouths of their tents, wet leaves tonguing the sides.

'Sorry. I'm Deirdre,' she said, extending a hand to the new lad.

He had a firm grip. 'Tommie.'

'I'm Mary. This is Emmett, Bob, Joe on dishes...'

'I assume you've all these tents water-proofed?' Tommie asked earnestly.

'Some of them are pre-coated. If you spray too much you risk damaging them,' Deirdre replied.

Tommie nodded and smiled. 'So what's the idea? Fuck

the man. I'm all for that. But what good's it going to do?'

'We hope by active protest, over time, we'll lodge our objectives at local and international levels,' said Deirdre.

Tommie was frank, direct, not aiming to antagonise. 'Aye, but sure aren't yous just catching the cold out here?'

'Well, sure Tommie, that's part of it,' said Mary. 'But this serves as a meeting point for direct action and co-ordination. Daniel! Would you stick the kettle on?'

'I'll get it,' said Bob, sounding upset.

He walked to the ten litre drum, unscrewed the cap and poured the water. Tommie stared and scrunched up his face, wondering briefly whether Bob was offended.

'He's a man of few words,' said Mary.

'Globally there are so many problems we're facing,' said Emmett. 'Only an assembly of the willing can change them.'

Tommie eyed far left. 'Aw shit. What're the cops doing here? Bastards. Always starting.'

The two police officers were at the raised parterre, a detached four foot square wall. Kiera sat there alone – her back against the small fence and shrubbery - holding a blue balloon on a string.

'Bit of a party here,' reported Barker, the big one.

'Bit of a celebration,' confirmed Corbett, the thin one.

'Could you hold this while I roll my fag?' said Kiera, casually.

Corbett held the balloon string stiffly, a stern look on his face.

'Well what do you think?' she asked, before licking the *Rizla* cigarette paper.

'You're not rioting,' said Barker. 'It's a far cry from the Twelfth of July.'

'No one has complained,' said Corbett

Kiera lit up and then took her balloon back. 'I'm Kiera. Most people call me Kiera.'

'Sergeant Oliver Barker. Constable Stanley Corbett.'

Kiera blew the smoke away from them. 'You should come and join us. When you're not working, I mean.'

Barker shook his head. 'My boss would have serious issues with that. If I don't report in an hour of my shift ending, she gives my dinner to the dog.'

Kiera chuckled. 'We could get you and her a double.'

'If she learned I was not having an affair it would be a disaster,' he said, keeping a straight face.

'Sir?'

'Yes, Corbett?'

'If home life is difficult...' he started, genuinely concerned, 'well, what I meant to say is, sir, the greater percentage of non-reporting domestic abuse victims are often male.'

'I was joking, Constable Corbett.'

'We're handy to your work-place,' Kiera told Corbett.

'Him? Oh, he's too fond of his television: all those HBO shows.' Barker put a hand over his mouth and whispered, 'Likes this American football too.'

'I don't think Inspector Tarbard would like us staying here,' said Corbett gravely.

Barker laughed. 'You're not in Barnabas Tarbard's good books are you? Last week, *someone,* phoned our supervisor at three in the morning with a pizza order.'

'Yes. He didn't get much sleep,' said Corbett innocently.

'Sounds like we'd be ideal for your boss. No sleep until the end of capitalism!'

Barker looked around and then asked her quietly, 'Did you fill in your 11/1s?'

'My what's?'

'Stan?'

Corbett reached into his pocket and brought out eight folded pages, stapled. 'We thought not. Form 11/1, Parades Commission. Due seven days before each march.'

'Are we in trouble?'

'No, no,' Barker assured her.

'We get so many papers it's hard to keep track,' said

Corbett.

Barker nodded. 'I'm sure this week's ones will turn up somewhere,' he said.

After the carnival there was loose rubbish which had to be tidied up and Galway promised he would get rid of the dirty wet couch. There had been plenty of donations: blankets, a rug, second-hand thermal clothes, three large wooden palettes and a five foot open metal bin which could be used to contain a fire. Best of all, enough money came into the collection tin to let them buy a marquee tent; much better protection than the gazebos.

Another addition was New John: a big bloke in grey jogging bottoms and an expired blue body-warmer. He barely spoke and no-one was sure where he came from. New John had thinning grey hair, looked permanently lost and he was genuinely confused when they offered him a tent.

'I think that fella has a problem with his bowels,' said Bob as he rolled a wet cigarette.

'You're not wrong,' Galway said. 'Still, he's being looked after here. That's got to count for something.'

Galway found a shop that was still open and selling coal, firelighters and wood. By ten o'clock the flames from the bin broke through the night air. The smoke did too, and got everywhere: coughs, splutters, watering eyes. Just when the victims had gotten out of its way, the wind changed direction.

By midnight Bob was enjoying the relative quiet: the spectral motors and fading steps and voices, yells from those going to and from nightclubs, and then, the campers returning from seeing Billy Bragg at *The Empire*. To his surprise – and relish – they all went back to their tents within minutes, leaving just the two older men sitting out.

'You know, Bob, it was just a few days ago everyone was ready to pack it in. Now look at us. Yes, the mood's really shifted.'

'Unstoppable,' muttered Bob gruffly.

Two full hours later, Eoghan and Leon dawdled down the path.

'What an evening! What an evening!' Leon exclaimed.

'Incredible,' said Eoghan.

'I'm breaking out the marshmallows,' said Bob sarcastically.

Leon wasn't having her enthusiasm dampened. 'No really, Bob. So he played *Never Buy The Sun* and *Power in a Union*. Loads. And before the encore we put an Occupy Belfast poster on the wall and the security guys, right, they took it down and they were gonna throw us out, right, and we complained, and one of them put their hands on me and Billy jumped off the stage and said, *No! No You can't do that, these people are my friends, and I said they could put that up.* Then he took the poster and he hung it from his mic stand. On the stage!'

'Is that really what happened?' asked Galway.

Eoghan laughed. 'Well, he didn't jump off the stage. But it's not far off.'

'Then straight into *Roll Over Beethoven*. He was telling everyone all about us, dead impressed, and they were all clapping and cheering,' said Leon.

'That's good. Good stuff,' said Galway calmly. 'Sure. It's been a long day. Why not get some rest?'

'Aye. The march, the carnival. You're right. God, adrenalin rush again, but at the same time I could sleep… I could sleep right through tomorrow. That's what I'll do. Don't let anyone wake me.'

'I suggest you go now,' said Bob firmly and he pointed past her to the cathedral. 'Tomorrow's Sunday.'

6

It was Halloween night: bangers and sparklers exploded in the sky around them. The fire from the metal bin made for an ethereal spectre. Levin Kirkwood watched. There were twenty-three at the meeting, under a large green marquee. Erected that day, it gave the impression of a barracks. The front was open with flaps tied to poles on either side. A pigeon bobbed as it marched along the front, stopping to scrutinise the markings on the chalkboard.

Levin watched Daniel beside him, nodding, with his thick mat of hair, grey wool and black jeans. Levin gazed out to the stacked palettes and the smoke stung his eyes. A sign in the shrubbery read *'Stormont Tax the 1%'*. It shook in the wind.

He counted eleven tents. The olive coloured ridge tent he'd learned belonged to Padraig and Fred. Padraig was the rakish fella with the braying laugh, who'd spent the evening cracking peanut shells and throwing them in the fire. Fred was the short and shifty black-haired lad who sat beside him, sometimes spitting shells on the ground where they sat.

'It's not just any tent,' said Fred. 'Its name is *The Love Shack*.'

Cat laughed. 'I didn't know you two were an item.'

Fred back-pedalled desperately. 'No! I didn't mean it *that* way!'

Most striking to Levin were the Anonymous, those in masks popularised by *V for Vendetta* and the Guy Fawkes inspired revolutionary, V. Half a dozen were men and one a woman. The Anonymi had bold expressions and sculpted, chilling smiles. They squirmed on the dank orange couch beside him. Others at the General Assembly wore Halloween horror facades: a devilish skull, a gargoyle and David Cameron. Kiera, the young red-headed girl, pulled off a rubber wolf mask and reached for her inhaler.

Levin became aware eyes were upon him. He looked to the striped gazebo at the side. The quiet old man stared, his expression set to grim. The assembly were talking about the *MTV Awards* which were coming to Belfast at the weekend. The event would coincide with their own *Carnival of Resistance*.

Some talked at great length. Levin had picked up on a few names. There was chestnut-haired Shay and confident blond Mary, heavy with make-up as David Bowie and a bloodied ghoul respectively. Eoghan seemed to be chairing the meeting and grew increasingly frustrated, rubbing the sleeves of his army surplus sweater and tugging on his red neck-tie.

And then Eoghan erupted. 'Forty-five minutes spent talking about clowns! Can we friggin' move on now?'

'We've a message from the Buddhist church?' said Cat. 'They're doing a prayer walk from the cathedral to City Hall. It's happening Thursday from noon.'

'Silent walk? That'll suit you Daniel,' said Shay, nudging him.

Fred lifted Shay's long locks. 'You not fancy getting your head shaved?' Shay batted him away and smiled.

'Mind if I speak?'

'Sure, Bob,' said Eoghan.

'It wasn't a question.' He waited for a moment, staring down anyone whispering. 'There was stuff nicked last night. A loudspeaker, a torch and some firewood. We need to be more vigilant.'

Most of the group raised their hands and wiggled them, signalling agreement.

'If I catch the bastards that done it I'll skin them alive,' said Bob.

'Tell me,' said Levin. 'How do you decide which protests

to take part in as a group?'

The English girl, Jack, brushed her short cropped hair. 'I think, correct me if I'm wrong, it's whatever the group decides.'

'Well, for argument's sake, what if someone decided to protest a movie?'

Eoghan grimaced. 'That doesn't really...'

'What about the *Twilight* movies?' said Padraig. 'Plenty of people are angry about those. And the new *Star Trek* one.'

'*The Phantom Menace* re-release,' declared Fred.

'What about *Passion of the Christ*?' said V.

'Oh, totally. A rare argument for censorship. Deviant sinful shit,' said Kiera, cracking open a monkey nut.

Around the tents others murmured in agreement.

Cat sighed and raised her hand. 'Can we talk about tomorrow and the BNP?' She caught Daniel looking puzzled. 'Stands for British National Party. Far right politics. Holocaust denial, *Campaign Against Islam*, inciting racial hatred...'

'*There ain't no black in the Union Jack*,' said Galway dryly. 'They were big in the eighties until Thatcher stole their anti-immigration voters.'

'What about them?' asked Levin.

'Tomorrow, the BNP are holding a rally at City Hall. We're boycotting it,' Eoghan told him.

'Good,' said Joe, and then he thought to check, 'By not going?'

'I mean we're counter-protesting it. We show up at their rally and call them out on their hate.'

'I'm up for it if you are, Padraig. I hate those BNP fucks,' said Fred.

'Economic downturn's ideal for predators,' sneered V.

'Their leaders all have criminal convictions: Nick Griffin, Jim Dowson...' said VI.

'I read Dowson groped a wee girl at one of their call centres,' said VII.

'Okay. In summary, BNP counter-protest tomorrow and the anti-Austerity march on Wednesday,' said Cat.

'Pardon me for asking,' said Levin, pointing to an Anonymi, 'but are you wearing those masks out of fear of reprisals? The BNP have quite a reputation.'

'We are Anonymous. We are not afraid,' said V.

'Aye, mate,' said Cat, accepting the bag of monkey nuts.

'We are everywhere,' said IV, firmly.

'And we do not forget.' said III.

'Some fucker'll nat forget my toe up their hole if they don't knock that shit off,' grumbled Bob.

'Anonymous values privacy,' said II.

Bob raised an eyebrow. 'Here, I know that voice.'

The smoke blistered II's eyes and she coughed into her mask.

Padraig broke out cackling. 'Mwah-ha-hahaha! It's Leon! Mwah-ha-hahaha!'

'We will not make ourselves vulnerable to fascism,' said V. 'Not to the corrupt forces of government.'

'Nor the right-wing media,' said VII.

'Well there we agree,' grunted Bob. 'I don't want no journo misquoting me. *Poking a camera in my face.*'

'ACTION!' yelled Padraig.

Bob jumped.

'Son, I'll fucking belt ye!' he bellowed.

'Mwah-ha-hahaha!'

Levin raised his hand. 'Shouldn't you be bringing in the homeless? You have all these tents. They could really help those that actually need them.'

'We have been doing that,' said Eoghan.

'Occupy Winemark, Occupy Russell Cellars...'

A peanut struck Fred on the temple.

Eoghan kept focussed on Levin. 'I mean not to be blunt but if you want to do something, you should do it. We're all just volunteers.'

'No, that's fair. I was just wondering. So what about drunks?'

'They're murder with the tent ropes. Mwah-ha-hahaha!'

'No drink, no drugs, said Bob flatly. 'If they've drink on them, they don't get in.'

'Though we always check to make sure they've brought enough to share,' quipped Cat.

Bob scowled.

Later that night the sky burst in rippling spits and bangs of salmon and blue. The passing rain, which had clung to them in molecules, was gone, and the wind had dropped to a cool breeze. Eight campers sat on the sofa and chairs around a crackling fire.

Eoghan looked up to the skies, a warm cocoa in his hands. 'They've almost got it out of their system,' he said.

'You don't celebrate Guy Fawkes night the same way, do you?' said Jack.

Eoghan shook his head. *'Remember, remember, the fifth of November. Gunpowder treason and plot.'*

'Unionists don't look kindly on Irish traditions like blowing up parliament. Mwah-ha-hahaha! Here: what did you make of those newbies? Yer man Joe?'

'Joe's okay. Blows a bit hot and cold,' said Mary.

'I don't know,' said Eoghan. 'What do we know about them really? And yer other man, with his twenty questions!'

A grey and green pigeon investigated.

Padraig rattled out his impression of Levin. 'Are people here going to stick it out? Aren't you afraid the cops will move you on? What about the cathedral?'

'So, Joe: cool. Thingy: possibly an MI5 plant,' Leon concluded.

Bob glared. 'Thingy?'

'Thingymajig. Kevin or Declan or whatever,' said Leon.

'Levin,' said Bob.

'That's gotta be a made up name,' Fred told them.

Jack found him quite handsome. 'Those thick arching eyebrows, Rhett Butler moustache and goatee…'

'Evil,' said Daniel with a knowing smirk.

'No more suspect than half a dozen people in Anonymous masks I suppose,' said Eoghan.

'His face did look just like one of those masks,' said Mary.

A gust of wind blew smoke into Leon's face and she coughed again. A few of them looked at her and she raised her arms defensively.

'I'll have you know I'm the lynchpin of Anonymous Belfast!'

'You realise the point of Anonymous is no-one is supposed to know who you are?' Eoghan remarked.

'Mwah-ha-haha-ha!'

'So, can you can hack into computers?' asked Jack.

'No! But I know how computers work!'

'Aye. Pornhub dotcom,' said Padraig.

Fred spoke up. 'She's just types *p*.'

'Well, it takes one to know one,' said Mary.

Fred stood and looked over the fire bin. 'You need more wood on that,' he said. He walked to the gazebo and picked up the axe.

Bob called out to him. 'Hey! I don't want that you swinging that thing near the new tent.'

Eoghan stroked the thick canvas of the marquee. 'Pretty good isn't it? When we clear the sofa, there'll be room for ten or twelve people under here.'

'Aren't you lucky the lads of *The Love Shack* came down to provide muscle?' said Padraig.

Leon snorted. 'You're just here because your electric has run out!'

Cat balanced the forms on her knee and wrote in black ink and all capitals. It was the following morning, a Tuesday, and random drops of rain spat on the ground in front of her. Eoghan provided direction as they worked through Parades Commission Form 11/1, for notice to protest. Daniel sat with them though he barely made eye contact.

Cat struggled. '*Organising body*... Occupy Belfast... *The*

Parades Commission may refuse to accept an incomplete form. Warning... if the requirements of notice have not been satisfied, the person taking part shall be guilty of an offence. Marshals must be informed...'

'Shit. We need marshals?' said Eoghan.

'We'll come back to that. Okay. *Reason for delay*,' said Cat. 'Current events?'

'That'll do. *Name of person organising, home address, telephone.*'

'You can put my name down. Eoghan McBride, 30 Riora Street, BT15 3BZ. 079018622879.'

'*Procession details. If you intend to parade out to a location, and then parade back from there, fully or even partly along your outward...* blah blah blah...'

'Put Writer's Square, along Royal Avenue, to City Hall and back. That ought to do it.'

'Purpose?'

'To draw attention to the illegal inflation of subprime mortgages by private investment banks as part of a global conspiracy against the blue collar labour force.'

Cat took a breath and urged him, 'Slow down.'

Gary cut across the man-made path where the bare roots of a tree was exposed among the tents. Daniel waved. Gary waved back and put his hand over his mouth as he yawned, then took a chair beside them. 'Alright. What are yous up to?'

'Parades notification form. One for today, tomorrow, Saturday...' muttered Eoghan.

'Forget I asked.'

'Hiya Gary. Eoghan, what do I put for dispersal?'

'When we leave City Hall? Say an hour?'

'I have that under dispersal of arrival. It asks for dispersal of return parade?'

'...Non-applicable?'

'Just put an hour,' said Gary.

Smoke billowed from the fire, right into Cat's face. She

coughed and flapped the papers around. 'The march leads into the carnival. Should that be four hours?'

They thought on this for a moment.

'The carnival isn't the protest,' murmured Daniel.

Gary nodded. 'Should you not be putting in the forms for tomorrow?'

'Nah. It's too close. Besides, the cop Kiera spoke to inferred they wouldn't bust our balls about it,' said Eoghan.

Cat gave a yawn that could've cracked her face. 'Jasus. Right, where was I? *Anticipated number of participants. Likely number of supporters.*'

Gary reckoned, 'It doesn't have to be an exact science. Just put thirty people down for each. Stupid system anyway.'

'No street collection, no uniform or regalia. Banners and flags?'

'Ah,' said Eoghan. 'We talked about asking the Socialists not to bring theirs. To keep it non-party political.'

'Yeah, but we'll still have placards and a banner,' said Gary. Then he yawned.

'*Marshals should pay attention to Paragraphs B, F and G of Appendix A,*' said Cat. 'Okay, page three. Huh. *Start time:* 12pm. Donegall Street, Royal Avenue. *Return journey start time.* What did we put, 1pm?'

'If we're doing this for every Saturday we should just photocopy this and Tippex the dates in,' Eoghan thought.

Gary shrugged. 'We should find out if we can do that but I don't think we can,' he said.

'*How many marshals will be in attendance?* It's asking for their names?'

'We can just put our own down,' said Gary. 'Assuming that's okay?'

'Want to be a marshal, Daniel?' He made a silly face at Cat and shook his head. 'Okay Daniel, would you make us some coffee? Thanks. So: Eoghan McBride, Gary Carell, Catriona Kennedy. Oh. Formal training? Gary?'

'Fraid not. Here: isn't the BNP demo starting?'

'Not until this is done,' said Cat. *'Form of identification worn by marshals. Armbands. Coats. Other.'*

Eoghan smirked. 'I'll be wearing a coat!'

'Coats it is. *What method of communication will be used:* mobile, radio, ah, verbal.'

'We got the mobile phone for the camp,' said Eoghan.

'I'll just tick verbal. *Part 3. Details of accompanying bands.* Skip. Page 6, same again. *Page 7. Details of further destinations.* None. Oh. *Declaration and signature of the organiser.* Over to you, Eoghan.'

'You sign it, Cat.'

'It's your name on the first page,' she said. 'Here.'

Gary said, 'I'll get a bunch of these from the station to do us for the weeks ahead.'

Eoghan autographed the back page. 'There you go. All done.'

'Good,' said Cat. 'I'm freezing my nuts off.'

Over the next hour Galway had been and gone, driving the mangy sofa in his trailer off to the dump. Levin returned, passing five Anonymi congregating on the roadside. Bob was chopping wood. Cat and Shay had been the first to return from the demo and Levin joined them and Mary inside the marquee. The space left by the sofa had been filled with ten fold-out wooden chairs in a rectangle.

'Are the others coming?' Cat asked.

'On their way. I think a few of them are giving me the cold shoulder,' said Levin.

'Never worry. They're just a bit suspicious until they know you,' said Shay.

'Oh Shay, I got you something,' said Cat. She reached under the chair for her backpack and from there unfolded a bright hi-vis jacket.

He beamed and wrapped it around himself. As requested, Shay gave them a twirl. 'Cool!'

'Suits you,' said Levin. 'Do you mind me asking, how do

you keep in touch with one another?'

Shay replied playfully. 'We pull one of the tents out so it catches the street-light there. You know. Like the bat signal.' He spread his arms upwards so the wings of his new jacket flowed like a cape.

Cat smiled. 'We've got a mobile phone for emergencies.'

Shay looked to the kerb where the Anonymi were keeping themselves to themselves: cold emotionless masks atop lanky frames and pot bellies. He walked over to them, putting himself in Bob's line of sight.

'What the hell are you doing with my jacket?' he bellowed.

Cat yelled back, 'I brought it from home this morning!'

'Cool jacket, Shay,' said one of the Anonymi.

'Thanks, Michael. Look guys. You're freaking everyone out. Just chill yeah?'

'Sorry, Shay.'

'The pot's near boiled. Come over and have some cocoa. Everyone appreciated your help at the BNP rally today.'

One of them, a lad with a crop of ginger hair, leaned in close to Shay. 'We are Anonymous. We are no-one's lackeys. We do not need cocoa.' He sounded quite serious.

'Okay. Well we have *Fig Rolls* and *Jammie Dodgers*,' said Shay.

The painted cheeks and emotionless smile capped each gravely delivered word. 'We do not want your *Fig Rolls* nor *Jammie Dodgers*,' said ginger Anonymous. 'We are unstoppable.'

Twenty seconds later he was still fixed to the spot, but alone. 'Huh.'

Others were filtering back now from the protest: Padraig waving his placard, *'We Won WW2'*, Leon with, *'The Other Is In The Albert Hall'*, and Fred, who refused to carry a sign on the principle he was only there for the banter.

'How was it?' Mary asked.

Padraig scoffed. 'Men with four chins and tan burns.'

'Fuckers weren't impressed,' said Fred.

Padraig imitated their monotone bellows. 'Suh yuh soon. Sleep wuf wan eye up end!'

'Those threats were probably hot air,' said Michael Anonymous.

'Nationalist gammons are all talk,' declared Leon.

'I could do without the bother,' said Joe, with a heavy heart.

'They said they were going to get us,' said Padraig.

'If they're making threats, you should probably tell Bob,' said Mary.

'Tell him, Padraig. The people on night watch should know,' said Cat.

'Why me?'

'Because,' she replied, 'I just told him a documentary crew are on their way. *He was RAGING. Then* I had to tell him a *Sunday World* journalist will be staying over this weekend. He really doesn't like journalists.'

Kiera, walking from the Royal Avenue end of the pavilion, paused in her tracks as Bob swung the axe over his head and brought it down hard on a defenceless wooden palette. The square echoed as it splintered into shards and dust. 'BASTARDS!' he guldered.

'Hmm. He *really* doesn't like journalists,' said Fred.

'Mwah-hahaahahahah!'

Kiera stepped past the mess. 'Jesus, Bob. Would you come here a minute? All of you better take a look at this.'

Kiera stepped into the marquee and reached into her satchel. She pulled out a laptop before planting herself down. 'I saw something at the library. It's got our faces on it.'

People crowded around as she flipped open the cover. The website was a brutal design of red and yellow type on black, much in block caps. Part-way down was a photo of Cat, Kiera and Daniel under the two gazebos.

'What is this?' said Cat.

'Redwatch,' said Leon.

'Red what?' enquired Levin.

'A right-wing creep site with ties to the BNP. They post photos of left-wing activists. Sometimes the subjects are victims of violent threats,' explained Leon.

A few people gasped. Kiera scrolled down the page. The pointer had been re-designed as a target with cross-hairs.

'They have a whole page dedicated to us,' stated Kiera.

'Your hair looks good in that one, Mary,' said Joe.

'Oh, yeah. I can use that for my profile pic.'

'They got you picking your nose,' Levin told Fred.

'Padraig's rubbing his balls,' he replied.

'Fucking scumbags,' growled Bob. 'Have me all twisted and vicious looking.'

Leon took the laptop. 'I remember that day, Bob. That's you laughing.'

He picked up his newspaper, and sat elsewhere.

Leon tapped down the page. 'Where's mine?' she asked and scrolled further and paged down again. 'Did they Photoshop me out? *I'm not in any of these!*'

Fred tapped Padraig on the shoulder. Together they walked over to the wall of the *Shac* flats.

'Would you look at your man Levin?' Fred whispered. 'I think he knows more than he's letting on.'

Eoghan rounded the corner. His face was sickly and pale. Fred signalled Padraig not to say anything. Eoghan's curiosity was already pulled to the cluster of people at the marquee. Padraig and Fred followed him over.

'They whitewashed me,' cried Leon.

Cat bobbed her head at Eoghan. 'We've been targetted by Redwatch.'

'We're pretty sure there's a spy in the camp,' said Padraig.

There were tears in Leon's throat. 'I *am* a prime threat to the right wing.'

Cat rubbed her shoulder.

'Are we sure about this? Do we know this isn't just one guy from the BNP?' said Eoghan.

'I heard a few of them talking among themselves. *We'll take care of them* sort of stuff. Then on the way back they were yelling at me and Leon. Like, threats, like,' said Padraig.

This made Leon feel better. She nodded and smiled.

'Oh for fuck's sake. I don't need *THIS*,' seethed Eoghan.

'What's *their* problem?' complained Levin.

'Geography,' said Leon. 'So many flags, it's like they need reminding what country they're in.'

Shay shrugged. He was laid back and seeming jovial. 'And meanwhile we're red from the fire, white from the cold and blue from the very very cold.'

Eoghan drew up to Amanda Anonymous. 'If you lot weren't taunting them, provoking them…'

'Don't blame me,' snapped Amanda. 'I didn't invade Poland.'

Eoghan looked over at Bob, who had his head deep in the *Belfast News Letter*. 'Bob? You're all about security. How do we respond to this?'

'Twenty across. Seven letters. *Devoid of all content.*'

Eoghan put his hand on his hip. 'Fuck's sake. Don't you ruffle a feather, Eamon DeValera.'

A little after half four – though it could have passed for late evening - vehicles rumbled by and a half dozen campers sat in from the drizzle. It came down on the tents sounding like a squalling child and sheened the footpath. The fire in front of the marquee delivered a thick fog of smoke. From the ether a tin whistle delivered an out-of-tune rendition of *'Danny Boy'*. Shay ducked under the canvas without missing a note. Bob shook his head, disdainfully.

'What's wrong? You don't like my playing? Cat? Daniel? My, my. All quiet at *The Swamp*. C'mon brothers, sisters, brothers. *Wassssup?*'

'All quiet 'cos Eoghan lost the biccies again,' said Fred, a little pleased about it.

'He lost the biccy barrel,' said Bob.

'Not cool. What was that about?'

Cat sighed. 'Tomorrow's Anti-Austerity march? The BNP have a new Facebook event up. They're counter-protesting us.'

Padraig spoke up. 'Twice.'

'What do you mean?'

'They're protesting our rally at City Hall, and also coming to the camp to protest,' said Jack. 'They're counter-protesting us for counter-protesting them.'

Fred imitated Eoghan's earnest panic. 'Eoghan hit the roof. Acted like it was only his problem. *I have to do everything around here!*'

'He's called an emergency meeting for after the GA,' said Bob, nonchalantly, and he sucked on his cigarette.

Cat mockingly gasped. 'Because apparently there could be spies at the GA!'

'Mwah-ha-hahaha! Sure, what are they gonna do? Tie up our camp phone now their wee call centre's closed? Mwah-ha-hahaha!'

Cat elaborated for Daniel's benefit. 'They tried to recruit members through cold calling out of a centre in Dundonald.'

'It's about seven miles east. Yeah, I know a girl who worked there. 95% of the mail they got was shit. Actual faeces,' said Fred.

'Hold on, hold on,' said Padraig. 'You know a girl?'

'I know your ma and she likes it up the –'

'It's Sturgeon's Law. 95% of everything is shit,' said Jack.

'Ya gotta wonder what that'd be like working there,' mused Shay. He held the whistle to his ear like a phone. '*Hello. Adolf Grobbler speaking. Can we interest you in hating your fellow man?*'

'*Subscription to White Supremacist Quarterly?* Mwah-ha-hahaha!'

'This city's full of call centres. I've worked for a few of them,' admitted Jack.

'I've done them all,' said Cat. '*Leperformance. Constipax Global. Convolutions UK.*'

'Padraig and I were at *Convolutions*,' said Fred.

Cat said, 'We'd ring people who couldn't understand Belfast accents. They thought we were Indian.' Cat laughed and waved the smoke out of her face. A moment passed and she found herself staring intensely at Padraig. Her jaw dropped. 'Wait, I'm remembering… Did you…? Where you the one who…?'

Padraig wheezed. 'Yes, yes. That was me.'

'You were… *that* guy.'

'I didn't know what else to do,' he pleaded.

Jack gasped and almost jumped out of her seat. Recognition spread over her face as well. 'You were *The Lone Voice!*'

Cat and Jack looked at one another with tearful delight, and back to Padraig, who had turned bright red.

'I couldn't quit. I would have lost my benefits,' he squealed.

'What are yous talking about?' Shay asked.

Cat laid it out. 'So, at Convolutions we had our little partitioned cubicles: our script, our computer and our phone. I was two cubicles along and I saw this lad climb onto his desk. Then, this almighty crack of wood, like he was going to go through it!'

Bob raised his head from the newspaper. Padraig didn't like how he was looking at him.

Jack picked up the story. 'He stuck his boot into the partition. Then there was another kick, smashing right through it.'

'That was my seat, but I was at the bogs and missed everything. It took them weeks to replace it,' said Fred.

'What did he shout? *Don't mention World Trade Centre building seven!* There he was, Shay: legs spread, fist raised to the ceiling.' Cat got up and stood on her chair, imitating Padraig's stance. *'Don't mention the melting point of steel!'*

Even Bob and Daniel were in tears with laughter. Fred clutched his sides.

'Everyone was staring. And Craig, the most useless line

manager ever, he didn't know what to do,' said Jack.

'And that's when Padraig starts singing. *They're coming to take me away!*'

Jack joined in singing with Cat. '*They're coming to take me away, ho ho, hee hee, ha ha!*'

'Craigs yelling, and there's two security guys calling for him to come down,' said Cat, 'And he yells…'

And again Jack and Cat called out in unison. '*They will not silence The Lone Voice!*

Padraig sighed.

'*I AM THE LONE VOICE!*' shouted Jack. 'And then the desk underneath him is cracking. He's ready to come down…'

Cat was laughing so hard the chair she stood on was shaking. Shay took hold of the back of it and steadied her arm as she stepped off it.

'His foot gets caught in the keyboard cable. He tugs it loose and slips. Falls face down.' Jack slapped her palm against her forehead. '*SMACK!*'

Padraig ran a finger down his temple. 'I've still got the scar, see?'

'You've no scar,' Bob stated.

Jack could barely speak for giggling. 'The phone comes down with him. The monitor smashes…'

'The whole office was cheering,' said Cat. 'Best fun we had there. And, there's customers, still on the line. They didn't know what was happening!'

Padraig shrugged. 'If I'd have quit I'd have been turned down for *Jobseekers Allowance*. My head was done in with phone monkey shit. It was the only way out.'

'The dole office don't pay quitters,' confirmed Fred.

He got up and threw the last of Bob's dismembered palette into the fire bin.

LEON

Leon's ready, revving revolution.
Anonymous union for action.
Stormont's cash convertors arrest time.
We say fight back, bring them to their grime.

A government of pearl counting bigots:
99% don't represent this tent.
Giving out alright: tea bank, care homes;
community backs justice in droves.

Understand as another raindrop, man,
slide tier. Damp faeces are Cameron
Toff's base anti-natal matrices.
So much future, denied of suture.

So left, she's right, but by god she is right.
Right sick of being gracious with fists.
Home the homeless in the cathedral
And tie a banner to the needle!

7

The John Hewitt – a pub named after an Irish literary master – was a stone's throw from the camp. A busy local haunt with an authentic attitude, the bar was full of punters and pumps, lit up bottles, and special offers on a chalkboard. To the right was an anteroom where Padraig, Mary and Fred sat pondering over pints.

Fred was revelling in the subversion of their secret meeting. 'Eoghan really wanted us to stay and plan for the anti-BNP thing.'

'Sure I'm not sittin' for another five hour meeting,' complained Padraig.

Mary groaned. 'We could have asked Joe to join us.'

Padraig shook his head. 'No, no. See, Joe's part of the problem. I mean, not Joe specifically. Well maybe, but the point is we don't know him.'

'He could be the spy,' mused Fred.

Mary laughed. 'Because he's new? I think yous two haven't gotten enough sleep.'

Padraig circled the rim of his pint with his finger. 'What about this practice of cops infiltrating the camp?'

Fred became excited. 'This could be a whole James Bond or Jason Bourne scenario.'

'Undercover, right. Like on *Spooks*. Joe with his tent, all primed and ready to go. And Declan, Levin, whatever his name is, with that just-too-perfect beard and moustache.'

'It's too perfect,' agreed Fred.

'He's gotta be a plant. A spook. Levin's well odd. Eoghan

isn't sure about him. Even Leon agrees,' said Padraig.

Mary stared at them. 'We're taking Leon as a barometer of objectivity? Goodness sake. A spook! What about Daniel? He never says a word. Or Jack? We barely know her. Is it because she's too pretty?'

Fred pondered this. 'Well, yeah?'

'She is pretty but here it is: we know you work at the hospital. We know Jack and Cat and Kiera are students. We know that Eoghan is… driven… but what do we know about Levin? Really?'

'So, you think Joe, or Levin, are going to set fire to our tents when we're sleeping?' asked Mary.

'Here: don't blame me if they both turn out to be MI5,' Padraig warned.

'Whatever.' Mary took a swig of her pint, and told them, 'Okay, look. I'll keep an eye on Joe. You two can check out Levin. If that's your bag.'

'Good,' said Padraig.

'We will,' declared Fred.

'We're not putting up with any spooks,' said Padraig.

'*Spook-busters,*' announced Fred in song.

'*Who you gonna call?*' sang Padraig.

Mary shook her head. 'No. No. No.'

'*Spook-Busters!*'

Faded green crayons denoted '*10 Days Occupied*' on the A1 free-standing chalk-board by the marquee. Joe secured a notice to the rails of a raised garden bed: '*End the Corruption of the 1% – Occupy Belfast St Annes.*' Under the marquee, Cat and Kiera smoked rollies; a long blanket covering their knees. They discussed holding teach-ins: small practical workshops on everything from resisting arrest to green living to non-violent civil disobedience. Leon volunteered to host the first one. The sessions had worked well in other Occupy camps. Shay was in his own world: bopping to the beats of Bob Marley inside his worn CD Walkman. Bob stretched out his news-paper and disappeared there.

The new fire bloomed red in the night air. Leon stabbed the smoking bin in front of them with a metal pole. Her black beret glistened from the damp of the day. 'Rain's off,' she said.

'Perfect timing.' Beneath the adjoining gazebo Eoghan cleared the table of pots and plates and set everything onto the wall.

Then he was rummaging through the thick plastic box of pamphlets. 'Where is everyone? Where's Padraig and Fred?

'Diddling themselves at Shaftesbury Square,' said Bob.

Eoghan stared at him. 'Bob, you've got to learn to be nicer to people.' Bob made a face like he didn't understand. 'The BNP plan to come for us tomorrow at City Hall. And at the same time, here: in our homes.'

'Their Facebook event has twenty-four people attending,' said Cat.

'Aye but according to Facebook there were five hundred people at Saturday's carnival,' said Kiera.

Eoghan set a sheet of paper on the empty table, and lifted it outside. 'Everyone gather round, gather round. This is our tactical strategy during the march.'

'It's what?' Joe asked.

Eoghan unfolded a tourist map of the city centre. Landmarks like Central Library, the Albert Clock and the Golden Thread Gallery were represented out of proportion along the arterial routes. Some locations were highlighted with red marker pen. They all gathered around, except for Bob who hadn't moved from his chair. Leon set down her metal pole and gazed over their shoulders.

'This is more like it,' she exclaimed.

'Bob will have a skeleton crew here, guarding base camp,' said Eoghan.

The old man yawned.

'The route of the march takes us to City Hall and back the ways.'

They leaned in and narrowed their gazes. Shay pointed

to the X marked over the cathedral on the map. 'Who's the kiss for?' he asked. Eoghan pretended not to hear him. Catching the chill now Shay warmed his hands over the fire.

Eoghan ran his finger along the route up Royal Avenue. 'Along the way one of us will break off at each side street and circle back. The BNP will be watching Royal Avenue, but we'll surround them,' he said confidently.

Leon beamed. 'Guerilla protest.'

'Glad you like it. I want you to liaise with Anonymous for back-up. And Shay? Can you bring your skate-boarder friends in on this?' Eoghan brought the plan closer to Shay, even as the wind flapped it in his hands.

'Mind the fire,' Cat told him.

Joe sighed. 'It all seems a bit... much?'

'It's fucking nuts,' said Kiera.

'This is how Che Guevara took Cuba,' said Leon.

'We're *taking* them *somewhere*? I'm really confused. What's the point of this?'

'I'll be clear, Cat. This isn't about confrontation. It's about controlling the narrative. The press will see there's more of us, and that we're better organised.'

'Right. You can't just piddle about doing good deeds and hope someone notices it. This is a strategy. Logistics. Opportunities.'

'Thank you, Leon. It's important you all memorise this,' said Eoghan.

Shay studied the X on the map, and the area around it growing a darker grey. 'Are you going to burn the map afterwards, like in the movies?'

'Eh? Of course not,' said Eoghan.

They leaned in and narrowed their gaze as the grey area on the map spread outwards.

'Map's on fire,' said Cat.

'Map's on fire!' said Kiera.

Joe tore it away from Eoghan, hurled it onto the path and stamped down on the flaming scroll. Bob chuckled.

It was after midnight and Shelby, the brown Staffy, ran from the planters round to the wide concrete plane. He bounded over paving stones inscribed with quotes from Louis MacNeice, C. S. Lewis and Michael McLaverty. Shelby found the softball and chewed it a moment, then turned back to look at the flames slapping the night air. Bob was watching the closing time detritus tumble onto the street in front, when the saliva sodden ball was pressed into his knee. He swatted it away, below the chair. Shelby followed. Bob stroked Shelby's coat and rubbed behind his ears, and the dog licked Bob's knuckles. Beneath the mist of the street-light two drunken yokels danced their way towards the camp. They were Padraig and Fred. Bob and Shelby fixed them with steely eyes.

'Yee-oww!'

'What are yous protestin' about anyway?'

Bob got to his feet and hissed. 'Do you two mind? There's people tryin' ta sleep here.'

'Bob! Bob!' cried Padraig, his arms outstretched. He stopped just short of hugging the grump.

'We love you, Bob,' said Fred.

'Read us a story,' Padraig begged.

Bob folded his arms. 'Get to bed. Now.'

'But... supper!' sobbed Fred.

'You'll get a stick smacked against yer arses if you don't settle.'

The street-light shone through the olive canvas of *The Love Shack*. The wind changed its shape from triangular to dome and back again. Spare clothes were piled in lumps brushing the sides which were moist from rain and sweat.

Padraig felt the cold uneven ground below as he struggled with his red sleeping bag. 'There's that same daddy longlegs crawling over my shit. I swear I've put him out at least twice, every day.'

There was no answer from Fred.

Padraig's head was spinning in a boozy haze. 'Hey Fred. Remember the pub?'

'Pub,' he mumbled, and turned over.

'We were going to set the world to rights. Remember? The real revolution?'

'Mmm, Cat.'

Fred's breath drifted off, and each intake grew louder until he was snoring. Padraig looked up at the leafy branches moving under the light like a shadow carousel. His head was full of ideas: for social change; political and environmental change; and each new idea kept the wheel in motion. Padraig found himself sitting upright. He pulled an A4 refill pad from under his pillow, and found himself a pen. Rolling over, balanced by an elbow, he began to write.

Dear Northern Ireland Executive, I am Padraig Mahon of the Occupy Belfast. You have forsaken your electorate and lied to us. I call on all MPs of parliament of all parties to resign immediately for the sake of peace without delay.

'Bastards,' he murmured, and added a spaghetti signature. Then he let the sleep take him.

Bob's was a vibrant blue dome tent, or it had been. Now supplies insulated the space: placards; firewood; spare duvets; Galway's hob, redundant as they used a grille over the fire. He was content with the arrangement. The tent was a donation of good size, and Bob didn't want company. Regardless that was what he got having chosen 'for security purposes' to pitch near the base tent. Galway and Daniel had relieved him from night watch at four that morning. He heard them chittering, and the songbirds chirping. The south-south-westerly wind clapped against the folds and changed course. Yet Bob was a heavy sleeper when he wanted to be. His brain filtered out the sounds of the road sweeper and campers sneezing.

The odd warning phrase triggered off his senses.

'A corporate enforcer for an arms manufacturer?' asked Padraig.

Leon retorted, 'That's Michael Knight and Knight Industries. Technologically aggressive intervention!'

He was still learning to block those two out. And Fred, hollering while bouncing the football on the pavilion. There were many foot-steps: the assembly for the Anti-Austerity demo and their departures. Bob was almost off to sleep again when, for a brief moment, he dreamed there was a reporter in his tent. He awoke with a jump.

Crawling outside on aching knees into a day which had turned dismal – an all-in-one screen of mist, rain spit and smoke – he heard Levin say hello to him. The wrist-watch read half twelve so Bob went directly to the pub for his morning piss.

Padraig sat next to Levin who sat next to Fred, exhaling their cigarettes and looking ahead. On the street casual passers-by walked and talked, some stared back at them. On the cathedral steps an obese man of forty years rested as sunlight crept towards him. Padraig's gaze was drawn to the perimeter of *St. Anne's*, bordering Talbot Street. Two large young men – one in a tracksuit, the other in a bomber jacket – had stopped beside a third man coming the other way. He wore a tee-shirt and shorts, despite the rain only a few minutes before.

'Don't say anything,' whispered Padraig. 'Look at them-muns there. Do you think that's them?' He cast a quick eye over Levin to gauge his reaction. There was no concern on his brow. They didn't see Bob wave to the men as he crossed back over the road, nor them waving back.

'Maybe scoping us out like they did for Redwatch,' Fred murmured.

Bob passed the marquee. The gazebo stored a ten litre keg of water container. He filled the kettle half way, picked up the cooking grate, and set both onto the fire. Then he sat down and picked up his *Daily Mirror*. Briefly he followed their gaze to the men on the street, now joined by a young woman with a pram, before taking in the paper's front page. 'Shite,' he said coolly. The lads glanced over as Bob turned the page. 'Shite.

Shite.'

Levin remarked, 'I wonder do they actually think about what news *is* when they're publishing. Little of it's actually news that helps anyone.'

'Shite,' said Bob, and turned to the next page. 'Shite, shite.'

That was how it went for the next five minutes. Bob's pronouncements didn't rattle the plump wobbling pigeon pottering around beside him.

Padraig said, 'I see you've found yourself a friend: Bob Pigeon! Mwah-ha-ha-ha-ha!'

Bob didn't react at all.

Padraig's 'suspects' on the street had already moved on. When he was ready, Bob took the kettle off the boil and made a cup of tea.

'Well... this is hardly the last stand at the Alamo,' Levin scoffed.

'The BNP could attack here, or at the march,' Fred assured him.

'Nazi fucks,' muttered Padraig. 'Here, we should take a selfie. To mark the occasion.'

Levin shook his head. 'No thanks.'

'Why not?' asked Padraig.

'I don't like selfies. They feel forced.'

'Ah go on,' sang Fred. 'Go on. Go on. Go on.'

Levin sighed. 'Okay.'

Padraig brought up the camera on his phone and held it an arm's length.

'Bob, do you want in on this?'

'He doesn't show up on film,' said Fred.

The old man was looking straight in front of them. Levin noticed and followed his gaze but saw nothing out of the ordinary. 'What are you staring at Bob?'

'BNP.'

Padraig gasped. 'What?'

'Been standing there ten minutes. Did you not see yer

man sat on the steps?'

Low under the cathedral one obese man was sitting with his sign between his legs.

Soon after, the protestors returned to base camp. Eoghan looked confused and was further thrown off balance by the sight of Padraig pulling leaves off random tents. When Bob relayed the detail of the lone timid BNP protestor Eoghan reacted the only way he could. He doubled over, laughing.

'One protestor! One protestor?!?'

Leon was in stitches too. 'The BNP sent half their forces here, and... one protestor? Oh lord! What happened to him?'

'Stuck it out for twenty minutes and left. No resolve,' said Bob.

Fred's tone was a little more sombre. 'Levin was going to talk to him. But the guy left when he saw him coming. What do we think of that?'

'Maybe he put the pee in the BNP!' roared Leon.

Eoghan was still chuckling too, and clutching his sides. 'One protestor!' he exclaimed, steadying himself on the marquee. 'One protestor!'

Padraig's wicked laugh echoed from the other end of the camp. 'Mwah-ha-ha-ha-ha!'

'Levin left ten minutes later. That's a little suspicious if you ask me,' said Fred.

'No-one did. How many of the BNP were at the march?'

'Five of them, Bob. Fourteen of us, and a half dozen cops,' said Eoghan.

'I bet they were pleased. And what about your great plan?'

Eoghan sighed and shook his head. 'No-one stuck to the plan.'

Leon spoke up. 'Shay and Cat disappeared.'

'Oh they're in Cat's tent. They got back ten minutes ago with burgers,' said Bob.

'It's that Levin one you have to watch,' Fred warned.

Eoghan looked over to the tents to where Padraig was raking leaves. He gasped, again, and for a moment had trouble forming the words. 'So… Padraig's… working?'

'I had a wee word in his ear and made him see it was in his best interests,' said Bob.

Fred raised his voice, demanding to be taken seriously. 'Levin keeps asking questions! *What's the plan this week? Do you write it down? Do you have a rota?*'

Bob chuckled. 'A rota!'

Eoghan's demeanour shifted: stern body language and a forceful tone. 'Now hang on. We do have a rota.'

Leon began laughing too.

'Am I the only one sticking to the rota?'

Bob stopped laughing, and replied in a monotone grumble. 'No, that's fair enough. I remember I'd get overworked in my time at the helicopter factory. Enough so the boss put me on rotas.'

He set Leon off giggling again.

'God's sake,' said Eoghan and he shook his head and started off to his tent.

Bob filled a large pot of water and set it on the fire grate.

By the tents near the roadside, around the Spanish War bust, Padraig called out to them. 'Leon! Bring us a bin bag!'

Fred rummaged in a clear baggie of tobacco, until he became aware Bob stood glowering above him.

'Right sunshine. There's a basin full of dishes there for you to wash.'

'Me? I'm not even part of this,' said Fred.

'Don't talk daft. You've stayed a few nights. If you're going to hang around you pay your dues.'

'Fuck's sake. Alright.'

'Well? Get started.'

The water was cold, brown, and stodgy, staining the sides of the grey basin. The wash-cloth was foul. Fred's hands searched for the cutlery, brushing against wobbly pasta and sodden tuna. 'This is horrible. Where's the rubber gloves?'

'Aren't none. Now, tell me about Levin,' said Bob.

'I don't wanna... do this,' cried Fred. The basin stank of rotten potatoes and in murky depths, something was moving. The gazebo roof spat rain upon his brow and his eyes watered.

'What do you know you're not telling us?'

A shoal of noodles swam over Fred's knuckles. 'I don't know anything. Eoghan and Leon said he was odd.'

'Keep talking. And keep your hands in the basin where I can't see them.'

'And Padraig, and Mary suspects him too... please, Bob.' Fred jerked his head away, and wretched.

'If they told you to stick your hands in the fire, would you?'

'No but... please Bob, I'm gonna boke.'

'I'm growing impatient, sunshine.'

'Well, Levin's all, *I'll do any job. I'm happy to help.*'

'So let's see if I have this right. He's more reliable than you, but bears watching, 'cos he's a spy?'

'That's right!'

'That water's getting colder, son.'

'Get off my case!' Fred squealed. 'Look, there's Levin now. Why don't you ask him?'

Bob's eyes widened. 'Why don't we?'

Fred shook his head. 'No, no. Don't tell him what I said.'

'I'll speak for myself. Hey Levin, come here a minute!'

Bob looked back to Fred and told him, 'You've a choice. You can stay here with me, Levin and the dishes, and continue this chat; or you can help your pal over there, sweepin' up the leaves.'

Five minutes later, Levin was at the edge of the camp, by the wall of the Shac flats, pouring the dregs of the basin down the narrow drain. He walked back to the base tent, and to Bob.

'There was some weird icky shit down there, Bob'

He nodded. 'Tell me. Are you working, Levin?'

'I'm taking a gap year from my PhD.'

'In?'

'Politics and international relations. At *Queen's*,' he replied warmly.

'And for your gap year you're pissing about at this?'

Levin laughed, as he sloshed cold water around the basin's filthy ring. He picked up a scrubber. 'Well, I did some teaching: Sociology and Politics; mostly for undergrads but a few A-Level students too.'

'Not much money in that.'

'You're not wrong. I worked as a line manager at a call centre for a bit. *Convolutions UK*.'

A light formed in Bob's eyes. 'Oh aye? Did you know Padraig and Fred worked there too?'

'Oh? I can't say I remember them. In any case, I didn't stay long. It was a horrible environment. The day after I left some guy went totally nuts: smashing up the cubicles, wrecking the machines...'

Mary had come out from the pub to the sight of Padraig brushing leaves into Fred's shovel.

'Well. Did you rule out Levin from your enquiries?' she asked.

'He fuckin' tricked us,' moaned Fred.

'How so?'

Padraig said, 'He's got Bob thinking we're spreading shit. Now he's making us do all this extra work.'

Fred wanted to know, 'What about Joe? Did you expose him yet?'

The large muscular man Fred had just asked about walked up behind Mary. He put his arms around her and she held Joe's hands at her waist.

'We're working on it,' Mary said.

'Excuse me!'

They turned around to see a woman with a clipboard and a lanyard around her neck. The badge identified her as a BBC journalist. Behind her, two men were hauling tripods, a camera and a boom mic.

'I was wondering if one of you could give us a few minutes to talk about living at the campsite, and what Occupy means to you?'

Padraig looked to Fred, smiled, and then pointed towards the marquee. 'You really want to see that older fella there.'

Fred nodded. 'That's right. Really helpful. His name is Bob.'

'Knowledgeable. Very photogenic. He'd be happy to give you everything you need,' said Padraig.

Leon wiggled out of her tent, and gazed over at the meeting on the kerb. A scrap of paper dawdled on the path in front of her. It was a hand-written letter which began, *'Dear Northern Ireland Executive, I am Padraig Mahon of the Occupy Belfast.'*

She called out to Bob. 'Would you get me out an envelope?'

Bob had his back to her and when he turned he saw the journalists advancing. 'Oh god, fuck's sake,' he said, his steely tone crumbling. 'Fuck, no.'

Eoghan was already part-way out of his tent. Hearing the fear in Bob's voice he quickened his pace. 'What is it? What's wrong?'

His face was simultaneously flushed and pale. 'Journos!' he whimpered. 'Journos everywhere!'

A half dozen campers sat under the base tent, unable to sleep. Beyond the slithering screen of rain water, the metal bin smoked from a fire beyond re-kindling. Eoghan strummed his guitar and sang to them.

'The BNP. got photos of V. They didn't get me. Or Leonie.'

He sat on his bum in the marquee and strummed.

'And Levin is just what we wished. He's not a spook, junkie or pished.'

Kiera and Galway John giggled.

'The TV crews gave Bob the blues. The big man does not tol-

erate fools.'

He slapped the guitar body, thrice in a hurry.
'If he's gonna be round, he'll have to tolerate those guys reporters and camera-men asking where and why.'
He picked strings like a master and the tempo got faster.
'I sing this song to a celestial ceiling for when we began the general meeting, the heavens opened on the tents, hard pishing,
we ran to get under cover and we ran all the way screaming!'

8

It was an hour since he'd gotten into the sleeping bag. An hour in darkness of wind battering the tent. Time spent perfecting the optimal sleeping position. Jonathan McCracken didn't know if the heavy moisture was from the rain, his sweat or aggressive sneezing. Mostly he felt like a prisoner to the tent. The ground was cold under him and his ear level with the coming and going of footsteps on concrete and the never-ending tires and motors on tarmac: wheels and wheels, so many wheels. At ten o'clock Jonathan gave up. He noticed a streak of mud all along his trouser leg, which was unusual as he'd been very careful. Jonathan crawled backwards out of the shuddering tent onto the cardboard doormat and into the night.

Eoghan sat at the fire rolling up a cigarette. 'I was thinking… the camp is growing. We could use a second marquee tent. Maybe strap the two together?'

It had worked with the gazebo, presently forming it's own section attached to the marquee. There, Levin Kirkwood scraped a plate over a bin bag hung from the fence. Levin agreed with Eoghan's assessment. 'We could use more shelter. Has anyone thought to email the council about getting us proper bins?'

'I'll talk to Gary – Jonathan! Good morning!'

'Aye. I wish it was,' he murmured. Jonathan kept his head low should they see how deprived he felt after an hour on the ground.

Eoghan knew it the moment he sat down. The reporter's thermal shirt, chequered earthy brown, was from a designer range. Jonathan was around thirty with a perfectly sculpted goatee and there was a whiff of product in his hair. Levin occupied a wooden chair beside him. Eoghan glanced up.

'Levin, I told you he wouldn't sleep. That's a pound you owe me.'

Jonathan chuckled, shook his head and asked, 'When do you get used to it? You've been out here, what, two weeks?'

'Two weeks tomorrow,' said Eoghan.

'With nothing to do but sit and think,' quipped Jonathan.

Eoghan glared. 'We all have responsibilities.'

'You've touched a nerve there,' Levin told him.

Jonathan acquiesced. 'Sorry,' he said.

Eoghan laughed it off and Jonathan was grateful. Earlier that day Eoghan had provided Jonathan with an unsolicited interview. Unsolicited because Jonathan was making small talk and Eoghan spoke on all aspects of the camp and the ambitions of the global movement and the weaknesses of Marxist theory in enabling an elitist tyranny as opposed to the libertarian anarchism of Mikhail Bakunin. Eoghan dominated the group conversation and though a trained listener, Jonathan found the whole thing uncomfortable. Late afternoon felt like half a world away.

Jonathan studied a placard on the wall by them covered in grime and bad green and red lettering. He took out his notepad – cautiously so as not to set Eoghan off – and scribbled down the words: *'A Revolution Will Not be Affected by Anything – Change Is Inevitable'*.

Leon McCallum came off the road via the path by the *Shac* housing shelter. In place of her loose fitting beret was a black beanie, long soggy black hair hanging out of it and down over a camouflage jacket. She passed the tree with it's rupturing roots in mud, and the soaked tents, with white splatters of bird shit on a few of them. Beside redundant hanging ropes she lifted a navy umbrella, upturned and partly dismembered, and carried it towards them. The street-light cast her shadow over wet concrete creating a dark mirror.

'Any grub left?'

'There's a pot in the back. Leave some for Bob,' Eoghan cautioned.

She carried on to the gazebo section. 'Sure. After all, I want to survive the night.'

It wasn't the first quip about Bob's temper Jonathan had heard. He thought he'd prefer to meet the oldest camper before making up his mind about him. He changed the subject. 'I read Billy Bragg was playing here last week.'

'Right where you're sitting,' said Eoghan.

'Cultural Mecca of Belfast this,' said Levin. 'Leon, do you remember we said the reporter from the *Sunday World* was spending the night with us? This is Jonathan.'

He gave her a wave. 'Hi, Lianne. What do you do around the camp?' Leon remained with her back to him; focused on the big pot of pasta, pesto and tuna.

'*Leon* helps with the demos and leaflet drops,' Eoghan clarified. 'She's also hosting our first teach-in. Our aim is to have a practical, participatory workshop a few times a week. So maybe we'll get something on green lifestyles, or resisting arrest. We're reliant on volunteers to teach in their areas of expertise.'

Under the gazebo Leon scooped a helping of food onto her plate. 'Martine and I are doing one called *Feminist Design in Technological Appliances*.'

Levin put his hand over his brow and shook his head. Then he slowly pushed his fingers through damp hair, reconciled to his place with these mad people.

'That's useful detail,' said Jonathan. 'And remind me about your General Assemblies? Those are every night at seven?'

'Every night,' said Eoghan. 'Oh god, every night.'

Leon sat on a chair in the corner with her cold plate on her lap, and scrutinised Jonathan.

By matter of fact Levin informed him, 'Last night at the

GA there was a call for a boycott on spiders.'

'And do you survive okay with your own money and the donations that come in? Do you have enough? Is there anything you need?'

Eoghan and Leon laughed. Levin flashed a smirk. Jonathan expressed confusion; raised his eyebrows.

'What's so funny?'

Eoghan laughed again. 'Sorry, it's just --'

'That's one of the things people say to us... all the time,' said Leon.

'That and, *what are yous protesting about?*' said Eoghan.

Leon answered in a squeaky falsetto. '*What's the big idea, missus? Missus? Missus? What's all this protest for?*'

'*Occupy Belfast you are filthy bums,*' squawked Eoghan. 'That's an internet favourite.

With a mouthful of pasta Leon managed in monotone, '*Uhhh get a job.*'

'Waster scum's another one,' said Eoghan.

'I will admit it,' said Levin.

Eoghan told Jonathan, 'We get a lot of help from donations and shop locally where we can. Okay sometimes the necessities includes the like of *Freddo* bars and *Tunnock's Teacakes* but you get my drift.'

Levin looked out to the two ash trees and the eleven ramshackle tents underneath them. They folded in on themselves, and fattened out, swayed and threatened to break. As for the trees a branch of the nearer ash had caught a plastic bag. It made a flapping sound as it squirmed in a tussle to escape.

'We've got a ghost,' said Levin.

'Aye. Ghost of capitalism,' said Leon flippantly, and put another forkful in her mouth.

Levin fixated on one tent particularly shaking. It seemed to rip apart as the large man burst out of it and stood on the path glaring. Bob was all in black: jeans, a rugged bomber jacket over layered jumpers and his flat cap. Little was said in the minute between zipping up his tent and arriving at the marquee. Jonathan bristled at the sight of him. Bob Barr stood in front of them, scowled and gave a sharp, heavy grunt. As if waiting for an answer to an unasked question, he puffed out his chest.

Levin, who already had his Bob-vaccination, greeted him in sing-song fashion. 'Good morning Bob!'

Jonathan risked an informal, 'How are you doing?'

Bob answered with a sharp, heavy grunt. 'Where's my breakfast?'

'Gazebo,' said Eoghan.

Jonathan whispered, 'Did he just tell me to piss off?'

'He said breakfast,' clarified Levin. 'It's an odd accent. I think he's from Lisburn.'

Eoghan got up out of his seat. 'Gentlemen, lady…'

'I'm no lady!' hissed Leon.

'Whatever. I'm away out of here; I promised Josie we'd spend some time together. Have yous got everything you need?'

Levin began to laugh, and Leon and Jonathan smiled.

'Fuck's sake,' said Eoghan.

'Good night Eoghan,' said Bob gloomily.

Bob spent the next fifteen minutes watching Jonathan like a hawk. He discovered the man jumped when he poured coal into the metal fire bin and made a point to re-stock it often. Eoghan and Leon had given Bob some training in what to expect in preparation for Jonathan's arrival. He took confidence knowing the reporter was on his turf, under his rules. He was dependent on Bob and Bob understood he could exert some control on the questions asked and answers provided.

'Why are you choosing to demonstrate in the way that you're doing?'

Leon did most of the talking. 'To draw attention to a system of financial brutality. The media elite doesn't care until someone's doing something drastic like setting themselves on fire. Being out here is horrible, but there's people all across the city who don't even have tents. Every single day. And they're ignored. So let me turn that around: why are you here? What do you think of what we're doing, Jonathan?'

Bob could barely conceal his relish.

Jonathan took a deep breath. 'Ask me tomorrow if I have the patience do it myself, but tonight? I think it's brave and honourable. Fair play to yous. It's an important story on a local and global level. My editor feels the same way, otherwise I'd not be hanging around.'

Levin smiled and nodded agreeably. Bob thrashed his hand against the billowing smoke.

'Do you take on specific tasks?' the reporter asked.

'We don't have leaders or assigned roles,' said Leon.

Levin elaborated. 'Though I think Bob ends up running security at nights, don't you?'

Jonathan looked from Levin, immediately friendly, to Bob, overwhelmingly unfriendly, and judging by the way he looked at Jonathan, his ire was reserved especially for him. He tried again to get the old man to warm to him.

'Bob, you must have a few good stories?'

'No stories here... things happen in stories.'

'He's got a point. This is just us; sitting,' said Leon. Suddenly her face contorted. She let loose a massive sneeze and then a second one, the chair rocking under her.

'Bless you,' said Levin. 'I'll put more wood on the fire.'

Leon let out another sneeze, this time like a full-blown scream, and then a fourth one.

'Bless you, and bless you again,' said Jonathan. 'Are the three of you really going to sit out here all night?'

'Not me. Not tonight at any rate,' said Levin, and he got to his feet. 'These two will be though.'

'Bob won't let a woman sit out on her own. He's a sexist pig,' muttered Leon.

Levin threw a bundle of firewood into the metal bin.

'I can't see how I'll sleep,' Jonathan confessed.

'Whoa!' exclaimed Levin. 'Did you see that?'

'What?'

'When I threw that log in? The shape of a man appeared in the smoke, in a gown...'

'Is this place getting to you already Levin?' Bob said gruffly.

Leon laughed. 'Lightweight.'

'It was sort of like Ben Kenobi,' Levin mused.

Leon screwed up her face. 'Who?'

Levin shook his head. 'Obi-Wan Kenobi. It can't be a good omen.'

'Why isn't that a good omen?' asked Jonathan.

Levin spread his fingers. 'Remember how in *Empire* Luke had a premonition of Han and Leia in danger and Obi-Wan told Luke not to go and save his friends?'

'Nice try but you're wrong,' said Leon. 'Obi-Wan was trying to protect Luke from Vader. But he didn't listen and... chop! Look ma, no hand.'

'Yeah, but if he hadn't have gone, Vader would have killed his friends,' said Jonathan.

Leon dug in. 'No. Lando's betrayal of Vader to save Leia and the others would have happened with or without Luke's intervention.'

'I always found that bit troubling,' said Levin. 'That an armed militia was taking advice from a ghost? Forecasts of Tony Blair and Iraq there.'

'Why,' enquired Bob earnestly, 'must you all talk such vast amounts of shite?'

Leon raised her shoulders and puffed up. 'Well I for one am glad we can partake freely in this important discourse.'

'The truth will set you free,' quipped Jonathan.

Leon opened her mobile phone. 'Hey, it's ten to eleven...'

Levin sprang from his chair cursing and ran quickly out to the path, the road, and disappeared.

Bob smirked. 'See the runs of him!'

'He's going to miss his bus,' said Leon.

Bob didn't seem to care. 'If only there were some place around here he could lay his head down for the night.'

Jonathan asked if they were low on tents. Bob said no. Leon stretched out, used to the finality in his voice. Jonathan waited for Bob to elaborate. The wind whistled and swept into the tents, scooping up leaves by Shac's wall and pulling the shoal to the back of the building. Exposed straps on tents slapped against the canvas as the campsite shook like jelly. Jonathan sniffed, as much to clear his nose as to punctuate the eerie sound-scape. He could sense Bob did not like him, and it made the hairs stand up on the back of his neck.

Leon yawned, and then made herself comfortable. 'The bars won't be out for a while. It's time to relax!'

'Get your feet off that chair,' snapped Bob. 'Do you think this is the job-centre?'

'Well, no. There's no plasma screen.'

Jonathan interjected. 'I don't mean to be rude, but what do you do all night?'

'The camp has to be a) safe, and b) tidy, for the morning. There's rules.' Bob got up and reached for the hard brush. 'Here, journo. Wind's died down. Give the front a sweep.'

'Sure.'

'Leon, there's more dishes out back.'

'Dishes? Away on! I didn't sign up for this woman in the kitchen crap. Chauvinist old --'

'If you want your worker's paradise,' said Bob coolly, 'you have to work for it. You know the gold on the Soviet star comes from the rewards system, don't you?'

'Are you sure?' asked Jonathan.

Bob nodded. 'Oh yes. We score those working hardest out of ten. The results are tallied between Occupy camps nationally and the winner goes on to the *Clean Dishes Championship* on Wall Street.'

Leon laughed. 'Right. So if I do the dishes, what are you going to do?'

'Chop more logs, secure the tents, tidy the supplies.'

'I'll do it,' she snapped, 'but I'm not following your diktat. I operate autonomously.'

'Aye, you do that,' said Bob.

Leon put a half dozen sticks in the fire bin. Post-pub traffic brought teenagers queuing at the camp for coffee. They wanted to know if Leon was going to try and convert them to Jesus. Leon said it wasn't her sins Jesus died for. The girls lost interest before the pot had boiled, and they wandered away. Across the street an eejit collapsed in a nest of blue bin bags. His friend spent six minutes giving therapy, and said six times he was going to leave. They parted together.

Accompanied by the marquee drip, Jonathan scribbled in the pocket notebook on his knee. Bob continued to scrutinise him. Leon gazed at the silvery pavement and supped from her coffee.

'You're protesting the *MTV Awards* tomorrow,' said Jonathan.

'Sort of,' Leon replied. 'We've our demo every Saturday. So we're using it to draw attention to Stormont giving breaks to MTV when they could be putting money into schools and hospitals.'

Jonathan finished writing and put his notebook away. 'Bob, have I done something to annoy you?'

Two dozen trees fell in the Amazon Rainforest.

'He doesn't like being interviewed,' Leon divulged. 'The other day he'd an encounter with a BBC documentary crew.'

'They shoved that flippin' mic right in my face.' Bob got up and stormed over to the gazebo section.

'He didn't know what to say,' whispered Leon. She imitated his mis-shapen awkward smile and held the expression for twenty seconds. 'We thought he'd had a stroke,' she muttered through a grin.

'Fucking BBC. Asking me about equipment being stolen. And tough labour? Bastards probably never worked a day in their lives,' said Bob.

'Padraig and Fred thought it'd be funny to stir the pot. Eoghan and Deirdre had to rescue you, didn't they?' teased Leon.

Bob kept Jonathan square in his view, as he sat back down.

'This camp is watched 24/7,' he barked. 'There's no question of safety. We try to give people as much privacy as we can, and we work to maintain what we do here.'

Jonathan took out his notebook again and began to write.

Bob waited for him to finish. Then his voice was cool, with softer tones. 'Look son, if you want to be useful, take a walk to the shop. We're nearly out of milk. There's an all-night *Spar* on Castle Lane.'

Bob gave him a few pounds from his pocket and they watched him depart.

'I saw what you did there, Bob.'

Bob hung his mouth open innocently.

'He could have gone to the filling station in half the time.'

Bob pushed out his lips and smiled.

'You sent him to an inconvenience store,' Leon said.

'Ach sure it gets him out of the way. Bloody reporters. Can't talk with them around.'

'They do like to have their own agenda.'

'Claiming we're all dirt. They're like gulls at bin bags,' he grumbled.

'Well they only want their own story. Failed novelists,' said Leon. 'Though I don't think yer man's too bad. I was all set to expose him – and I will if he pulls some shit – but he's a good bloke.'

'Oh he is, is he?'

'Lighten up, man. You think he's getting paid hourly for sitting here? It'll be his weekend off. The way the press are going he's lucky to be on staff. I think he might do us fair.'

Bob murmured something unintelligible.

'So! What was it you wanted to talk to me about?'

'Those election boards Gary brought down for re-use. A few of them were vandalised: broke in half; scrawled over. What do you know about it?'

'Nothing. Hey! Gary's alright by me. Sound as a pound. One of the rare politicians who actually gives a shit,' said Leon.

The old man thought for a moment. 'Tell me about Fred and Padraig. Don't you live with them?'

'In the flat above them. They're a bag of dicks.'

'That's what I thought.'

'I wouldn't put it past them to have done it.'

Bob pondered this. 'Well I heard wee Fred talking shit about Gary.'

'Oh that's him. Slabbers behind people's backs. Always at it. Noisy fuckers too.'

Bob shook his head.

'I'm sure you've had many sleepless nights in your time Bob. What did you do for a living?'

'Worked security.'

'Where was that?'

'Can't tell you.' He saw her scepticism and added, 'For reasons of security.'

'So you worked in security your whole life?'

'I've worked my whole life. I was on the milk float at fourteen, straight from school.'

'You left school at fourteen? You rebel.'

'Wasn't much use to me.'

'When did you start smoking?'

'Fourteen. I shouldn't have started.' Bob paused; gave her a mean side-eye. 'What is all this? All this one hundred and one bloody questions?'

'Well we're sitting here in the cold and rain. What else are we going to do?' The wind howled and the fire convulsed, flames rising like arrows towards them. 'You're a man of few words. Tell me something. Do you have family? What did they do?'

'I don't see how that's any of your business.'

'*FUCK'S SAKE!* This is blood from a stone. You know a good bit about me...'

'*AYE, COS you do not stop YAPPING.*'

'*...AND I KNOW NOTHING about you.* How am I to trust you if that's the way it is?' Bob laughed. Leon looked him in the eyes. 'You don't trust me, do you?'

'Don't trust anyone,' he replied glibly.

'Why? What is it makes you say that?'

Bob looked along the path to a puddle capturing the reflection of the trees. His bones were crystallising in the bitter chill.

'Okay, general knowledge,' said Leon. 'What do you remember about World War Two?'

'World War Two? How old do you think I am?'

'About seventy?'

'Not far off. But sure I was just a nipper.'

'It's just a game. Come on. What do you remember?'

Bob exhaled. 'I remember the ration booklets. And my ma, when she didn't have to use them no more. Chuffed to bits she was.'

'Bet she was the type of woman that spread butter on her toast once the rationing was over. Cut it like cheese so you could see your teeth tracks in it?'

A smile spread over Bob's face. His cheeks were red and his blue eyes sparkled with magic. Then the mugginess brushed his face, beginning his drift back to his usual state.

'We didn't have the opportunities you lot have. With the bombs, and the streets full of litter. The power and lighting cut. That oul' bitch Thatcher ordering her army to murder us in the street, and breaking up the unions.'

'I missed that. What about your dad? Was he around to see all that?'

'Right. Tea,' said Bob sharply.

'You fancy a cuppa? Am I making?'

'Go on. My knees are killing me.'

'Sure we'll have a cuppa and then you can tell me all about that oul' bitch Thatcher.'

Several hours later the first paw of light crawled into the city's dark streets. There came a gale – wrestling their tents and muffling their words - although it was a short burst. The wind wore itself out and rested. Bob left for the shop to get tobacco. Jonathan looked out into the dim light, shivering; frustrated that the darkness had looked so long into him.

'That tent's moving. It's not the wind,' he said.

'That's Mary and Joe. They're very close,' said Leon.

'And that one?'

'Joel. Snoring.'

Leon walked past the gazebo to the wall and lifted the ten litre cannister. 'These water drums need filled. Will you be okay on your own for fifteen minutes?'

'I think I can communicate with the hordes,' said Jonathan sarcastically.

'Bob should be back soon.'

'What's the protocol if someone's looking to cause hassle?'

'There'll be no hassle, trust me. Fifteen minutes.'

Jonathan sat a few minutes before stoking the fire. He looked East, the direction of home. He tried to circulate heat around his body by arching his feet from his toes and bouncing his legs up and down. He watched the eleven tents and smiled thinking of the people inside them under his protection. The tents pattered and puttered under the wind.

It felt longer than fifteen minutes. He checked his phone, but couldn't remember when Bob or Leon had left. The gale returned blowing chip papers and polystyrene tubs into the camp's wind trap. Jonathan heard the sounds of footsteps close by.

'Hello? Is somebody there?'

Two police officers loomed large over the fire, casting their shadows into the base tent. The bigger of the two, Sergeant Barker, peered down upon Jonathan. 'Are you responsible for this encampment?'

'It would be bad if you weren't,' said Constable Corbett.

'No,' said Jonathan. 'I mean yes. Yes. I'm responsible. How would it be bad?'

Sergeant Barker rubbed his broom moustache and put his hands on his hips. He looked around. He had a big, authoritative voice but the wind was blowing so furiously Jonathan strained to hear him. 'Then the camp would be unoccupied and – well, I'm afraid you'd have to take it down.'

'Ah no. I'm in charge. I'm not committing any crime,' said Jonathan defensively.

'Thank goodness. Inspector Tarbard wouldn't have us manning the place,' Barker said, as best as Jonathan understood him.

'Tarbard would think we were informing on departmental corruption,' Corbett said cheerily.

'Constable, have you got the cuffs?' Jonathan heard Barker say.

Corbett reached into his jacket pocket.

'Now hang on. You're not putting hand-cuffs on me! I'm just observing, I'm —'

Jonathan stopped as Corbett held out not hand-cuffs but a pair of ear muffs. He changed his expression to an over-compensating smile, but still hesitated before taking them.

Barker raised his voice. 'There's rain expected later. And rising wind speeds. You'll want to make sure all those tents are fastened down.'

Corbett sniffed as he fumbled in his trouser pocket. Then he straightened up, having found three folded pairs of slim gloves. A single teardrop ran down his face. The sorrow caught in his throat. 'I thought finger-less gloves would be easier to work with. They made fun of me at the station for this,' he blubbered.

Jonathan took the gloves as well. 'Thank you, officer.'

'See, Stan? He loves them! I told you he would. Now,' said

Barker firmly, 'I'll leave you to get on with whatever it is you're plotting. Don't be spray-painting City Hall pink! No prank calling *The Kevin Trojan Show!*'

'Ah, right, no. Of course not,' said Jonathan, still on the defensive and taken aback by Barker's humour.

Barker slapped Jonathan on the shoulder and said goodbye, then led the sobbing Corbett away with him.

'He thought I was going to hand-cuff him?' murmured Corbett.

'He didn't mean it. He's just been at that camp too long. Let's get you feeling better with a healthy walk. It's good for you.'

Jonathan was still processing the encounter ten minutes later when Leon returned.

'Where did you go for your cigarettes? Colombia?' he asked sarcastically.

At almost the exact moment Bob reappeared from the other direction.

'Fifteen minutes you said!'

Bob simply shrugged. Jonathan looked back and forth between him and Leon, who replied, 'If we'd known you were that scared, Bob could have left one of his glass eyes with you!'

The black sky turned grey monotone, camouflage for stars and for sun. Within every five minutes a car passed. Then it was four minutes, then three. Jonathan was watching the fire and waiting for the kettle on the steel grate to boil. Leon walked in front of him with a tea towel in her hands. She picked up the kettle and moved it to the side where there was less heat.

'Oh come on. Can't I even have a cup of tea?'

'Poor bloke,' she said sarcastically, and walked away.

Bob was under the gazebo rummaging through the bag of groceries he'd brought back from the shop. 'We'll all be slaving away to sunrise tomorrow. No sleep, no sleep, while you're off in your nice warm bed.'

There was a clattering of metal from the gazebo and Leon returned to the fire with a large frying pan, sliding oil around it. It went down on the centre of the grate. Bob followed her out with a plate of cut soda bread and sausages.

'You get bacon?' Leon asked.

'Sausages, bacon, eggs and fresh bread,' said Bob.

Jonathan was confused. 'I thought we were down to leftovers.'

'You can have pasta if you want,' grumbled Bob. 'Either way, night shift gets offered a proper breakfast. That's in the rules.'

The sausages began to sizzle, and after the kettle whistled, the cracking of eggs. The yolk dripped through the potato bread on Jonathan's lips and he felt whole.

BOB

His chest empty finds a hacking cough.
A few old flames didn't burn for long
Stub one butt out and pick up two.
The wind spinning canopies of blue.

Fingers of a man who worked the soil
The dirt of coal draught, 'hey, kettle's boiled'
'It would freeze the bollocks off ye.'
'Look hard enough there's CCTV'

(The missing after Demetrius
The Milltown Babies and the job
at the car park; no one seemed to
hear the morning I woke up screaming)

Berates woeful rollie making skills.
'Sure, too old to be at that: tools!'
Guy-ropes on green and black he scouts
Always something else to see about.

'Losing my wits so just to talk with youngsters'
'Compassion is me being a sucker!'
Let's see how The Sun likes the flames
We keep some respect about this place

The candle and the moon, streets serene,
Clouds soft, coasting and air I breathe
Night bird speaks in swaying stark tree
Early riser camaraderie

9

Eoghan stank. Leaving behind 'the marqueestas', paper-thin tents, cathedral and park with three buoy sculptures, he hurried – with a corrosive need to piss – to the art college's door. Saturday sun gilded coloured windows striking his damaged eyes. A guard buzzed him through, the same guard Cat introduced Padraig and himself to the previous week.

Along the long hall noticeboards were overstuffed with aspirational posters for studying abroad. It had been a long night. A long fortnight. Lack of sleep and constant noise. He'd seen things that weren't there; heard voices in his head: random gobbledegook. It all seemed to drift away when the lights flickered on over a large clean empty bathroom.

He set his bag between the urinal and another door. Hours of stored urine flooded into the bowl: relief, liberation, *revolution*. When Eoghan finished, he touched a door which drifted open. It was the door of promise. The shower door. He undressed, discarding the flesh of the world; turned on the tap and heard the rush of organ pipes: Händel's *Messiah.* Then came hard cold pelting, continuous. It sounded like trumpets. And it was all around him, flapping, singing the song of of the Seraphim.

Hallelujah! Hallelujah!

Eoghan trembled in holy water: immersive, baptismal. There were violins, cellos. He lathered and the shower spirit warmed his bones; he rinsed his chest and his heart was made to glow.

Hallelujah, Hallelujah. Halle-lujah!

In the incandescent glory of the rapture pained legs were whole again. The ass cleansed by the angel. All the sins – mucus, old hair, the smell of smoke – all were cast from him. He massaged his head, unblocking his crown chakra, and when he opened his eyes Eoghan could see once more.

And he shall reign forever and ever.
King of Kings, forever and ever.
And he shall reign Hallelujah, Hallelujah. Halle-lujah!

The shave, his first in two weeks, started by reclaiming the skin under his chin. The goatee came away by short strokes around the lips, with and against the grain. Sideburns he cut level with the top of the earlobe. He discovered his desired width was achieved by running the blade parallel from the eyebrow down – taking untidy edges off both. He found a new smile in the mirror. Eoghan thought about taking a complimentary *2000 AD* or *New Internationalist* from the rack, but knew he'd imagined them.

'Now. Some soap, and a rinse,' he said to himself.

'Certainly. Will it be the Jasmine, Orange and Cedarwood again, sir?'

Eoghan had also imagined a tall, elderly attendant with receding dark hair and a pencil-thin moustache.

'That sounds perfect, Jarvis.'

He held out his hand so Jarvis, in black shirt and chinos, could squirt the fragrant liquid soap on his palms. The scented soapy cream on his face and then the cold rinse was like a few breaths of nirvana. Jarvis presented him with a navy blue towel made from Turkish cotton and it was warm on his face.

'Mint or gum, Master Eoghan?'

'Neither thanks, Jarvis. Could you roll me a ciggy?'

'Very good. Filtered or unfiltered, sir?'

The wind picked up though the sun remained for most of the day. The midday march would be be a collaborative effort between Occupy and Anonymous. Under the gazebo Leon, wearing her V mask, scrubbed a filthy wire pad against food welded to a plate. Padraig took the soapy dishes from the rack and dried them. Fred walked up behind him and wrapped a mask around Padraig's head. From the marquee, Galway John watched gathering masked figures pose like superheroes for photo shoots, and he sighed.

In a short amount of time everyone was marching. The Anonymi drove a passage through Royal Avenue. They'd dubbed the November 5th event *Operation Stand*, and they pushed out their red and black striped leaflets. Anonymous called for a protest of the *MTV Music Awards*, claiming MTV enjoyed subsidies from the city council. The march was all over the middle of the street. Stalled motorists yelled abuse above bass speakers thunking out Britney Spears and *Circus Spide*.

'Bloody dole scum!'

'NO MORE CUTBACKS! NO MORE CUTBACKS!!'

'*OOPS I DID IT AGAIN, I PLAYED WITH YOUR HEART...*'

They pushed up past the pound shops and the *Tesco*; every sixty seconds fast food bar looking to attract children with the enthusiasm of a pederast. Gary had the megaphone and beanstalk Cat and bubbly little Kiera at his side. Anonymous also had a megaphone and the amplified chants cut into one another and the followers who repeated them.

'WE DEMAND THAT STORMONT DISTRIBUTE THEIR FUNDING TO MAKE A BETTER SOCIETY...'

'TO MAKE A BETTER SOCIETY...'

'REMEMBER, REMEMBER, THE FIFTH OF NOVEMBER...'

'AND EQUALITY FOR ALL!'

'THE FIFTH OF NOVEMBER...'

'AND EQUALITY FOR ALL!'

'WE ARE ANONYMOUS, WE ARE LEGION!'

'INSTEAD OF RECOURSE TO INVESTING IN THE COMMERCIAL INTERESTS OF PRIVATE INDIVIDUALS...'

'INSTEAD OF RECOURSE TO...'

'GET OFF THE ROAD! You're not allowed to do that!'

'*AYE*, mate. FUCK THE DUP!'

A manicured man – a Young Unionist – looked disdainfully at the provocateurs from his seat outside Asher's Bakery. An Anonymi, knowing Asher's was run by religious fundamentalists, raised a pagan horn sign over his head and sneered. Eoghan, Levin and Galway John watched the scene play out.

'Not the element we want on our marches,' groaned Eoghan.

The large Southerner admitted, 'I'm sixty-two years of age. I've seen all these shenanigans before. *Why all that gunpowder, sir?* To blow you Scotch beggars back to your native mountains.'

Levin rubbed his brown beard and ruminated. 'People always talk about Guy Fawkes in terms of trying to blow up parliament and being hung. No one ever mentions the massive austerity measures he was reacting to. Or that he was horse drawn backwards by his head to the scaffold.'

'The sort of regime that does that to a man? Something wrong there,' said Galway.

'He tried to warn a few people too, didn't he?' said Eoghan as they passed the Vodafone store. 'Even back then the establishment had it in for the miners.'

'A man of peace pushed to desperate measures,' mused Levin.

'YOU SAY CUT BACK, WE SAY FIGHT BACK!'

'WE ARE LEGION, WE ARE EVERYWHERE.'

'*I GOT A DIRTY MIND, I GOT FILTHY WAYS, I'M TRYNA BATHE MY APE IN YOUR MILKY WAY*'

'What is that dreadful racket?' asked Galway.

Levin reasoned, 'It could be any number of offenders: Chris Brown, Miley Cyrus, Bruno Mars, Kanye West...'

'It's Kanye,' cursed Eoghan. 'I think it's coming from The Odyssey Arena.'

'All the way across the river? God save us. And you mean to say you listen to that dross?'

'No! But you can't go anywhere without being bombarded by it,' said Eoghan.

'It's ghastly. In my day, music was music. Not the noise

of ten year olds with attention deficit disorder.'

'For sure it's worth a protest,' said Eoghan.

'I dunno. I heard *The Chillis* are playing,' said Levin.

Two hours later they were back at Writer's Square and the pavilion was filling up. The Anonymous were waltzing and twisting as Eoghan played his guitar, and long-haired Shay tooted on his tin whistle. The second gazebo had been erected, where Cat painted Fred's chunky yet ratty face. A sign behind him read *'Revolution Begins Here.'* On the back steps the reporter, Jonathan, was interviewing Gary. Then the time came for Gary to address the crowd.

'People are here to protest different things: MPs expenses, bankers bail-outs; the environmental issues, and the closure of Accident and Emergency wings. We're all angry. We've been let down by people who claim to act for us, but do very little unless it will line their own pockets. I'm going to open up the floor to anyone who wishes to speak. Okay I see a hand. Cat Kennedy, one of our regulars. Cat!'

Cat climbed up the steps and took the megaphone from him. Her dyed green hair hung down over a worn pink cardigan to blue drainpipe jeans.

'Thanks Gary. Thank you all for coming to our second Carnival of Resistance. We've been here two weeks today. I'm sure many of you have questions. John and Mary at the main tent will be happy to answer them.'

There, Galway John turned to Bob, and said, 'She left your name out of it. Isn't she good?'

'We'd love for you to join us here, camping out,' said Cat. 'Phil Allen will be hosting a teach-in on community gardening and permaculture at three. That's open to everyone. You're welcome to join us after five for a meal.. beans on toast probably...' They laughed. 'And you can attend our meeting – which we have every night at seven – to decide camp policies.'

Fred watched her with adoration. He remembered looking into her thoughtful eyes when they were under the gazebo;

how her cheeks curled; how she playfully wore her make-up over lightly freckled skin, and how she carefully painted his face. Fred's own face was all brown dots, and whiskers inked over his lips. He imagined he'd never wash again.

'The MTV Awards are at the Odyssey tomorrow night. A display of shameless greed. Millions of pounds flushed into the River Lagan by the city council.' She was screaming now, rough smoker's chords around the edges. 'A council in favour of prioritising shite music over homelessness and poverty. Well, this is our festival!'

'Yeah! Fucking yeah!'

Martine, Eoghan, Joe, everyone applauded her, and Fred clapped the hardest.

Leon pushed her way to the front and took the loudhailer from Gary before it could reach his lips. She yelled, 'Revolution, YEAH!' The applause barely stopped. Leon looked out to the members of Anonymous; to the trade unionists and those from the Socialist Workers Party. She saw a lot of people she didn't know, but all gathered in common cause for revolution, and talking excitedly, raring to go.

'Leon's really great at this sort of thing,' said Kiera.

'Those Scientologists will be quaking in their boots,' said Martine, rubbing her hands gleefully.

'I heard she's *Truth Live*'s Northern Ireland source,' said an Anonymous.

'She could lift my awareness any day,' said Joe, looking up at her with admiration. 'But why are no words coming out of her mouth?'

'Oh that's one of those sophisticated yoga techniques,' explained Daniel with authority.

Cat nodded. 'She's making a point about suffering in silence. And ending the silence.'

Gary screamed, 'YEEE-OHH! LEON, SOCK IT TO THE MAN! YOU ARE THE 99%! YOU ARE THE 99%!' Galway John repeated Gary's chant while punching the sky, and that was when Leon realised she'd been imagining all of it. Everything that had happened over the last minute.

The crowd before her were actually silent, waiting for her to speak.

Gary, the real Gary, walked up the steps and put his arm on her back. 'It can happen to the best of us,' he said gently. 'Let's give Leon a round of applause for having the courage to come up.'

He clapped and the others followed suit, pitifully. Leon wandered off the steps in a daze.

'We'll leave it there,' said Gary. 'Unless anyone has anything they want to add?'

Fred marched up the steps. His short spiky hair was brushed to the back and sides, looking like cat ears over his feline make-up. Gary handed him the loudhailer.

'I don't agree with the budget. Meow.'

Deirdre took off her cycling helmet and shook her blonde curls. She listened to the laughter from the square behind, before ducking under the marquee. A half dozen people were there. Thin dark-haired Daniel sat at the far end and acknowledged her with sparkling eyes and the nod of a broad chin, but as usual said nothing. Big Joe looked up and smiled. Mary fed Shelby a biscuit and the dog licked her puffy cheeks and flaxen hair. Jack stroked his coat firmly. Bob kept his distance, preferring his own counsel. Galway John looked over to Deirdre's bike leaned against the lamp-post and over to her.

'Well, Deirdre, what have you been up to?' he asked.

'I'm just back this from the Greenisland Greenpeace meeting, *through* the green-way, en route to the Green Party meeting,' she exclaimed.

Bob didn't react. 'All these extra people. Tents will have to be moved,' he said firmly. He emptied the water cannister into the kettle and unscrewed the next one with some disdain.

A sturdy man dressed in black pullover, jeans and a bomber jacket strode into the tent. Mary's cheeks expanded. She recognised him from the first carnival and his hairline: receding, though styled short.

'Mind if I sit?' he asked.

'Free world,' muttered Bob.

Tommie was fifty-two years old and fit, so could easily have passed for younger. He took a seat beside Daniel. Shelby fussed over the newcomer who rubbed the dog's head vigorously, before putting his hand in Shelby's mouth.

'You were here last week. Tommie isn't it?' Deirdre asked warmly.

Shelby closed his mouth down on Tommie's hand. He pushed his hand forward and Shelby pulled away. He withdrew his hand and then tried for it to be re-captured. 'That's right. And you're Deirdre. Mary. Bob.' He turned his head to look at Daniel. 'How are you big man?'

'Not so bad,' said Daniel, who wasn't big, and took the remark with his usual plain stoicism.

'And who's this lovely lady with the sparkling eyes and fine dress?'

'Oh. Straight in there,' said Jack.

'No point beating about the bush. Who doesn't like a compliment?'

Jack gave her name. They shook hands. Tommie said it was a pleasure. Bob snorted. Tommie's nose curled up and he looked at the dog suspiciously. 'What's that smell? Smells like shite?'

'Might be Shitty John,' said Mary.

'You really shouldn't call him that. Call him New John,' said Galway.

'It's just to distinguish him,' she said.

'Who?'

Jack said, 'Some guy; he just started hanging around. No-one knows where he came from.'

'Terrible thing when you get old,' Bob said. 'Bits start falling off. And when the body decomposes --'

Joe came over from the crowd and took a seat next to Mary.

'Well, it all begins to leak. Not just faecal matter and urine. All the innards turn to chemicals.'

Galway shook his head. 'That's something I'd rather not dwell on Bob, if it's all the same to you.'

Tommie studied Mary and Joe. 'Were you two an item already, or did yis meet here?'

'You two?' Jack asked.

A smile spread over Bob's face. 'Did you not catch that one, Jackie?'

'I guess I need a new gossip radar,' she said.

'Yous all living together. Of course it'll happen. Glastonbury vibes, free love and that,' said Tommie.

'Never you fuckin' mind free love sunshine.'

Tommie whipped his face round and fixed on Bob. 'Have you some problem me being here?'

Joe was looking out in front of him and suddenly he jumped to his feet. 'Hey!'

'What the bloody hell?' shouted Deirdre, on her feet just as fast.

'Yeeeowwww!'

A large bald man was straddling Deirdre's pushbike. He was mid-thirties, wore a black tee showing off the muscles in his arms and was as large as Bob or Galway. The pedals fell from underneath him as he tried to climb on them and he shook the frame in frustration.

'Put the bike down!' screamed Deirdre.

The man lifted his leg back over the frame and let the bike tumble to the ground beneath him.

Deirdre yelled. 'How dare you? That does not belong to you!'

'Red on the rag, red on the flag,' sniped the thug, and spat on the ground. He gave the bike a hard kick.

Bob got to his feet and stepped towards him. 'OY! Come on now!' he barked.

The thug met Bob's gaze. 'OR WHAT?' he demanded.

'There's no *what* about it,' said Bob.

He laughed. 'I'd break you in two you aul shite!' He looked over Bob's shoulder as Joe stepped forward. 'You steppin' up to me, fuck-face?'

The jerk jerked. Joe flinched. He eyed Joe up and then turned his gaze to one of the tents. It was *The Love Shack*. He kicked the front of it with his industrial boot. Padraig yelled from inside. Suddenly, Tommie flew past Joe and Bob, grabbed the thug's arm and twisted it behind his back.

Tommie was the smaller of the two, but stronger, and he quickly grabbed the provocateur's other arm. The man screamed in pain.

'I know who you are. Name's Headfat Turtleneck isn't it?' Tommie tightened his grip until the man was bent over and squealing. 'I think you'd better move on now,' Tommie hissed.

'Get off!'

Tommie pushed Headfat down the path to the kerb, keeping a vice grip on his arms. 'I'm going to let go in a moment and then you're gonna to start walking.'

'I'm gonna kick your head in!'

Headfat squealed as Tommie tightened his grip. 'Try me. Try me and see what happens. You are not gonna come back here, son.'

He squealed again, and gasped. 'Fucking, fucking --'

'COMPRENDE?'

'Aye. AYE! Get off!'

At the kerb Tommie pressure-squeezed Headfat's right wrist, so the aggressor's palm opened and he could not form a fist. Then, he let go. Tommie stood back, ready for the worst. Headfat took a step back and shook his arm to get the circulation flowing.

'FUCKING CUNT. I couldn't give a fuck about a bunch of hippies and babies!'

Tommie looked at him with scepticism. 'Fuck off and sober up.'

He stood there until Headfat was off down the street. He knew Bob and Joe were behind him, but didn't acknowledge them until he looked them in the eyes.

'Nicely handled,' Joe told him.

'Thank you. Are you okay?' asked Deirdre.

'No worries.'

'That's all well and good but what if he comes back? Ay? What if he brings a few of his mates?' said Bob dourly.

'His mates are keeping a low profile... after he brought the cops to their doors the other week.'

'Right,' said Bob.

'You know him?' asked Joe.

'Aye. And now he knows me. He'll not be long asking to find out he doesn't want a rematch.'

Mindful of Cat, Padraig and a half dozen occupiers converging at the kerb, Bob lowered his eyes and spoke softly. 'Thank you Jimmy.'

'It's Tommie.'

'Tommie. Okay. You dealt with that quickly.'

'And without breaking his jaw,' said Tommie, and offered to shake Bob's hand.

Padraig was the first to reach them. 'That was excellent!' he roared.

'Well done,' added Mary.

Eoghan was in a tizzy. 'What's going on? What was all that about?'

'Yer man here was brilliant,' cheered Jack.

Cat's pupils grew large and her speech was rapid and excited. 'Tommie is it? Oh god. That was amazing. Would you be up to running a teach-in on self-defence?'

He checked his wristwatch. 'I've to see a fella from work at four – actually, I might have something else for you – I'll swing by this way around half seven and we can arrange something.'

'Whenever you have the time. Yeah. We can get together and slot you in,' she gushed.

'Cat, you're drooling,' said Padraig.

Leaves on the trees brushed together and the tops of

tents puffed up. Dark clouds passed, re-colouring the square from gold to grey and gold again.

The sun hung its embers like shedding skin and the moon drew up beside it. Fred said when the sun and moon were out together it wasn't natural. The occupiers, and Anonymi, and ten other visitors – almost thirty people in total – drew round the fire for the General Assembly. Cat took the minutes, though the GA evoked thoughts of long hours. There were bags under her eyes too and her unholy yawns drew Kiera's concern.

Gary thanked everyone for making the carnival a success and they thanked one another. Then the floor was given over to Bob. His tongue was sharp and his stern demeanour dialled to ten.

'Your night shift rota isn't working. It needs a person from the night watch overseeing it, with reliable people on board.'

'Well you're our Director of Homeland Security,' Eoghan joked.

Bob opened his stuck out his bottom lip. 'I don't see anyone else volunteering to take charge.'

'Aye. Hang on,' interjected Padraig. 'Once we start giving people titles instead of names, chaos reigns.'

Leon sat bolt upright. She was surprised the sensible objection came from Padraig, of all people.

Gary brushed the smoke from his eyes. 'That's true, but the way I understand it is there's times now when one person is alone on night watch.'

'That's right,' the curmudgeon blurted out. 'And I'll tell you what else. We need lights up. Proper lights so people can see what they're doing.'

'Does anyone object to this being put to a vote?' Cat asked.

'On whether we have lights?' sniped a muffled V-mask.

'On Bob as Head of Security,' she said.

'Now I'll do my three nights a week,' said Bob, 'and I'll

make sure the boys clean up for the morning.'

'The boys? The boys?' asked Leon, aghast. 'Patriarchal framing!'

'I don't mind girls doing nights but I won't have them out here on their own.'

'What else would you want to do?' Levin asked.

'I'll get trusted volunteers and put teams together to make sure the shifts are spread around.'

'Well...' Gary shuffled uneasily, 'I don't know if it's wise giving someone a leadership type role. Then again, you've proved yourself more than capable of managing this.'

'If we were to put Bob in charge of security we should probably put it to the vote,' suggested Cat.

There were six against the idea, ten abstentions and twelve in favour. This was deemed too close to call. Eoghan asked for those in favour to raise their hands again. 'Ten out of twelve are full-timers,' he pointed out, referring to the shorthand they used for permanent campers. Of those who opposed the motion none were actually living there. The motion was passed and only Anonymous Alexander complained.

Bob ignored the masked man. 'First things first. There's a lot of extra people around here. What would help is if we could organise the space better.'

'I'd help if I could but I'm going to have to go and knock on a few doors this week,' said Gary.

'Knock on doors?' Fred asked.

'He's focussing on his constituents,' said Levin.

'Another election's going to come up in West Belfast. Before that's announced I want to spend more time with the people there.'

'I'm seeing my niece tomorrow,' said Eoghan

Padraig balked. 'Surrender control to the police and surrender responsibility!'

Leon nodded. 'Who decides how the camp is re-organised?'

'Mwah-ha-hahaha! Right. Decisions taken away from us!

And before you know it they're designating borders, saying who can and can't stay. Mwah-ha-hahaha! Sure I'm only pulling your leg, Bob.'

'Oh I know, Padraig. I didn't want to have my boot on your rear while you were talking through your arse.'

'Going forward we need focus on organising demos and flash-mobs,' said Cat. 'Someone was talking of protesting the BB –'

A sudden bang drowned out her voice, an explosive sound sweeping the area. It lasted a few seconds. Hearts jumped. People jumped and pigeons too. A few folk got to their feet.

'What the fuck?'

'*What the actual fuck?*' shouted Kiera.

'Sounded like a bomb,' said Shay.

Immediately, there was a second burst. Cat shook. Mary and Joe took one another's hands. People on Donegall Street looked around them. The traffic continued on in light rain as it had been. Those on their feet surveyed the road looking for fire or broken glass.

'*IT'S A FUCKING BOMB!*' shouted an Anonymous.

'*BOMB!*' shouted another.

Padraig stumbled back to his chair, his brow wet. 'Fucking hell.'

Bob got to his feet. 'Gary, come with me. The rest of you: sit tight.'

'*CALL THE COPS!*' yelled the Anon.

'Oh Christ,' said Leon.

'I don't like this,' said Kiera.

'*IT WAS CLOSER, THE SECOND ONE WAS CLOSER,*' Leon screamed. 'Oh Christ. They've come for us.'

'Were any of you actually born during the Troubles?' said Eoghan.

Some of the activists were stuck to their chairs, waiting for news. Two pigeons sat atop the walls bordering the planters and looked out onto the street.

'I saw a flash before that second one,' said Anonymous.

'Let's wait until they get back with some answers,' said Galway coolly.

'*IT WAS A FRIGGING BOMB!*' screamed Anonymous Doris.

'It might have been just a car back-firing,' said Levin.

'No way that was a car!' yelled Shay.

'I hope no-one was hurt,' said Jack.

'Might have been a tear gas cannister, like in Oakland?' said Leon.

Eoghan gave her a look of disbelief. 'At *Caffe Nero*?'

'That's not far from the cop shop,' Fred reasoned.

Eoghan said, 'We don't even –- there. They're back. With yer man, Tommie.'

'What happened?' Cat asked.

Gary was shaking his head. Bob blinked, as if surprised to see them all still there.

'Oh no worries,' said Tommie. 'No worries. It was only fireworks for Justin Bieber getting out of his limo.'

10

On the morning of Wednesday 9th November, 2011, light rain fell from broken clouds. The fire billowed and the radio crackled. Levin waved in the direction of the marquee. Fred's football whizzed in front of his face. It struck the green dome tent.

'*OY! YOU MIND?*' Kiera screamed from inside.

Leon, Cat and Jack sat under the canvas, mugs and cigs in hand, each greeting him with an 'Alright, Levin.'

'Morning all. What are we listening to?'

'*Swampy, SWP, and their friends in Tent City: a mob of unwashed worms who've closed streets, damaged property, brought on the coming of Satanic Forces...*'

'BBC Five Live,' said Leon. 'Mouth off local, transmit global, with Kevin Trojan.'

'And the soothing tones of commentator Dovid Vonce,' said Cat.

Jack said, in her proper English diction, 'He sounds jealous of us. Us, wriggling about in the mud with our sneezes and diseases.'

From the pavilion a clap of fast feet echoed until Padraig rounded the corner. He slowed down and found Fred's ball on the path. He dribbled with it and came to a stop at the marquee. Jack was wearing a refined blue and white striped dress. Padraig looked her up and down. 'Jack, it's ten o'clock in the morning. How come you look so well turned out?'

'Thank you, sweetie.'

'*Anarcho-communist street rabble...*'

Padraig looked at the radio. 'This is about us, isn't it?'

The host, Trojan, had a voice that was chummy and pragmatic, but raised in argument. *'Okay, okay. Let's get back to the church report on ethics issued today.'*

'What about the excrement found on the carpet of St. Paul's Cathedral?'

Padraig got to his feet and turned in the direction of the pavilion. 'Fred!' he bellowed. 'Come hear this! There's a priest's crapped himself!'

'Excrement!' screamed Vonce.

'If Jesus was alive he'd be in a shelter. Or in counselling,' whined Leon.

'Did Jesus even go to church?' Cat asked.

'The bible says he went to the temple two or three times,' said Levin. 'Remember? They kicked him out?'

'Excrement!' screamed Vonce again. *'That's what the Anglican Church gets for collusion! Excrement!'*

'You'd think St. Paul's would have toilets,' Padraig remarked. 'While we're on the subject, why does my piss always smell of Sugar Puffs?'

'Have you eaten Sugar Puffs lately?' asked Jack.

Fred rounded the corner and slid the ball away from Padraig.

'Mr. Vonce,' said Trojan, *'You accuse the BBC of bias towards Occupy...'*

'Because you indulge in shadow puppetry instead of cogent, rational analysis!'

'Vonce is always on the BBC complaining about not being on the BBC,' said Levin.

'Tuberculosis Britain is descending into Sharia Law!'

'I'm sorry,' said Trojan, *'but we have to wrap it up there.'*

'Sharia Law!'

'Thank you for your time, Robert Dunlop from the Socialist Workers Party, and political blogger, Dovid Vonce.'

'Hang on?' said Leon. 'There was somebody from the SWP in that interview?'

'I didn't hear anyone else speak,' said Cat.

'Bloody BBC!' Leon dropped her voice to a murmur. 'We should boycott the fuck out of them.'

The playful brown stray, Shelby, dandered in. He pulled an empty *Tesco* bag from the floor of the gazebo, and wrestled with it in his jaw on the way out, before letting it go by the fire.

'Good boy,' said Leon. 'Yes. Yes. With Tesco, very little helps.'

Shelby ran over to her and moved around her legs. She patted him and he jumped up, his wet paws up upon her knees.

'Get down! Bad dog!'

'Is that a Labrastaff?'

'It's a Labrador Staffy,' Padraig sneered at Levin.

'The news at eleven o'clock. The government have agreed to a £9,000 cap on university tuition fees. The decision – which allows universities to charge three times as much as before – has been met with criticism.'

Levin threw his hands up in the air. 'Jesus Christ!'

Leon's tone was resigned. 'I think I'll clean up around the camp. I don't want to give the media elite any more ammunition for their mad *fucking* imaginations.'

'Sure I'll give you a hand. Where do we start?' asked Levin.

The sun spilled celestial rays over the North Street buildings. On the pavilion the boys continued to kick the ball while Leon and Levin surveyed the placards around the wall and fence. One sign bent over the railings, read, *'No House. No Job. No Fear'*. Another lay buried in the shrubs, its frayed split string trailing behind it: *'99% don't get why the 1% just won't take responsiblity.'*

'Someone needs a spell-checker,' said Levin.

After tidying the signs and making a list for painting, they circled back around to the marquee. The football flew just over their heads.

'Sorry,' yelled Fred.

'He's very sorry,' Leon told Levin sarcastically.

Kiera was awake now, under the marquee eating a bowl of corn flakes. Cat was beside her, and talking about their afternoon class. Jack was rolling a cigarette.

Leon ducked under the marquee. 'I'm thinking we should make another big banner. Maybe hang it across that tree there. Cat, where's that stack of duvet covers?'

'The ones your mum donated?'

'That big stack of sheets?' enquired Jack. 'I'm fairly sure those are in Bob's tent.'

'We've got one or two in ours,' Kiera chirped.

'Can you get them? I'll replace them when Bob gets up.'

Five minutes later, Leon was shaking up a black spray can. The women and Levin held the four corners of the white linen up in front of her as she painted the words. Against the soundscape of the football bouncing on the concourse and the motor buses and treble bass cars, they cut off string and threaded it through the edges of the sheet. Levin gave Jack a foot up to tie it to the branches on each of the two trees, so it hung visibly across the camp.

'THE World has enough fore verybody's need but NOT enough 4 everybodys greed! - Gandi'

'You can't spell for shit,' Cat told Leon. 'Apart from that, it looks good.'

Full of pride, they set on returning to their seats. The football struck the fire bin with great force, and nearly turned it over. Leon whirled around to the pavilion.

'HEY!' she screamed.

Shay and Daniel put their heads out of their tents.

'Sorry,' yelled Padraig.

'SORRY WON'T CUT IT!' she yelled back.

He'd just rounded the corner and almost tumbled with the sudden stop.

She was spitting. 'FUCK SORRY! MARCHING IN HERE...' Leon threw her crotch forward, and began shaking it about. 'OH, I'M A MAN, I CAN DO WHAT I WANT. I'M GONNA WAVE

MY DICK AND MY KNUCKLES WHERE I LIKE. And screw EVERYONE else!' She whipped a fist across the air and screamed, '*How ABOUT you FUCK OFF and PENETRATE SOMEWHERE ELSE?*'

Padraig left the ball where it was, turned around and walked away. When he'd rounded the corner into the square and out of sight, the others fell into hysterics.

'Leon, that... was awesome,' said Cat, gushing.

'YEAH. YOU BETTER RUN,' Leon yelled.

They disappeared from camp for the rest of the morning. An hour later the women had gone elsewhere too. Eoghan arrived at the marquee. He fancied a kickabout though the ball sat clamped under Shay's foot. Levin explained what happened. Shay took persuading that there was plenty of safe space for a kick about. Daniel declined Eoghan's offer, and stayed in his tent.

Eoghan showed off his dribbling on the concrete pitch. 'Levin, back to me!'

Shay passed it back and Levin shot the ball against the back steps.

Ten minutes into play, a dark haired woman in a long coat approached. It was Josie, Eoghan's partner, with a large plastic bag at her side. After a few moments of not being noticed, she called out a reprimand. 'Ah, so this is what you've been doing!'

'Josie!' Eoghan brightened up and left the game.

'What's this, Eoghan? Have Lehman Brothers started a staff football team?'

Eoghan kissed her. She recoiled. 'Aw don't be like that,' he said. 'Levin, stick the kettle on would you? Did you bring us clothes?'

'They're for you. Not for giving out to some randomer. And I don't want you coming home and giving me the flu.'

'This is amazing!' He pulled a stringy green pullover out of the bag. A grey wool cap fell out onto the damp concrete.

Josie picked it up and pushed it to him. 'You can dry that

off. Were you planning on coming home anytime this winter?'

'Of course, of course. Is this new?'

'I got it from the filling station.'

He thanked her and pushed the sweater back into the bag. Eoghan rubbed the cap against his jeans and fitted it on his head.

'Early Christmas present,' she said.

'It's been really busy. We've a piece coming in the Sunday World. The BBC shot some footage...'

They sat down under the main tent. Levin smiled and said 'hello' and Josie nodded in recognition. Shay excused himself with a want to go down to *The Waterfront*, a popular spot for his skateboarding posse. Levin exchanged pleasantries with Josie and then asked Josie how she liked her coffee: milky, one sugar. Eoghan told him not to use the blue mug. Levin had learned this already. The blue mug had blue mold.

'We have to spend more time together if this is gonna work,' whispered Josie.

'I know. But it's not like I'm difficult to find,' quipped Eoghan.

This annoyed her. 'I don't want to come out in the freezing rain to have a conversation with you.'

This annoyed him. 'Ah come on! I'm not asking you to do that!'

Levin put the handle of a hot orange mug into Josie's hands.

'Levin, would you give us a few minutes?'

He gave Eoghan an understanding nod. Levin went to the tents to fix loose pegs and ropes.

Cat swayed towards them, singing. *'Walk on, walk on with hope in your heart...'*

Eoghan pleaded, in urgent whispers. 'This is a part of my life, Josie. You know that.'

'Yes, but...'

'And you'll never walk alone,' sang Cat. *'You'll never walk alone!'*

Eoghan rolled his eyes and sighed loudly. Cat shifted the little table, skraking it on the concrete. Levin called out to her.

Cat and Levin climbed the steps of Belfast Cathedral, under the Spire of Hope. Light poured through the stained glass windows, even on this muggy day, gilding the viaduct-like archways and six stone columns either side of the large basilica. The pews were rows of single wooden chairs on a footprint damp camel floor striped with darker hues. At the end of the hall were two raised inset chambers, with the pulpit and a row of flickering candles, the only sign of life. If there was anyone else around, they would have had plenty of places to hide.

Cat shivered. 'I don't know why it's colder in here.' She heard her words as she spoke them, warmer and softer, bouncing off the Romanesque architecture around them. 'It's beautiful, mind.'

'You've never been here before?' Levin asked.

She shook her head.

They walked the aisle flanked by semi-circular arches. Levin took in the glass-work. He noticed the repeated theme of harp, crown, and eagle, and laughed inwardly. Cat was overwhelmed by the silence. She'd grown used to the constant drilling of traffic and could feel this sacred place re-wire parts of her brain where connections were frayed. There was that moment, when she was ready to accept Jesus into her heart. She rejected the notion when a rambunctious group of twenty tourists struggled to enter the vestibule all at once.

'No flash photography, please,' the tour guide announced.

'WOW,' barked an American.

'Bell Fast Cathedral.'

'In 1776 a Parish Church called St. Anne's was consecrated on this spot. Work on the Cathedral began much later, in 1895, under architects Drew and Lynn.'

'It's so beautiful.'

'Is that Saint Patrick?'

A camera went off.

Cat and Levin moved quicker, towards the altar. They found themselves by the chalices and the seats of the choir. On the wall behind hung an indigo pall with a cross, patterned with speckles and smaller white-gold crosses.

'I read about this,' said Levin. 'It's a memorial to the Titanic. Irish linen, silk...'

Cat flashed her eyebrows. 'Looks like velvet.'

Another camera clicked. The tour party were gaining on them. 'The roof represents earth, fire, water and the hand of the creator, raised in blessing. This is symbolised by one hundred and fifty thousand pieces of glass.'

'Gee!'

'Glad we can put a number on it,' murmured Cat. She looked to the Baptistery chamber's three stained glass windows, and stepped up to the lectern.

'I was reading about this,' Levin recalled. 'That's the Book of Prayers. The pages are made from rice paper. It was written by a Korean War POW.'

Cat had been about to touch it, but drew away. The tour were upon them, and she walked back down the steps.

'The font is made from marble,' stated the guide. 'Black at it's base for original sin, red marble columns for the blood of Christ upon Calvary...'

'Shall we go now?' asked Cat, though it wasn't a question.

'I thought we could follow these ones around for a while,' he deadpanned.

An elderly lady tugged on Cat's arm. 'Excuse me dear, would you mind taking my photograph?'

It had been raining. When they returned Josie was gone, Bob was awake and Padraig sat in the marquee wearing his red sleeping bag, zipped up over his padded coat. He was shaking. His glasses were steamed up with his thermal cap pulled over them and his skin was pale white.

'He's wearing his guddies *inside* the bag,' said Eoghan.

Levin balked. 'His trainers?'

'The fire's out,' said Cat.

'That's mist,' said Bob.

'So cold, so cold. I can't do this any more,' cried Padraig.

Cat pointed out, 'Well you've slept over, what, seven nights maybe? You must be doing something right.'

Padraig pulled his glasses off and wiped them furiously. 'Cars going past all hours. Getting rained on. It's only one o'clock and I'm here shivering. Fuck this!'

Bob looked Padraig up and down and laughed.

'I'm sick of this. Fuck it all!'

'Oh. I need Mummy to come and tuck me into my electric blanket,' Bob teased.

'Piss off.'

Bob balled his hands into his eyes. 'Boo-hoo. I can't cope without my computer games.'

Padraig gritted his teeth. Bob put his thumb to his cheek and made slurping noises. Padraig opened his mouth but was seized by the compulsion to sneeze. It was like a scream.

'Guys, I've to go round to the cop shop to hand in the 11/1 forms,' said Eoghan in a no nonsense tone.

Padraig despaired. 'Isn't anyone going to say *god bless you*?'

'Who wants to take a walk round and keep me company?' said Eoghan.

Levin said he would. Bob told them to come back quickly as he needed help with re-organising the campsite.

They crossed Donegall Street, Eoghan saying he wasn't sure if they just left the forms in or were interviewed about them. 'To be honest I don't like being in police stations by myself.'

'I understand. How did it go with Josie? She seemed a bit pissed off.'

'Ah, she's coming round. She'll be fine.'

Behind the cathedral they walked the cobblestones of

Hill Street and Talbot Street, gentrified by new cafes and bars. 'I was thinking I'd join yous. You know, camping,' said Levin.

Eoghan smiled. 'Really? I'm glad you said that. I was about to ask.'

'I'll have to get a tent. And it'll be the weekend, after my dole comes in.'

'Is that the only thing stopping you?'

'Pretty much. I mean I don't know how I'll get on with sleeping --'

'Right, stop right there. Just a suggestion but you're perfectly welcome to share my tent. Plenty of room. You can bring some clothes down. There's a spare pillow. Have you a sleeping bag?'

'I can get a duvet from the bedsit. Thanks, Eoghan. I appreciate this.'

'Don't mention it.'

They passed the *Ramada* and rounded onto the busy A2 link road leading to Victoria Street. Eoghan went on to tell him about the teach-ins. 'We get people with various areas of expertise to teach for half an hour, forty-five minutes. You should host one. Put that Politics Masters to use. I'm doing one later on how democracy works. It'd be great if you could come.'

'Sure. I think I can get to the flat and back by then,' Levin reckoned.

They came to the crossing opposite Custom House Square and the Albert Clock. Musgrave Station was beyond, surrounded by a grey corrugated fence, with stripes of red and black.

'Levin, you know when they rebranded the *Royal Ulster Constabulary* as the *PSNI*? They were going to call it the *Northern Ireland Police Service*. Then they realised that spelled out as *NIPS*.'

Levin laughed. 'That's an urban myth. Like *Police Enquiries: Northern Ireland Service. PENIS.*'

The cars were whirling around from Chichester Street, the main artery of the city, and flowing out east. Eoghan let out a sneeze. Levin said bless you. Eoghan sneezed again, and again. Levin said bless you twice more. They walked to the traffic lights and the green man signal retreated when they were halfway across. There was a hatch in the front of Musgrave Station with Constable Corbett behind the grille. Eoghan waved the papers. Corbett hit a buzzer, releasing the lock on the black steel gate. In the yard there were two PANGIs, the old armoured land-rovers used during the Troubles, recently decommissioned.

The entrance to the main building was threadbare, not unlike a port-a-cabin. They took a seat in the waiting area. It had white walls, a noticeboard behind a potted plant, and another behind their heads. The posters, five deep, brushed the back of Levin's neck. Each were full of phone numbers, emails and serious warnings.

'Loving the décor. But you'd think a police station would be the last place they'd need to remind people about security,' said Levin.

'You'd think so,' said Eoghan.

The person being dealt with left the counter and they got up. Whichever officer was there had gone already. Eoghan leaned forward, his head to the holes in the plexiglass.

'Hello?'

'No-one there? There's a switch.'

Eoghan laid his finger on it. An officer appeared at the back of the room but seemed to ignore them in favour of going through the mail. 'Hello?' Eoghan was ready to rap the window when another man appeared. He was swarthy and grey-faced, with bloodshot eyes. 'I've got these 1/11 forms, for permission to march.'

'Slide them through the hatch.'

The constable picked them up and leafed through them.

'There's one for this Saturday, and some for the next few weeks,' said Eoghan.

'Okay. Your contact details are on these?'

'Yes, there's a few points of --'

'We'll be in touch if there's any problem then.'

'Is that it? We can go?'

'Is there a problem that you know of?'

'Not as far as I know,' said Eoghan.

The officer stepped away from the desk. Eoghan looked to Levin.

'I think that's it,' said Levin.

'He barely looked at it.' Eoghan tapped the glass. The officer at the back didn't respond. Levin said they should go.

They parted ways outside. Levin walked straight along Victoria Street where traffic entered the city by St. George's Market. He kept by the main flow: Cromac Street and the A24, where cars and lorries came in from the East. A furious wind pushed against him.

He turned right at the fire station on Ormeau Avenue, its other side lined with red brick offices. There was greater shelter there even where broad side streets opened up glimpses of the back of City Hall. He turned left at the junction, away from the BBC building. All in all, it took him about forty minutes: through Shaftesbury Square; climbing Dublin Road; climbing University Road, climbing the steps to his small room on Camden Street, where he nearly fell through the door.

It hadn't rained during the mile and a half. Somehow Levin found himself taking off a wet coat. He lay back on the bed. Now at rest, the pain in his legs flared. Levin could feel his eyes roll and lull him to sleep. He took his phone out, brought up Occupy's Facebook page, and turned on his side to read it. The three most recent posts were links to socialist songs on YouTube: Eoghan posting, he reckoned. There was a link to a story from the previous Saturday. Six hundred thousand Americans had closed their accounts with major banks in a co-ordinated action. It was unclear why the post had been duplicated.

An extensive wish-list was posted requesting tents, sleeping bags, roll-mats, pillows, firewood, firelighters, coal and marker pens. A comment from Bronagh Boyle asked, '*How do I get to the camp from Great Victoria Street?*' Ginty McGinty had written, '*Look left.*' Bronagh replied, '*I'll be there at 6pm on the 9th with a box of supplies.*' McGinty replied, '*The camp's open 24/7.*'

There was a post declaring Occupy Belfast's support of the public sector in the 30th November strike. Martine McHale had commented, '*Occupy will stand up in the national strike and never abandon the working and oppressed mothers and daughters of the world.*'

Levin rolled on his back and glazed over the next comment from Richie Keen. '*With the greatest respect Martine, you seem very young and while it is admirable you choose to stand up and make your voice heard, the romantic notion that millions will be taking to the streets and overturning the will of the government is just not reality.*'

Leon McCallum replied. '*With the greatest respect Richie, the strike on November 30th will be the biggest strike in the UK since the 1920s.*'

Padraig Mahon had commented. '*With the greatest respect Richie, you seem terribly mature and experienced. I respect your scepticism but I must dutibly point to the fact you are full of shite.*'

The Facebook animation showed someone else was typing. Levin sat up and threw his legs over the bed. There was already a new comment from Jack Hughes, and he was drawn back into it. '*Richie, this is a strike of members of all professions, backed by the unions, and the general public.*'

And Bronagh Boyle again, '*There will be millions in the streets, Richie.*'

Then yet another new comment! Patrick Keogan had written, '*what do u think u are doing u are never going to change anything lol occupy a job shitbags.*'

Levin tossed the phone on the bed and looked around. There wasn't much in his room: his laptop; the table and chairs; the basin; the hob; twelve books, half of them study texts. He'd limit himself to taking one book, Klein's *No Logo*. He was halfway through it. Levin opened the wardrobe and found the holdall, which his duvet almost filled. He squeezed in a pair of jeans and a shirt, three tee-shirts, five pairs of boxers, and four and a half pairs of socks.

Levin noticed sludge built up around the camp and the pathway. The tents had been brought close together, and raised onto palettes. He laid his holdall down in the marquee. A pigeon hurried out of his way and Bob and Galway John watched it as they supped their tea.

'Oh there he goes! Columba livia, the rock pigeon, Bob. Did you know they're descended from doves?'

'A rat with wings.'

'Very clean animals, actually.'

Eoghan had a small group on the other side of the fire for his *How Democracy Works* teach-in. Levin took a chair over and joined them.

'There was... Nixon's adviser. The Trilateral committee fella. What was his name? Fuck. That's going to annoy me. Anyway. He thought there was too much...*'unreasonable'* political input in government. The public, ha, they thought it was a democracy and were sending millions of letters. He didn't want that. So he brought people in to insulate the political class. And that's how we have the International Monetary Fund and the World Trade Organisation.'

'Fucking WTO lizards,' sniped Fred.

Cat sighed. 'Then you have private finance...'

'Right,' said Eoghan. 'That's the framework. So the thing is, democracy can't run on investment. Money, too much of it, undermines the process. It becomes a swamp. Take PFI, the Private Finance Initiative. We have private companies with contracts buying schools and hospitals from the government. These public institutions have to pay vastly inflated rent over thirty years to take back control of their properties.'

'It's kind of like a mortgage,' said Levin.

'Exactly, exactly. And it's a snake that swallows it's own head. Our obligations to performance and success dictate what we get from the system. Think about how they've implemented the dole benefits. If you don't take a low paid job you're cut off. This is them policing the poor,' said Eoghan.

'We're all in the computers, like Big Brother. There's no human element to the decisions. It's all just numbers.'

'That's right, Fred. And if we go back to Nixon's man… Samuel Huntington! That's his name! Huntington and the private sector, policing democracy… their problem is us. History has shown democratic outbreaks always follow state incompetency. *Stop the War*. Solidarity in Poland. East Timor versus Indonesia.'

'Tiananmen Square,' said Daniel.

Eoghan continued. 'A strong democracy goes beyond voting day. What we're doing with our meetings is globalisation from below. Hijacking political process as the political class hijacked it from us. Popular power shaping decisions. These changes need to be long-term to form institutions.'

'How long?' Leon wondered.

'Yeah, how long? I'm really hungry,' said Fred.

Crossing Rosemary Street, Levin had two empty plastic tubs in his arms, each two foot long. Fred carried one, because he was shorter. The tubs were from *Brown's*, an Asian fast food takeaway, which from the previous night had been supplying the camp with leftovers.

Levin tried to break the ice by asking Fred if he was politically active. He said no, that was more Padraig's thing. He was only there for the lark, and the hot birds. Though he admitted he'd learned some things he found interesting.

The takeaway was on Corn Market, a pedestrian thoroughfare and popular spot for city shoppers resting and skateboarders bouncing off the plinth. *Brown's* had only three tables. Tommie, the street-smart muscle they'd met at the Saturday carnival, was behind a tight counter serving youngsters. When it came their turn, he took the tubs and came out of the back a few minutes later with each of them filled.

'I'll try and pop round after my shift ends,' he said.

Levin's eyes nearly popped out looking into the big steamy boxes of egg fried rice, chips, noodles and sweet and sour chicken. It was hot on his fingers as they walked back to High Street.

'Why are you shaking the tub around like that?' asked Levin.

'There's only two spring rolls. I'm hiding them in the rice so I can get to them before the others do.'

'Spring rolls! Don't you love the way the pastry holds it all in like a packet?'

'That's it. It's like getting mail, but instead of bills and shite, you've meat and peppers and noodles. Dee-lish.'

'Crunchy too.'

'When you get that thin, flaky stuff in with it...' Fred mused on it. 'I like that. All my food mixed together. Gives it extra flavour.'

Kiera found herself quickly bored with the general assembly and asked if she could mark up the chalkboard for days occupied. Levin did the maths. The occupation had been set up nineteen days beforehand. This spurred Padraig – revitalised by the meal – off on an Occupy-themed adaptation of Paul Hardcastle's *19*. He body-popped as he sang.

'*All those who remember the camp, they won't forget it was wet and unclean. Insomnia of men in Occupy, whose average age was nineteen. N-n-n-n-n-nineteen.*'

'I don't know what that is?' said Kiera.

Eoghan felt that was inappropriate, but catchy, and moved on to talk about the national strike which was only three weeks away. Leon rubbed her hands together gleefully and gave the traditional Northern Irish call of approval. 'Yeee-ohhhh!' Others joined in.

Tommie suggested they raise their profile in the run

up to the strike. Cat proposed running a week of teach-ins, if she could get help. Levin said he was willing. Eoghan wanted to focus on the demos. He was interrupted by a woman who introduced herself loudly as Bronagh Boyle. Bronagh wore her hair back in a bun, had fat red cheeks and a plain black dress right to the ground. *She was large and in charge,* as they said in Belfast. Her husband was with her. He didn't speak, but his arms were filled with blankets and pillows and a roll mat was tucked against his chin.

'I have more for you in the van,' Bronagh announced. 'Oh no, don't worry. It can wait until after your wee meeting.'

'I guess we should wrap it up soon,' said Padraig, and he let out his trademark ghastly laugh. 'Mwah-ha-hahaha!'

'Okay,' said Eoghan. 'I'd heard some talk about protesting the BBC this week. *Oh shit!* Shit! I forgot to pick up the new forms! The 11/1s.'

'Mwah-ha-hahaha! What? We're playing by their rules now?'

'Yous should be able to protest where you want,' said Tommie firmly.

'Well that's not the way it is,' said Bronagh. 'They have control over when you can and can't speak out. Where are you marching to?'

'City Hall,' said Daniel.

Fred shook his head belligerently. 'Is it gonna be there every Saturday?'

'It's about establishing a pattern for newcomers,' Jack told him.

'You could always protest at the new *Invest NI* building,' declared Bronagh.

Leon clapped her hands together. 'They've the offices of the New York Stock Exchange on the ground floor.'

'Well that's what you want then,' said Tommie. 'Take them yuppies to task.'

'They'll get what's coming to them,' said Bronagh.

Eoghan took a vote and everyone was in favour of adding an *Invest NI* protest to the camp diary.

Eoghan turned on the light of his phone for Levin, crawling bum-first into the tent.

'Walking on all fours will take some getting used to,' he quipped.

Yanking his shoes off, he set them under cover of the flysheet. His bunk-mate was already cocooned, laid on his back watching an ant crawl across the ridge pole. Levin unbuttoned his jacket, and took off his shirt.

'Tents are quite cosy when it comes down to it.'

'That's because we've got prime real estate. Padraig can't say the same. He had a big grumble with Bob over his tent being moved closer to the drainage. Bob said it was his own fault as he hadn't been around to help. And then Cat and Leon had a go at Padraig too.'

'Oh? What was that about?'

'About him kicking the football around. And now they've decided there's a match on Saturday: girls versus boys.'

'That might be fun. Count me in.'

Levin took in the folds of the groundsheet, and the green tint of the walls against the street-light, then got down on Eoghan's spare ground-mat and pulled the duvet over him.

'Hey, your teach-in seemed to go well.'

'Hit and miss. We had to put up with Leon complaining that the government want to take away her *Farmville*. I can't figure out that girl. Sharp as a knife one minute, total air-head the next.'

'That's a bit unkind,' said Levin.

'Her *Farmville* unicorns! The Tories were going to take away her *Farmville* unicorns!'

Levin laughed. 'Well, here, I thought I wasn't going to sleep right away but you see after that dinner...'

'The all you can occupy buffet.'

'Aye. I'm ready to go.'

LEVIN

People come in from the street, tell me their truth
I tell them mine. I never
was met before by hundreds saying yes
These are cold age matters of fact

Housing benefit barely covering rent.
Seven GCSEs, two
degrees: of five hundred applications
Only twenty have gotten back

I'll ask at encounter intuitively
what we can accept within
our means; cautious talking, and listening,
Scholar explorer, puts at ease

When I awake with dew upon my face and
from eyes down I've been branded
Lines fade in the air of steaming coffee
Voices of love, smoke and story.

11

The sun spread heat through passing clouds. A light breeze filled the camp on Thursday morning. Mary had her class at *Queen's* and Joe would brave the South Belfast hills with her. They waved goodbyes to the old men and lads under the marquee, who sat with their cuppas. Leon sat with them, anxiously checking her phone.

'I barely slept a wink,' said Eoghan. 'Did you get sorted, vis a vis the accommodation?'

'The new fella? We put him in with John,' said Galway John.

'Mwah-ha-hahaha! Shitty John? Good luck with that! Have any of yous seen the Facebook lately?'

'Bog standard toxic masculinity,' griped Leon. 'Excuse me, I've to make a call.' She stepped around the ropes of the marquee and walked around to the rear of the *Shac* building.

'Facebook, Jesus,' groaned Levin. 'There's people on there who don't know they can use lower case.'

Eoghan put his fists on his hips and pivoted campily. *'Occupy is an NWO plot!'*

Padriag turned to him and flapped his arms about. *'I'm User 46397. Occupy is a Communist front. Stalin killed thousands!'*

'Yous don't half talk some bollocks,' said Bob.

Galway John got up and walked to the table in the gazebo.

'No,' squeaked Eoghan. *'Hitler killed more!'*

'No, Stalin!' squealed Padraig.

Eoghan rasped. 'You're a traitor because you don't support your government. Why do you hate them?'

'Would yous ones shut up for two fucking minutes?' growled Bob.

Galway came back with the radio on, and the local shock-jock selling his concern. *'You're listening to Kevin Trojan. Our topic today: the Occupy movement – conscientious citizens, or dirty filthy layabout bums? Phone lines are open to take your calls.'*

Eoghan jumped to his feet and called out, 'Leon, Daniel, everyone! Come and hear this!' He looked at the others with furrowed eyebrows. 'Did Trojan reach out to us?'

'I heard nothing,' said Galway.

'We have Ron on the line, from Cullybochan, Ballymean village.'

Padraig whipped a pen and miniature notebook from his pocket. Galway John turned the radio up. Ron sounded urgent, like a man literally dying from the words he'd kept inside. *'I don't think it's right that these waifs are camped out on the King's highway.'*

'The King's dead, Ron,' said Trojan.

'Whit?'

'He died in 1951. Besides, it's a public highway.'

'Well, who-ever owns it... if they want to make things better, why don't they join the army? Fight in a war then you'll see--'

'Which war?' Trojan asked.

'A disgrace is what it is.'

'Which war, Ron?'

'It doesn't matter, they're dirty hallions. And there's rats there!'

Levin rolled his eyes, and looked to Padraig. 'Wait. Did you make a bingo card?'

'Dirt. Rats,' murmured Padraig cheerily, as he ticked off the words in his notebook.

'Did you see these rats?'

'I don't want to see rats!'

'Okay Ron. We have another caller. Lianne claims to be a

representative of Occupy.'

'Leon,' she said.

Bob's eyebrows shot to the back of his head.

Galway John sunk his face into his hands. 'Oh Lord, no,' he cried.

'Firstly,' said Leon. *'I don't claim anything. I AM a member of Occupy, opposed to your pro-government propaganda --'*

Ron interrupted. *'Is there something wrong with supporting your government? Do you support your country?'*

'That's a false paradigm and a fraudulent dichotomy.'

Padraig raised his hand, cutting off Bob before he could query what Leon meant. 'Bob, I haven't a clue.'

'What do you say to people who say the campsite is an eyesore?' asked Trojan.

'No-one's saying that. No-one but muckrakers,' said Leon.

Trojan laughed. *'But what about the muck? And the noise? What do young kids make of that, Lianne?'*

Leon's pitch dropped by an octave. *'That's right. Lie. Smear. Make fun of my name. Distract...'* A car engine roared, really roared, the length of Donegall Street so that the next thing they heard Leon say was, *'...police brutality and slush funds.'*

Eoghan left Padraig ticking boxes and walked around the side of the tent. 'LEON!'

She emerged by the rear wall with a hand over the speaker. 'I've got him on the ropes,' she whispered.

Ron asked, *'Why is it you do these things? Behave like thugs and criminals?'*

'Well Lianne?' asked Trojan.

'That's not true. And it's Leon.'

Trojan said, *'It's hard to trust you when many of you hide with masks and scarves over your faces.'*

'The scarves are because we'd been out all night one degree above freezing!'

Ron said, 'Why don't you get a job?'

Padraig jumped out of the seat with his bingo book and

screamed. '*Yeee-oh! Full house!*'

'*I do have a job,*' said Leon.

Ron became quite irate. '*What's your job then? What do you do?*'

'*I'm a-an educator. And an anarchist,*' said Leon.

'*A, what, an artist? Yeh sound like a piss artist,*' exclaimed Ron.

'Mwah-ha-hahaha!'

Bob glared at Padraig, 'Do you want a smack round the ear, sunshine?'

'*Okay Ron, this is a family show. I'd ask you to mind your language or I'll have to hang up the call. Lianne. You're an artist. That's what you do? Watch paint dry?*'

'*When did you last have a bath?*' asked Ron.

'*I thought this was a serious interview where –*'

'*I'm going have to stop you there: Lianne, Ron. That's all we have time for. What's the verdict? Occupy, a menace! You heard it here, but the conversation continues...*'

Leon wandered back to the group looking angry and humiliated. She sat next to Padraig who lurched away in faux terror. He cupped his hands round his ears and made an O-shape with his mouth. Leon kept her head down. Padraig drew his lips together, wickedly, and began to speak. Bob raised the flat of his hand, cutting him off.

'Earn some brownie points and put on a pot of tea would you?'

He nodded and went to the gazebo section. They sat in quiet a moment listening to him pull the teapot open with a *tang*, the *glug-glug* of the water cannister, the *clank* of the grate on the coal fire. Bob kept Padraig confined to the gazebo with his icy stare, and he dried cutlery into the rack.

'He's not going to silence me,' snapped Leon.

'It was a set-up from the start,' said Levin.

'There is a question of personal honour at stake now,' admitted Galway, irritated.

'Trojan's honour is fairly questionable,' said Eoghan.

'Let's get it before a General Assembly. Maybe we can write him an open letter.'

Bob said, 'I'd knock the pastie-gobbed troll's balls off.'

An ambulance siren wailed a few streets away. 'Ah sure he's not worth it,' said Galway.

The kettle boiled, and Padraig re-entered their orbit. Eoghan reiterated his point. 'We send an open letter about representation and the damage done by sensationalised stories. And we can use it to address other issues with the BBC.'

'Like their pro-Israeli bias and complete disregard for the illegal occupation of Palestine,' said Levin.

'The propaganda war on the miners,' added Galway.

'Covering up the behaviour of Jimmy Saville,' said Bob.

Leon was roused to listing others. 'The institutional racism, sexism, homophobia, transphobia and Islamophobia.'

'Exactly! So let's go to the GA and see if Trojan doesn't change his tune when it's in all the papers.'

'Maybe Leon shouldn't take the mic next time,' said Padraig, as he presented her with a piping hot cup of tea.

She glared at him and made him wait with it until the tea scalded his fingers.

The camp was unusually quiet for a time: Cat and Kiera were at college and Daniel was sleeping off night watch. Jack was at home, Galway John was going home, and Bob laid down in his tent just as soon as he could. Leon and Padraig went north to their building to gather supplies: Fred was there alone, and was lonely, so they took Shay with them to cheer him up.

Levin watched four pigeons spontaneously scatter. 'I'm going to pick up a few things from the flat later.'

'No problem. You're free to come and go as you please,' said Eoghan.

'Answer me this. If I wanted to take an action that affects the group, would I have to wait and run it through the general assembly first?' asked Levin.

'Not necessarily. Say something needed to be done in a

hurry. An individual could act and it would later be discussed at the GA as to endorsing it as a collective action.' Eoghan put his hand over a yawn. 'Excuse me!' His black rim glasses accentuated the bags under his eyes.

With little else to do they brainstormed text for the open letter. They tried alternate phrases and discussed the impact of their decisions, but ultimately they had a lot they wanted to say. Over cheese and tuna sandwiches Eoghan floated the idea of calling the BBC. To his surprise, he quickly got through to Trojan's secretary, Angela, who arranged to call them back ten minutes later.

Angela called just as Kiera appeared, briefly, to throw her satchel in the tent. Cat picked up the ball from the gazebo, and vanished. Then Deirdre, in luminescent cycling wear, sailed off the street and glided towards them. Eoghan spoke quickly and positively until the call wrapped up.

'What's the good news?' asked Deirdre.

'Well, Kevin Trojan's radio show is booked up, *but* there was a sudden cancellation on his TV show. We're on tomorrow night.'

'That's fantastic,' she said.

Eoghan looked at Levin. 'I was thinking you and I could go on Trojan.'

Levin laughed nervously. 'Me? *Yeah, right.* Wouldn't Gary be more appropriate?'

'Nah. He's all tied up with some community thing. Sure you put in the work on what we want to say. And it's a good formula – old camper, new camper...'

'I don't know... what about you, Deirdre?'

She was distracted by the ball bouncing on the pavilion. Cat and Kiera had gone straight to practice for the game at the weekend. 'Sorry Levin, did you mean me? No, no. That television show, it isn't my cup of tea. All that screaming and hair pulling.'

'Hair pulling?' asked Eoghan.

'They had a guest on that tore a man's centre parting.

Tore it all off,' said Deirdre.

'A toupée,' said Levin.

'No, no, it was real. And Trojan says, *'Well you've taken that, why stop there?'* He actually sent his producer out for an electric razor!'

Levin gasped. 'Jesus.'

'Anyhow, I'm busy tomorrow,' said Deirdre. 'Cycling down to Roscommon for an anti-fracking rally in the afternoon. Then tea with someone from *Indymedia* to talk about improving education on renewable energies, and a candlelit vigil in Castlederg.'

Cat rounded the corner, her legs wobbling and face and arms glowing bright pink. Four pigeons flew away and she slumped down into a chair next to Eoghan.

'Have you seen the camp diary anywhere?' Eoghan asked.

Cat was out of breath and just shook her head, sweat dripping from it.

'Maybe Bob moved it yesterday,' said Levin.

Levin turned away when Eoghan let out a yawn close to a spasm, and waved over to Mary, before her head disappeared into her tent.

'You're not going to last to the GA,' said Levin.

Cat shot him a disappointed look. 'We've loads to get through.'

'Maybe put your head down now for a couple of hours,' said Levin.

Eoghan grumbled. 'I don't know if I'm going to sleep. I think I'll go up home and lie on a warm bed for a while.'

'Sounds like a plan,' said Levin.

Eoghan went to his tent to pack some dirty laundry.

'FOOTBALL PRACTICE!' yelled Kiera.

Cat sighed and got to her feet. Mary wriggled back out of her tent. They got Leon to join them, having come back to camp ahead of Padraig and Shay.

Levin sat alone a while until he was joined by two of

the homeless campers: Shitty John and the new fella, Tall Paul. John was in his late forties with swarthy skin, clothes loose fitting and heavily stained. Paul's dark woollen clothes were tight on his lanky frame, about six foot three inches. His eyes were somewhere else, somewhere distant. Although Levin tried to engage them neither man said much more than a nod. When he offered to make a cuppa, John tapped Paul on the shoulder and repeated the question outright. Neither man joined Levin to watch the women play football.

He sat on the pavilion wall with his coffee while they dribbled and volleyed. Jack had joined them and hammered the ball through the coats they used as goal posts.

'There's a taste of what you're gonna get on Saturday!' she said.

'The spy has come to check out our tactics!' yelled Kiera.

And Leon, 'You're gonna be doing the washing up 'til this time next year, son!'

Levin took it all in good humour. He finished his coffee and wandered back to the gazebo. Tall Paul and John were talking. It transpired they knew each other from the *Salvation Army* shelter. The conversation trailed off when Levin joined them.

'He's a bit quiet, sorry Levin,' said John.

'Hey, you're alright. It must be confusing. New surroundings and new people.' John nodded. 'They're a good bunch here. And dinner's coming in a few hours. Did you get something last night?' John nodded again.

They sat in silence a while longer until Levin said he had to go home to pick up a few things. 'Will yous be okay to sit here until the girls come back round?'

'Aye,' said John. He patted Tall Paul on the back. 'Won't we?'

Paul nodded.

That night there was an ethereal moon, a cool snapping wind, south to easterly. At one in the morning Leon returned to Bob and Daniel. She'd been up to the food van, five minutes away, by *The Kremlin* nightclub. Her chips were topped with cheese, eggs, bacon bits and mushrooms. Bob briefly looked up from his book, disgusted, as she burrowed into the polystyrene dish, wolfing it down.

'You should try these, Bob. Go on. Daniel? No? Suit yourself.'

'What did they talk about at the assembly?' asked Bob.

'I dunno. Had to miss it,' said Leon, a mushroom dangling from her bottom lip.

Daniel spoke quietly and slowly. Hearing him use a sentence of more than five words, Leon was struck by the colour of his Spanish accent. 'There were a few people missing: Gary, Eoghan, Levin. It was mainly about the BBC demo tomorrow.'

'Is that in the morning or tomorrow night?' asked Bob.

'The night. Cat knows more about it than I do. Someone mentioned the possibility of an interview with them.'

'With the BBC?' asked Leon. She struggled to keep her food in her mouth as if the concept was anathema, despite their being interviewed by the BBC twice already.

'Perhaps. No-one was sure when it is, or if it's happening at all.'

Bob held his book in one hand and reached into his pocket. 'We're nearly out of milk. Daniel, would you mind making a run to the all-nighter?'

Daniel waved him off. 'I'll get this.'

'Take the money,' Bob insisted. 'Oh and I think the garage is out. You might want to try the *Spar*.'

Daniel drifted into the wet air of the street. Leon stared at Bob, really stared. Bob put his head back in the book. It was a blue hardback A5 diary.

'That's the camp diary. Eoghan was looking for that you know.'

'Fat lot of use it is,' said Bob. 'This operation doesn't know it's brain from it's arse.'

'What's got your knickers in a twist?' Leon asked.

'See that gazebo? Everything under it is soaked. We were supposed to have another of these marquee tents up. It was supposed to be here yesterday. Not that Eoghan or you were about to help. It's not even in the diary.' Bob put his head back in the book.

'What does it actually say in there?'

Bob sighed. 'Well, my little socialist power friend.' He took a look at her, and bent back the pages. 'Once upon a time there was a commune of hippies. They thought they were going to save the world. So they invoked Bob Barr, a man so strong he could turn hippies into heroes.' Leon laughed. Bob continued his pretence of reading. 'However, on meeting Bob the Brave, the lazy free-loading bastards chained him to the camp for all eternity; with a sign which read, *'Not to be moved.'* Rotas were promised. But no relief arrived, to deliver the King from his long dark night of the soul.'

Leon laughed again. 'You're the King now?'

Bob looked up. His face was unusually soft, and kind and his lips broad, as if he was trying to smile. 'Do you doubt it? Well, on the night after Thor's Day, Bob got hold of Prince Eoghan's magic book of spells. His magicks were thwarted by Leon the Feeble that dutiful nocturne. And so multiplied the tiger's wroth.'

A piece of paper fell to the ground, unnoticed by Bob as he slammed the book shut.

'I didn't have you down as a *Game of Thrones* fan,' said Leon.

'What are you on about now?'

'It's like Tolkien, but with sex and violence. Jesus! You must know! Most everyone in this camp has been in Game of Thrones.'

Bob shook his head. He noticed the paper on the ground. Leon lifted it and unfolded it. It was a printout of an email addressed to Eoghan, from Angela, *The Trojan Show* booking agent. A glow spread across Leon's face. Bob took it from her, and read it himself.

Leon couldn't contain her excitement. 'Oh, this is good, this is good!' She tried to take the printout back but Bob moved it out of reach. 'Bob, we're going to be on Trojan's Show! On the telly!'

Bob arched an eyebrow. 'We are?'

'I meant… well, that could be *us*. Balancing the scales, taking charge of the narrative. I'm up for it if you are… Bob the Brave.' Leon reached for it again, but Bob kept it to himself.

'It's Eoghan's name at the top of this piece of paper. No-one else is mentioned. Did he not tell anyone?'

Leon shrugged. 'Maybe not. If he wasn't at the GA and it doesn't seem to have come up. *And* it's not *written* in the camp diary. His tent's empty, so we can't ask him tonight. Maybe he is keeping it to himself.'

'Everything has to go through the GA. When was he planning on telling us? After all the rigmarole I had to go through to organise night shift!'

'We should do it, Bob. Eoghan's always doing the press stuff. And you got on okay with that Sunday World guy last weekend.' Bob contemplated the matter. The rain was getting louder. 'Let's do it Bob. Me and you, facing the Trojan virus!'

He handed the printout back to her. She looked disappointed. Then, to her surprise, he said, 'Okay. Right. I'll do it with you.'

'You're going to face your fears?'

He laughed. 'I'm not afraid of him. Trojan's nowt but a big slabber. Someone needs to teach that boy a lesson.'

At that moment, Daniel came running through the rain with the jug of milk in his hand. Leon quickly thrust the paper into her pocket.

12

Levin awoke too early the following morning in his bedsit in the student quarter. He sat in pyjamas and emailed the university about a supervisor for his dissertation. The laundry was taken out of the washing machine and hung on the clothes horse to dry. There would be just enough room for them and the spare blanket in the holdall. A pigeon precariously staggered across his windowsill and got comfortable with it's back to the room. Levin's plan was to leave at noon and walk to Writer's Square to go over the interview strategy with Eoghan. They'd attend the GA and check in at the BBC by half eight. As Eoghan let him share his tent, he didn't need to buy one. However, Tall Paul and John were in his thoughts and Levin decided to buy one to donate to the camp. It would be an investment. But as he lay back on the bed his eyes rolled and he slept.

The high pitched chimes of his mobile phone shook him awake shortly after four, when the rain was heavy on the windows.

'Oh God, I'm so sorry, Eoghan. I'll be at the camp in a half hour.'

'No, no, don't panic. I haven't been down at all today. Josie wanted us to spend some more time together and I think I'm going to have my dinner here. So look, I'll tell you what. Let's meet at the bus station near Blackstaff House around half eight.'

'That should be fine. We know what we want to say.'

'Great. I'll see you then!'

Levin took a shower and fried two eggs and ate them

with tortilla wraps. He folded and packed his clothes. The rain kept on. He went online – consciously avoiding toxic Facebook – to search for his tent. There were many contenders. He spent too long comparing sizes, styles and prices but eventually he found the one he wanted and paid to collect it on the Monday. He was rubbing a mucus ball from his eye when he noticed the time. He nearly put his eye out.

Levin scrambled for his shoes, put on his coat, and found the phone under the bed. Speed walking on soaking pavement, he caught sight of a bus at the lights. He ran, alongside heavy traffic, and got to the stop opposite Queen's University, its Gothic and Tudor front muted behind the plexiglass. On the bus a stream of water in the aisle spread and trickled. Levin checked his phone on a seat by fogged up windows. It was only two stops, but half a mile, and Blackstaff House was only a minute away, across busy Great Victoria Street.

Eoghan was waiting. 'We're still in good time. Did you find the camp diary?' he asked.

'Shit! Should we go to the camp for it?'

Eoghan tapped his head. 'Ah sure it's all in here.' He looked across the road to Blackstaff. 'Saturdays against Austerity! And if Kevin starts giving us shit...' Eoghan found a gap in the traffic and led the way, shouting, 'Well then, I'll tell him we're protesting the BBC next week.'

Levin laughed. 'You wouldn't dare!'

'We've got to address the issues. Engage the audience. Don't let him off the--'

He stopped mid-sentence, mid-crossing. From the City Hall end, a group of thirty people rounded the corner. A speeding motorist came within inches of Eoghan. Drivers palmed their horns in anger. When the two men did reach the other side they were literally frozen in place. The crowd were protestors. *Their protestors.*

'*Fuck!*' exclaimed Eoghan.

'No way.'

The oncoming force was fronted by Anonymous. They

waved placards: *'Occupy Belfast', 'End Anti Palestine Bias At The Beeb', 'No More BBC Blackout On Occupy'.* Everyone was there: Padraig, Fred, Mary, Joe, Kiera, Daniel, Jack, Sadie, Terry, Dee, Jim, and they gave approving nods as they walked past. Gary and Cat stopped to talk with them.

'I was wondering if yous were going to show,' said Cat.

Eoghan shook his head, almost in a state of shock.

'Let me get this straight,' said Levin. 'We're on the BBC tonight, *while* we're boycotting the BBC.'

'What?' asked Gary, nearly dumbstruck.

'They're *giving* us a platform to speak?' said Cat.

Eoghan squealed defensively. 'I didn't know! My home internet was down so I couldn't see the minutes. And I'd have seen the clash if the diary hadn't went missing.'

Cat was fuming. 'Why the fuck did you not tell anyone else about this?'

Eoghan and Levin turned to one another and said, 'I thought you were going to.'

Cat pressed her palm to her forehead and rolled her eyes. 'Melters!'

Levin scrutinised the protest as it surrounded the studio. 'Do you think we can make it through to the front?'

Gary was uncertain. 'The police have arrived. You might have to talk to them.'

The reception of BBC Blackstaff House was dark carpets and grey fabric walls. A large friendly looking man, in a sharp white shirt and tie sat behind a cola-coloured glass desk. Leon took the printout from her pocket and slid it across the desk. 'We're along for the Trojan Show tonight.'

Bob took in the lay of the land. 'Good set-up,' he said and he drummed his fingers on the counter.

The receptionist dialled an extension. A minute later a small, middle aged woman opened the barrier for them. She seemed glad to see them and spoke in a sing-song fashion. 'I'm Angela. Glad you could make it. This way, please... Eoghan...

and Levin?'

Leon blurted out, 'My name is Levina.'

'Oh crap,' sighed Angela. 'Okay, we can fix this.'

They followed Angela down the hall. Bob's head was turned briefly by a broad blond security woman going the other way. Angela opened the door to the Green Room.

Bob was beginning to get anxious, ready to object, when he took in the sight before them: vibrant coloured firm leather seats; a small fridge with miniature wines and beers; baskets of wrapped chocolate and cheesy biscuits.

Angela said, 'You'll be called when The Beast is – is -' She stopped herself suddenly. Her cheery expression was gone, her face frozen in grave expression. 'W-When M-Mr. Trojan, Mr. Kevin Trojan is ready, you'll be called to join Mr. Trojan on stage shortly.'

Angela had barely closed the door behind her when Leon was at the table, pocketing a bunch of thumb-sized pens. She quickly made her way to the fridge.

'God's sake,' growled Bob.

'It looks like we're going to be front and centre. Are you okay with this? You're not going to space out again are you?'

'The fuck I am. Hey! You don't have to take anything that isn't nailed down. We're here to make the camp look good.' He lowered his voice to a murmur. 'Though it'll take some effort.'

Leon rubbed her back, like a cat, against the lounger and she cracked open her beer. 'Swish gaff this. Bob, shove some of those teabags and shortbreads in your coat.'

He shook his head, 'no', and poured milk up to the top of his styrofoam cup.

Leon prattled on. 'You know I was at this party once. We ran out of mixers, and used milk in place of vodka. Tasted like boke.' Bob withdrew the cup before it reached his mouth. 'That was the University in Coleraine. Crazy days. Non-stop at Old Mill Grange. Eggs thrown at walls. Someone put a Chinese takeaway in the microwave. The foil dish! Minutes later the thing was on fire.'

'Good for you,' he muttered. Bob cracked open a tiny whiskey, opened his throat and inhaled the scents of wood and grain.

'The cops were always raiding the place. Never found anything though.'

'I'm glad my taxes went to such good use. Did you actually learn anything?'

'I was taking Sociology and Media Studies. Had to drop out at the end of the first year.'

'I wonder why,' said Bob. His knees cracked as he sat and he gave a sharp yelp.

'That's education. Anyway, there was an academic matriarchal conspiracy against the left. What a surprise! So what are we thinking here? Bring up his pro-Unionist bias? Those legal injunctions that we'll get into trouble if we mention their existence?'

'You bloody better not embarrass me.'

'For the Republic of Occupy!' she yelled, and raised her beer in the air.

'I'm warning you, Leon.'

'How could I embarrass you on a BBC show? These are the bastards that let Jimmy Saville run wild for four decades.'

Bob seethed. 'Fucking disgusting.'

'We're way down in the rabbit hole here,' said Leon.

'How anyone could have caught a whiff of that and turned a blind eye. Sickens me to the pit of my stomach.'

'Not just him. Rod Hull, Rolf Harris, Benny Hill. They were all here.' Leon noticed the bottle shaking in Bob's hand. 'Don't fret about this, Bob. Just get on there and do your thing. If he steps over the line, we'll take no prisoners.'

The large friendly receptionist left the front desk and was replaced by the stern woman Bob had taken a liking to in the corridor. Eoghan and Levin moved forward in the line until it was their turn to be seen.

'We're from Occupy?' said Eoghan.

'Our names are on the list.'

Eoghan handed over his passport. She examined it, and then the list, but couldn't find their names. However they were let through and directed to join a line of five people in a nearby hallway. Before they could present their queries to the staff member at the door, he impatiently hurried Eoghan and Levin inside. The door shut firmly behind them.

They found themselves in the studio, squinting before the harsh lights of the stage. Eoghan moved towards it but an usher motioned them back into the black ascending rows of the audience. Eoghan tried to object but the floor manager had taken the stage and was whipping up the audience.

'When Kevin humiliates the smelly students I want your applause to shift tectonic plates!'

'I need you to take your seats. Top row, on the right,' said the usher.

The floor manager got everyone to shout as loud as they could and after they did he called out, 'Now let's practice trolling. Give us some gaslighting. Say it with me. NO! NO, YOU DIDN'T!'

'NO! NO, YOU DIDN'T!'

Confused, Eoghan and Levin climbed the steps. The walls and floors were painted black. They turned back to the stage to see Bob seated there by Trojan's desk sneering at the assistant fitting him with a mic. Leon was there too. She stood up and tried to help Bob, and got batted away for her trouble. Seeing this, Eoghan nearly fell on his fingers there on the steps.

'Back row. Two seats by the aisle. Quick, quick!' cursed the usher.

They were seated, their protests unheard. Onstage the floor manager was waving his arms around. 'Very good! Can you clap again? Clap for Kevin Trojan! HARDER! CLAP LIKE YOU MEAN IT! *CLAP LIKE HE SAVED YOU FROM DROWNING!*'

Amid the applause the host took the stage, clambering like a dazed baby elephant. He nodded and smiled, his triple chin brushing against the top of his tailored jacket. Though fifty years old his face was full of acne and his receding hairline contained traces of a long-departed quiff. He sat down and spun in his swivel chair like it was part of an amusement ride. The floor manager counted him in, directed the applause to fade. Trojan circled again with the chair and clawed his way to the desk.

'Welcome to the Kevin Trojan show. Welcome. Now. Twenty days ago, a group of protestors erected tents in Belfast's Cathedral Quarter. They said they wouldn't leave until their demands were met. Some call them concerned citizens. Others say they're public nuisances. Or lazy terrorists. For one night only, we've got them to leave their posts. Welcome, from Occupy, Miss Levina Kirkwood...'

'Thank you, Kevin.'

'And Eoghan McBride!'

'No fucking way,' muttered Eoghan.

'Let me start by asking the question that must surely be on everyone's lips. Levina, what are you protesting about anyway?'

Leon threw her back up.

Her words came out on automatic. She was on her feet ten seconds later. Her chair almost fell behind her. 'Are you a complete and utter moron? Really? Do you have a researcher? Do you know what research is? Are your audience so doped up as to not have the slightest inkling you're lying to them? Well, Kevin No-One?'

The audience were on their feet now, clapping and screaming. She reached over the desk and pulled Trojan's hair, using it to drag him across the table.

She felt Bob kick her foot, and snapped out of the daydream. 'You're doing it again,' he murmured.

'Well presumably you're unhappy about *something*?' said Trojan.

'We're protesting cuts to housing,' said Bob coolly. 'And MPs lining their pockets with the sweat of our brows.'

'There's schools and hospitals closing,' said Leon. 'Cuts to the emergency services. Record homelessness and crime. The people won't stand for it!'

The audience did applaud this time: a third of them pounded their palms enthusiastically and others not so much. Levin joined in, to Eoghan's annoyance. He was not enjoying this.

'How do you propose to achieve your ends?' asked Trojan. 'A couple of tents in the mud? And what about the thousands of man hours spent policing you?'

'It's a lot easier than policing your nights on the town,' Leon blurted out.

The audience gasped. Bob kicked Leon again. She shot him an angry look.

The floor manager whispered into his ear piece. 'Cut the mic on the feminist.'

Trojan wasn't phased. 'I have no idea what you're implying, but any more of it and we'll end the show with my legal team delivering a writ. I hope I've made that clear.' Leon put her head down and sunk into her chair. 'Now Eoghan. I'm wondering why a man your age would get involved in this tent occupation? What would make someone want to do a thing like this?'

Bob drew his gaze from Leon, looked at Trojan, and thought for a moment. A long moment. He was still, his expression was dour. Then he looked out into the audience.'S-sorry. Did somebody... say something? I thought... I'm getting old now, and I can't hear too well.'

Whispers floated around the studio. 'Old guy's not well.' 'He's losing it.'

The floor manager whispered, 'Did we cut the right mic?'

Trojan raised his voice. 'I asked why you would --'

'SHHHHH!' Bob's was a warning shush and Trojan flinched. 'Did anyone else hear that?' he whispered. A malevolent grin spread over his old face. 'Anybody? I thought I heard...

crying... gurning... *a little pipsqueak mama's boy?'*

There was an eerie silence for a moment. And then, suddenly, small groups exploded in laughter around the studio. Others were infected by the humour and sniggered.

Trojan frowned and raised his voice again. 'Who's clapping? Don't! Don't pander to their needs. These are juvenile parlour games.'

Leon lifted her head up, her eyes widening and sparkling with confidence. 'Daddy,' she cried, in a child's voice, 'Daddy, the big boy at school said I'm mean.' Her microphone was still on. Again, sections of the audience began to chuckle. 'Daddy, would you tell him off? It wasn't me! He started it!'

In the back row, Eoghan permitted himself a grin.

Trojan slammed his palm on the desk. 'Alright, alright! Seeing as how you're so fond of showing off in front of our audience, let's take questions. Second row. Wait for the mic to come to you!'

The man Trojan selected was forty with a complexion of someone twenty years younger. His chestnut hair was newly cut, like that of a child's, and his bone structure tumbled in on itself. 'Don't you realise you're causing an obstruction? What about the effect on local businesses?' His questions were followed by weak clapping.

'Those are very good questions,' said Trojan.

Bob replied firmly, 'My arse they were. We're in no-one's way. And local businesses do alright from our custom.'

'What about litter?' asked the conservative man-child.

Leon made a face like the man-child had a screw loose. 'Duuuuh! That's what bins are for!'

Bob scolded him. 'No Blue Peter badge for you.'

Trojan wanted to move on, but the man-child asked another one. 'How can you say the government are wrong when the majority of people in this country voted for them?'

'Same as the majority have been with your ma. It's still wrong,' said Bob.

The audience booed. Bob seemed to have seen it coming

and let out an enormous yawn, stretching for effect.

Trojan waved a chunky finger at him. 'Now I've asked you once already to refrain from personal remarks. This interview will terminate if it continues. They can show a repeat of *Mrs. Brown's Boys* in place of this. Okay, back row, aisle seat. Wait for the mic!'

Levin leaned forward. 'I have a question for Levina? Could you tell me about your role in the running of the camp?'

Leon hesitated.

Trojan spoke up. 'He asked what is it that you do?'

'Ah... s-sure, well... I tidy, and h-help with meals. I get up at dawn. B-Before everyone wakes I read Marxist macro... Marxinomics.'

Trojan laughed. 'That sounds fascinating. Back row again! The fellow next to you.'

The floor manager gave Eoghan the mic. 'My question is for Eoghan, I think he said his name is Eoghan? That's funny. That's my name too.'

'Well I hope you're politer than this one,' quipped Trojan.

'A good deal, Kevin, a good deal,' said Eoghan. 'Anyway, I work in security so it's something I think about a lot. If I wanted to join your protest, how could you convince me your camp is secure?'

'How can you ensure there's not people who will wreck the place?' said Trojan.

Bob creased and furrowed his brow. 'There's at least a dozen people there during the day...' He was becoming flustered. 'We have it set so three, four people arrange to watch... it is watched, the camp, is watched every night.'

Eoghan said, 'You seem very sure of this. So, what do you do if someone's given you a fake name, or if they've an ulterior agenda?' Levin kicked Eoghan under the seat.

'And who's watching these tents if you're here?' asked Trojan.

Bob felt around for the words, the furrows multiplying,

the crow's feet murdering. 'I'd guess... those papers would have to... step up into the light...'

'We have to hurry you,' said Trojan.

'The... we have people... a loop of people... shouldering consequence...' said Bob.

Trojan took a deep breath. 'Well, certainly something to think about. That's all the time we have tonight. I'd like to thank my guests from Occupy Belfast, my wonderful audience and you at home. I'll be back next week for more cutting political discourse. Don't miss it!'

Leon went straight home afterwards. Returning quickly to camp, Bob took up Galway's offer of a night off, and crawled into his tent. The clouds shepherded the night with wind and rain, sprinkling upon the canvas. Eoghan found the camp diary stuffed in with the other papers in the gazebo and used the pages to feverishly scribble out a new song. Afterwards he got his guitar and strummed for them.

'*We had a tussle with Kevin Trojan, slabbery big head like a wet mountain*

A bully and a scally and a rogue and it went on so long we was countin'

What would Eoghan ask Bob if he was Bob and what would Bob ask if he was Eoghan?

My name's Eoghan, I'm the singer of this song, and I'm still not sure about Trojan.

What would Bob say to Eoghan (that's me), if he was Levin and Levin was Leon?

Glad I only asked a few 'bout that, 'cause if I asked everyone I'd be no one.'

BRONAGH

A tabloid journo's hat's in the ring
and everyone's throwing their copper and silver in
You did your best with family and gave all that to charity;
Come down to cruel glassy stars with heated soup
Come down from on the hill above
Square up to yer tea-towel, yellow cuff yer gloves

Saturday's promise of jasmine abandoned
to humid cloying
and friends in the downpour
Water pressure cleans stains, glassy frothing up
Heavy passing truck
Weather slinging accusations and excuses
tapping keyboard whingers enough
This city is a puddle of sleepers
out rough

Raid the storage box for linen
and sleeping bag of relief
laundered to the touch
You go crazy mash potatoes; fry oil before petrol,
wing in paella and fork off tuna
Tents' push and pull, be a getter
You know what needs done, let's wade on
how long the trough before we're all laid off?

13

Between fifty and sixty people walked to City Hall that afternoon. The severity of Belfast's winter put pressure on their ears, blocked their noses and ached their joints. A few passers-by sneered, others joined the march. Photographers took shots for their portfolios and websites. Some who couldn't make the demonstration sent messages of support. Narcissistic 'conservative' writers shit out eight-paragraph-treatises on mass hypocrisies of 'hippies with grubby bed-sheets.' In their bubbles the hacks passed by corporate and political investigation and blame to pair Palestinian advocates with Nazi sympathisers, to frame George Monbiot as a modern-day Ayatollah Khomeini.

In the square they danced to keep warm. The chords of a composition by David Rovics rocked out and Luke the busker followed Eoghan's string-plucking fingers note for note. Cheers went up when Gary said nine thousand were protesting, that moment, at the Central European Bank in Frankfurt.

Cat was noticing a discoloured stain on her shirt when Kiera found her outside their tent.

'*Carnival of Resistance 3: The Occupy Football Championship!* Well done!'

Cat looked unsettled. 'Me? I didn't do anything.'

'Come on. You came up with most of our strategies. And I sat next to you while you were tweeting and blogging about today.'

'I hate to admit it but *The Trojan Show* appearance gave us a boost.'

'Even before that! Messaging dozens of people one at a

time! How come you're so organised?'

Cat laughed. 'I wouldn't say organised. I used to post my drawings on *Livejournal* and *Flickr*. Then I was selling them. You know *The Black Box* does that art market on Sundays?'

'Oh aye. My mate Hanita had a stall there. Dead cheap it was.'

'I didn't want to be just another needy artist so I promoted my stall on Facebook during the week. A few other stallholders asked me to do the same,' said Cat.

Bob, Galway John and Tall Paul were sat inside the marquee, watching the kids on bikes ride through hoops.

'Four seasons in a day,' said Galway.

'It's all up the left. John, do you ever feel like we're the only ones doing any fucking work around here?'

'It has crossed my mind from time to time, sir. It has crossed my mind. Tell me Bob, I heard a wee rumour you were on the television last night.'

'Sure neither of us even have a television, John.'

'True. I couldn't tell you what's on it it these days.'

Cat brought over a middle-aged woman in shiny black fake leather, and introduced her to the older men as Sarah. Sarah looped the handles of her carrier bag into Cat's pink hands.

'Awk God love yis. Sittin' out in this bitter wind. People haven't forgotten about you.'

'We're expecting a tent that'll be much better for shelter,' said Galway.

'It should have been here by now,' grumbled Bob.

'Awk ye poor souls.' Sarah lifted Tall Paul's hand and gave it a squeeze. 'You're to keep warm now, ye hear?' The big burly man shook, and looked up at her with sorrowful blue eyes.

Tall Paul was in his fifties but had a baby's face. They still couldn't get much out of him other than he'd been homeless and had problems with his hearing. When Levin offered him a new tent he said he didn't have any money. Tall Paul spent most of his time with Bob, but staring into the distance and not saying anything. He didn't seem to understand why they were camped there.

'Do you think he's afraid of us?' asked Kiera, as she unpacked the donations in the gazebo.

'He's probably used to being around people he doesn't trust,' whispered Cat.

Shay joined them, blowing his tin whistle, and wearing an Italian coat: gold and brown wool with flecks of black and white.

'Shay, that's much too big for you,' said Kiera.

'Really comfy though. Get anything good?'

'Oh it's all posh stuff. Mostly tins: chickpeas; more beans; ugh. Hmm, steak and macaroni. Oh, oh, I call dibs on the olives!'

'Olives are evil,' said Cat.

'Olives are great,' said Kiera. 'I saw this documentary this one time about people in the Mediterranean who ate olives five times a day. They were all a hundred years old and playing badminton.'

'Paul!' Shay called out. 'Do you want an olive?'

He declined with a shake of his head

'Ooh, pesto,' said Kiera.

Eoghan strummed Tommy Sands' *There Were Roses*. A car door slammed. Bronagh emerged with a supermarket box thrust in front of her. Tommie made a beeline to the kerb, passed the bust of the Spanish War volunteer, and took it off her hands.

'There's extra blankets, and tea towels,' she told him as they walked back up the path. 'Those ones you were using are stinking. Fling them or give them to me and I'll take them home and put them through the wash.'

'We're grateful,' said Cat. 'Bronagh, can I ask a favour?'

'What is it?'

'The football. We're having a bit of a contest: boys versus girls. Padraig has been taunting us and --'

Bronagh refused, dourly shaking her head. 'Oh no. I'm not getting drawn into all that. And I don't think you should talk about Padraig behind his back.'

'Hang on,' said Cat. 'You think I'm slagging people off behind their backs?'

'Well it sure sounds like it to me,' said Bronagh. 'I don't have time for petty rivalries, Cat. I saw the television last night. Eoghan and Levin taking the hand out of poor Bob and Leon. The whole country saw it. We need a bit more unity around here.'

Cat muttered through gritted teeth. 'All I was asking for was an impartial referee for the game.' She turned around to the marquee and when there was enough distance between them, she continued muttering. 'Fucking aul bitch.'

Bob saw Cat coming and hid behind his *Daily Mirror*. Galway John was more malleable, although it took some pleading before he relented.

'I hope I'm up to the task, Cat. It's been manys-a-year since I refereed a football match,.'

Shay held out his tin whistle to him. Galway wiped the mouthpiece on his shirt and blew a long shrill toot into it.
The lads: Eoghan, Levin, Padraig, Tommie and Fred took the half of the pavilion nearest the road. The lasses spread out over the upper half: Cat, Jack, Kiera, Leon, and Mary in goal by the steps. The crowd were lined from the Police Ombudsman's building at the far side of the square: passers-by, friends and families, some with hoods up against the drizzle. The pavilion held most of their signs with things written on them like *'Peace', 'People United', 'No More Bailouts'* and *'Go Away I'm Sleeping.'*

Galway John brought Padraig and Cat to the centre and addressed the pavilion. 'Right now. I want a nice clean game. No questioning my decisions. No kicking. No biting.'

'No Surrender!' Padraig shouted ironically.

'That's a warning right there,' said Galway.

He blew the starting whistle. Padraig kicked to Tommie. Tommie took it around Cat, back to Eoghan, around Jack to Padraig. Jack pursued him. The ball went to Tommie. He took the ball around Kiera. Mary came out to the goal-post coats and Tommie saw his opening. Then, a last minute save as Shelby invaded the pitch, barking excitedly. The crowd awwww-ed. The whistle scarcely reached Galway's mouth when four laughing children stormed the pitch. Padraig was too forceful pushing Shelby away. The Staffy stepped back and shook his coat, raining wet dog into Padraig's mouth.

Play resumed. This time Jack intercepted. She passed the ball to Mary. Forming a triangle with Cat they drew Tommie and Padraig in, sailing it over their heads downfield to Leon. Levin closed in on her. His stoic calm transformed to a new intensity. He strained with the rain rattling like acupuncture on his face. Levin was between Leon and the goal so Leon kicked the ball as hard as she could. The ball struck his cheek. He nursed the stinging sensation and looked to Galway John, who did nothing. Leon kept with it. Car horns were honking. Shelby was barking. She took her shot.

Fred fumbled the catch but quickly scooped it up. The ball went out to Levin who made a few shows of passing it so the girls stayed marking the centre forwards. He was on a clear line to the goalmouth. Mary came out and he put the ball past her. Kiera came in from his left. Levin went right, looked up, and spotted his mother waving on the sidelines. Leon intercepted, and turned the ball around. Padraig tried a dirty tackle but she skipped past it. Galway John shook a stern finger at him.

'Ya capitalist, Leon,' shouted Padraig, 'Ya lousy fuckin' capitalist!'

Leon ignored him, passed it to Cat. Fred saw her, her bouncing breasts and green hair, charging towards him. Her slim frame, flush cheeks and elfin pink ears, warm and panting. He saw the woman of his dreams. He went right. She went left.

Galway John raised his hand and blew a warbling toot on the tin whistle. The crowds danced and applauded. The pigeons flapped.

Levin played the ball to Eoghan. He wanted a quick equaliser. He found Padraig, feeling similar. He kicked the ball high and far: beyond Tommie; beyond Mary. It hit the top of the steps and took its time to bounce back down. Five minutes later Cat took possession and tried for a second goal. It went too far again, onto the road this time. A few spides fucked around with it until Fred threatened to lamp them. He threw it to Eoghan, who winged it to Tommie to Padraig.

Galway blew the whistle twice. 'Off-side, Padraig.'

'The fuck I was!'

'That's three strikes.'

'Bullshit. Name them.'

Cat shouted, 'Do you not know the off-side rule Padraig?'

Under the trees at the touchline Sadie, Martine, Steph and Katrina sang. *'You're not singin', you're not singin', you're not singin' anymore!'*

Fred stepped forward to take Galway to task. Behind him Shelby rummaged inside his coat, dragging the goal mouth wider. Daniel took the dog by the collar and pulled him away, Shelby's mouth full of biscuits.

'You're not serious, big man!' insisted Padraig. 'Wise up.'

'Referee!' complained Fred.

'What have I told you?' Galway cautioned Fred, and then told Padraig, 'You're off the field.'

'For fuck's sake!' he yelled and passing Eoghan, muttered, 'Wanking wanker.'

'You're the wanker,' Eoghan said.

'You're an arsehole wanker,' Padraig said, seething.

'Referee, can we at least bring Joe on?' asked Tommie.

Galway shook his head and awarded the girls a penalty. Leon ran at the ball with a warrior's scream. The instant she struck it the drizzle became audible. Fred leapt and grazed his shin. The ball passed through the goalmouth. It hit the top of a post lining the road, bounced back and struck Fred on the back of his head. Galway blew the whistle. The crowds cheered. The sound was cut by a sudden downpour and spectators stormed the pitch, running to the marquee for cover.

The following night, after the cathedral bells faded, a healthy compliment turned out for the General Assembly. Orange licking flames from the fire bin oscillated, blowing smoke easterly. Bob waved it away with his *Sunday Mirror*. Behind him the branches of towering ash trees swayed, though not so ominously as Friday. On the cracked pavement a lone tubby pigeon with a small head took it's short legs to the chalkboard which read '22 Days.' It was a humid night and with the threads of the BBC fiasco spilling out, tempers were boiling over.

'The Occupy movement is never going to be seen in a positive light because of internal conflict. Leon and Bob messed things up for everyone.'

'Do you hear that everyone? Eoghan's peeved. Never mind that we stood in the cold and rain two hours, despite getting more BBC airtime than we were asked for,' said Cat.

'You're lucky Trojan didn't mention the protest on air,' said Bronagh.

'What did any of it actually achieve? We looked like a laughing stock,' complained Mary.

'It's probably best to just move on,' said Levin.

Shay and Daniel agreed.

Eoghan disagreed. 'Except the thing is, we know it was intentional. What were you thinking, Bob? Leon?'

Leon looked up, agitated, with a ridiculous expression. 'Are you serious? We apologised. It's done with, and this is a waste of time.' She cast a long glance across the assembly, now bearing her teeth and screwing up her face. 'Are we going to talk about Portland? Nearly a thousand cops took down their camp. Fifty arrests. Or what happened in Denver? Jesus Christ.'

'I was just coming to that,' said Eoghan.

'What happened in Portland and Denver?' asked Padraig.

A few others shrugged.

Leon spelled it out. 'Riot gear. Batons. Pepper spray. Two dozen arrests in Denver; fuck knows how many in hospital, beaten and bloody. Do you know how many tents they had?'

'Denver? I guess, I dunno. Fifty?'

'Three tents, Levin. Three tents. Three tents against an armed militia of two hundred.'

Eoghan said, 'I had a chat with Gary earlier. He proposed a response demonstration on Tuesday, midday. We talked about doing something at the *Invest NI* building on Bedford Street?'

Hands went up in agreement all round.

'There's a BBC building on Bedford Street,' Kiera teased.

'So we'll have an alibi this time,' quipped Joe.

'The Invest NI building is one of those Tory PFI deals,' said Levin.

'What's that?' Shay asked.

'Invest NI: Northern Ireland's economic development body,' said Levin.

'PFI is the Private Finance Initiative. Government procurement through a mortgage which lets developers make a killing,' said Eoghan.

Kiera shrugged. 'It's all Greek to me.'

Levin explained. 'They bill the government for construction costs, maintenance, leasing; a ton of other stuff, including interest.'

'Right, right, now I get it,' said Tommie.

'Twenty-five year contracts. Think of it as a buy-now pay-later pawn shop arrangement, but with buildings,' said Levin.

'We had a protest there, at Invest NI, the week before we set up here,' said Eoghan. 'Gary told me this year they paid out over four million pounds: twice the market rate. Bob, you wanted to say something about next week?'

'Later. No, this is about the second marquee. Whoever promised to collect it last week messed up. Meanwhile we're all crammed into this one. It's been dry today but that'll change soon.'

'If there's the money in petty cash I can go and pick it up in the morning,' said Bronagh.

'That would be a big help. But who's going to put the thing up, that's what I want to know.' Bob looked around with a penetrating gaze.

'I'll make myself available,' said Eoghan.

Bob nodded. 'It's a four person job.'

'I don't know if I'll be about,' admitted Padraig. 'Fred definitely won't: he's currently on an *Assassin's Creed* marathon. And he's not too happy about yesterday. Someone put wet dog biscuits in his coat pocket.'

Kiera avoided making eye contact with Padraig and looked out to the darkened street where the traffic passed like a never-ending locomotion, a low constant drumming. It hadn't rained but the marquee smelled of damp and smoke.

'I'll help,' murmured Daniel.

'I've got school tomorrow,' said Kiera.

'You don't go to school,' said Cat.

'I was there Friday,' she said.

'You were in the canteen picking up boys and then we went out for a smoke. You were marked absent.'

'Yeah. The tutor got it wrong?'

Kiera coughed and Bob coughed as the smoke from the fire blew in, stinging their eyes. Bob charged expletives in his mouth.

'I'll check my work rota,' said Tommie.

'It shouldn't come to that, Tommie. It seems you work hard enough as it is,' insisted Bronagh.

The blue rock pigeon at the assembly nodded disapprovingly. It decided the meeting had gone on long enough and flew off for home. Levin balanced the notepad with the minutes of the meeting on his knee and the pages flapped against the dark frosty air. Bob's attention was drawn over the road to the locking of the cathedral doors.

'Not one churchie came over this evening. You'd think they would, after subjecting us to those bloody cathedral bells: every Sunday; morning and night.'

'I spoke to the Dean but he wouldn't move the service,' said Cat.

'Mwah-ha-hahaha!'

Joe sneezed. Mary blessed him.

'Didn't the Dean say we could host meetings inside the cathedral during bad weather?' asked Ryan.

'Don't get me started. There were all sorts of conditions,' said Eoghan.

'Is it Galatians or Ephesians we have to memorise?' said Leon.

Eoghan shook his head. 'It was stupid. No meetings before 7pm. A maximum of ten people. So that's general assemblies out.'

'*Yes, I gotta have faith,*' sang Shay. '*Ooh, I gotta have faith; because I gotta have faith, faith, faith.*'

Padraig drummed the side of his chair in tune and the intermittent drip off the front of the tent joined in. New/Shitty John smiled.

'Alright, guys. Joke's a joke, but knock it off. Religion's left at the door,' said Eoghan.

Leon got up and stretched. She walked to the gazebo section where she pulled out half a dozen wooden sticks for the fire. Daniel rolled a cigarette and passed it to Tall Paul.

Bob cleared his throat, loudly, and got everyone's attention. 'I've decided to take a few nights off so I don't go stark raving mad. Now the nights' rota has been drawn up in advance, and if there are any issues you're to see Galway John, or Daniel here.'

Eoghan addressed the assembly. 'Bob's been working flat out – almost every night for over two weeks, and we're all very grateful for your efforts.'

The campers applauded and waved their hands in agreement.

'Bob, are you ill?' asked Mary in jest.

'Mwah-ha-hahaha! Right enough. It could be any day now,' said Padraig.

'I don't want to go away and come back to a shambles. So would you all, please, do me a favour and be a little bit more vigilant?'

Padraig conceded. 'No, that's a fair point. A few days ago there was a car sitting just down there, by the printers, with blacked out windows. It was there for hours.'

Bronagh swore under her breath. 'I was by this afternoon and this place was deserted, but for Daniel in his tent,' she said crossly.

'We all have lives outside this place,' said Eoghan.

'That as may be, Eoghan. You or someone else should have been visible,' she said. 'It was an open invitation to thieves. It could have been vulnerable for hours for all anyone knows.'

Eoghan's tone reached a higher pitch. 'Hey. I spend most of my time here. I don't appreciate you raking me over the coals. Especially as you've just got here.'

'No one's doing that to you Eoghan. This is for your benefit too,' said Bronagh.

'Excuse me?' said Kiera. 'I was here this afternoon. So was Shay. And Levin. Remember those weirdo blokes in suits that came by?'

Shay broke out in a shiver. 'Oh, that was mad. Two men: dark hair, combed in side shades, but like, the mirror image of each other.'

'God Squad,' Leon asserted.

'At first we thought they were Jehovah's Witnesses. You know how they're like twins,' said Shay.

'They didn't have name-tags though,' said Kiera.

Shay thought to himself. 'What did they call themselves? Zach and Chaz? Right enough, I had problems staying awake at the time. Maybe I freaked out a little. But these twins, they had the strangest skin tone: pale, almost silver.'

'And they asked really odd questions,' Kiera added.

'Their questions weren't so odd,' said Levin.

Shay asked, 'Did their teeth seem extra sharp to any of you? And their eyes!'

Levin raised his head back and lifted an eyebrow.

Shay continued. 'Their eyes seemed to have a reddish glow, like when someone's taking a photo and the light bounces off the retina. The scariest of it was they said our records were in their database.'

Kiera shook her head no and confirmed by muttering, 'No, no.'

Padraig howled. 'Mwah-ha-hahaha! Shay, you need to get yourself to sleep! Mwah-ha-hahaha!'

'I swear I heard him say, *we want to sup on the poison in your sacs.*'

'I remember this exactly. They said we needed *sufficient lozenges and macs.* Okay, so that was odd,' said Levin. 'We asked them what they did. One said he was in insurance and the other one said he sold used cars. So Shay puts his hood up, and Kiera goes silent. I tried to talk to them but after a while they sensed the hostility and left.'

'Failed infiltration,' reckoned Leon. 'Maybe they were trying to seduce you, Kiera.'

'Sounds like the Federales,' said Padraig.

'You said the same thing about me,' Levin noted.

'Aye.'

'On the basis that I have a beard.'

Tommie rubbed his moustache that wasn't supposed to be there. 'Are we...' His words trailed off as he was overtaken by a yawn, that changed into a draconic gurgle, and he stretched out his arms to be free of it. 'Are we done here?'

'Only two more items left,' said Levin.

'Well it's gone on long enough for me,' Bob retorted and he got up and walked to his tent.

Tall Paul repeated Tommie's question. 'Is it over?'

'You can leave if you want to,' said Padraig.

He did, and his friend John followed him. The street was empty now, distant traffic sounding in a lazy vibrating moan. Eoghan looked up to the sky and saw the moon. Levin strained to read the agenda in the poor light so Tommie brought up the torch app on his phone.

'This just says, *Dublin Castle Wednesday.*'

Cat clarified the matter. 'That's the protest against third level education fees in the Republic. Occupy Dame Street invited us to send a delegation.'

'How much is it on the bus?' said Padraig.

'Ach! Sure never mind going that way!' barked Bronagh. 'I'll drive us down. My people carrier takes six. Would you like to go, Daniel?'

'I think I would enjoy that,' he said.

Leon stuck her hand up. 'Oh me, me!' she screamed.

Mary raised hers and Joe's arms up too. 'Sure come on, Joe. We'll go for the ride.'

'That's six. See. That wasn't so hard,' said Bronagh.

The fire crackled weakly. An owl hooted in the distance.

'I think Shay's asleep,' said Tommie.

'Final item is an admin update,' said Levin. 'Cat?'

She rubbed her damp green hair out of her wet pink face. 'I'm going to the library tomorrow to set up the Facebook event for the demo and carnival to recur weekly. I've typed up the contact details people have left us, with notes about particular resources or insights.'

'Very good,' said Padraig.

'That's all in the spreadsheet, and the data has been exported to the mailing list.'

'I wasn't aware there was a mailing list,' said Leon.

'There's ninety-seven people signed up, but it hasn't been used at all.'

Eoghan was embarrassed and scratched his beanie. 'Cat, could you use it to put the word out about Invest NI on Tuesday?'

'Yes, but I'd rather someone else did.'

Mary wondered, 'What's the plan for making use of this mailing list?'

'I've given it some thought,' said Cat. 'We've a back-log of offers for teach-ins: people willing to speak on workers solidarity, activist safety, a talk on epilepsy. I was thinking we could run them consecutively, every week-night.'

Eoghan strained with apprehension. 'It's a bit much.'

'There's really no hurry,' said Kiera.

'I'm thinking of it as a special one-off. To get people's attention.'

Leon backed Cat up. 'Education's one of our key aims.'

'Nah. I don't like it,' said Eoghan.

'Two more slots to fill and a bit of promoting and it's ready to go. It's an opportunity to show something's really being accomplished here.'

'Yeah but we don't want to spread ourselves too thin,' said Eoghan.

'Who's we? I'm doing the whole fucking thing on my own.' Kiera put her hand on Cat's arm. She shrugged it away. 'And another thing. There's an activity log on the shared drive. Is it too much to ask people to update it with what they're done, so we're not going over the same jobs?'

Bronagh sneered at Cat and shook her head. 'Do you not remember what I said earlier in the week about how one or two people couldn't be doing all the work? It's a noble ambition but it sounds like a disaster.'

Levin was conciliatory. 'I was thinking about this idea. Do we really need the publicity a week of teach-ins would bring?'

Out on the road, the door of Galway John's jeep slammed behind him. He studied the bust of the Spanish volunteer, its chin held high; sad granite cheeks and tired bronze eyes. He continued on up the path, using the faint flames of the bin to guide him. His boots slowed as he grew nearer, counting ten, no twelve, no fifteen people around the marquee.

'Is this still the general assembly?' he asked.

Eoghan and Kiera nodded.

Padraig sniffed. 'Yes.'

'Then,' said Galway John, 'you all ought to catch a frigging grip. It's nearly midnight for Pete's sake! Dear help us, you need your heads examined! You're not in your right mind, any of you!'

Padraig raised his hands and waved them in agreement.

14

Cat went to bed immediately after that marathon General Assembly. Most occupiers did. She felt faint yet heavy, as if sleep wouldn't be an issue. She lay in the tent with her eyes closed, the pressure pressing on her lids like they were stuck with glue. For three minutes she was completely offline, blank slate, in a resting place. An hour beforehand, Bronagh had driven Kiera home as she wanted to use the morning to prepare for the college seminar: typography; the Bauhaus; imitations of Josef Muller-Brockmann; the vortex of topics swarmed and rotated in Cat's head. Specks of mucus softened in the passage of a tear running down her cheek. People yammered at the marquee. Air filled her tent. Rowdies on the street. An argument. An Englishman's laugh over the noise of cars. The tug of a rope on her tent. She opened her eyes. The slither of plastic around her forced itself inwards. On a whim it left her again. The noise never left. Her brow was too hot, feverish. Cat shivered and covered herself with Kiera's bedding, which was cold to the touch. No sooner was everything arranged than her head jerked forward with a sneeze: a convulsing, spitting scream of a sneeze and another one. *She was so tired.* She tried hiding under the covers to wait for sleep to find her.

    She heard Galway John, in softer tones than the Englishman. 'The bark of ash is pale brown to grey, with fissures as the tree matures.'

    'Fuck! That tea's scalding hot!' She heard every word the Englishman said. 'CHEERS. So here's what I don't get. This is a protest camp, I know that. I've seen it on the telly. Why is it all

kicking off now?'

Galway's voice was considerably less soothing than it was three weeks before. 'The crisis was brought about by the banks inflating the value of all subprime mortgages. And well, the government let them have their way and run wild.'

Then Tommie, louder. 'The government let them crooks have their way. Tipping wee'uns out of their homes onto the street. Then shutting down the hospitals.'

The Englishman spoke again. He couldn't control his own volume. 'I'm no expert on politics like you guys are, but fuck those cunts, I say! Bastards in government are the reason I lost my job and wound up in that place. I wonder if a few of them got taken out, would the rest wise up their act?'

'Is it all self-contained flats in *Shac*?' asked Tommie.

'Yeah. Got my own living room with the telly and sofa. Bedroom's no more than a box room though. Fucking pokey.' Cat disassociated her mind from his story and fixed on sleeping. 'And don't get me started on the bathroom: big fella like you could barely get into the shower. Tight squeeze.' Or maybe she'd sleep when he was finished. Or she'd wait for him to leave, and go home herself. 'Kitchen's no better but sure call up sometime and I'll return the favour.' He raised his voice to a shout. 'I'll get the kettle on!' She turned over, cursing them, and herself. She knew how to sleep. It was a certain curl of the legs, a particular angle on the pillow. 'Anyway, I should go. I know I said that three times already!' He was still shouting. 'Goodbye, Bob. Tommie. Goodnight John!'

'Bye, Nige.'

'Goodnight.'

The door of Shac slammed behind her and she heard Bob mutter, 'Keep an eye on that one.'

Minutes later she heard two noisy males in the street only yards from her tent.

'Fuckin taig bastards!' shouted one.

She heard them move on. Then it was Tommie's voice, in a low conversational tone. *'You're a fucking taig bastard,'* he said sarcastically. 'Where's the megaphone? If he wants to go toe-to-toe...'

Galway John interjected, annoyed. 'I'll never get that. Why do folk have us down as Catholics just because we're protestors?'

Tommie spoke with intensity. 'Stupid fuckers,' he said.

Galway mused lyrically. 'We'll never exchange Ulster's grey skies and black smoke and burning houses for the green green grass of the Republic.'

Cat heard a hint of metal, unscrewed caps, and water slooshing into the kettle. Tommie spoke next.

'Sure the DUP were a leading terrorist recruiter. Just as much as the Shinners, and where was their sense of social justice, celebrating the murder of working men and women?'

Bob said, 'It's sardines to them. Like how they barely talked about Protestants who couldn't find work during The Troubles.'

'It doesn't suit the narrative,' said Galway.

'What narrative would that be?' asked Tommie earnestly.

'Buggered if I know,' came the smooth Southerner's response. The three men laughed. Cat turned over. Her sleeping bag twisted. 'I'll tell you, Thomas, it's the young ones I feel sorry for. Wee Kiera and Shay and Cat. I thought there was new hope but it's looking like little to nothing for them. And it's getting worse.'

'You're a bundle of joy you are,' grumbled Bob. 'This is a new era for Northern Ireland sure!'

'How did you get involved in all of this, Bob?'

'Joined the union in seventy-eight, Tommie. Transport and General Workers Union. Not that I give a fuck about the English, but when I saw later how they treated the miners? Whole towns decimated and their babies in poverty? The hell I'll let those wankers run roughshod over us.'

Cat felt sick. There was nothing warm. Despite the wind the smoky stink clung to her. The rain was just spit, but the noise of it, the eternal tapping… a signal never reaching the receiver, never ending. She tossed the blanket aside, unzipped her sleeping bag cocoon – saturated from condensation – and felt around for her coat.

Tommie's voice was low at the fireside. 'My kid? I provided. I spent time with them. Then all this shit happens. There's nothing I can do. Just wait and hope she remembers. Stands up to her ma.'

Cat unzipped the front and crawled out, bandy legs first. She wrestled with her trainers, faltering with the topline on her way to the marquee.

'Oho! Here comes the walking dead!' said Galway playfully.

Cat didn't respond, just sat down and took the transparent bag of tobacco out of her pocket. The night shift were used to folk resurfacing in the middle of the night to take a half hour with them by the fire.

'You'll have to sleep. Haven't you college to go to in the morning?'

'In the afternoon, Bob. I was thinking I might go home.'

'Sure is this not your home?' he asked.

'Don't take it personally,' she said, sucking on the wet cigarette straw.

Tommie offered to walk with her, but she wouldn't hear of it. Cat needed to be thinking about graphic design, and the 11/1 forms for new protests. She walked past the Kremlin and St. Patrick's, up the steep incline to the Antrim Road passing the street ghouls and the shops which had been closed for a long time and a short time. Paper sheets and crumpled specks whirled past her. The gate of Alexandra Park came into view. Familiar trees seemed to hold new intent as she passed underneath.

Cat heard the vacuum seal break when she opened the door; felt the warmth in the hallway flood out into the street. She closed it, turned the key in the lock again and climbed the steps. Almost to her room, Cat's mother stepped out onto the landing: hands on her hips; shaking her head. 'What time do you call this?'

'Time for bed.'

'Out all night at this protest, you ought ta have your head examined. You'll catch pneumonia and god knows what else.'

'Mum, please, I'm tired. I just want to sleep.'

Her father piped up, presumably still in bed. 'Your mother's just worried about you.'

'You could have been raped, or robbed. For all we know, you might have been lying in a ditch somewhere.'

'Cat, anything could have happened,' he said.

'That's right, anything,' insisted her mother. 'Anything!'

Cat opened her bedroom door and closed it behind her. In darkness, she made her way to the bed.

'You see, Alan?'

'Cat, your mother was talking to you!'

'She doesn't want to know us! We're not worth her time!'

The bed squeaked as Cat pulled off her shoes and socks. She lifted the blanket, and was about to get in when she thought a change into a fresh tee and knickers might be a better option.

'She doesn't care. She couldn't give a monkey's! Nothing matters but Catriona. If we want to go to sleep we have to run it by her.'

Cat raised her voice. *'GOODNIGHT!'*

'Leave it Ellen, she's only upsetting you.'

'That's her mission in life!'

She rolled over in the bed and pushed her face against the pillow in an embrace with silence.

Bronagh delivered the new marquee just after midday, as Padraig and Eoghan nursed their coffees. 'Where is everyone? How are we supposed to put this up?' she asked.

'I heard Bob getting up so he's around somewhere,' said Padraig, wearing a Russian winter cap with ear flaps.

'He'd better have gotten a sleep,' she declared.

'Mick and Daniel took the second night watch. Cat was by for the protest forms. She's taking them to the peeler station.' He raised his large brown mitts, like baseball gloves, and waved at Levin who was crawling out of his tent.

Eoghan wore the beanie cap Josie gifted him and swatted at a bluebottle buzzing around it. 'Joe's on his way. Galway too probably,' he said.

The Assembly had decided on taking down the gazebo and erecting the new marquee in its place. It would be an extension of the present marquee, utilising the space behind to form an L-shaped super-tent. Padraig and Eoghan began folding the chairs and setting them on the walls at either side. The gazebo was lifted to the edge of the pavilion. There had been chip wrappers and crisp packets packed behind it which were caught in the wind and littered the path. Bronagh tutted. Bob swore. They re-stacked plastic boxes underneath the gazebo, along with the stepladder, the table, the coal and the chalkboard, which read '23 DAYS OCCUPIED.' Atop the boxes they set the basin and drying rack, plates, bowls, cutlery and packs of firewood. An empty water container was docked by putting the axe on top of it.

Their marquee was untethered too, with a heave up from the corners. The four men tried to keep in step with each other as they carried it to the path beside Shac, with Bronagh directing as they passed the stacked chairs. Canvas walls bent and flexed, the roof slid out a little trapped water. It was roped up again so it could stand temporarily, making use of the railings and wedging a peg into the hole of a drainage slit.

Eoghan and Galway stared at the empty space where their base had been.

'It's like we're beginning again,' said Padraig.

The new marquee was the same dark green canvas as the original. No-frills industrial shafts slotted into one another with a sense of permanence. Everything had to be kept in perfect balance. The tallest of them, Levin and Joe, went under the canvas to align the poles and indented holes for thick green ropes to be tied at fixed points. The marquee was drawn back to where the gazebo had stood and the back of it was fastened against the railings.

'Blast it!' cursed Galway. 'Blast it to bloody tarnation!'

'What's wrong?' asked Bob.

'Joe, go and get me some chalk and the stepladder. We should have cut the front partition before we put this fucking thing up.'

'Oh no,' declared Bronagh firmly. 'John, you're not climbing up there. You'll crack your knees!'

'It has to be done properly. Measured precisely.'

Bronagh retorted, 'And do you think I have the time to drive you up to the Royal Victoria hospital? Catch a grip!'

He settled for holding the ladder and fussing over the operation. 'Just take your time. It has to be precise. Eoghan, is he keeping in a straight line?' Joe worked downwards along the chalk line with the Stanley knife. 'That's it, Joe. Good lad. Just like you're cutting carpet!'

Once the canvas was divided in two, the inner flap was roped creating a half-wall and tied to the fence. The front flap was left open to the wind.

The original marquee was brought back and slotted at a right angle against the new one. Galway fussed some more until he was happy with the alignment. To the rear of the original marquee, the ropes had to be taken off the poles and tied to the poles of the new marquee. The canvas there would remain loose, creating a partition 'gate' between the tents.

'Super-tent,' said Bronagh.

'Super-tent,' agreed Bob.

The store under the gazebo was brought in and they rounded up spray cans and spare palettes. Daniel came out to help them cart the supplies from the gazebo. Some items were taken through to the partitioned 'room', two spare palettes filling half its ground space. Bob brought out the placards and spray cans stored in his own tent.

The gazebo's already muddy white plastic bases were held down with boots and the steel poles were pushed upwards. Lodged free, the green and white striped roof was angled down so Eoghan and Padraig could detach it. Padraig said it was a little sad to see this piece of history come down so quickly, but then it was shite at keeping the rain off. As punishment a dribble stream ran all the way down past his elbow and into his armpit.

A kilometre away Cat and Kiera rounded the corner of Ann Street and Musgrave station. Petrol fumes blew in the wind over the River Lagan. They followed the steel fence, painted with diagonal stripes of red, black and two tones of grey, stopping at the spring gate by the vehicle barriers. The gate slammed shut behind them.

As they crossed the yard Cat turned officer's heads with her lanky frame and green shock of hair. 'I've to go round the printer's later. Want to come with me?'

Kiera pushed open the smoke tinted door. The draft of hot air hit them. 'Is that the one a few doors from the camp?'

'They're good, but they take forever. It's one guy, working two dozen jobs. *Oh hold on, it'll just be a minute* he says, and you're standing with the USB stick in your hand.' They queued at the window, until Sergeant Barker put his head above the person he was dealing with and pointed them to the seats.

Kiera began to unbutton her dark blue duffel-coat. 'Anytime I walk past that printer's the place is filled with boxes,' she said.

Cat kept her gloved fingers inside the silver puffer jacket. 'It's like an episode of *The A-Team*. Yer man's always hopping over the boxes. I thought he was going to go on his ass one time.'

'You'd think they'd have more staff in,' said Kiera.

'It's a small shop: sure city centre, the rent is high; cost of machines and maintenance. They know their stuff and do a good job but it's like, *call at four,* then *call at four thirty*, and more standing about.'

'Good thing we're local.'

Sergeant Barker called over to them. 'You're up, ladies.'

Cat approached the hatch and slid the forms underneath. Barker flipped through them and tossed them in the tray.

'All in order. I'll see these are filed, and a good day to you both.'

The women smiled, bewildered, thanked him, and just as they turned away he said, 'Hold on.' He brought his voice down to a whisper. 'If you like you can put one of your protest flyers up on the public notice board.'

'Ah, thanks, but we don't have any with us,' said Cat.

Barker seemed relieved.

A dozen campers sat inside the new super-tent with plates of egg fried rice and sweet and sour chicken. Their hands were wet from the steam, and the plates rested on tightened pairs of knees. Daniel noted how Shelby hadn't been seen for a few days. The campers had made up posters to search of Shelby's owner. The photograph on it was cribbed from one of those taken by Redwatch.

'Cosy as this is, I'm looking forward to getting off to Dublin on Wednesday. Three protests in a week. *Rock and roll!*' exclaimed Leon.

'I couldn't be arsed with all the chanting,' said Fred.

'I don't chant,' Levin told him.

'What do you mean you don't chant?' asked Cat.

'All that *you say cut back* seems a bit...'

'Sheep-like,' Padraig reckoned.

Levin nodded.

'It's a means to an end,' said Joe.

Joe had been feeling the chill, but as he ate, his shaking subsided. His first chip was like hot cake: completion, utter fulfilment. He took in another: the smooth fried crisp skin collapsing like a spread pillow onto mash potato; creamy, dense yet delicate. He looked to Mary, sat beside him with a fork of egg fried rice. He thought of the warm and cold intertwined within her in moments of sensuality, consummated.

Bob turned the radio on. '*QC Robert Jay says he has seen evidence twenty-eight News of the World journalists were involved in criminal activities...*'

The cold tapped on their shoulders and their eyes watered from the smoke of the coal fire. Tommie took Tall Paul with him to the back of the marquee and made sure to fill both their plates.

'You don't chant at all?' Kiera asked.

Levin chewed quicker. 'Nope. *You say fight back.* What? Mixed signals there.'

'Fighting back against the system and those fat-cats running things,' said Leon.

'*News International's James Murdoch was questioned extensively by the Commons Select Committee last week.*'

Their clinks of knives to forks sounded above the traffic. Padraig slurped the chicken, awash with red sauce. He chewed the fat and calories, crisped, promising to add to his muscles. The meat writhed in his throat, the garlic and crushed chilli flakes glowing through his face. Shay put in fork size portions of salt chilli chicken against his teeth, emulating the rubbing of bones; hot and salty. The rain dripped off the marquee's front: a slow, steady drip. Drip. Drip.

'That really filled a hole,' said Daniel.

'Grab more if you want it,' Eoghan replied.

'*Fighting back*,' said Levin with contempt. 'Isn't this supposed to be a peaceful demonstration?'

Cat worked through a spork harvest of long yellow noodles, bringing yellow pepper with it. A green broccoli sprig breathed on her tongue. A missed pea jumped into her trouser fold. 'Levin, tell us how you really feel,' she said.

'You're giving it too much thought,' said Eoghan.

He shook his head and Cat pointed her fork at him.

'It's like singing in church,' said Padraig.

'It's nothing like church,' exclaimed Leon.

'*O Lord Almighty*,' sang Fred. '*They say cut back. O Lord our God, we say fight back.*'

Cat and Eoghan found themselves looking at one another and laughing. Soon everyone was laughing. Even Bob managed one of his rare smiles. Most were caught unaware, surprised Fred had the wit in him, and he was surprised by the wave of acceptance.

'Nice,' said Levin. 'Church is a good analogy all the same. It's peer pressure. I don't want to bother with it.'

'Fair play,' said Padraig.

'*Thirteen individuals have been arrested so far. Robert Jay praised the Telegraph for the MPs expenses scoop and The Guardian's reporting of the phone hacking scandal.*'

Bob pushed sweet and sour chicken, staining orange on the plate and picking up white beads of rice and sesame seed. In his mouth it was gilded pineapple, and sticky, like a lover who wouldn't let go. Levin gathered steamed white rice, egg yolk pills, carrot cubes and corn. He'd almost cleared the plate. The last forkful was dry, and a little tepid.

'Do what I do in church,' said Shay. 'Just sing the bits you agree with. For example: *they say... fight back. We say... back.*'

'You could mime,' suggested Kiera.

'*In Oakland police have dismantled the protest camp belonging to the Occupy movement. The action occurred in the early hours of the morning. The Police Officer's Association thanked protestors for dispersing peacefully, although thirty-three arrests were made. In Barnslow, a chihuahua has married a rabbit.*'

'Scumbags,' spat Tommie.

Eoghan screwed up his face. His tone was angry. 'I'll tell you about church. Fourteen of those arrests were made in Oakland's faith tent: people praying.'

Leon chinked her fork onto the plate. 'I am so *fucking* tired of this.'

'Sorry. I thought you knew,' said Eoghan.

'It's co-ordinated action,' said Bob. 'How many cities is that raided this week?'

'Dunno. But for sure there's a boardroom somewhere full of fuckers pulling strings just because they can,' snarled Tommie. The fire crackled beside him.

'Oakland was a hundred and fifty tents,' murmured Daniel.

'Aye and they sent in nearly a thousand police,' snarled Eoghan.

'The courtship of three year old lop-eared rabbit, Bugs, and Rover, a chihuahua of the same age, was accelerated by their owner, Harper Twelvetrees, who does not believe in sex before marriage.'

Bob turned the radio off. 'They'll probably be drafting in a private security firm for the next step,' he said.

Padraig gasped. 'That's six or seven cops taking down one tent.'

'Well we're doing something about this,' Leon announced.

'We've got Bedford Street tomorrow,' said Eoghan. 'Who's willing to back me at the GA if I propose an emergency action for Wednesday?'

'I will. But won't we need more forms in to the police?' Levin asked.

'Fuck the police,' said both Leon and Eoghan.

'We ought to write to politicians and ask them to speak out. Don't you think?' said Cat.

Leon, Tommie and Padraig laughed.

'Mwah-ha-hahaha! Like any of them give a fuck. Here! How many Yank cops does it take to screw in a lightbulb?'

'I dunno,' Fred said.

'All of them. One to screw in the bulb, one to break it. One to screw in the bulb, one to break it. One to screw in the bulb, one to break it. Mwah-ha-hahaha!' His cackles resounded across the street.

The following morning over fifty protestors gathered at the campsite. The sun shone in their faces and they took up placards and walked. Gary led them by megaphone: Jack, Tall Paul, Martine, Galway John, Greenpeace John, Monty, Michelle, Ryan, Steph, Katrina, Joel, and a few Anonymi. The pigeons walked with them.

'Two point six million unemployed. The highest figure since 1994,' boomed Gary. 'Youth unemployment, the highest since 1986. At one million!'

Deirdre got off her pushbike when she caught up to them at the top of Bedford Street, behind City Hall. She weaved through to the middle of it and found Cat and other campers, cold all over, and weary. 'Good morning,' she sang.

'What's good about it?' asked Cat.

'Sorry. Are passions running higher than usual?'

Eoghan seethed. 'They raided the Wall Street camp.'

'Zucotti Park?'

'Six o' clock in the bloody morning,' said Levin.

The Invest NI building had a landmark style: a round glass front two-floor reception area, with three round glass levels above that. They stopped outside where the path was set in off the road. Fred gave Levin his placard so his hands were free. He pulled moist, stringy tobacco from a transparent bag. Levin asked Fred to make him a rollie. Others brushed past, off the pavement, to the L-shaped twelve storeys of heavy glass. Eoghan walked off toward Gary, who was not his usual cheery friendly self. He looked tired, wounded and guarded. His hair was ragged in the wind. He handed Padraig the megaphone who toyed with it before giving it over to Eoghan.

'GOOD MORNING,' he said. 'Thank you all for coming. We gathered here a month ago as part of an international day of protest. A week later we decided to occupy Writer's Square in solidarity with thousands of cities the world over. We are in the throes of a global uprising but how have the government and their friends in merchant banking responded?'

Fred passed Levin a cigarette. He tucked it behind his ear.

'In the last few days, disproportionate and excessive force has been used to take down camps in Utah, Missouri, Portland, Denver, Vermont, and Oakland. And as of early this morning, Occupy Wall Street at Zucotti Park. Two hundred arrested. People given only twenty minutes warning, before riot police kicked down their homes. They dragged folks out of tents serving as medical centres, and pepper sprayed people in soup kitchens.'

'Fucking bastards!' yelled Bob.

'The whole world is watching!' yelled Levin.

'That's right,' said Eoghan. 'America's ugliness is exposed for the whole world to see. They thought to make us go away. Instead their brutality has given the anti-Austerity movement it's biggest recruitment tool. We stand in solidarity with our brothers and sisters there, and we're going to keep going. They say cut back...'

Levin yelled, 'We say fight back!'

'They say cut back...'

'We say fight back,' Leon yelled.

'They say cut back...'

'WE SAY FIGHT BACK!'

'We are the 99%!'

'WE ARE THE 99%!'

'WE ARE THE 99%!'

'WE ARE THE 99%!'

15

It was eight o'clock in the morning and Padraig sat in the super-tent puffing in tobacco through a tiny cotton filter. He watched Daniel secure his tent under the nearest ash tree. Padraig's legs were cold. His shoulders and arms were cold. His head: cold. He envied Bob with his leathery skin, and Mary and Joe, who had sewn their two pullovers together to form one tight fitting poncho. Bronagh bumped the maroon people-carrier up upon the pavement and opened the driver's door.

Padraig sprung to his feet. 'I call shotgun!' he yelled. He raced for the front but Daniel, oblivious, was already clambering in to the front passenger side and he slammed the door behind himself.

Bob tapped on Leon's tent. 'Leon, come on now. Wakey wakey, girl.'

The zip came down. She crawled out on on all fours, fully dressed. She'd slept still wearing her black beanie. She looked up and a fat raindrop slapped her forehead.

Bob smiled as she tugged on her shoes. He remembered Leon's excitement the previous day. A minister in the Irish Parliament, the Dáil, had resigned in protest over finance cuts hitting the neediest.

'Big news from Dublin last night,' said Bob.

She stood up, groggy, but her mind fired. 'From the Dáil? What is it? Has something else happened?'

'It was bad,' said Bob.

'What? Tell me!'

Bob paused for effect, then revealed, 'Dublin and Estonia

drew one-all in the second leg play-offs.' He chuckled to himself and walked off.

'Leonie, come on!' yelled Bronagh.

Bronagh's people-carrier had two seats for each of its three rows. Mary and Joe jumped in the back. When Leon was inside, Bronagh called on them all to belt up. The car was as cold inside as it was out. It was relatively new and when the heating got going it circulated a scent of sandalwood. Padraig drew a cock and balls on the steamed window. Leon was not impressed.

On the Westlink out of the city, Daniel put his head outside to wipe mist from the wind-shield. Bronagh followed the M1 by Dunmurry and Padraig and Leon got into a game of spotting red cars and yellow cars. The game's prize was getting to punch the other's arm.

'It wouldn't steam up if you two weren't talking so much,' Bronagh told them.

'It's them two back there,' said Padraig.

'Excuse me?' asked Mary.

'They're horny devils, Bronagh. You shouldn't have turned the heat on. It's an aphrodisiac to them. Here, did your hubby not want to come with us?'

'Brian and I aren't married yet,' declared Bronagh. 'Sadly, he's stuck at work today.'

'What's he do?' asked Padraig.

'Brian's with *Translink*, driving the buses,' she said.

'So long hours, low pay,' he said.

'It was hard for us to both get the day off,' she said.

The car in front quickly cut into their lane. Bronagh dropped speed and hammered the horn three times. '*You fucking idiot! Fucking arsehole!* Can you believe that?'

Daniel shook his head. 'Where do you work, Bronagh?' he asked calmly.

'The further education college over at Blackrock.'

'Is that not a bit out of the way?' asked Padraig.

'It is, but we get a good influx of students. Of course now

they're tripling university fees students who would have come through us for their entry grades won't even bother! That's another part of why today's march is so important.'

'I didn't think about it that way,' said Leon.

'Oh they don't care that we're already under-funded and under-staffed. I'm the only one in the admin department who does any actual work. The rest are a pack of space cadets too busy being afraid for their jobs.'

'Fucking Tories,' Leon scowled.

'I'll be okay. I've driven taxis; been a care worker; a classroom assistant… if there's any trouble your Auntie Bronagh will land on her feet.' Passing signs for Lisburn, she kept her eyes in front, following the A1 stream towards Dromore.

'Bronagh! Are we there yet?

'Hardy-har, Padraig. We should be in Dublin inside two hours. Daniel, are you working?' she asked.

'No. I had a job as a kitchen porter for a while.'

Joe put his head forward. 'You're from Madrid, right?'

'Alicante,' said Daniel.

'Alicante?' wondered Padraig. 'What did you want to come here for?'

'I came over in 2004. I'd heard Belfast people were friendly.'

'Mwah-ha-hahaha!'

They all were laughing. Bronagh nearly swerved off-road with it. 'From the mouths of babes,' she said. 'Would you open up the glove compartment? There's a bag of fudge in there. Take some and pass it round.'

'Thanks, Bronagh,' said Daniel.

'So are you on the dole then?' she asked.

'No. I don't need the hassle.'

'You should be claiming benefits. You're legally entitled to them,' she said.

'Before, I got paid cash in hand. I'm not on their system for benefits.'

'What do you survive on?' she said.

'Donations coming into the camp. Odd jobs here and there.'

'And you're homeless too? That's not right.' Bronagh sighed.

'Daniel, if its an address you want you can put down my place,' said Padraig. 'Just make the trek up every two weeks, give them your autograph, and collect your signing fee.'

'Thanks, but I'm surviving. It's good enough for Eoghan,' he said, passing the fudge back to Leon.

'What's Eoghan got to do with it?' said Bronagh.

'He says it's beneath his station to accept money from a corrupt government,' Leon informed her.

'He refuses to sign on,' said Padraig.

'As far as I'm concerned, it's money they don't spent on guns and bombs. Give it all to me,' said Leon.

'Right.' Bronagh's tone was firm. 'Daniel, you want to take Eoghan with a pinch of salt.'

'Why's that?'

'Eoghan, he's always trying to take control of things. It all has to be about him. And then he makes decisions nobody wants: like that protest, and the issue with the printer.'

'I think he's going through a break-up,' Padraig said, and he turned around to pass the bag of fudge to Mary. She and Joe were locked in a passionate embrace. 'Oh, for fucks sake.'

'Daniel. If you know what's right you'll be up to the Social Security first thing tomorrow,' instructed Bronagh. 'I'll drive you.'

'I'm grateful but--'

'No buts. You can put Padraig's address down. Or mine. And see when the camp gets too much? You come stay in your Auntie Bronagh's spare room.'

'Thank you,' he said. 'I may do that.'

Leon looked out of the circle she'd cleaned in the window, and sighed. 'Banbridge. The state of it. Dreary hole. This place is all God-botherers.'

As if in response the car was battered with buckets of

water from the skies, which kept up, chasing them out of there.

There was a glimpse of sunrise towards Newry, though the Mourne Mountains were covered in clouds of grey static. Joe said they'd be getting ready for the march back in Belfast. Following more trouble in New York, and fresh arrests in Zurich, the General Assembly called for another emergency demo, this time to the Belfast Stock Exchange. Padraig said he'd never noticed a stock exchange on Bedford Street. No-one had.

Suddenly all five mobile phones beeped.

'Oh fuck, what the fuck?' cried Leon.

It was a text message telling her she was now on the Irish phone network and call charges may vary.

'Well Daniel. What do you think? Two countries, two capitals, two hours apart,' said Bronagh.

There was no visible border and only little differences: dual language signs; car registrations; an alien petrol station franchise. The road wound around Ravensdale, where Leon called their attention to a sign. 'Look. The Hill of Faughart.'

'Fuck art. Hmm,' said Padraig.

'I'll do you one better. There's a hill in Meath called Faughan,' said Joe.

'Fuckin' Hill! Mwah-ha-hahaha!'

Mary told them, 'They've a River Faughan in Derry. And just outside it there's a place called Muff. Swear to God. They have a sign says, *You are now entering Muff.*'

Padraig's trademark wicked laugh was catching.

Five minutes on, they were waiting in line at the toll booth. Bronagh scooped euros from the cavity under the gearstick.

'Why are you called Leon?' Joe asked.

'Because she's a hermaphrodite,' said Padraig.

'Red car!' exclaimed Leon and smacked him on the arm.

'OW! That *fucking* hurt!'

Joe chuckled. 'You deserved that.'

Bronagh raised her voice. 'OY! No fighting back there! Padraig, apologise to Leon.'

'I am not a hermaphrodite, transgendered, transsexual or a lesbian,' declared Leon.

'That *really* hurt,' whimpered Padraig.

'I'm an openly identifying female bisexual Marxist anarchist.'

'Righto,' said Padraig.

'Leon sets me apart. My name hijacks labels of masculine status, allowing me to reclaim that power as a woman.'

Padraig looked round to Joe. 'She thinks we're powerful. You can tell she doesn't know a lot of men.'

Leon sneered. 'Fuck's sake.'

'Tell it to Kevin Trojan!' said Padraig.

Bronagh snapped at him. '*PADRAIG!* I won't warn you again. I'll pull over and stop the car and you can walk home.'

Leon stuck her tongue out at him. Padraig lowered his hand so Bronagh couldn't see and he gave Leon two fingers. She ignored him.

'Most people think it's short for Leonie. Actually, its a derivative of Lee. There were too many Lees at the school I went to. So I changed it, in honour of Leon Trotsky.'

'You named yourself after the revolutionary who opposed Stalin,' said Joe.

'Didn't you say he got killed by a Spaniard?' Padraig asked. 'Here! Good thing you're sat behind Daniel, and not the other way around.'

Mary reached over the seat and punched Padraig on the arm. 'Red car!'

'HEY!'

'Actually, we have a city called Leon in the north-west,' said Daniel. 'It's the capital of a province which is also called Leon.'

Bronagh wound down the window to put the coins in the slot by the toll machine. The barrier lifted and she drove through. The clock on the dashboard read nine thirty. 'Is that near Alicante, Daniel?'

'It's near Bilbao. By the Bay of Biscay, but further in from the coast. They speak Leonese.'

'Mwah-ha-hahaha! I'm never visiting!'

'Sounds like a clued in place,' said Leon.

Bronagh followed the lorries out of the toll road; onto the M1 and the sign for Dundalk.

'Aww, who farted?' spluttered Padraig. He waved his hand about. 'Goodness sake.'

'That's it. Get your male toxicity everywhere,' said Leon.

'He who smelt it dealt it,' sang Mary.

Padraig teased her. 'You picked the wrong time to come up for air, Mary. Hey Bronagh, you shoulda been here the first time they had sex at camp.'

Bronagh sighed.

'There were four or five of us under the marquee watching their tent wobble about; like it was nearly ready to topple. We ran over to it 'cause we thought someone was having a seizure.'

'Padraig, stop telling tales,' said Bronagh.

Leon piped up. 'He's telling the truth this time. Everyone ran over to it, everyone except Bob that is. He knew what was happening and just sat there laughing. Galway John unzipped the front of it and got an eyeful of them at it.'

Bronagh laughed. 'Don't embarrass them.'

'We weren't embarrassed. It was a really good fuck,' said Mary.

'Before and after,' said Joe.

'Front and back.'

'You've opened Pandora's box,' said Daniel.

'And all her drawers,' said Bronagh, laughing.

Leon groaned. 'Can we stop soon? I'm dying for a piss.'

'Me too. If we don't stop I'm gonna get a bladder infection,' squealed Padraig.

'Suck it in!' exclaimed Bronagh. The tone wasn't obviously a joke, perhaps meant callously, playing with her prey.

'It's agony! My dick's gonna fall off! At least let us roll down the window for a cig?'

'Yeah, okay. But one at a time. Another half hour and we'll stop.'

'Look! Six kilometres to Hackballscross. Mwah-ha-hahaha!'

A cold breeze filled the car as they passed by the twin churches of *St. Patrick's* in the town of Dundalk. Padraig blew out smoke to the Louth Courthouse and the Marshes Shopping Centre. Then Leon sparked up on the edge of town, by the Crowne Plaza Hotel, its eight storeys dwarfing everything else. It was twenty minutes along the road to Castebellingham, occasionally catching glimpses of the sun on the Irish Sea. They followed the country road inland to Dunleer, green fields and blue skies ahead.

Ten minutes on the motorway led to Tullyallen, on the outskirts of Drogheda. Bronagh followed the slip road to a retail park with car dealers and coffee shops, department stores and sports suppliers. The women queued at the toilets and Padraig puffed on his second smoke. Then he leapt in the front. Daniel didn't even shrug in response.

They passed a sign for Balbriggan, which brought laughter. The traffic grew thicker on the road to Dublin and it took them forty more minutes to reach the city. The were rewarded by the sight of a notice pointing to Slutsend. In the centre of Dublin, Bronagh found herself driving round and round the same streets. Pavements were heaped with parked cars blocking her view. A Ford backed out of a small bay and she pushed her way in to the parking space. Daniel, once he'd gotten free of the squeezed together cars, let out a yawn. With Bronagh walking to the ticket machine, Padraig and Leon rolled and lit their cigarettes. To get out of the tight space, Joe literally had to lift his knees to his chest and Mary stretched, pivoting back on her ankles.

They found a very tiny cafe across the street. Dark wooden tables and benches with feel-good signs hanging off low ceilings and a spiralling staircase in the middle of the floor.

Both the upstairs and downstairs were packed. A waitress took their orders while they waited for seats to become free. As luck would have it they didn't wait long. Two downstairs tables were pushed together, although they sat almost on top of one another.

'I hope they're alright at the camp,' said Daniel.

'That new bloke Tommie… great guy, but he looks like he could seriously fuck you up,' exclaimed Padraig.

'You'll want to stay on the right side of him then,' chided Joe.

'Mwahahaha! You know what you mean though? You look in his eyes and you can tell he's seen a few things.'

'You all want to treat Tommie with care,' cautioned Bronagh. 'It's awfully good him arranging for your meals every night.'

They all agreed.

'He's the means of consumption,' quipped Leon.

'I wonder are him and Bob related. They've got that same intensity What age do you think Tommie is?' asked Mary.

'I dunno. I think he's not much older than us but then he's got all those Chuckle Brothers wrinkles. Going on attitude, I'd say him and Bob are related,' said Joe.

'Tommie's still learning about activism. I think Bob's been in socialist circles since the nineteen-seventies,' said Leon.

Joe nodded. 'He covers it up but there's a lot of heart to him.'

'Mwah-ha-hahaha! What about that epic rant last week? *Kiera, I was out standing on picket lines before your parents had even met!*'

'Which politician do you suppose is slagging us off in the press today?' asked Bronagh.

'Dovid Vonce?' said Daniel.

'Very probably. After all, it is Wednesday,' Mary replied.

'Why is it more likely on a Wednesday?' asked Joe.

'It's a weekday,' she said.

'My bet's on Unionist Schutzstaffel officer Nigel Dodds,' remarked Leon.

'I don't know him,' said Daniel.

'The man believes the planet was built last week by a piece of sky with clouds for a beard.'

A big basket of toast was sat down for them to share and a wholegrain bloomer loaf with seeded crusts. Then their fry-ups arrived.

Leon exclaimed, 'I love the smell of revolution in the morning!'

Mary cut her potato bread and eggs up, placing bite size portions together. Padraig's took a deep sniff of his thick sliced bacon, but turned his noses up at the sausages. They were an odd colour and too thin. He poked at the eggs which were sprinkled with green herbs and then leaned in and whispered, 'Who the fuck puts parsley on a fried egg?'

'Shay's talked about becoming a cook. It's the sort of thing he'd do,' replied Mary.

'Or Eoghan. He's a vegan, isn't he?' said Joe.

Leon laughed. 'Not at all. Bob calls him that to wind him up.' She craned her neck and gritted her teeth in snarky imitation of Eoghan. *'I am not a vegan!'*

Around the table, laughter, all except for Padraig who didn't want to risk spitting out his bacon. However, this didn't stop him talking with his mouth full. 'Thuh pruhtest's at Dublin Cuhstle. How fuh out is it?'

'Right here in the city. Twenty minutes walk,' said Joe.

Leon rolled her eyes. 'It's on Dame Street? Did you think Dublin Castle was in the countryside?'

Padraig wolfed down his sausages and later he told the waitress they were delicious. The bacon was chewy: tasty but it took forever to get through. Bronagh said it was the best she's had in years. Mary particular enjoyed the tanned potato bread. It was floury but absorbing the fried egg yolk with it created the perfect synthesis.

It was after midday when they trekked to Parnell Square where activists climbed off coaches from Donegal and Sligo and as far as Galway and Cork. Padraig watched the marshals in their yellow jackets direct them. A long line of police cars were parked along the kerb and officers in black padded jackets scrutinised the arrivals.

'There's a few guardee around already,' said Padraig.

'The Garda,' said Leon.

'Garda Síochána,' said Joe.

Padraig tried to repeat the words. 'Guarda-sheer.'

They were laughing again.

'Sounds like you're sheering sheep,' said Bronagh.

'The po-po,' said Leon firmly.

They met a man from Kerry who talked and talked about the route of the march which would be the same route he'd walked on a demonstration a month before. There was a young couple from Tallaght and Bronagh cooed over their 'wee babbie.' The sky was overcast, another winter afternoon which looked like it was evening already.

A familiar luminescence rolled towards them on a bicycle: Deirdre Hoffman. 'Oh hello there! Are you all ready for the big march?'

'Aye! Ready for revolution!' exclaimed Leon.

'Deirdre, if I'd known you were coming I could have squeezed you into the car.'

'Oh, that's alright. Bronagh. I took the Enterprise from Great Victoria Street this morning. May as well support the only piece of Northern Ireland's rail service that works.'

Padraig stared at the bottom of a placard, obscured by other placards. He read the words aloud. 'Edna Kenny, Keep Your Promise.' Kenny's election photograph came into view and Padraig gasped. 'Edna Kenny is a man? Since when? Edna's a girl's name!'

'Enda,' said Daniel, smiling.

'Enda?'

Leon taunted him. 'You're such a numptie, Padraig. He's the Taoiseach. Here! Try saying Taoiseach.'

'Tea shock?'

They followed the Luas tram lines around the corner to O'Connell Street as part of a rolling sea of people and banners; whistles and screams of bodies moving underneath the granite statue of Labour leader James Larkin, arms outstretched now like some kind of prophet; the chanting beyond the nearby Spire of Dublin, rising, and the General Post Office of the Dublin Rising: the pensioners' groups; lobbies for transport and essential services; the Students Union; the teachers' unions; the dock-workers and the fire service.

'NO IFS, NO BUTS, NO EDUCATION CUTS!'

'RUAIRI QUINN, KEEP YOUR PROMISE!'

'YOU SAY CUT BACK, WE SAY FIGHT BACK!'

Banners and flags swirled alongside those lining Grand Central Bar. They passed the O'Connell monument and crossed the busy bridge over the River Liffey and swarmed right over D'Olier Street, though a few hundred took the short cut through tourist trap, Westmoreland Street. The Garda wanted them to stay in line, their fluorescent jackets disappearing amid those of the marshals. They would estimate fifteen thousand protestors that day; the Union of Students said there were over twenty thousand. Another body would report fifty thousand. Groups trying to keep together inevitably integrated with those around them: Mary, Joe and Deirdre were separated from the others, disappearing in among the groups carrying Anonymous and Socialist Workers Party flags.

The fenced off corner of Trinity College came out to the roadside, rounding onto College Green. The march grew. Parliament House stood opposite: a semicircular building fronted by grand steps and classical columns. Since 1803 it was home to *The Bank of Ireland*, on the corner of Dame Street where Dublin's Occupy movement had pitched their tents. In that distance of a hundred metres up to Trinity's gates the crowd went wild: a samba band; high-pitched whistles; cheers;

chants; screams and tambourines; bicycle bells and honks of car horns.

The extra bodies packed tightly together brought the march to a slow crawl. Padraig tried to roll a cigarette and the wind blew it into the folds of someone's rucksack. Leon got her heel trodden on, and she screamed.

'Watch where you're fuckin' going,' she yelled as she whirled round.

'So sorry, so sorry,' said the man in the wheelchair.

Leon turned bright red and apologised profusely.

The appearance of Dublin's streets was subsumed under brown coats and green coats, faces rough and reliable, resistant to advancing as their number deepened: an elderly decorator in a puffer jacket; a twenty-something coder in light denim. Cameras moved about above the throng. Helicopters whirred higher. At the bottom of Merrion Street the crowd stopped and were addressed by Gary Redmond, the president of the Union of Students in Ireland.

'Nine months on and its the same old false promises! The Coalition have fallen silent on their pre-election pledges to students.'

'Shame on them!'

'Yesterday we heard the Tánaiste Eamonn Gilmore committed to education, as part of the bailout agreement. Yet fees have not been reversed, in despite of his pre-election pledge nine months ago!'

All around the National Museum the crowd roared, shaking their placards in the direction of the Merrion Hotel.

Leon told Bronagh, 'That's where the IMF delegation are staying.'

Redmond continued. 'Let us see the budget! If it is true, let's see the proof, because we are sick of lies! One point three billion euros of the seventy billion spent by the government went to higher education. We have the second highest fees in Europe, right behind the UK.'

'Fucking UK. Who'd wanna live there?' carped Padraig.

'Monkeys, that's who,' said Bronagh in self-effacing bluster.

'In the UK, only three out of ten have access to higher education,' shouted Redmond. 'It is six out of ten of our youngsters. We don't want a situation where only the wealthy elite have access. Eamon Gilmore keep your promise!'

'EAMON GILMORE, KEEP YOUR PROMISE!'

On the way back to Parnell Square there were people swimming against the tide of the march. Talk had circulated of a doorstep sit-down in Upper Mount Street where the conservative coalition partner, Fine Gael, had its offices. On Clare Street there was a lad in his underwear with a sign, *'Can't afford trousers let alone fees.'* There were fresh young faces of hope, a contrast from Belfast where everyone looked scared or depressed. The Carlow group were all in face paint. One was in a dog costume. Another was dressed as a gorilla holding a sign reading, *'This Shit Is Bananas.'*

The demonstration thinned out, and the fences of Trinity College revealed themselves. On College Green there were thousands of red shirts and gold banners. The march stopped outside the Central Bank of Ireland. Mary, Joe and Deirdre were there, under a banner which read *'Think Contraception – Because the Government Intend to Screw You.'*

'Where were you three?' Bronagh asked angrily.

'Sorry. My fault,' said Deirdre. 'We met anarchists from Athlone and the Waterford water tax demo. Then we got chatting to autonomous collectivists from a Cavan caravan, and my friend Dennis from Ennis.'

'Oh! We should go to the Dame Street camp,' said Leon excitedly. 'Can we? Can we?'

Bronagh groaned. 'Oh no. No. My feet are aching.'

'It's only ten minutes away,' Leon pleaded.

'You'll not get near it. Every other group that's turned up today wants to see them,' she said.

Suddenly, Padraig raised his arm and pointed through

the crowd. 'Look. There's Gary!'

Bronagh's face lit up. 'What? Our Gary?'

Gary spotted them too. He made his way through the crowd, beaming. 'Ah Bronagh, Mary, Daniel. Goodness, half the camp seems to have made it.'

'Gary you should have told me you coming. I could have chucked one of these eejits out and given you their space,' said Bronagh.

He put his hands up to his face. 'It was touch and go to the last minute. Leon, Joe, how are you?'

'Can't protest,' said Joe. 'Well, can protest. Did protest.'

'I think I got on TV for all of about three seconds,' said Leon.

'Three seconds too much! Gary, what's this about another camp setting up?' asked Padraig.

'There's about forty people with tents going to the Department of Education building on Marlborough Street.'

'Really?' said Leon.

'Just until the morning. Here, I'd better be off. I'm going to try to catch the ten to five train.'

'I'll go with you,' said Deirdre. 'Will yous be at the consulate demo in Stranmillis tomorrow?'

'I doubt it,' said Bronagh. 'I'm so tired they'll be lucky if I don't drive us into a tree. Right, let's go, you lot! Off to the Bronagh Bus!'

Leon felt the weight come off her feet as soon as she sat down in the car, and wished she could get her boots off. It took them an hour to get out of Dublin, red tail-lights in the night already upon them. Daniel brought the fudge from the glovebox and passed it back. The road was too dark for the passengers to say where they were and as night closed in the conversation closed down. The heat and the new car smell circulated. Padraig tried hard to stay awake. Daniel was telling Bronagh about his life in Spain: something about moving because his family were hounded; barely grasped conversation about stowing away in the back rows of university lectures. Padraig's eyes were dry and heavy and he gave into the urge to close them. Within seconds, openings in his eyelids filled with water. Basal tears fell silently down his cheeks. He didn't understand why; that his body was recuperating from stress and tiredness. He felt embarrassed, briefly, reckoning no-one would notice in the dark. Padraig opened and closed his eyes a few more times until they'd finish streaming, and then decided he would sleep it off. Within minutes his head had fallen onto Leon's shoulder. He awoke an hour later to Cave Hill, maternally signalling a return to Belfast, its peak like the edge of a womb.

16

Fred said he'd help Eoghan with the placards and Leon knew she was dreaming. It was Thursday 17th November, though she didn't know that, only that she was still tired after the trip to Dublin. She lay in her tent with sunlight streaming in through wavering walls, a paper-thin groundsheet above mud which was as hard as cold concrete. Leon heard their sneezes and footsteps; a car rev down Donegall Street; the flapping of canvas; Galway John explaining the route they were to drive, from right outside her tent.

'The American consulate is in Stranmillis but no you couldn't walk there.'

'It's out past Elms Village. On the right. The street's called Danesfort Park,' said Gary.

Levin said, 'What do they have it away out there for?'

Galway John said, 'It would not be unlike the Americans to put themselves beyond reach when it suits them. Their foreign policy, after all.'

'I need another set of hands here,' called Eoghan.

'Fuck off, fuck off, fuck off,' moaned Leon.

She grabbed her pillow and thrust her head down in the damp. The wind blew a tiny money spider from tenuous moorings, dropping onto her dark hair and crawling in her scalp. Outside there was the scraping of wood. A sharp tug. Someone tripping on the guy rope.

'Where's Padraig?' asked Fred.

'Bronagh dropped him home. He wanted a night in his own bed,' Mary replied.

'That's what I thought,' said Fred.

'Well why'd you fucking ask?' shouted Leon.

The morning sun grew bolder and pierced the canvas. A car honked its horn three times. There was a mass of footsteps and then the clattering of a half dozen placards on the ground. A boot kicked against the side of her tent and Fred's rushed apology met her ears. Doors slammed and engines started. The camp was quiet, or with the waves of cars what passed for quiet.

Yet ten minutes later the echoes rattled in her head. A hundred metres away on Royal Avenue a car backfired, tuning her into the painful constant rumble of traffic there. She tried to centre herself and find the calm in her breath, but produced an out-of-tune throaty whistle.

'Alright Tommie... you've literally just missed them,' said Shay.

And then a stranger's voice. 'What are you protesting about?'

Leon clenched her elbows over her chest and curled into a ball.

The guard at the barrier said Danesfort Park was private property: there was no public parking. Galway John and the three drivers behind him - all there to protest America's crackdown on Occupy camps – reversed back down the hill and onto the main road. They found a spot a few streets away but it was a fifteen minute walk back. Under over-hanging trees raindrops dripped onto Cat's temple. Kiera was hunched up, shivering, as they passed the bus shelter.

'What a load of bollocks,' cursed Eoghan. 'This road is private property. *You hear that, son? Just pack up your whopper and thick-shake and ride on out.*'

'Confederate country,' said Levin.

Fred tried his hand at a cowboy drawl, '*You're new in town, and we don't like strangers.*'

'Santander have more than enough parking space,'

noted Galway.

Like much of Stranmillis, Danesfort Park was leafy and suburban: a posh cul-de-sac, unassuming except for the security barrier. The guard, a stern and stocky jobsworth, directed them left. It was a sliver of a pavement, bordered by wet shrubs. The consulate was on raised ground: a grim red brick four-storey place.

'Come on now. Keep on the pavement,' said the guard.

'It looks like Bedlam Asylum,' said Levin.

The building was sealed off by a barrier and Gary stood as near to it as he could. Cat and Eoghan walked towards him. Levin and Fred hung back to greet the new arrivals: Terry, Michelle, Gerardy and Auld Joel. Galway hung back while Kiera took some air from her inhaler. All the while the guard uttered his mantra.

'Stay on the pavement. Stay on the pavement.'

In gamely defiance, Kiera tapped her foot on the empty road.

'I do not want to ask again!'

Galway John did the same.

'This is your last warning!'

'Terribly sorry. My mobility isn't what it used to be,' said Galway. The guard turned away. Galway continued in the same soft tone. 'As I advance in years, orientation becomes increasingly difficult.' The guard was now harassing someone else. 'You must pardon me if I flout the requirements of irritable shit-birds such as yourself.'

Kiera gasped, and then exploded in a fit of laughter. She threw her head into his wet coat and hugged him. He threw his head back, surprised.

'Sorry, John. I just really needed that,' she said.

'Can you all hear me?' shouted Gary, through the spitting rain.

The crowd murmured.

'Okay! Today is an international day of protest against the forced removal of Occupy camps across America. On Tuesday under cover of darkness, New York Mayor Mike Bloomberg ordered police to make mass arrests. They seized tents, clothing and cooking equipment. Among the subversive materials found in Zucotti Park were five thousand books, now in police custody.'

Fred yelled out, 'Have they DUP men on the city council?'

There was laughter, and Levin gave him a Cheshire Cat grin.

'We're here today to make our voices heard. We stand in solidarity with Occupy Wall Street, and in solidarity with our comrades across America and Europe. I want to hand over to Cat Kennedy from our own camp, to say a few words.'

Rain came down in a skin of drizzle. Cat stepped up to the top of the kerb. Gary noticed the guard striding towards them, and tapped her elbow. She took a few paces down, and focussed on the moist folding papers in her right hand. She looked over the fifty assembled: friends; strangers; Socialist Party salesmen.

'This afternoon I'll be writing a letter to support our sisters and brothers in New York. We can send your message too. There's been a black-out on press coverage. Reporters for the *Wall Street Journal* and other papers were among those arrested. We've heard stories of mass beatings, the use of tear gas and pepper spray. Zucotti Park has been reopened but police are searching bags. Turning away anyone with camping equipment. Let's get the message of solidarity out. New York, we stand with you. To St. Paul's, facing legal action, we stand with you. We stand with occupiers in Africa, South America and Asia, united. We are the 99%, and the 99% have spoken!'

They applauded. Gary shook her hand. Although she was freezing, in the relentless drizzle, she didn't feel the cold – only the warmth of swelling pride. She felt high.

'WE ARE THE 99%!'

Galway John looked right before taking the jeep back out onto

Stranmillis Road. Behind him sat Fred, letting them all know he thought Cat was amazing, before reclining in a state of bliss. His head almost collided with Eoghan's arm, as Eoghan pushed out a bulbous yawn.

'Sounds like you need your beauty sleep, young Eoghan: if you're to be up bright and early on Saturday,' said Galway John.

'What's happening on Saturday?' asked Fred.

Kiera looked at him in the mirror, raised her eyebrows and rolled her eyes. 'It's the march to City Hall. And the carnival. Were you not paying attention?'

'That's five protests in a week,' noted Eoghan.

'I don't know where you youngsters get the stamina, but if you know you should bottle it for me.'

'We'll have to get a breather in before the thirtieth. It's less than two weeks away,' said Kiera.

'That's the one with all the unions,' said Fred.

'The National General Strike,' declared Galway.

'The college is closing down for the day. All the schools,' Kiera remarked, looking out the window as they passed Queen's University.

'Everyone is out over pension cuts. Prison officers, nurses, engineers, bus drivers. Even the managers,' said Galway.

'Though it's about more than that,' said Eoghan. 'It's about wage freezes and everything costing more. Austerity, and the sustained attack on the working class. We'll have to step up getting flyers; use the media and talk to as many people as we can. It'll be the biggest strike since 1926.'

'Ah yes,' said Galway. 'When Protestants and Catholics came out together to support one another. They were fighting the same nonsense back then.'

'John... What's it like in Galway?' asked Fred.

'I've not been to the home city in many-a-years. There are plenty of good bars. Friendly people. The sun setting over the harbour is beautiful; though you wouldn't want to get too close. With the wrong weather you'd be blown away. Why do you ask, young Fred?'

'Levin was talking about visiting the camp there.'

'Yeah, he was. Deirdre went. Their set-up's meant to be perfect. Clean and tidy, people sticking to rotas...' mused Eoghan.

'Why'd you leave, John?' asked Kiera.

'I bet it was a woman,' said Eoghan with a smile.

'Was it a woman?' said Fred.

He laughed. 'That's none of your beeswax. And besides, a Galway woman would eat you boys alive!'

The following day was Friday 18th November, 2:44pm, according to the monitor screen in Central Library's computer suite. Eoghan had just logged into one of the terminals wrapping around the room, below a poster on the wall which advertised job opportunities overseas. He'd come across a video of the anti-Austerity protests in Madrid, and plugged in his earphones. The camera panned across the Spanish capital showing people laying flowers at the feet of riot police. They used human microphones, the repeating of a speech through chant, so those furthest from the speaker could hear what was said. They raised hands, and hand-signs. *'People of Europe Rise Up!' 'Ya! Ha empezado!'* Eoghan's favourite placard read, *'No One Expects The Spanish Inquisition'.*

He used the phrase in a status update when he linked to the video, logged into Facebook as Occupy Belfast. He took out his earphones and scrolled down the group page. It was the usual assortment of trolls and counter-trolls. Someone called Sneaky Weasel had written, *'Any monkey can type but few can talk politics in a tent in the rain.'* He gave it a like and scrolled down.

One minute ago someone else had posted using the Occupy Belfast account. *'March against Austerity tomorrow. Meet at Buoy Park, by the Art College, at 12 Noon. Followed by Carnival of Resistance at Writer's Square, and a teach-in on fracking. Have *an idea for a teach-in? Get in touch.'*

Eoghan heard a familiar cough and turned round. He made out Cat, her back to him. He said her name in a loud whisper. She didn't respond. Then, mischief seized him. In a comment under her post he typed, *'This isn't the blog or twitter I'm not sure its credible.'*

He waited a few minutes, and watched her, but there was nothing. Eoghan got up and crossed the room. She was fixed on his comment. 'We are everywhere,' he said.

'Are you have a fucking laugh, Eoghan?'

He was caught out by her anger. 'Uh, that was the idea.'

Cat stayed focussed on the screen. 'I could do without it. Do you not think I've enough to do?'

'I'll delete it. No problem. Lighten up!'

She deleted it, hard, and then turned in her chair, bearing her teeth. 'Lighten up?'

'Yes. You're yelling at me for no reason.'

'No reason? People are supposed to be on outreach for the Carnival but no, muggins here has been left to carry it while you all gallivant off to god knows where. You know what? Never mind!'

'Don't be like that. I put in the order to the printers. I'll collect it later and check the emails. It's fine. Don't worry. Cat?'

'Okay, right,' she said. 'Just... leave me to get the blog updated.'

'I don't want us to fall out,' he said.

'No, it's fine. Don't worry,' said Cat, though from her tone it didn't sound like it was fine.

Saturday 19th November: Leon scanned the front of *The Guardian*. It told the story of father of six, Mark Duggan, killed three months beforehand by members of the London Metropolitan Police. The headline read, *'Revealed: man whose shooting triggered riots was not armed.'* Leon opened the pages and buried her head within reports of Cairo in flames during the police assault on Tahrir Square. A timid winter morning sun crept over camp. It offered no heat, and glared into Padraig's lenses. Shay, noticing Padraig was trying for his attention, hit pause on his white CD player.

'Sorry, Padraig. Were you saying something?'

'He was asking where Fred is. Fred and Levin went to Galway,' said Leon.

'What, Galway in Ireland? When?'

'Yesterday afternoon,' said Shay. He just said he was bored and they were away. Off in search of adventure! Spur of the moment thing.'

'Wee man owes me a fiver,' said Padraig.

Nearby Bob squeezed water out of a sock. 'Aw, poor Padraig. His wee chum has left him. For another man too!'

Daniel grinned. Leon got up and fetched the water cannister to fill her nearly empty bottle of mineral water. Down the path, Jack zipped up her tent. Her industrial boots, though pressed against the mud, were spotless. A new long skirt led up to her tanned skin and restyled golden curls. If there was one person at the camp who seemed impenetrable to the elements it was Jack.

In received pronunciation she asked, 'Are we ready to object vociferously to the bourgeois contamination, darlings?'

The patch of green and concrete between the cathedral and art college was known, until the early eighties, as Cathedral Gardens. The maritime safety group, Commissioners of Irish Lights, donated three buoys to the city council – thick steel plated giant sculptures which eighty years before would have been used by sailors to find safe channels to and from Belfast port. There was a red can, a black conical buoy and a red spherical striped buoy and their iconic status quickly saw Cathedral Gardens rechristened as Buoy Park.

Cat and Eoghan moved through the eighty people gathered in the space, making sure each got a dozen flyers with details of the National Strike. There were so many people and Cat felt dizzy distributing to them all. A pigeon on the ground looked up at her sympathetically. When she and Eoghan regrouped a moment later, Bronagh was upon them.

'I told you I was doing a batch from home,' she asserted, with an accusatory tone.

'It's a big demo. I don't see the problem,' said Eoghan casually.

Bronagh looked away to the buoys. It was an intentional move, as if Eoghan's strategy of printing extra flyers was beneath her. 'The problem is the camp has no need to waste money.'

Cat got in between them. 'This was agreed by the GA.'

'Yes, and I emailed to say I'd do it. Excuse me if I have other responsibilities,' said Bronagh sarcastically.

'How about you give out yours and we give out ours?' said Cat.

The rounded red striped buoy, once marking the junction in the channel, was erected further back from the others. Leon and Shay ducked underneath it, the three tonne sculpture offering protection from the sun. With tired eyes they looked down on the concrete where they sat, and they rolled up their cigarettes. Leon puffed hard on her smoke, as if doing so was a small act of rebellion against the sun.

'Before he left, Levin was saying he wants us to occupy a building,' she said.

'Aye, that'd be alright. Imagine a bit of warmth around us, and not being rained on 24/7. Though the fuzz wouldn't be too pleased,' said Shay.

'There's squatters' rights. It's written into law. If we do it right they can't touch us.'

Shay took out a small bag of pills.

'What's those?'

'2C-B. Psychedelic. Puts you in touch with nature. Want one?'

Leon scanned the area to make sure no one was watching. 'It might cheer me up some,' she admitted.

'Have you done psychedelics before?'

Leon took a pill right out of Shay's hand. 'Aye. Loads of times,' she lied.

Shay was suspicious. 'Uh-huh. Give it back.'

'Okay, it was only the once. If I take this, will I be dancing to the cathedral bells tomorrow? Am I going to hallucinate?'

'Naah, bud. You'll just be really happy for three or four hours. Or really sleepy.'

Leon unscrewed the top of her water, put the pill in her mouth and swallowed. Shay took her water, and did the same.

'I wish I'd stayed in Dublin, or gone with Levin to Galway,' said Leon.

'Maybe these will take you there,' he replied jovially.

They both looked up to Cat's oncoming shadow She was in a foul mood, gripping a pile of leaflets.

'Shay, did you put the word around about the rally today?' she asked.

'Ah. I forgot. Sorry, love.'

'We'll be okay. The rising is almost upon us,' said Leon cheerily.

'Right, right. Everyone will rise up with their dreams and unite hand-in-hand. Fucking get a grip.'

Shay squinted, trying to make out Cat's face against the sun. 'Are you okay, bud?'

She scowled at them a moment, and then said, 'I'm sorry, sorry. I'm just, Christ, juggling certain peoples' egos, trying to do a hundred things at once.' Cat thrust flyers at each of them. 'Would you give these out?'

'No bother, mate,' Shay assured her.

They watched her make a beeline for Deirdre and Amanda Anonymous.

'Poor Cat. She's going off her rocker,' said Shay. Despite the phrasing, his tone was quiet and concerned.

'We're the only sane ones in the place,' murmured Leon.

Their attention was drawn to the corner, where the park met Royal Avenue, and the booming of Gary with the megaphone. 'Alright! It's ten to one. Are you all ready to march?'

Shay yelled back, 'I forgot my sash!'

'Again! Are you ready?'

There was a muted 'yeah' from the crowd. Gary brought down the megaphone and waved it at Eoghan. Eoghan laughed and took it from him. He raised it to his mouth and stepped towards Royal Avenue.

'No more bankers' bail-outs!'

'NO MORE BANKERS' BAIL-OUTS!'

While the parade advanced on City Hall, Bob and Tall Paul were at camp unpacking a gazebo. The *'Occupy Belfast'* cloth banner tied to its poles breathed with the wind, greeting the marchers on their return. They drank and smoked and caught up with friends. Bronagh ladled out her delicious vegetable soup for Jack, Paul, Galway, and New/Shitty John. Leon's absence was felt. On the way back from the march she'd wandered into the library, and spent the afternoon there. Shay crawled into his tent and witnessing this, Bob thought it was as good a time as any to chastise Padraig for his want of 'a wee lie down.' Kiera didn't stick around either, leaving for home after six consecutive sneezes. Folk brought more donations: a thick beige throw, and a few pairs of gloves; teabags and a family pack of biscuits. All in all, a hundred and fifty people passed through the square on their fourth Carnival of Resistance.

On the steps at the back of the pavilion, Luke Devlin and Eoghan stood with guitars slung over their shoulders and Joe between them with the megaphone, speaking his protest with conviction. The time flew in. Deirdre had been due to present a teach-in on fracking which they decided to postpone until after the General Assembly. However there were plenty to clap and hoot when Padraig marked up the chalkboard: *'28 Days Later... Still Occupied!'*

Two dozen people hung around for the teriyaki beef and chicken curry, which Tommie and Sean brought back from *Brown's*. Over steaming hot orange rice the campers praised the two of them for making it happen. But Tommie was fed up with food he'd looked at all day every day. He boiled the pot for his Pot Noodle.

The first item on the agenda at the General Assembly was Tommy Sands. Tommy was a veteran disc jockey at *Downtown Radio* and wanted to host his show, *Country Céilí*, live from the camp the following Thursday. He was well known as the songwriter for *The Sands Family*, an influential folk group performing live from the early seventies. Some members of the camp knew of his solo work and his great reputation as a peace activist. Eoghan said he'd organised a *Citizen's Assembly* of leading cultural figures during The Troubles, and played Carnegie Hall. Galway John knew his name from *There Were Roses*, a song based on the true story of the murder of a Catholic man, and the murder of his best friend, a Protestant man, in reprisal.

The next matter concerned preparations for the National Strike. Cat was worried by the scale of it, potentially overshadowing other camp activities. Gary, and Deirdre, diplomatically told her not to think too much about it. The media team had made good contacts and they could talk about the teach-ins and assemblies on Downtown Radio. Conversation moved to the health and social services sector, and then the Minister responsible, Edwin Poots, of the DUP. Poots had been at the centre of the local news cycle that weekend after he was discovered to have been charging £50 for a 'health workshop.'

'Bog standard DUP gay-hating seven-day-world prick,' said Leon.

Eoghan looked to Fred and said, 'Poots wants an end to free prescriptions.'

'Those are services his constituents should have been getting for free,' said Galway.

'He's the one looks like a leprechaun?' asked Fred.

'An elf with a face like an arse and hair that's been spunked on,' said Padraig.

'Well now we have consensus,' said Gary cheerfully, 'can

we turn back to the subject of direct action?'

'Leon, did you manage to update our media pages?' asked Cat.

A barely perceptible vibration of the head said she had not.

'You were in the library all afternoon,' said Cat.

'I guess I was just hanging out... in front of screen, like you do.'

Light rain pushed by an east wind sprinkled onto the twenty people inside the marquees. They discussed the excess of strike leaflets. These would be given out in Royal Avenue during the week. Padraig, Eoghan and Leon volunteered for that. The south wind blew droplets onto the pages of the camp journal, rested on Cat's knees. She shared December's events: the carnival on the third, the student protest against tuition fees on the ninth, and *International Human Rights Day* on the tenth. Tommie put the kettle on. The west wind blew campfire smoke, drying and reddening their eyes, and stinking up their clothes. Bronagh said she'd cook turkey and trimmings for those who were staying at camp over Christmas. Some were keen to talk about focussed protests.

'We could boycott Coke,' suggested Eoghan.

'Boycott Nestlé!' exclaimed Leon, adding, 'That one's good for Easter too.'

'Haven't we more pressing things? I mean, right now,' said Cat.

Tommie made eye contact with her. He smiled compassionately. Cat nodded and buried her anger.

Eoghan quickly said, 'It'd be good to do something big for the thirtieth, something eye catching.'

'You can't get more eye catching than tens of millions on strike as far as I'm concerned,' said Bronagh.

'What about making room for a few more tents?' asked Galway.

'I mean something that says we back the strike. Like a banner over City Hall. I don't mean we should do that, but y'know, like that,' said Eoghan.

'Chain ourselves to the railings of City Hall,' said Leon.

'Or kidnap Edwin Poots? Mwah-ha-hahaha! And we don't hand him back until the IMF pay us… one meelion dollars!'

Jack shook her head. 'It sounds as if they'd pay us that to keep him.'

Without looking up from the fork in his second Pot Noodle Tommie replied solemnly, 'Are you for real? For a job like that you're talking four men, an unmarked vehicle and a few heavy duty bats.' The hard lines in his face were pronounced in the glow from the fire and years of pain which seemed, albeit matter-of-factly, to want to unleash that pain on others. 'You'd want duct tape, as much to stop the screams as so you don't have to look at the ugly bastard's mouth. And he'd have to be stored off-site of course. This place is much too central.'

A few people laughed, some nervously, and there were one or two gasps. Eoghan and Bob seemed uncertain how to take it. Gary was mortified.

Leon just stared at him a moment before embarking on her own distraction. 'How about we boycott Pot Noodle?'

'Aren't Pot Noodle owned by Golden Wonder?' asked Eoghan.

Cat tapped a pen on the camp diary. Tommie rolled his eyes. Bronagh looked completely confused.

'Pot Noodle are owned by Tayto Crisps,' said Gary helpfully, then regretted fuelling the tangent as soon as the words came out of his mouth.

'Tayto Castle in Tandragee also makes Pot Noodle?' asked Padraig. He pointed to Tommie's top-bulbous snack pot. 'I suppose that would explain why Mr. Tayto has that big yellow head.'

Galway John sighed and rubbed his eyes. 'I'm giving up my bloody time for this,' he muttered.

Deirdre chimed in. 'About five years ago Pot Noodle were

owned by Unilever. Is that what you mean?'

Gary lowered his brow. Leon smiled and her head bobbed.

'Greenpeace have Unilever linked to the depletion of Indonesian rainforests. They're one of the larger emitters of greenhouse gases,' Deirdre explained.

Gary slowly raised his head. 'Actually, this is relevant. The Indian government released a report a few weeks ago into Unilever dumping two tonnes of toxic waste in densely populated townlands.'

'They refused to take responsibility for it,' said Jack.

'That's right!' exclaimed Eoghan. 'There were, like, sixty deaths because Unilever won't clear it up. A third of them children too. It was mercury poisoning from one of their factories. Real Bhopal Dow shit. The court threw the case out. *Loss of memory, and teeth, birth defects? No! It couldn't be the mercury!*'

Padraig interjected. 'Now, hang on. You're saying Tayto crisps is killing kids?'

A tight band of stress lines formed on Cat's forehead. Eoghan let out a heavy sigh.

Leon jeered. 'Numb-nuts, how do you connect mercury poisoning with Tayto crisps?'

He shrugged. 'You're a numb-nuts. You're saying Pot Noodle did this?'

Tommie abandoned his fork and set the Pot Noodle on the ground.

'It was crushed glass in a thermometer factory,' said Eoghan.

'How was I to know?'

Leon scowled. 'You're a fucking idiot, Padraig.'

He shrugged, and smiled. Leon reached under her chair to an open bag of firewood and threw a piece at Padraig. He put up an elbow and deflected it.

'Hey now!' shouted Bronagh.

'For God's sake,' moaned Galway.

Cat frothed. 'This is a waste of time,' she said, and sunk

her head into her hands.

Padraig threw the stick of firewood back at Leon.

'Missed, dickhead!'

'Could we please treat the subject and each other with more respect?'

'Gary's right. This is serious stuff. Many of the victims are still suffering neurological disorders,' said Eoghan grimly.

'Mercury's bad news,' said Tommie. 'At school we had this teacher who kept a glass box of it: on top of a cabinet, right at the front of the room. She only brought it down once. We weren't allowed to touch it. She said if the mercury escaped the box it would eat through human flesh.'

'Would All Of You Shut The Fuck Up?' bellowed Cat.

You could hear a pin drop. Even the wind fell silent.

'See Deirdre there? She was due to give a talk on fracking! Three And A Half Hours Ago!'

'It's okay, really,' said Deirdre.

'NO. It's not! Ninety fucking minutes. Chittering about Pot Noodles and kidnapping Mr. Tayto or whatever else.'

Eoghan and Gary each formed a T with their hands, signalling time out.

'She's right. We've been getting nowhere,' said Bronagh.

'We do have to get through a lot,' said Jack.

'And people are all over the place,' said Bronagh, who had patiently held off her latest rant. 'This demo, that demo. All talk, and then when it comes to action, well somebody has to be there to make it happen.'

As she spoke, Galway John got to his feet. He crossed through the circle of chairs, and walked away. There were a few confused looks.

Padraig ignored him. 'What if we move the camp? In time with the strike. That'd make a statement.'

'That wouldn't help,' said Gary.

'Jesus!' shouted Cat. 'Have you not been *fucking* listening? I'm wasting my breath here!'

She got up, whipped her coat with her, and pushed her

way through the assembly. She walked into Donegall Street, past Galway John at his jeep, and kept walking.

17

Levin clung to sleep, fixed on the coach's LED display stuck at 03:45, though he knew he was outside in mild air and moist odours. He heard splashing rain, safe, like a nearby waterfall. He heard traffic. The light increased. Voices reminded him of the energy of nightclubs where he'd searched, not alone, not so intimidating. The quest ended in a sense of comfort and he felt someone holding him. Snuggling further, Levin embraced the sleep which dreamed warmth, and spoke with contentment.

'Your hair… Cat, so lovely.'

He prised Fred off him and back to his side of the tent, ten minutes later. They both woke up immediately after. Fred apologised. Levin reassured him.

'Eoghan talks in his sleep all the time. Anyway, we were wrecked when we got in.'

'I don't remember much. We found the camp. We're in Galway.'

'It was dark when we got here. Friendly reception, organised marquee. It was very dark.'

Fred pulled his boots to him. 'I guess we should get out and have a look.'

They emerged to blue skies and green healthy trees. A high metal sculpture represented six sails of a Galway Hooker, fishing boats unique to Galway. Water fell there from the Quincentennial Fountain. Nearby was a grey limestone archway extended upwards with a frieze and an oriel window. They understood they were in the heart of the city surrounded by shoppers and motor traffic; but also that this was a place of rest.

Fred zipped up the front flaps. 'Whose tent is this?'

'I have no idea; I thought you would know. Saying thank you could get embarrassing,' murmured Levin.

They saw the green marquee tarpaulin of the meeting place. Beside it stood a large wood-framed solar panel, on a raised platform buttressed by sandbags. Beside it was a table with blue tarp and ten pots: Levin smelled basil, onion, coriander and chives. The tents were circled by a fence of three foot high planks, painted white with green at the base. Activist's notices were nailed around the paddock's exterior, and a chalkboard which read *'Day 36'*, a week ahead of their Belfast counterparts.

At the entrance to the main tent, actually a built hut, was a fixed neat banner proclaimed OCCUPY in gold on blue. There was an information table by one of two broad open wooden doors. Flyers and photos were pinned to them. They entered. Inside was all wooden-framed, giving the area some stability. Only the overhanging green canvas flapped, providing air circulation. Levin gasped. Fred too.

'My god...'

There was a colour scheme. Red-pink for the felt noticeboards, lounging chairs and carpet in the meeting area, though the remaining floorspace was grey vinyl. There was much use of pine: from the supporting structures, to the makeshift frame holding tight the plexiglass window, and the coffee table and clerical and kitchen workspaces. Under a hanging whiteboard, a wooden bench supported a hob, chopping area and cutlery drawer. There was a condiment rack and wide neat storage shelves. A sturdy marble table at the far end was clear to allow for thorough preparing of ingredients. The walls were decorated with postcards of support, photographs, post-its, hanging lanterns and hand-made decorations. A man in a grey parka with a light blue thermal hat rose from his lounger and introduced himself as Emmett. His handshake was warm, although Fred and Levin were still transfixed by the space.

'I'll get you both a cuppa. There's cereal over there.' said Emmett.

Fred roared. *'It's a clubhouse!'*

On Sunday evening the bells of St. Anne's were received by the antennae of leaf-less trees lining Donegall Street. Although only thirty shades of grey are visible to the human eye, Eoghan and Kiera were aware of many more. Grey saturated the red letter brick buildings and four shutters scrawled with graffiti tags. They passed every scuff and piece of gum, dog turd and cigarette butt, loose brick and firm weed. Eoghan was complaining about Bob and his reluctance to follow through on a break from the camp. Kiera said nothing for a while. A particular question was foremost in her mind.

'Cat didn't come back last night. What exactly happened?' she said.

He was flippant in his response. 'Ach, you know General Assemblies. People can't stay on topic. Can't work things through without blathering to midnight.'

They passed the derelict car park's blue painted fence round to Waring Street. The cathedral bells continued to echo. Overhanging lights from swanky cafes shone out to a dark, damp street. Beyond the abandoned *Northern Bank* they crossed into Rosemary Street: the sandwich bars; *The Red Barn Gallery*; the *First Presbyterian Church*. The bells of St. Anne's dimmed until the overlapping rings lost their melody, sounding like a jumbled disco beat.

'I was thinking of getting Leon onto the media team. She's not organised, but she knows how to make herself heard,' said Eoghan.

'Yeah. Leon's really stable, Kiera deadpanned.

'Honestly, I could do without the drama.'

'Hold on Eoghan. Cat's been nothing but pleasant to you. She's done all that social media stuff...'

'I'm not disputing that, and I like Cat, but...' Eoghan stopped, and sighed. 'I'm sorry. Josie and I broke up. And I'm just-- just--'

'God. Sorry to hear that. Is it fixable?'

His eyes half closed, the lines underneath pronouncing his twenty-nine years. Admitting the truth to Kiera he was, for the first time, admitting it to himself. He heard his own voice cracked and vulnerable and quickly changed his tone to affect bravado. 'I moved my stuff out. She doesn't want to talk. Isn't open to working anything out. Doesn't want to talk compromise.'

Kiera took a breath from her inhaler, and replied, 'I don't understand how two people in love can't stay friends. Was it the camp?'

'Yeah. She kept saying, *we're too different.* As if I'd want to be with someone the same as me.'

'Right. If you were after that you'd shag your cousin. Did she use the old, *it's not your fault it's mine…?*'

'Jesus! Yes! Like she was making some heroic self-sacrifice. Which I'd no say in!'

Outside the *McDonalds* on Castle Place, puffer jacket people wobbled as children tried to keep their screaming parents in line. Eoghan and Kiera entered the *Spar*: the tiny convenience store at capacity with only twelve people. Shelves of multi-pack chocolate bars bore fluorescent stickers marking them out as bargains. And there were more: coffee, toilet roll, sandwiches and milk, all on very special offer.

'*It's not your fault, it's mine!* I knew that was bullshit,' moaned Eoghan.

'It's a bit sarcastic,' said Kiera.

'Worst of all she dumped me by text. The lowest of the low.'

'Seriously? Sounds like she hasn't a clue about relationships. You're better off without her.' Kiera threw a granary loaf into their basket.

He shook his head. 'I don't feel that way. And I'd give up the tent, and go back to her, if she'd have me.'

'Would you not regret it?'

'Probably. I'd have a lot more time on my hands for sure.'

'You could take the laptop into the bathroom to answer our emails,' said Kiera.

Eoghan couldn't even manage a smile. He looked down to his feet and said, 'You know what? I'm just tired of leaping from one crisis to the next. For what? Catching the cold and coughing up phlegm. Fuck this shit. Fucking just arrest me already.'

He lifted his head and realised the staffer behind the till was waiting patiently. Eoghan raised the basket onto the counter.

Encased candles hung emitting soft light around the Galway meeting hut where Levin nestled into the lounger. All around him were the beautiful accents of Galway women. There was no rain or wind. He took in the neat shelving units and the antique writing bureau; the bookshelf and the stereo speaker above it. A typeset notice, *'No Alcohol, No Drugs'*, was prominently displayed. Fred lounged beside Levin: head laid back and smiling.

'If I hadn't been here for two days I'd swear I was dreaming,' he said, eyes closed.

'Do you think we should be just sitting here? Except for the march we've hardly been outside the camp.'

'We went to the shopping centre,' Fred replied. 'I'd say we're probably even.'

'Even?'

'With Bronagh and the others. Them getting to that demo in Dublin, and leaving us behind. Hell, we're in the lead.'

The women were clearing out. One of them smiled and waved to Fred in passing and he returned the gestures. He reached forward to the oak coffee table for hot tea from a hot mug. Levin looked around to make sure they were alone. There was desperation in his voice.

'We are so fucked. I don't know how we're going to get home. We could be trapped here. Here in Bizarro Occupy. I've never met a bunch of more genuine people.'

Off-the-cuff, Fred remarked, 'Ah it's Occupy Paradiso. We could ask them for the money for our trip home and it'd be fine. Come on. It'd take us a week to walk back.'

Levin paused, and then suddenly exploded with un-Levin-like laughter. 'Bwah-ha-ha! Bwah-ha-ha!'

'*It's not funny!* And that laugh? You know, you sound just like that ginger guy from the teach-in.'

'Right, Patrick. It *is* an infectious laugh. And no, we're not going to ask them for money. We got ourselves stranded here.'

Fred got up and took his mobile phone from the charger at the bureau, and reclined back into the lounger. 'I was thinking about this. We have enough to bus it to Dublin. Let's figure out our next step from there.'

'I suppose the plan was for this to be an adventure.' Levin looked to the clock atop the office desk. 'It's after eight. We have less than four hours otherwise we're here another night.' Then he drew in closer to Fred, and whispered, 'Are the people here, maybe, too nice?'

'They treated us like heroes at last night's GA.'

'*You're welcome to stay as long as yous want.* And we smoked in here. No one else did. Nobody said anything.'

Fred shrugged and wondered, 'Aye. What was that about?'

Levin was sounding increasingly concerned. 'Big helpings of steak and chips. They did our dishes, because they have their rota. More cups of tea than I could drink.'

'Right! It felt like I was being ambushed by tea!'

Levin looked over to the cushioned chairs, the uncluttered workbench and the sealed and stored boxes of tools. 'How long before they figure out we're impostors?'

Fred conceded. 'He's not saying it, but I think yer man wants his tent back.'

'And what about the creepy polite guy who led the march yesterday?'

Fred sat up. 'He looked almost exactly like Gary, except his side-shade was combed the other way. And the goatee...'

Levin gave a sly grin. 'Maybe he was a spy. You know, a spook.'

In mornings so grey, Bob's shut eyes had no need to distinguish from the night. Tobacco neutered his sense of smell in sleep. He pretended he was immune to the moisture in the air. When he laid down his body throbbed with intense pain, as if rats were biting his feet to the heels. Bob's aches lifted in slumber, each passing car driving them away, for time reinvigorated him. Relief was punctuated by the stray missiles of the nonsense he heard them talk. This time it was Shay, asking about the chalks, and the clanking as the chalk pieces hit the edge of the metal tin. Soon after there was the sound of chalk on stone tiles and Daniel joining Shay. At least he could count on Daniel, thought Bob, and he drifted back to sleep. It was Shay, jovially greeting 'officers' which brought him to wake.

'Vandalism of a public by-way is a criminal offence.'

A laugh from Shay, who said playfully, 'Do you not think it's colourful?'

'It's a disgusting sight,' said another deeper voice sternly.

'I'm instructing you to remove it,' the first man snapped.

'What? Seriously?' Shay asked.

'Do you people know how to scrub something?' one sneered.

'Fuck,' muttered Bob, after a deep, deep breath.

'It's funny to you toe-rag? Do it. Or you're both going to Musgrave for booking. Five, four...'

Bob's boots were already on. He threw back the door flap. The first thing he saw were the chalked letters each to a tile in bright purple: *'OCCUPIED.'* Daniel's tan had drained and he was as white as a plastic bag. Shay was shaken, but hiding it. The two officers were large, in black padded gear, dressed for a riot. One was fat faced and balding, with red rosy cheeks and three chins. The officer in charge was the smaller of the two, more muscular, with a broad chin and groomed moustache.

Bob demanded answers. 'What's the problem here?'

'Are you the leader of this little group?' sneered groomed moustache.

Bob looked down at the pavement and then at Daniel. 'Is this the issue? Go and find a mop and sponge and you,' he said looking at Shay, 'you go and get a keg of water.'

Groomed moustache evil-eyed Bob as Shay and Daniel left for the marquee.

Bob called after them. 'Grab the brush too!'

'I do not want a repeat of this incident. Are we clear on the matter?' said groomed moustache sharply.

'Crystal. It's on record,' said Bob.

Shay poured out the bucket of water over the chalk. Daniel brought the wire broom down, scrubbing over the slosh. Satisfied, the two officers nodded, and walked away.

It was a blowy, overcast, late afternoon in Dublin. The camp was set back off the street so it didn't block access to the busy thoroughfare. Pedestrians constantly flowed by; cars paused and buses stopped. There were twenty two-person tents, enclosed by a fence at the foot of the bank's steps, bordered by a vibrant red, blue and white banner reading '#OCCUPY DAME STREET.' Placards rattled on lamp-posts: 'We Are Your Crisis', 'Enough is Enough' and 'Tremble Ye Bankers. The People are Coming!'

Fred was alone, a stranger among a dozen people: youthful grandmothers; a lucid speaker with dreads; gentlemen in suits and hip middle-aged city lasses. People from Tipperary and Porto, Hackney and Sligo. Fred sat on one of two full couches under their marquee, transparent white with window decorations, strung to the fence of the Bank of Ireland. It was missing a roof and two walls. Strings were blowing. A broad white banner blew so hard he couldn't read it, though he had been in its vicinity for six hours. The only thing that didn't move was a bronze gold-coloured sphere sculpture, raised on a pole ten feet off the ground.

People talked constantly. 'I had my own business. I was a well paid IT consultant. I played by the rules, and what do I get for it?'

'You've got to remember that inside that building there, is a full-time unelected official from the IMF, running our country's economic policy.'

Fred piped up. 'My friend and I are from the Belfast camp. We got in from Galway about six this morning.' His audience of a dozen people looked intrigued and so he carried on. 'Levin's been here six or seven times, including to Trinity College. He has a Masters. But we still took hours to find this place!'

His exclamation was met with dead silence, and then someone said, 'I hear they sent men from the Central Bank to look us over. Robbins said they were in the new kitchen. It's the first time the bank sent anyone in an official capacity.'

Levin walked towards them and Fred got to his feet.

'Bad news. Minimum withdrawal is twenty euros.'

'You're fucking joking me,' said Fred. 'You're fucking joking!'

'What's wrong?' asked a young Dublin protestor.

Sounding slightly brittle, Levin replied. 'We're broke. Why didn't we take some out over the counter? Before the bank shut?'

'The irony of it,' said the protestor carelessly. 'The bank being right here on our doorstep, I mean.'

Upset, Fred caressed his face. 'I haven't had a shave in a week.' Suddenly he had their attention again. All eyes upon him, he carried on. 'The thing is, we came from the Belfast camp on a cross-camp embassy thing, and we've no money to get back. We wondered if you could lend us the fare?'

Levin rolled his eyes and pointed Fred to behind him: the fenced yellow-coloured shed which served as a small meeting place and kitchen. The actual subject of their attention were two Gardai officers chatting to a fella at the doorway.

The young Dubliner turned back to Fred. 'We've a good relationship with the peelers but I've never seen those two before. Sorry, what where you saying?'

Fred gulped. 'Our bus fare home. It's about twenty-five euro. But we have *some* of that, right Levin?'

'We've got two euro.'

All around the group, people murmured that they couldn't help out, though they wished they could.

'Not yous personally. I was thinking about the camp funds,' said Fred.

'Janey Mac! From donations? I hardly think so,' said one of them.

Another Dubliner said, 'The treasurer's not here. The best I can offer is if we put it to a vote at the General Assembly.'

Levin and Fred looked at one another, dumbstruck. Fred sighed and took his phone out of his pocket, handed it to Levin. 'It'll sound better coming from you.'

They were interrupted by the occupier that had been chatting to the Gardai officers. 'We've just had a visit from our legal people. It's bad news,' he said.

The Belfast camp got busier as Monday wore on, with a dozen or so gathering round in preparation for dinner. The rear of the marquee would ordinarily be in darkness, but for a few hanging lanterns. They'd also tucked the partition flap in above the ridge pole, letting light in from the twilight sky. Steam rose over the basin as Kiera washed and Tommie dried.

Outside, Padraig was holding court, loudly. He'd devised a game where a person in a tent had to guess whether the sound they heard was the weather or the traffic. The second player, the lookout, would hold their head outside the tent. Padraig was coaxed into demonstrating and crawled into his own tent, but Leon zipped it up before anyone could join him inside. Meanwhile, Bob chopped. Wood splintered and tumbled. Bob chopped. The axe tore the palette apart, echoing around the square. Eoghan approached, looking disappointed.

'Fuck's sake, Bob, that's the eighth palette today. You're going to send your blood pressure through the roof.'

'Just sit back down and have your drink, Eoghan.'

'When we talked about your taking time off --'

The old man raised his voice. 'I didn't realise there'd be people doing breakfast dishes at five o' clock! Get off my back, will ye?' Bob hurled wooden wedges into to the fire, clanging on the metal sides as they fell.

Eoghan heard the weak descending ringtone of a Nokia. He set down his coffee and felt his pockets for the phone. He'd left it in the rear tent, from where Tommie arrived with it in his wet hands.

'Thanks, Tom. Yello! Levin! What about you?'

Tommie pulled the tea towel from his shoulder and joined Kiera in the rear marquee. However she'd just washed her last dish. She handed it to Tommie, and dried off, and took a seat out front with Bob and Eoghan.

'Levin, slow down and speak up.'

Kiera took out her beaten silver case and fed tobacco into the built in rolling machine.

'All done, little Kiera?' asked Bob.

'Doing the dishes relaxes me.'

'Wish there were more with that attitude,' he said.

'Christ. Well, I'll need the money back first thing. And the library's closed,' said Eoghan as he sprung out of his seat. He walked away from the marquee and the noise of the street traffic.

'Bob. You're pretty good at solving problems,' said Kiera cheerily.

'I like to think so. What are you after?'

Kiera looked into his leathery old face with the cig beside it clasped in hardened fingers; his green eyes that had seen too much conflict and were tired from four or five night shifts a week.

'Let me buy you a pint,' she said.

'Pardon me?'

'I'm offering to take you for a pint.'

'What's the catch?'

'No catch.'

Every well guarded wrinkle dropped. Alarm bells were ringing in Bob's head.

'Anywhere you like,' said Kiera.

'I see. You were listening in to what Eoghan said. *Take a break, Bob.* Whose idea was this?'

'Don't be daft. I'm fucked off sitting here all hours, Bob. I need a pint and you need a pint. So come on, let's go.'

'Are you even old enough to drink?' he enquired.

'I'm eighteen.'

'Thanks, but no thanks.'

Tommie joined them. 'That's the drying done. Did you say you're going to the pub?'

'Wanna come?' asked Kiera.

'I'd love to get out for a while,' he said.

'Will yous be back for dinner and the GA?' asked Bob.

Kiera shrugged. 'Meh. I'm not that hungry, really. Missing one GA won't do much harm. Probably would do some good, Bob.'

'…Give me a few minutes.'

Gourmet burgers and beer battered wedges were brought out over the chequered floor to the patrons of *The John Hewitt.* Kiera took out her purse at the bar, where every bottle seemed to light up. She forced a tenner into Bob's hand, and left to blag the camper's usual seats in the alcove. There was an open arched entrance, a medium sized table, and a longer fixed one beside it, with a bolted in pew of soft furnishings seating three people either side. The men joined Kiera soon after, with pint glasses and bottles of *Erdinger.*

'See a hard day's grind and a well made pint or two? Perfectly sympatico,' said Bob. He examined the poured beer a moment, and then took a long satisfying mouthful.

'They balance each other out, no doubt,' Tommie said.

'Well, Kiera. What's on your mind?' asked Bob.

'The other night. Has either of you heard from Cat?'

They both shook their heads: no.

'What about John?' said Tommie.

Bob waved the matter away. 'Oh he's just taken a strop. He'll be back, right as rain. The second or third week, sure didn't he leave after something Martine said?'

'Martine's a cow,' asserted Kiera. 'She got Cat's back up slabbering to people on Facebook.'

'If she wasn't a wee girl I'd gub her,' said Bob, which made the other two laugh.

'You wouldn't. Wimmen think they know me, but they don't understand me,' said Tommie.

'Aye, well, guys are mostly weirdos in my experience.'

'What about school? Did you not see her there?' asked Tommie.

Kiera shook her head. 'Maybe she'll be in tomorrow.'

'I wouldn't worry. Sounded like Padraig and themmuns deserved a good bollocking. Cat will get over it. She's no dozer,' said Bob firmly.

Kiera knocked back a third of her pint and screwed up her face. 'This stuff tastes funny.'

Tommie scolded her with a raised finger. 'Don't rush it. Erdinger's a wheat beer. It has to be refrigerated and poured from the bottle, as if its going in a straight line.' He swirled the remains in his bottle and poured. 'The last action picks up any yeast sediment left over. Gives that first mouthful a powerful taste.'

'Like *Guinness* then?'

'Guinness is a stout,' said Bob. 'That's poured different. You get it at a forty-five degree angle, pour slowly, then tilt the glass until its half or three quarter full.'

'To let it settle,' said Tommie.

'Exactimundo,' said Bob. 'Do you know how you should

drink a Guinness?'

'Slowly?' said Kiera.

Bob raised his glass, keeping his elbow extended. 'Slowly, and at the same angle it is poured. But unlike the barman, the drinker never looks down into his pint.'

Kiera asked about the altercation with the police. Bob confessed he had to make a big show of being hard on Daniel and Shay 'to get the peelers out of their hair.' That conversation was a blip because for the next half hour they didn't talk about the camp at all. Kiera brought out her sketchbook full of portraits in graphite pencil. She'd drawn pop stars and TV presenters. There was one of Levin, and Daniel, and four consecutive pages of smaller sketches of campers and visitors. Tommie and Bob's features were among them. The men were heartened by the likenesses. They were near perfect. Her buildings and statues weren't as good.

'I'm shit at horses too.'

'It's not bad,' said Tommie.

'The head isn't quite right but you can see all the muscles,' said Bob. He pointed gleefully at the torso and two of the legs. 'You should be proud of this.'

'My mum liked us to take holidays out in the country. I'd take a deck chair and sit at the gate of a field with my sketchbook,' she said.

Suddenly Bob looked up to the alcove's arched opening. Jack stood there in a dark satin jacket with a glass of red wine in her hand.

'I told you we'd find the dissidents plotting in here,' she purred.

Leon was behind her in ripe black thermals with leaves stuck to them and a lager in her hand. Kiera blushed and packed her sketchbook away quickly. Jack sat down beside her.

'Well, my darlings, how are plans formulating to topple the oligarchy filth?'

'Setting the world to rights, Jackie,' remarked Bob, rubbing his index finger on the rim of his glass. He noticed Leon wasn't sitting down. She was staring at him, a dangerous grin on her face.

Leon chided him playfully. 'I saw Padraig. Oh, but you're a bad man. You're a bad, bad man.'

Under the light of the alcove, Bob looked almost angelic. After a moment's deep thought he was still perplexed. 'What the fuck did I do?'

'Bob doesn't think I'm up to to it. Bob doesn't think I can stick it out,' said Leon, in Padraig-voice.

Jack smiled. 'Padraig does seem to like his home comforts.'

'That's an understatement,' said Kiera brusquely.

Leon continued. *'I'll show Bob how wrong he is. I bet I'll last longer than him too. If I have to spend the next six months or a year in that tent I will.'*

Kiera laughed. 'Not a fucking chance.'

'To be fair he's there a lot of the time,' remarked Tommie.

Leon planted her bum down next to Jack. 'Well now he's not budging.'

'Occupadraig,' said Jack.

The five of them were in fits. Bob could hardly keep his eyes from watering. Then, he looked up and saw Cat at the end of the table. Her skin was pink and frail and her hair, which had been dyed blue, was soaked and stringy.

'Uh-Oh! Here's trouble,' he said loudly.

'The agitator,' quipped Leon.

Tommie moved up to let her sit with them. She didn't.

'I'm sorry I flew off the handle the other night.'

'You didn't go far enough,' said Leon.

'Someone needs to keep us on our toes. I was worried sick about you, love.'

Cat blushed. 'I'm fine, Tommie. And I'm sorry.'

'We were all worried,' he said. 'And don't be sorry. We all lose our cool from time to time. I've blown my top more times than I care to admit. God's sake, sit down. Come on. Oh! Oho!

There's the other one. John from Galway.'

Galway John had three pints in his hands and he set these on the table. 'Good evening, folks,' he said dryly.

Bob craned his neck forward and raised a suspicious eyebrow. 'And what's going on here? You and this young girl leaving with each other, and now you're arriving together?'

Leon giggled. 'Aye. Is there something you want to tell us?'

'Oh aye,' said Cat. 'I took him to meet my parents. They didn't like him: so he's definitely *the one*.'

Galway John pushed the two tables closer together and then remarked, 'We married on Sunday, when the clergy don't charge, and walked barefoot on the sandbanks of the Lagan.'

Seeing Jack buckle over with laughter, Bob responded, 'Jackie's jealous. She likes the older men I hear.'

'I like your hair,' said Kiera.

'Oh aye! It's blue!' said Tommie.

Cat pulled one of her new blue strands down her face. 'Just like our wedding night, right John?'

He turned bright red but saw the funny side.

'I'm guessing the other pint's for the best man,' said Tommie.

'That's for young Eoghan. He's on his way over,' said Galway.

Bob rolled his eyes and let out a low growl. 'God save us. Yer man's always running around. This has to be perfect. That has to be in order. Won't give my head a moment's piece.'

'I suspect we're all for a slap on the wrist for ditching the GA,' said Jack.

Cat shrugged. 'Nah. There was barely anyone there: Joe, Mary, Daniel, Tall Paul and us. They were just talking about boycotting Coca-Cola over Christmas.'

'It lasted barely fifteen minutes. That must be a new record for a GA, perhaps a world record,' said Galway John.

Kiera chirped. 'Oh! Speak of the devil.'

Eoghan entered the alcove, shivering. He greeted them

and took off his glasses which were all fogged up. He went to wipe them on his clothes but everything was too wet so he put them on the table.

'That pint's mine? Thanks, John. Listen, I just heard. They're threatening the Dame Street camp with eviction.'

'Wankers,' blurted out Leon.

'The Bank of Ireland are filing for an injunction with the High Court tomorrow.'

'Bastarding wankers,' repeated Leon, through gritted teeth.

'What in Christ's name's wrong with these people?' John asked, disgusted.

'The politicians responsible need to be put out of their fucking homes,' said Jack by matter of fact.

'It's not a problem yet. In fact, it's not been properly announced. There's time before the case goes to court,' said Eoghan.

'How serious is it?' asked Tommie.

'The land their camp is on isn't public. It's owned by the bank,' said Galway.

'What's our source? Did we get a message from Dame Street?' asked Cat.

'In a round about way. Levin. He called to ask me to send some cash for him and Fred to get home. They got as far as Dublin and ran out of money.'

Leon got out her notepad and scribbled. 'I'll draft up a message of support tomorrow morning.'

'Aw, the poor boys,' said Kiera sarcastically, and Leon laughed.

'Fred's extra twitchy. He bartered most of his tobacco away. Something about stinky sausage rolls.'

Leon smirked. 'We should hold a fundraiser for them. *Help save The Occupy Two!*'

'You could hold a fundraiser for me,' said Bob.

'How about a sweepstake on how long Padraig can stick it out?' asked Galway.

'A week?' asked Jack.

'Five days,' said Cat.

Eoghan pondered. 'Do you think so?'

Leon threw her arm up, and four fingers. 'Four! Four! Wait. I'll write this down.'

Bob made a two fingered victory sign. 'Two hours.'

18

Leon quickly forgot the quirks of the weirdos sharing the library computer suite and the labour of the group announcements she had to write. She read every line on the screen as the roll of filth dripping onto The Guardian website live-feed filled her heart. Everything she knew, and suspected was coming out of the Leveson Inquiry. The top news was James Murdoch's resignation from the board of News Corp, and each short paragraph was some new damnation – bribery, suicide, persecution, intimidation – by the time the smoke cleared, she thought, every UK town and city would act like post-Hillsborough Liverpool, a nationwide blockade shunning tabloid incursions.

'Burn in hell, motherfuckers,' she said.

She clicked on the pop-up notification about the allowed hour for browsing, and extended the session. Job #1 was to post on the evening's teach-in, which she was looking forward to. Job #2 was writing text copy for the Occupy mailing list:

Greetings, comrades!

We're only days away from Occupy Belfast *hosting a two hour live broadcast with Tommy Sands and Downtown Radio. Tommy is a folk singer and activist, celebrating thirty-five years at Downtown. You can take part by joining us around the fire at Writer's Square from 7pm this coming Thursday.*

We're also gearing up for the National Strike next Wednesday, 30th November. This week we'll be running a placard building workshop and series of teach-ins on protest related activities.

If you're around tonight, John Travis is hosting a teach-in on survival techniques at 8pm.
SOLIDARITY
Leon McCallum
Occupy Belfast, Writer's Square

Morose clouds gathered. A constant spit of rain fell on the tent frames. A pool had gathered on top of the mega-tent forming a low hanging belly, which dribbled where the two marquees were joined. The towering fire snapped. There were about twenty people out, all eagerly anticipating the presentation. Cat drummed her pen on her notepad and Bob watched them all very carefully.

'How was the big adventure in Galway City?' asked Shay.

'Pretty good. We went on a march to City Hall to protest the water tax: really strong turnout,' said Levin.

'I heard someone say there were about three hundred of us,' Fred informed them.

'Were the streets made of gold?' asked Leon.

'Streets were freezing,' gurned Fred.

'That's the North Atlantic current and the Gulf Stream coming in,' said Galway John.

'Dublin was a bit of a washout: you know, congested capital city, bigger populace, central location,' said Levin.

'But Galway was quite good. We got lots of ideas,' said Fred.

'Yeah. There's things I'd like to implement here: use of solar, more solid construction. Oh, and they were lovely people too.' Levin was distracted by a sudden hard splat down on the path, a fresh deposit of white bird shit.

'Did you meet Emmett?' asked Mary.

'Oh yeah,' said Levin. 'He was asking about you. And you, Tommie. The Galway group are all really into sustainability. Oh, and there was a guy with a really mad laugh. Do you want to guess what his name was?'

'Not Padraig?' asked Daniel.

'Close enough. It was Patrick,' said Levin.

'There's only one of me,' exclaimed Padraig.

'No way! I think my head's going to explode,' said Kiera.

Cat raised her voice. 'Okay, everyone! Everybody! I think we're ready to start the teach-in. Tonight's session is on survival techniques, presented by John Travis.'

Her formal introduction was interrupted by twenty people clapping and stamping their feet.

'Yeeee-ohhh!'

Galway John smiled, raised the palms of his hands and slowly brought them down again. 'Okay, okay. Thank you. I'll try to do justice to that reception. Now... Winter is almost upon us. Very soon temperatures are going to drop and I have put together a few items, examples to get you thinking about how to endure the coming months. Firstly: footwear. Thermal woollen socks. Or two pairs of normal ones. You can see I'm wearing elasticated waterproof leggings.'

He lifted his leg, and began peeling back layers. Padraig sang to the tune of Daniel Rose's *The Stripper*.

'Ta-Dada-Da, Da -Dada-Da!'

Others joined in, and clapped too. '*Ta-Dada-Da, Da-Dada-Da!*'

'Show us some skin!' yelled Padraig.

'Get the petty cash. Fiver in his codpiece,' hollered Fred.

A stern intensity spread over Galway John's face. 'When you're all quite done...' he said, and he said nothing more until they were silent.

'Thank you. I am wearing jogging bottoms for manoeuvrability. See how my socks are pulled up over them. Insulation is important.' He lifted up his arms and patted each of his jacket's six pockets. 'Waterproof jacket. Pockets for gloves, a compass, a torch, your hand warmer, and a whistle: useful during fog, or for keeping Fred and Padraig in line.' From the last pocket he pulled a blue cloth, which unfolded into a cap that he put on his head.

'The winter range from Versace!' exclaimed Kiera.

'What's in the box?' asked Tommie.

'Is it the bread?' asked Levin.

Galway John slid the red and white picnic box out from under his chair. He unfastened the lid and pulled out a white, unsliced loaf. He unwrapped it from the cling film, and turned it to show yellow plastic packaging in its centre: a sealed bag of *Tayto Cheese and Onion* crisps, which he pulled out from the hollowed loaf. They gasped.

'Derren Brown,' said Cat.

He gave the bread to Leon.

'That is a stew glove. You can fill it with meats, cheeses; even soup.'

A thermos flask came out of the box next.

'Vacuum sealed hot water for tea, coffee or chocolate. Bottled water. Hydration is of prime importance. This next item you can only get from outdoor supply centres...'

Galway John lifted out a small rectangular plain white packet.

'White chocolate?' asked Tommie.

'Heavens, no! White chocolate raises your risk of heart disease. No anti-oxidants and full of fats! White chocolate is butter, milk and sixty percent sugar. This, this... is one hundred percent purity!'

Padraig said to Fred. 'Do you hear that? *One hundred percent purity!*'

'Cake?' asked Leon.

'Kendal mint cake,' said Bob.

'Open it up. Just one square of this provides a pure energy source. It's what Edmund Hillary used on the first successful ascent of Everest. It is also used as part of the Irish Defence Forces 24-hour ration packs.'

'It's cocaine,' said Shay.

'Looks like it,' said Padraig. 'Tastes like... Type 2 diabetes! Mwah-ha-hahaha!'

'It provides a rush of carbohydrates,' said Galway John.

The fire's smoke changed direction, pushing relentlessly at Eoghan, Daniel and Joe, who coughed and coughed. Daniel drank from the cup he had with him, and Galway John nodded with approval.

Levin said, 'Were you in the mountain rescue, John?'

'Oh, no. One of the few services I was not employed in.'

'He used to work the traffic lights,' said Cat.

'Installation and maintenance,' said Galway John proudly..

'Tell me this then. Why is it I am only two steps on the road when the green man disappears?' asked Padraig.

'Well young Padraig, in times gone by the pedestrian light signalled the right of way, extending by proxy until the walker had completed their journey.'

'Not round here,' said Leon.

'Why does the red man come up then?'

'Bureaucrats and their policies, Kiera. Elements I had no control over, sorry to say.'

Tommie put his hand round his lighter and sparked it three times.

'Traffic lights were originally gas-lit. They were invented in Westminster, in 1868, by a man called Lester Wire.'

'Did you know him?' asked Padraig cheekily.

Bob sneezed.

'Bless you,' said Mary.

'Isn't it true that, originally, they didn't have the colour yellow?'

'That's right, Cat. Not until the 1920s,' said Galway John.

Levin informed them, 'In the future traffic lights will be able to talk to your car: tell it what speed to go at; how many pedestrians there are.'

'Like *Knight Rider*?' asked Padraig, semi-serious.

'They'll change colour based on the amount of GPS signals,' said Levin.

Galway John shook his head. 'It'll never work. There was a traffic jam in Beijing last year. It was ninety-seven kilometres long. Think about that. Over sixty miles of vehicles.'

Eoghan said, 'I remember reading people were selling food and water to drivers for ten times the usual price.'

Shay asked Galway John if he'd ever hot-wired a car. He said no, but explained how he'd recalibrated his trailer with a four flat plug and by splicing ground wires for lights and brakes. Tommie nodded emphatically as he talked about test-lights and volt-meters.

Kiera asked about Galway's other jobs. He talked about the stationery warehouse where he was a union rep and his time with Northern Ireland Gas. He didn't like the road diggers. Said they were the road mafia, and they thought they ran the country.

Bronagh arrived at rant's end and Tommie brought out a chair for her.

'Am I too late for the teach-in?'

'Galway John used to be a pub landlord,' said Kiera

'Oh, that was a lovely little spot. Just outside Bicester, before it became a retail park. I was my own boss until the building was bought out from under me by some fool, completely clueless. He wanted to run it himself and sacked the lot of us. But I made some good friends there. Cathy, the first aider, with long black raven hair, and a great sense of humour. Arsalan, a massive fellow who managed the nature reserve, and then there was…'

Two days later, and Padraig followed Bronagh into *The Windmill*, a belt-and-braces greasy spoon ten minutes walk from the camp. It was always packed full, and chaotic, but it was hard for the waitresses to miss Bronagh. She ordered two Ulster Frys and a pot of tea. Padraig's legs shook under the table. The light at the window beside him was already gone. He rubbed at the three stains at the top of his jeans, partly to keep moving.

'So c-cold.'

'Tonight should be interesting,' said Bronagh as she checked her makeup in a hand mirror. '*Downtown Radio. DTR.* Never mind the BBC. All those great names: Eamonn Holmes,

Big T, Candy Devine. Doesn't matter who you are, everyone in this country listens to Downtown. So tell me, what did I miss at the GA?'

Padraig shrugged. 'Hardly any regulars were there. Ach. They need flyers for the Coke action tomorrow.'

'That's a bit short notice. I'll see about it. Why are we protesting Coke?'

'Beats me. Eoghan said something about pollution. Someone was meant to ring you.'

The back of Bronagh's chair shook. She turned and took a good hard stare at the back of someone's head. Servers seemed to climb over diners. Every table was a conference, chair legs scraping and cutlery clanging. The tea arrived. Bronagh opened the pot and gave it a good stir.

'So now they want my help, but last week I was told to keep my nose out of it. I'm sick of it to tell the truth.'

'Who said that?'

'Eoghan. Not in so many words, but more or less. Tea? I tell you Padraig, I pull my weight, more than my weight, and I get the impression I'm not wanted.'

'Ah that's rubbish. Eoghan... he works hard but he's bloody single minded.'

'When Leon dragged Bob onto the Trojan Show, and Eoghan tried to show him up? Scandalous!'

'He's been a bit of a dick to me since we got back from Dublin last week. Though he's worked really hard getting more people involved in the camp.'

'Well we should all be involved in talking to these people. Then there's Cat. Oh, she's right cheeky.'

'The smurf's all over the place.'

'The smurf?'

'Cat. Cos her hair's blue. She's just stressed. Levin's helping her start up the teach-ins again. That'll chill her out.'

'It's more than that. She's always talking about someone behind their back. God knows what she says about me. She seems to have it in for me. I take people as I find them.'

A plate smashed in the kitchen. The diner quietened for a few seconds, before the noise rose louder than before.

'See Bronagh, it's only the full timers are active on group actions.'

'Full timers?'

'Like Daniel and me and Bob. Campers. And the likes of you and Gary who are regulars. Actually Gary's more of a part-timer lately. Problem is some full-timers are totally clueless, like Paul, because they've nowhere else to go. And Mary, Joe and Tommie all have jobs too.'

Bronagh took a sip of hot tea. 'Daniel's a nice lad.'

'He is. Good bloke. I think he was a bit rattled by those cops on Monday. I heard him tell Galway John there were some problems with his visa when he moved to the UK. He's here legally, mind.'

'Ah. Poor fella. Asks nothing of no-one. Tell me something, Padraig. The strike is less than a week away, and I've not seen Gary since Saturday.'

'He's trying to drum up support for the next election. Fair enough, he's been talking about the strike and the camp when he's going door-to-door. Problem is, half the women in West Belfast have a crush on him. Mwah-ha-hahaha!'

'I can imagine. Thanks,' she said, when two steaming hot all-day breakfasts were sat down in front of them.

'Cheers, love. I'm famished!' exclaimed Padraig. He lifted his knife and fork and attacked his bacon and eggs, before shovelling them into his mouth.

'Could we have a top up of hot water for the tea, please? Ta. Oh that does look good.'

'Suhduh brud's cholesterol ecstacy,' said Padraig.

'We all need to come together for the strike,' said Bronagh.

'Right. Und thur's lots to do. Nuh punt squbblung whun thuh country's buhund us!'

Seven hours later the fog gathered at the street light. Underneath it was parked a black *Downtown Radio* broadcast van. The logo was mixed case and italics in white and red. From the camp's metal bin came arms of orange flames reaching up over the rim two feet high. There were nearly thirty people there, gathered around Tommy Sands. Sands had long white hair and blue eyes and wore a brown leather jacket bearing the words *'Hate is not a strategy.'* On the back it read *'I will not dishonour my soul with hatred but I will offer myself to heaven as an architect of peace.'* His voice was tender, and calming.

'We're gathered around a fire that's really beginning to brighten up here in Occupy Belfast... and rosy cheeks are beginning to appear now on hitherto coldish faces: Terry, Michelle, Mary, Gerardy, Mick, Jim, John, Bronagh, Joel, Dee, Sadie, Bob and many more, and each will be giving us a piece of philosophy or a poem. You may hear a guitar in the background. We're going to have some music and song. The wind is lapping on the side of the tent, you might hear that. And there's a little pigeon there, reading the chalkboard which says 'Day 33.' Well done. He, or maybe she, is impressed too. Levin, that's a good warm fire. What's in that fire?'

'It's a mixture of charcoal, smokeless fuel, and wood. It's been keeping us warm so far. We try to keep the amount of wood down because the smoke can get really horrific sometimes.'

'Tell me, how many are here permanently at the moment?'

'Thirty? Thirty plus figures. We have twenty-one tents here now. Some of us are sharing. In the last few days we've had four new members. The numbers keep going up. It's accelerating.'

'There's a man coming in out of the cold. He's got a cap on his head which is a good idea on an evening like this. Why did you come here?' asked Tommy.

John said, 'I came here because the Occupy movement, as far as I can see, is the only thing addressing the problems of the working class at the present time. We're just doing what we can.'

Sands didn't stay too long on any one person: live vox pops in a tapestry, flowing easily from person to person.

Katrina said, 'For years I knew the system wasn't right. I was recently made homeless and came to camp three days ago. It's everything I stand for. The stuff that I had to go through, I didn't have a safe environment. This is everything. This is right.'

'I imagine people who don't have a home to go would find a certain hopefulness here with people who care about what's going on,' said Tommy.

Shelby barked at that.

'There's a dog. Would he bite?' asked Tommy.

'This is our leader,' said Fred.

They laughed.

Steph said, 'The system we live in is completely unjust. One percent of the population are pulling the strings. We are engaged in a quest for equality and change in the system. It's not just one city, not just one country, it's a global movement.'

'I see a sign there that reads, *New York, Belfast, Rome, Berlin.* Are you in touch with the groups in other cities around the world?'

Leon said, 'We've visited people in Dublin and Galway and gotten shout-outs from Portland and New York as well.'

Tommy prompted Eoghan to take up the guitar. He'd made something up the night before, strummed to the tune of *House of the Rising Sun,* and Levin and Fred sang along.

'There is a tent in Writer's Square
They call the Occupy
Where many a man will stand up
Solidarity to the day they die.'

The brief performance was followed by clapping and calls of 'yee-oh!' Tommy prompted one of the full-timers, earnest and passionate Barry to talk about what the movement meant to him.

'I arrived here three or four weeks ago. I was very intrigued and I wanted to know the full ins and outs about it. These one percent of bankers are tearing everything apart. What damage it's doing to the communities! What damage it's doing to the children! The poverty. It's a disgrace, a literal disgrace, and I stand up for the rights of the Occupy movement and I will stand until we get a reform of the government and a change to the policies that we have.'

Everybody around him whooped and hollered.

'There seems to be people here from all sides, and from every walk of life in a sense,' said Tommy.

'There's an agreement that you leave your politics at the door,' said Monty. 'It doesn't matter if you're Protestant, Catholic, male, female, white, black.'

Eoghan said, 'Exactly! None of that matters. We're here to support Occupy at Wall Street and everywhere else: in Egypt, people in Libya and Syria.'

'I'm sure people are curious. What do they say to you?'

Tommie Murphy answered him. 'It's universally supported. The support we've got is just humbling. It's unbelievable. I never expected it. They're driving and they see us, and they toot their horns. They find wood or biscuits or something.'

'It's such an exciting time globally. Everyone knows they're in the same struggle,' said Hanita.

'Sometimes whenever you're here and you're wet and you're cold, it's a long time since you've had a proper night's sleep, it really lifts your spirits to know there's other people supporting you,' said Cat.

'People are optimistic there's some really big change just around the corner,' said Fred.

'There's a certain sense of democracy about how you operate here. Eoghan, you said you already did plenty of interviews and you wanted to share the experience with newer people coming in. What sort of structure do you have here? Padraig?'

'We've got the general nightly meetings, our assemblies,

where we make our decisions, and the elected co-ordinators. The community has guidelines and rules.'

'Eoghan, you did some singing for us earlier. Could you give us another?'

Eoghan sang his rendition of David Rovics's *Behind the Barricades*. Tommy joined in for the last lines.

'The more we hold each other up the less we can be swayed, here's to love and solidarity, and a kiss behind the barricades.'

Calls came from all around the campsite.

'Well done!'

'Well done!'

Katrina read her poem. It was rhyming couplets, full of emotive vulnerability. It was real, sentimental and conveyed desperation. It was optimistic, and indestructible. It was followed by applause and wolf whistles. Everyone managed to find something different to say.

'The expenses scandal, the dodgy dossiers, the duck pond thing? It's disgusting,' said Leon.

'There's absolutely no need for mass poverty in the world. Thirteen billion could end world hunger but globally bank bail-outs are forty trillion. I mean... *what?*' asked Cat.

'Over two thousand cities and they're all pulling for the same thing,' said Bronagh. 'The idea that you can pass on austerity to people for the crisis you've caused... it's an absolute crime.'

'We're giving hope to people. I think it's hit something,' said Joe.

'There's a great sense of friendship here,' noted Tommy.

Levin agreed. 'It's unbelievable.'

'Friendship and solidarity,' said Tommy.

'Absolutely. We are brothers and sisters here,' said Levin.

Shelby barked at that.

The last bars of Pete Seeger's *We Will Love or We Will Perish* played, and Tommy gently repeated the last lines.

'Dare to touch, dare to danger. Dare to touch the hand of a stranger.'

They talked: of the Iraq war demonstrations, the biggest the UK had seen; and the coming strike, the biggest in British and Irish history. They talked of how Occupy was made up of people of all ages, and from all parts.

'We're making a difference here and now,' said Bob.

'Here's people that are willing to give up everything in their lives,' said Levin. 'They're willing to leave their house with a rucksack and not know when they're coming back. For a crazy hope that one day the world's going to get better.'

'We're not talking about dismantling capitalism or what we're going to change the future into,' said Eoghan. 'But we know that at the start of this century, by defining it here and now so that when our great grand-kids come around the system is much better, much fairer for them, then we will have won. We won't see any victories for years but… if this movement's going where I think it's going, it's got to be a good place.'

'We got to start somewhere,' said Padraig.

'We got to start somewhere,' said Eoghan, and everyone was clapping again.

'You heard Dick Gaughan with Your *Daughters and Your Sons*, and with the wind flapping on the tented walls here and the fire crackling in the grate of a small, black reddening stove we go leave our newfound friends in Occupy Belfast, warming the cold and brightening the darkness of a Belfast November, 2011. From me Tommy Sands: oiche mhaith, goodnight.'

19

On Royal Avenue, beneath McDonalds' yellow arches stained by time and the city, shoppers walked around the leafleters. Eoghan gave a twirl, showing off the brown leather jacket which Tommy Sands had given to him. Levin reminded Eoghan he hadn't stopped talking about it. Their leaflets bore the logo for Coca-Cola with a bar across it. Few wanted to know about the company's links to Guatemalan death squads.

'We'd have more joy selling five lighters for a pound,' said Eoghan.

'Coca-Cola linked to the droughts in India! Sir? Ma'am?'

'Boycott Coke!'

'Standing here's putting me in the mood for a milkshake,' complained Levin.

'I don't blame you. One of my earliest, happiest memories is from McDonald's. My dad took me on a long car drive and we stopped, and he came back with this strawberry shake as thick as glue. It seemed to last forever,' said Eoghan.

Friday's lunchtime shoppers changed their routes. A large man waved them away. A track-suited young spide – his hand in his trousers feeling his balls – limped by and swung open the doors.

'I've been in McDonald's five times: once for a Big Mac, two visits to the lavvy, including just now, and twice leafleting for unionisation,' said Levin.

'Remember the McLibel trial?'

'Of course. Longest running libel case in English law.'

'For a flyer claiming Ronald McDonald was responsible

for deforestation, and animal cruelty. *Duhhhh!* Like it isn't at all obvious.'

'Right. The European court overturned the verdict because our own justice system is too corporate and corrupt to do it themselves.'

'Coke in Mexico: fraud; exploitation; diabetes!'

A woman with six bags passed by. Her rebellious child took a flyer from Eoghan's hand. Five minutes later the two men had had enough and crossed the road to Poundland, where Bronagh and Shay were leafleting. In the front window stood a tall cut-out of a policeman, a cardboard scarecrow for shoplifters. Eoghan pushed the flyer against the glass where it stood.

'Officer, aren't you going to investigate Coca-Cola's links to kidnappings in Colombia?' he said.

'Explain to me again about the Supreme Court,' said Shay.

'Which one?' asked Eoghan. 'Coke's been brought up to loads of them. In America, India…'

'Get a job!' scowled some old sulk on her way into the shop.

Eoghan called after her. 'What about Coke's twelve hour work-days in Hangzhou? Prick!'

'Boycott Coke,' called Bronagh. 'End their use of child labour! It's a disgrace!'

They offered flyers to people from all walks of life. An elderly woman offered a leaflet exchange: she learned of Coca-Cola's links to the Turkish Special Branch in acts of torture; Levin received a pamphlet on the good news of accepting the Lord Jesus Christ as his saviour.

Shay danced and sang as he offered the flyers around. 'Better think once, better think twice, they're gonna find out who's naughty or nice, Supreme Court is coming… to Coke!'

On the other side of the city was Custom House Square. A pavilion as bleak and empty as Writer's Square, it was lit up by bright fairy lights lining the borders of the red Coca-Cola truck. There was a merchandise stand. Adults and children lined up for freebies. A roulette wheel offered one in five a free bottle of pop. They paid little attention to Leon and Cat with their packs of leaflets flapping in the wind.

'Eight spoonfuls of sugar in each can,' cried Leon, parroting the words on Joe's placard. 'God, I'm dying for a piss.'

The ten activists stood in a huddle: Daniel, Kiera, Fred, Miriam from Queen's University, and Filipe, the tall Polish newcomer. Padraig was with them, his 'Boycott Coke' placard lowered to the paving.

'See, Kiera, I'm not like you. I've got the stamina to keep going. I don't run home any time I can't hack it,' he said.

'Oh. So you won't want me to wash your clothes. I hear you,' she said.

Leon joined them and with Fred looked up to Albert Clock: it was a quarter to four. The clock was famed for its lean, and infamous for prostitutes meeting sailors in bygone years. Daniel looked the other way, out to The Big Fish, a mosaic sculpture at the edge of the River Lagan. Cat walked towards the huddle.

'Do you think you might try to make an effort?' she asked.

'I'm not sure what we're actually protesting,' said Kiera.

Cat was gobsmacked. 'Did no one do any research?'

Joe shrugged. 'These flyers don't really tell us much. *Collusion with death squads. Drought. Fraud.* What do we tell people?'

'Right. Eoghan set this up. I haven't a clue what this all means,' said Padraig.

'Okay. So I'm hearing only Leon and I know why we're doing this?' said Cat.

'Ahhh,' said Leon. 'It's... not really my area?'

'Sorry. I thought yous would tell me,' said Miriam.

Cat fumed. 'Well that's just great. You know, I really feel nobody cares about the work I put in.'

'No. That's not true,' said Kiera.

'It's nothing personal. I just don't like work,' said Padraig. 'And Fred, he's a lazy bastard.'

Fred began to nod, but slowly stopped as he comprehended Padraig's words.

'Hang on,' said Leon. 'We support the teach-ins.'

'You do, and Levin does, but no-one else does. Unless it's to take the piss.'

'I've been helping with the admin. And Eoghan too,' said Leon.

Cat glared at her, seemingly ready to erupt.

'I think you're still taking too much on, Cat,' said Kiera.

A tree rustled as the wind blew hard sending splattering rain their way.

'Maybe you should talk it out in the meeting. Get some help,' said Fred.

'Yeah,' said Cat coolly. 'Right. Excuse me, I've something I have to do. See you later.'

She handed Leon the flyers and walked away. Kiera followed her.

'She's probably on the rag,' said Padraig fondly.

Miriam shot him a look of disgust. Leon hit him a hard smack with the flyers across the back of his head.

'You're on the rag,' said Fred.

The coal fire was stinking. Bob brushed loose tobacco threads off his jacket. He tilted his cap and looked up to grey clouds sailing over stars. Earlier that day the council had brought them a large metallic dumpster for general waste, and one with a green lid for recyclables. The rumbles of their arrival woke him up, so he was no happier. The coming strike would bring great numbers to the campsite and plenty of reasons for him to be anxious. Galway John held a piping mug in each hand. He gave one to Bob, and sat down beside him. Fred watched Eoghan, who explained the chords on his guitar one by one.

'Well the bins seem to have led away that bluebottle.

Young Leon nicknamed it Dovid Vonce. No Thomas to join us tonight?' Galway asked.

'Working. All weekend. Boss gave him a warning over missed shifts,' said Bob.

'Now listen how it all comes together,' said Eoghan. He began to sing and strum. *'Friday nights and the lights are low... to Austerity Occupy says noooo...'*

'Has anyone seen Cat?' asked Fred.

'She's not around. She's learned she has a stalker,' said Bob.

Eoghan looked across to Bob and let out a tight lipped grin, erasing it before he turned back to Fred.

'What? Who?' said Fred, panicked.

'Ignore him, young Fred. Mr. Barr is in mischievous form,' said Galway.

Fred gazed out past the fire and saw Cat, by the sculpture of the Spanish volunteer, coming in off the street.

'Anybody could occupy... Night is young and the camp is drry...'

'Eoghan, down a notch,' warned Bob. 'Don't make me break your guitar.'

Galway laughed. 'It sounds like it's already broken.'

Fred got up and walked towards Cat. She was hunkered down, unzipping the front of her dome tent. 'Hey Cat.'

She didn't look up.

'I was reading in the Telegraph about the education cuts.'

'Yeah. Shameful.'

'I'm glad you're organising the teach-ins again.'

'The teach-ins are dead,' said Cat, and she climbed inside.

'Everyone loved John's one on Tuesday, and isn't Tommie doing a talk on security next week?'

'Fred, I don't want to talk about it.' She zipped up the tent behind her.

'If you're having problems, maybe we could sit down

with Kiera and --'

'Goodnight Fred.'

In the marquee, Eoghan yawned a long, guttural rattle and said he'd go to bed. They wished one another good night. The wind blew a stinging plume of coal and wood smoke right in their eyes. Galway flapped his arms to steer it away.

'Cat was near sobbing,' said Fred quietly as he re-took his seat. 'She said there'd be no more teach-ins. What the fuck?'

Galway John was concerned. 'I know she was upset that I'm departing for Dumfries but that would hardly be it.'

'She's her knickers in a knot because the sugar-daddy is leaving her for some Scottish schoolmistress,' said Bob.

'Janey is my sister. Her house is in need of structural repair and she can't take time off work. If I can be there to accommodate the situation, I will.'

'Now,' said Bob. 'With the more experienced man out of the way, it's time for you to swoop in, young Fred.'

A whoosh hit the gazebo. The side flaps punished the pole repeatedly. The low-hanging ceiling slobbered out a fat stream of rainwater onto the concrete. The fire bin shook violently, nearly overturning. Bob sprung to action. He put his boot to the edge of the base, nudging the metal bin inwards. It caught on the paving. He extended his sleeve over his hand, and pushed. He screamed.

'FUCK!'

'*Cryin' out loud man!*' Galway snatched up oven gloves, ran out, and shunted the hot metal bin toward him.

The bin was out of the wind trap when another strong gust hit them hard. The pool of water remaining on the marquee roof swam back, and forward. It fell, splashing on their shoulders. Water trickled down Bob's back and along his arse and down to his knees. He took off his cap, and squeezed it dry.

Shay had the best sleep a lad could have. The firm pillows and mattress rejuvenated him. He awoke at eight to a knock on the door of the spare room. Bronagh asked first if he was decent.

When he replied he was she entered and set a cup of tea down on the bedside table. Shay was to come down for breakfast when he was ready. The tea was perfect.

Bronagh's was a proud home: clean patterned duvets and fresh bed linens; the bathroom fittings shone and signs spread inspirational homilies; family photographs in silver frames were glimpsed passing the couple's bedroom door; no dust mote in the narrow stairway and the living room window was open, illuminating the gold-patterned wallpaper. He walked beyond the sofa to the table at the end of the room. It had on it a couple of plates, glasses, cutlery, a carton of pure orange and a butter tray. The air was hot with the scent of scrambled eggs.

They ate there from full plates.

'I slept fantastic, Bronagh. Is Brian away already?'

'Brian was out to work at five this morning. You probably didn't hear him, he's as quiet as a field-mouse. Do you want me to put you on more toast?'

'One more, yes please,' he said.

She got up and put on two rounds. 'How long have you been homeless, Shay?'

Shay finished chewing his little egg and toast envelope. 'You don't beat around the bush do you?'

'I do not. Did you have no place to go until the camp arrived?'

'I didn't have anywhere for eleven months. It's not so bad. Mates let me stay on their sofas. Sometimes I'm sleeping on the carpet. Better than the concrete.'

Bronagh held the kettle under the tap, timing the flow to finish before Shay began to answer her question. 'And how long did that last? Sleeping on sofas?'

'A few weeks with Boone, and Leo. A few nights with others. I don't want to impose on people. I've been back to my mum's a few times.'

'Is she not worried sick?'

'We don't really get on.'

'I would think she'd want to see you.'

Shay shrugged. 'Ach. She knows I've friends who help me out.'

Bronagh stared at the pale, slim lad, with his flowing hair and easy-going expression. Displeased, she shook her head. 'A mother's love is never ending, Shay. Did you say you were staying at a shelter?'

'Yeah. I spent some time at *Centenary House*. I'd see Daniel there, not to talk to. And Tall Paul and Shitty John.'

'You shouldn't call him that. I've been meaning to get Daniel up in the spare room.'

'He'd like that. Bob too.'

Bronagh raised an eyebrow. 'Was Bob in a shelter?'

'Nah. He told me, but don't say I said. The same day the camp set up, he got home to find an eviction notice nailed to the front door. Turned out the letting agency went bankrupt.'

'And they put him out on the street?' asked Bronagh, incredulous.

The toast popped up. She glanced over but ignored it and paid careful attention to Shay speaking against the rising noise of the kettle.

'They gave him thirty days notice. It would have been repossessed last week. I asked why he didn't sit it out. He said he'd not give them the satisfaction. He took the keys with him too. Said it was a two-bedroom place, about this sort of size. *Here, Bob's still got the keys! We could turn it into a squat!*'

Bronagh facepalmed. 'Oh dear high heavens, saints save us! What am I going to do with you lot?'

Saturday was a bright day, blue skies with cream clouds. Once again they walked to the dirty green copper dome centred over Belfast City Hall. *'BANKS & CORPORATIONS CORRUPTED POLITICAL PROCESS'* on one placard and another read, *'End the Greed, Invest in the 99%'*. Gary spoke at the gates, and then Eoghan, framed by the three columns over the front door, and the triangular gable above.

The Cathedral was set in its brightest beige showing its off splendour of palisades and archways, watched by Luke the busker as he sang *Ain't No Military Son*. Underneath, the ground was dry and clean, the trees unashamed. Tents of colour, weathered by other times, sat in the sun with purpose and cool. A board fixed on the railings read, *'APATHY IS VIOLENT. STRIKE! OCCUPY! THINK!'* in tidy black handwriting, and the ferns peeked out from underneath it.

Kiera and Cat had taken £15 from petty cash and returned from the cheap shops with markers, paints, brushes, card and glue. The placard art workshop was a great success across all age groups. The many results would feature at Wednesday's National Strike, and replenish the camp as many previous signs were wilting.

'No More Bailouts. There Is A Solution: Occupy Belfast'
'We Are Many'
'Just another brick in Wall Street'
'Occupy Now.'
'You Better Occupy.'
'This is What Democracy Looks Like'
'End Wanker's bonuses'
'Oh Go On'
'We Have a Duty To Disobey Unjust Law'
'I love you'
'Baby, baby, they're ain't no fortune in war, yeah.'
'Revolution Starts Here!'

They were lettered in a variety of colours, sometimes on the same placard. Kiera noticed some painters put in more detail than others. Eoghan's was a prime example:

'Facts From This World:
- (In red) More than 2 billion people live in extreme poverty with an income less than $1 per day (1 in 3 people worldwide)
- 400 people own the equivalent of half the world's wealth
- (In blue) 1.02 bn. people are suffering from chronic, permanent

malnutrition, which 16bn are overweight
- (In red) *Over 10m children under 5 die every year from malnutrition*
- (In blue) *Every 3rd human is forced to drink contaminated water from which 3m people die per year*
- *12% of the world consume 85% of the world's clean drinking water*
- *£800bn (57% of annual global expenditure) would be enough for access to basic education, sufficient nutrition and drinking water'*

However, Shay created Kiera's favourite signage:

'*Free eye cheqs
for the unem
ployed are at
risk do so
mething
argh!'*

A band of pigeons walked round and round the new signs reading each letter with interest.

Almost everyone was happy to be there, with exceptions. A gammon-coloured two-toed sloth on the street yelled at them to get a job, setting Eoghan off on a tremendous rant in Cat's ear.

'No job? No job? Mary works at the hospital. Joe's part-time at the car wash. Tommie and Sean are at *Brown's*. I'm pretty sure Daniel's starting as a kitchen porter. You and Kiera and Jack are students. Bronagh works at a college and Deirdre doesn't sit still for a minute!'

There was a snooty local blogger who took photos and drew Bob's ire. The tension between them worsened as Bob listened to the man audio-record his reportage.

'*Occupy Belfast's Carnival of Resistance 5: Signs of the Times* is devoid of the vibrancy of their previous features and fails entirely as a trailer for the forthcoming National Strike.'

He didn't stay for long.

There was the wide-eyed young man who sat in the marquee. He described himself as an online commentator, though he refused to name anywhere he was published. He described himself as a libertarian and told them Occupy's ideas were all fragmented.

'What do you mean?' Levin asked.

'Well one minute it's education, and the next minute three or four of you are talking about nursing. Or then you want parliamentary reform.'

'Mwa-ha-ha-ha. What?'

'Silly me. Your stance on teaching conflicts with my goals about providing for the National Health Service budget,' snarked Leon

'Banking reform is more important,' said Padraig, and he gave her a toy-punch on the arm.

'What about press reform?' said Levin, and he toy-punched Padraig.

The sky was darkening. Gary approached, giving Levin the nod. He went out to the path and announced the teach-in on the banking crisis was beginning. The libertarian commentator left. Daniel pulled spare chairs from the rear marquee.

'Sorry, Gary. Don't take it personally but I'm going to have to pass on the teach-in. I'm not in the mood for a lecture and I really need a kebab,' said Padraig.

'We'll be getting tubs from *Brown's* after,' said Fred

'I can't hack eating that same shit every night. Coming?'

'Are you paying?'

The visitors arrived by the marquee, numbering two dozen by the time they gathered: Dee, Joel, Jack and others. Bronagh watched Padraig go and she asked Fred about him, who complained that the 'fucker wouldn't even offer to share his meal.' The fire bin was streaming the tears off their eyes, and Joe moved it away.

Kiera nipped into the last free seat. 'Hey, where's Cat?'

Joe answered. 'She took one of those police forms to the library to photocopy. Said she was going to work ahead on the other ones.'

'We don't need one for next weekend. Sure, it's Human Rights Day. It's filed for,' stated Eoghan.

'Okay so, the financial crisis of 2008,' said Gary, 'The crisis was caused by a market that overpriced mortgages and bonds, and in turn, the security this gave them.'

Shay put out the palms of his hands. 'Okay. Slow down. Slow down. What are bonds?'

'You shee,' said Eoghan, affecting the tones of Sean Connery, 'the bondsh are like an IOU with a contract; a license to bill, one might shay.'

'It's money Shay,' said Bronagh.

'Although bonds come with conditions,' said Gary. 'They're based on fixed incomes and are traded differently. For example, Fred knows he's getting a fiver a week for ten weeks. He sells that assurance to Levin and Levin, if he needs cash quick, can offer to sell it on to Leon based on how valuable he thinks that IOU might be.'

Leon shook her head. A few of them laughed.

'Okay, bad example,' said Gary.

'You shee,' said Eoghan-as-Connery, 'the document shtatesh – if Fred doeshn't pay it back – whether it'll be a cashe of lashersh... or sharksh.'

'Literally, it was sharks. Lehman's was thought to be too big to fail,' said Gary.

'Like The Titanic,' said Bob.

'But without the commemorative key rings,' said Miriam.

'They were completely unregulated. Nothing was certified,' said Gary.

'But how did this happen? There were rules, right? I know banks have loads of fine print,' said Kiera.

'I tried to open a Co-Op bank account the other week. They wanted to know if I had shares in British Gas, North Sea oil and arctic drilling, mink fur, arms companies, nuclear arms companies... it was a really long list,' said Levin.

'Bear Stearns operated for ninety years; Lehman's, a hundred and fifty. People just assumed they were professionals. They're bundling up all these IOUs as if, well... take the example of Fred's £50 bond. There's interest and it's exaggerated so word goes around Fred's going to repay £200. And so is Levin. And Shay. And Kiera. And off the back of that £800, or a grand, the wee lady up the road will lend you five grand.'

'I've got eleven pence in my pocket,' said Fred.

Gary smiled. 'That's relevant. Thank you, Fred. That's exactly the point. This all operated on false collateral. A false economy.'

Bronagh said, 'And then you throw into the mix other types of securities: stocks; shares...'

'Foreign exchange. Derivatives claiming assets,' said Levin.

'Much of it speculative. Poor mortgages --'

'Sorry Gary. You still haven't answered my question. How did this happen? How did they --'

'They were blasé, Kiera. It was all risk, risk, risk. They were addicted to it.'

'Global trading between states and mega-corps was going unchecked every day,' said Leon.

Eoghan chimed in. 'At that level, the failure was catastrophic. It's like lots of deadly volcanoes going off and in no time Europe's economy was destroyed. And Russia's, North and South America, all over.'

'What do they mean by the Celtic Tiger?' asked Filipe.

Joe explained. 'In the decade before the crash, the South was going through genuine rapid growth in transport, education, information and communications technologies. The Republic of Ireland was matching the Asian markets. But even in among all that genuine growth, you had these imagined resources.'

'It was a boom and so the sudden downturn was that much harder,' said Gary. 'The Republic was one of the worst affected areas, but the stories there are the same as all over the world. People had their homes taken away from them. One in every six or seven lost their jobs. Folks had to leave one another and emigrate to find new jobs. Literally, kids out on the streets, begging.'

'And it happened because instead of addressing the street level problems, governments stepped in and funded those who caused the massive problems,' said Joel.

Gary nodded. 'With our taxes. And so the cycle continues: pay freezes and public cuts, personal debt and poverty. To be continued.'

Sunlight stroked the tents camouflaging the rains that would beat them cruelly from west to south. The wind dropped speed and the cathedral bells rang again. The skies cleared, and reverted to their usual greyness. Bob was ensconced in his *Sunday Mirror,* until he heard their footsteps. The pages fell slack and he peered out over the masthead. The two police officers arrived in industrial boots and padded service jackets with attached radios. Their heads were raised tall and Eoghan stood up to draw level with them.

'What are you two protesting about anyway?' asked Eoghan.

Sergeant Barker gave a deep hearty laugh. Constable Corbett seemed confused.

'Bob, what are you doing working on the Lord's Day?' said Barker.

'Somebody's got to get these blighters into their worker's paradise,' he grumbled.

'Ah sure God doesn't exist,' said Corbett, and quickly added, 'Sorry. Sorry. That's not my place to say.'

'I should think not,' said Barker. He spied the tin whistle in Shay's hand and said, 'I hope you have a public performance license for that, young man.'

Barker was joking but Shay put it away and brought his earphones and CD player out of his pocket. Corbett's smile dropped and he sniffed. A pigeon walked from the chalkboard towards him.

'Cup of tea?' asked Bob.

'We better not. It's just a flying visit to see how you're all doing. Some nice new placards I see,' replied Barker.

Cat lifted her head up. 'There's two dozen more out the back. All the community came around to paint them, but Bob won't let us put them out.'

'Because the ones that are out are a mess,' he said.

'Sergeant Barker, where you aware the cost of policing has gone up 25% in the last decade?' Eoghan asked.

'Blair Gibbs, London School of Economics,' said Constable Corbett.

'Yes, thank you, Stanley.'

'And yet, the government have announced a 20% cut to your wages,' said Eoghan.

'And the resources we have to do the job,' said Corbett.

Barker sighed. 'Where is all this going?'

'When the nation goes on strike on Wednesday, it'll be for your jobs. You should probably join us,' said Eoghan.

'The law forbids serving police officers from marching or striking,' said Barker.

'I thought it was worth an ask. The last time I was at Musgrave, I saw a flyer for our camp on the noticeboard. I wondered who put it there,' said Eoghan.

'That's been taken down now. I'm afraid we can't get involved in the political aspect of this. Police policy is not to discuss these things. We're here to enforce the law,' said Barker. Then he drew in close, his broom moustache almost touching Eoghan's ear and he whispered, 'But between you and me son, those criminals in Westminster should be in front of a judge facing life sentences at Belmarsh and I'd arrest them myself if I could get close enough.'

Barker drew away, all smiles, and said, 'Well if everything's in order we'll be moving along then!'

Bob stood up and addressed him. 'Actually there is something you can do for us. A couple of officers came by the other week. No damage done but they were a bit heavy handed with their approach. I wondered if you'd heard anything?'

'What did they look like?' asked Barker.

'Full riot gear. Both fairly large. Daniel, you got a close look at them.'

Daniel shrugged, as if he'd never been there.

Bob tutted and shook his head. He tapped Shay on the shoulder. Shay took out his earphones.

'He wants to know about the officers last week. Remember when you had the chalks out?'

'Those guys… they were large. Yeah, large.'

'That's a big help,' said Bob.

'One was smaller than the other, and he seemed to be the guy in charge,' said Shay.

'Did he have a moustache like mine? Big broad chin, and muscles?' said Barker.

Shay nodded.

Barker rubbed his moustache and ran his finger over his lip. 'And did the other one have a fat face and three chins?' he asked.

'Aye, he did.'

Barker informed them, 'That sounds like our super, Inspector Barnabas Tarbard. And his junior, Constable Klaus Louse.'

'Oh, they're terrible men. Absolutely terrible,' said Corbett.

'Makes our lives a living hell. He's full of shit and the man has his head stuck up his own backside,' said Barker.

'His name was in a report on brutality that someone leaked to the press last year,' said Corbett.

'He's not too fond of you lot either. Wants yous gone. It wasn't helped yesterday when he found a poster for Occupy Belfast taped to the front of his locker,' said Barker, staring accusingly at Corbett.

Corbett looked up to the sky where a half dozen swallows were circling. 'Oh, look at those birds. Aren't they beautiful?' he said.

Cat put her hand up and got to her feet. 'Oh! We've got some 11/1 forms here! Would you mind?'

'Sure. Give them to me and I'll make sure they're filed where Tarbard can see them,' said Barker.

'Where the sun don't shine?' asked Bob with a smile and a twinkle in his eye.

20

It was Monday evening, forty-two hours before the National Strike. The associated anxieties earlier that day led to an unpleasant mood around the camp. Bronagh and Eoghan, especially, were at each other's throats. Eoghan accused her of digging into his business and talking about him behind his back. Bronagh wanted everything done right away, and because it wasn't, she said there was a conspiracy against her. Shay was tired of it and quietly decided he'd couch-surf elsewhere a while. Deprived of Galway John's soothing company, Bob was at his wit's end by the time the assembly came around.

'Would you two get off each other's backs and listen to me. Come Wednesday, this place will be swamped. We need our own people acting as marshals to maintain and secure the camp. It's a mess as it is!'

'I'll give you that. But what's this about you nearly setting the camp on fire?'

'You can pick up the next bag of coal, Padraig.'

'Perhaps after this is over you should take a holiday, Bob. *An actual holiday*,' said Eoghan.

'We'll handle it,' Tommie assured them. 'First thing's Tuesday night watch. What about a three-shift rotation so all of night watch can go on the march? I'm doing my teach-in on personal security so I can take first shift.'

He'd already spent the last few days jotting down pages of notes, spending much time fussing over what he should and shouldn't include.

It wasn't just Bronagh and Eoghan's feud that was the

problem. During the GA Levin talked about the functionality of Occupy Galway and proposed they look for a building to squat in. There were some concerns and discussion morphed into moving the camp to a new location.

'What about around by Price Waterhouse Coopers?' asked Leon.

Eoghan was aghast. 'Beside the river, in the winter? With rats everywhere?'

'Utter nonsense. Are you right in the head?' said Bob.

'Have you forgotten the train tracks right beside it?' said Levin.

'We should make a statement on the eve of the strike,' said Padraig, and quite a few people warmed to that. 'Perhaps we could move right away,' he said, and quite a few people froze over.

Ten said it could work. More than a dozen said it was insane and voiced their objections at the same time.

During all of this Cat lay in her tent, face pushed into the sodden pillow, muffling the noise. She'd remained in the tent alone for most of the day and left only to get a drink and to use the toilet. She prayed the ground frost would take her.

The following morning, Eoghan stood outside her tent, and tapped on the wet green flysheet.

'Cat? Do you think you might get around to updating Facebook today? We've Tommie's talk tonight, and an announcement about the strike. I wouldn't ask, but my hands are full.'

'I'm not well, Eoghan. Would you get someone else to do it?'

He couldn't make out much through the two mesh windows, only that she was alone there.

'The only free hand we have is Padraig. When's Kiera due back?'

'I don't know.'

'Okay. Let us know if you need anything. I swear, half

the time I spend on Facebook seems to be dealing with trolls. That guy, Ginty McGinty. I suppose it's a guy. He was criticising how we organise ourselves. Said our Coke demo was a shambles: makes me wonder if it isn't someone here.'

'Leave me alone,' she said.

When he'd gone she sobbed.

She heard him argue with Padraig about it. Padraig got really cross and said he'd earned a place on the Media Team. After ten minutes of impassioned arguing back and forth, Eoghan relented and agreed.

Kiera returned later that afternoon. At first she didn't understand why Cat was sleeping so long. Her skin was pink but for black rings around her eyes. There were tissues everywhere.

'Come on. They might not deserve you, but they will. If you get out there and remind them of all the things you've done they might calm the fuck down. Maybe just go out to grab a shower? You'll feel miles better.'

Leon rapped on the tent door and peered in. She sang, 'Dreaming of a revolution.'

Cat snapped at her. 'Leon, would you just go away? Seriously, just fuck off?' Cat asked.

Kiera squeezed Cat's hand and then put her hands on her shoulders.

'Okay. Pub. Now,' she said.

Beside the marquee, the fire caught the wind and gnarled and snapped. A dozen orange tendrils warred with themselves, each spearing the grey sky, and a few lobbed burning pellets onto the slimy tiles.

Bronagh was furious with Levin. 'You want to up sticks and move the camp in the next eighteen hours to some airy-fairy location? Am I hearing that right?'

'It's a bit short notice,' murmured Daniel.

'I didn't say anything of the sort. You're blowing it all out of proportion,' said Levin.

Jack pondered the notion. 'I suppose they'd have to sit up and take notice.'

'We're all about having no hierarchy. What if we put it to the vote? Those who want to leave can leave,' said Padraig.

Eoghan crumpled up his empty *Rizla* cigarette paper packet. 'Padraig, you and Jack can leave if you want. This is bullshit.' He hurled the packet into the fire.

'For once we agree, Eoghan,' Bronagh raged. 'This is setting us up for a fall. And I notice nobody's mentioned or given a second thought to Bob, Daniel or Shay and the others whose home this is. What about all the work they've put in here?'

Shay had returned but half wished he hadn't. 'Would you mind leaving me out of this?'

'Me too,' said Bob.

'How about two camps?' Jack asked. 'This as the main one, and a smaller settlement. We're hardly in anybody's way here.'

'I don't want to be in anyone's way,' said Tall Paul in his usual subdued manner, not quite understanding the discussion.

'You're not, Paul. Why on earth do we want to get in anybody's way?'

'I don't know, Joe. I don't know why we would want to create more problems for ourselves,' said Tommie.

Fred waved his hands in agreement. No one else did.

'Could we all just cool down for a moment?' asked Levin.

'Joe, what I was trying to say is we're on the edge of the city. It's hardly the doorstep of a powerful financial institution,' said Jack.

'It'd help if you had a plan for implementing this.'

'We're not talking plans, Mary. It's just an idea,' said Jack.

Shay leaned back in his chair. 'Don't let it be a bother. I'm happy enough with whatever yous decide,' he said.

However, Eoghan was determined to be heard. 'Well God forbid we should use this time to talk with Gary or the wider community or the union leaders. Has anyone thought about that?'

Padraig interjected. 'What do we need their approval for?'

And then – for the first time – Levin lost his cool. *'This fucking talk is fucking going round and fucking round: it's going fucking nowhere!'*

'You're right,' said Bronagh. She took a deep sigh. 'How about we take this over to the pub and try to sort it out there?'

'Do that. And give my head some peace,' said Bob.

Leaving Bob, Tommie and Paul on watch, the others crossed the street. The John Hewitt was quiet, and they lined up at the bar. The staff sped into action. A few occupiers went on through to the alcove. Cat was in the corner with Kiera and Leon guarding her. Initially they barely acknowledged the others but in a few minutes the room was filled with heated debate. Kiera took a suck of her inhaler and endured the noise.

'Where are we going to have this second camp?' asked Fred.

'There's vacants all over the city,' said Levin.

'You need your bloody heads examined,' carped Bronagh.

'What about office blocks?' said Jack. 'Can we have a look at those?'

'ENOUGH!' shouted Kiera. *'Look at the state of this poor girl. Running around doing everything for you.* It's no wonder she's burned out and depressed. Not one of you besides Leon thought to check on her. No. You fucking repay her by making up more problems. Bickering over petty crap *on the night before a national strike!'*

Those entering the alcove froze, or moved very slowly. There was quiet until the girl ran out of breath to express how rubbish they all were.

Then it was Leon's turn. 'Do you want to talk about comradeship and social welfare? Well we're listening. Go on then. Tell us how we're all ready to move the camp tonight because we're all in such good fucking health!'

'Sorry, Cat,' murmured Shay.

'I thought you'd gotten help. I'm sorry I wasn't more attentive to your needs,' said Jack.

'Sorry,' said Fred.

'I know I'm in part to blame. Tell me what I can do to make it right,' pleaded Eoghan.

Cat nodded solemnly as one by one they apologised.

Levin tried to clarify matters. 'It seems to me Cat and Eoghan are doing most of the organisation. Wouldn't it be an idea to break that down, so the burden isn't only on a few people?'

Levin proposed streamlining management into teams, just like they were doing in Galway. There were already people responsible for Media, but Admin encompassed so many areas. Joe got a pen and paper from the bar and began to take note of Levin and Fred's suggestions.

'Okay, so for campaigns, a Direct Action team; Outreach, also looking after teach-ins. I think that should have some sort of mental health focus,' said Levin.

'Yeah.'

'Oh absolutely.'

Others signalled agreement with a wave of hands. Daniel mentioned an informal team had sprung up around Bob and the physical development of the camp. They called this the Construction Team. Bronagh left to get Cat and Kiera fresh pints, putting the order in just before the bar filled up. The mass of bodies in the alcove warmed them quickly and a few people took off their jackets and pullovers.

'We should have a legal team in place. There's going to be trouble from *The Man* sooner or later,' said Leon.

'Sounds fair. But what do any of us know about the law?' asked Fred.

'We can learn enough to find someone who does.'

'Aye but Cat love, we're broke,' said Shay.

'There's people who'll do it pro bono. I've got a number

somewhere. That's another thing. We're always scratching the bottom of the petty cash. Shouldn't we have a fundraising committee?'

'Write it down. Fundraising committee. I want my holiday in Ibiza. Mwah-ha-hahaha!'

In her usual blunt manner Bronagh said, 'All these committees sound all well and good but I'm worried they'll be stepping on each other's toes.'

'I've been thinking about this,' said Levin. 'We've six groups on paper. That's six nights a week. What if on the seventh night an elected representative from each group bring a report to a committees assembly? Or to the General Assembly?'

'Can I cut you off there?' asked Eoghan. 'Before we start adding people to these new groups? We should wait and do this at an assembly meeting after the strike. Are we sure we've everything in place for tomorrow?'

'It's all sorted. There's no need to do anything else,' said Cat.

Padraig threw his head back in his chair. 'Flip's sake Eoghan, would you stop worrying?'

People nipped out to the toilets, and for refills from the bar where a folk band were setting up on the small stage.

'There's a debate on fracking at Stormont next week,' announced Levin.

Leon knew of it, having heard the news from Greenpeace John and Deirdre. 'It's less of a debate, more, *we're going to bombard the Fermanagh wetlands with our big fucking dicks and we're only here to explain it's our God-given right to do so.*'

Levin unearthed the pocket notebook he'd been searching for. He scribbled down a possible anti-fracking action for Monday and made mention of the coming Saturday's demo. Cat said there was a student protest against tuition fees on the following Friday. Eoghan told them Gary was involved in that, and Miriam, who was a *Students' Union* representative at *Queen's*. Jack volunteered to reach out to her. Saturday week was International Human Rights Day. They discussed contacting Amnesty International to incorporate their activities on the day into their usual Saturday event.

Suddenly Bronagh looked regretful and annoyed. 'God save us, it's half nine already! We forgot about Tommie's teach-in!'

'Shit. We should probably get over there,' exclaimed Levin.

Eoghan necked his pint, and got to his feet. Mary, Joe and Daniel went too, squeezing through the dense crowd.

The night was cold, with stars on the pavement and the street was empty. Bob stood over the dying fire. Levin asked where Tommie had gotten to. Tall Paul shook his head.

By noon the following day, Donegall Street and Writer's Square were transformed. It was as if a rock festival had descended on a tiny village. Over six hundred people gathered on the pavilion and around the camp. Bob embraced Galway John and shook hands with Gary. Bronagh re-introduced them to her husband, Brian. The workshop placards were handed out by Kiera and Fred.

Eoghan and Levin were reunited with Tommy Sands and eager in discussion with the union heads. Deirdre tried to interest Shay in the work of the Green Party. Leon's estranged friend, Martine, was there and they excitedly pitted off against one another over left-wing gossip and news of government disinformation. Tall Paul got caught in Martine's verbal crossfire and was forced to listen to details of Health Secretary Andrew Lansley's many lies surrounding health reform.

Tommie was nowhere to be seen. Bob had made sure to make them all feel guilty the previous night, but now it was pushed to the back of their minds. New and old faces swarmed together: Cat's cousin, Cian, a champagne punk, and her partner, the rocker Imelda Zen; her Auntie Amy, a hipster, and her bookworm Uncle Robin, who chatted with Deirdre about bike lanes. Later, Cian's sister Jenny showed up. She was tall, androgynous, and clad in camouflage wear. Her boyfriend Glenn

Bean was well known in the local prog rock scene, and Padraig and Fred ate up his every word. There was Conor, Philip, Monty, Hanita, Miriam, Michelle, Dee, Filipe, Barry, Mick, Jim, John Donegal, Gerardy, Gerry, Terry, Sadie, Kev, Kelly, Cara, Joel, Katrina, Steph and Ryan.

They looked around the tents and the bust of the Spanish War volunteer, reading the inscription, 'No pasarán!' At the rear of the square, Gary shook the hand of Eoghan's grandfather, before climbing the steps. He called out for people's attention but his voice was drowned out. A union leader with a megaphone announced it was half past and they should make their way to City Hall.

Most of the occupiers marched together: Bob with grim defiance; Eoghan adamant, giving his all to every chant; Shay, for whom Occupy was his union, and Tall Paul, who they took under their wing. It was his first demo. It was a first for many. They passed the offices of the Belfast Telegraph, with its iconic clock jutting off the wall to the street. Marchers jeered and booed, for the Telegraph had been playing up the damage the strike would cause. Gary and Levin mingled with the teachers' unions passing the derelict Bank of Ireland building and crossing onto Royal Avenue. It was more a shuffle than a march. Kiera and Imelda gelled right away, and spoke of mutual friends. Padraig got separated from his tribe. He was uneasy, alongside the gruff, elderly woman who he signed on in front of at the dole office. He hid his face under his scarf, from time to time peering out at the last person he expected to be a socialist firebrand.

They fed in from the Mater, north on the Crumlin. They came from the east, bussed in from Dundonald and the trains to Central Station had brought people in from other counties. In South Belfast they descended from Stranmillis and the Lisburn Road, passing the City Hospital and from the Royal Hospital west-side on Grosvenor Road.

The Workers Solidarity Movement would number fifteen thousand at the protest, and *The Guardian* would claim there were five thousand. Everywhere there were people with heads held high and defiant expressions. Winter woollies and fluorescent jackets pushed together against Royal Avenue, Donegall Square, and the side streets around. There were banners for *Unite, the union*; black and white. The blue emblem of the *NASUWT*, the teacher's union, streamed as they waved it.

There was the red, white and black of the *Workers Solidarity Union*, and the placards of the LGBT community with every colour on them. Galway John stood with his old electrician friends, under the flag of the *International Congress of Trade Unions*. He shook their hands enthusiastically. One of them recognised Bob and they waved to each other in good cheer.

Despite the law forbidding his attendance Constable Corbett was there, head held low and his uniform left at home. Barker, Tarbard and Louse were all on duty, watching the troops of bin-men, safety inspectors and care assistants. Sinn Fein flags waved and a few booed and heckled them. Four miles away at the Stormont parliament, their co-conspirators in the DUP got the same treatment as they crossed the picket lines.

'Always some toss-pot politicians on the bandwagon,' said Levin.

'I've never seen this many flags,' said Cat.

'Not since the twelfth of July at any rate,' noted Bronagh.

'There's not that many in proportion to the people,' said Eoghan.

The media raised their cameras and boom poles. They filmed tax inspectors, paramedics, midwives and probation officers. The banner of *NIPSA*, the public service union, flew over Donegall Place and Leon punched the sky. Like NIPSA, the *Irish Congress of Trade Unions* had a large presence. The ICTU were a cross-border alliance, built around corporatist agreements and social partnerships. Their logo was a circle of joining blue ellipses. Government cuts two years before decentralised their power and control, yet the social bonds remained and members had doubled their efforts.

When Bob called out to him, Tommie was with his mates from *Brown's* restaurant, and a loader he'd known from Sailortown. The old man pushed through the crowds and Galway John and Daniel followed his wake.

'Ah, Bob. What's up?'

'Good to see you, Tommie. I was worried about you after you took off last night.'

'Ah, no, I'm fine. It'll pass. Fuck 'em. And thanks again for taking my shift. Sorry I couldn't provide cover today,' said Tommie.

'You needn't worry. That's sorted. Fred's keeping an eye.'

He gasped. 'Fred?'

From City Hall, a loudspeaker thundered, and then screeched in blasting feedback.

'God, would they ever sort that?' moaned Galway.

A man of sixty with a hanging grey fringe took the platform. He introduced himself as Peter Bunting, Assistant General Secretary of the ICTU. He was too far away for a clear view.

'Today we are putting down a marker that we will oppose the austerity cuts that have not worked and will not work!'

'I'm sorry about last night, Tommie. It wasn't intentional. We lost track of time,' said Daniel.

'The public sector is being sacrificed in the name of an ideology which favours the one percent. We need a Plan B!'

'Same old shit, Daniel. No hard feelings,' replied Tommie.

They shook hands as Bunting spoke of other demonstrations in Magherafelt and Downpatrick, Derry, Omagh and Cookstown; Craigavon, Newry and Ballymena.

Bronagh spotted Tommie but even with her large stature and willpower she couldn't get over to him. They were pushed in so tight. The city, like the interconnected state of things, had reached a bottleneck.

'Belfast has not seen a demonstration like this since the

1932 Outdoor Relief Strike. Then, Catholics and Protestants stood together, as we do now, against the injustice of Austerity.'

Bunting spoke of their solidarity with two million public sector workers across Britain. Hundreds of thousands of messages of support had come from Europe and the colonies, video messages from government workers in Nicaragua, and emails from garment workers in Bangladesh. The generations gathered in Belfast that day were familiar with the word 'no'. All their lives they'd been told it. No, said the churches. No, said the terrorists. No, said the politicians. No pay rise. No sanctuary. On the 30th November, 2011 the people sought to change that mantra.

'No more cuts. No more cuts. No more cuts!'

'No pasarán! No pasarán!'

21

The morning after the strike the camp was thick with frost and the three girls in the marquee sat in a wafting mist. Regardless, there was colour in Cat's cheeks. She and Jack were talking about where they went for bargain clothes. It transpired they each went to the same charity shops. Kiera said they dressed so differently she'd never have realised it to look at them.

The interruption introduced himself as Alex. He was well groomed, and dressed in a sports coat and slacks, smiles and winks all round. Alex sat down a little too close to Jack for her liking, but she let it go. Alex kept his his options open, making eye contact with Cat.

'God, yous are game, camping out in this weather. So are yous into politics then?' he asked unironically.

Cat responded dryly, and disinterested. 'Nah. Whatever gave you that idea?'

'Ha! Did you hear about that strike yesterday?' he asked.

'Well duh,' said Kiera.

'They said the UK could be on the brink of another recession,' said Alex.

'That's the word. Not just us: Europe, America, Asia,' replied Jack.

'Yeah. It's all starting up again, honey. You've got to wonder.'

Eoghan zipped his tent closed and wandered up the path, bleary eyed.

'Alright Eoghan,' said Kiera.

'It's all engineered,' said Alex.

'Morning,' said Cat.

'What's happening?' asked Eoghan.

'Am I detecting some animosity here?' asked Alex.

Eoghan threw his head back, puzzled. 'No. No animosity,' he said.

'It's okay. Eoghan's a friend,' said Jack.

'Oh. Just a friend? Nothing more?' enquired Alex.

For a moment no-one spoke.

'What's up with you this morning? You're looking worse for wear,' noted Cat.

Eoghan sniffed. 'Ah, just tired and fucked off.'

'What's the matter?' she said.

'Ach. The usual. You-know-who is sticking their oar in again and we've all this shit to do before the rally on Saturday *and* I haven't had a day off this week.'

'That's what they want though, isn't it? They all get together and decide,' said Alex.

'Same old shit,' said Eoghan, and he began to pour out a bowl of cereal.

'Wait. Who decides?' said Jack.

'Well, that's it,' said Alex. 'Labour and Conservatives argue over which of them go to war. They get India and Pakistan to agree to fight. It's the Illuminati.'

'Oh, the Illuminati?' said Cat.

Eoghan moved slowly to take his seat.

'It's true. That's how they see consensus. War: good for the economy, good for technology. We're in the middle of things they set up three hundred years ago. Go and look it up on Wikipedia.'

'Aye. Wikipedia it, Cat,' said Jack sarcastically.

Kiera turned her face away from them and broke out in a huge grin.

'I don't think they're capable of planning that far ahead,' said Cat.

'The Illuminati,' said Eoghan. 'A secret organisation

causing chaos in the world, though not doing a very good job of disguising themselves.'

'It's true. This current situation is all carried out by finance capitalists pretending to look weak. They manufacture a narrative that they're hard done by so that they can turn round and do it again in five years time.'

'He has a point,' said Cat.

Fred staggered out of The Love Shack, one shoe crushed under the weight of his sweaty heel. The new streams of drizzle slapped his creased face. He hobbled on the slimy path a bit before fixing his shoe. Eoghan looked at Alex with scepticism.

'That's balls. You're saying they didn't get caught with their hands in the till, but they wanted to get caught?'

'They staged it. They rule us by division. Even this movement of yours! Capitalist society is run by the secret elite. They're dedicated to preserving bloodlines --'

Eoghan mimicked an English aristocrat. *'What? Capitalism is a boys club, filled only with the wealthy? And the rich people only marry other rich people? My god, does anybody know? Does Lenin or Trotsky know?'*

Fred took a bowl and filled it with cereal and milk, and sat down next to Alex.

'It's fucking obvious,' Eoghan ranted. 'Princes marry Princesses, they become Queens and Kings. That's the whole system staying in place!'

'Alright Fred. Are you off somewhere?' asked Kiera.

'I've to sign on in ten minutes. It's twenty minutes walk: uphill all the way.'

'It served a logical purpose possibly at one time,' said Eoghan, 'but it wasn't a great system. People were trying to overthrow it for years.'

'Well it's true,' insisted Alex. 'The Illuminati are going to take over the world and kill everybody.'

Eoghan raised his voice as he became increasingly frustrated. 'There's no such fucking thing as the Illuminati! Look. Have you ever read the books by Robert Anton Wilson?'

'I don't read books, said Alex.

'You don't read books? You don't read books?' yelled Eoghan.

Again, no-one spoke. Fred froze with his spoon before his mouth, milk dribbling off it.

'Ah!' exclaimed Alex. 'Sure it's all the fucking Jews anyway.'

Everyone was staring at him except for Fred who got to his feet and slammed his bowl and spoon onto the chair behind him, splashing milk onto Alex's trousers.

He glared at Alex. 'That's what I like to wake up to in the morning. A good old bit of anti-Semitism. Who doesn't need a bit of beat-the-Jew over breakfast? Fuck this. I'm going back to bed.'

On the second day of December, Bob watched a seagull pace through the mud and pick at the litter around Leon's tent. He wondered if he might train it to pick at her skull instead. She was rabbiting on about all the Murdoch family filth coming out in the Leveson Inquiry: the stalking, and the man framed for murder, the undeniable proven links between their journalists and suicides. Bob watched the gull on the concrete getting bolder. Bob barely spoke all morning: he was in one of his moods. He just sat and watched the once pale brown ash trees which had taken on a more sinister shade. Galway John arrived and had barely said hello before Leon told him all about News International hacking into the Civil Service.

'Well, someone's been reading,' he remarked.

'You're right, John. It's sick. And intimidating grieving parents? They've left paedo priests in the dust for new lows.'

'Where is everyone?'

Bob shook his head. 'I sat through a three hour meeting just so I could put cleaning this bomb site on the docket. *Yes Bob. We'll be there for you Bob, We'll all pitch in.*'

'Are you sure the site tidy-up was marked for today?' Leon asked.

Bob spat. 'Yes I'm fucking sure. Bad enough the way it is. Tomorrow there'll be people all over here again, trailing this shit on the soles of their feet.'

'That's not good.'

'To hell with it, John. Line up the gas cylinders. I'm going to burn this place to the ground.'

'Well Bob. That's a bit... extreme. Now, I've a box of cleaning materials in the jeep: bin bags, a new rake...'

'What's the point? They want to live in filth and squalor they can go right ahead,' grunted Bob. 'I wont be staying long.'

'Surely there's people in those tents willing to help,' said Galway.

'I'll ask around,' said Leon.

Leon stood at the entry of the olive coloured ridge tent which Padraig, in a fit of zeal, had spray painted with *'Tax the 1%.'* She got no answer calling his and Fred's names, and unzipped the front to find Padraig fast asleep.

'Padraig, get up! We need help cleaning the camp. Come on, man. It's the middle of the afternoon. We're all going to pitch in. Less work?'

'Sure, sure,' he said, and rolled over and snored less softly.

She moved on to the olive green ridge tent where Levin was tucked into a copy of *Manufacturing Consent.*

'It's a mess and we have to band together. We have to show those leeches in Stormont and Westminster that we don't have to live like pigs!'

'We don't?' he asked.

A black funnel tent was occupied by Daniel. Leon stood at the front as the flap blew open. In contrast to The Love Shack, it was organised, clothes all folded and matching socks rolled together. She began to talk to him about the organised tidy-up when Daniel said he remembered it being discussed at the General Assembly, and of course he was still willing.

'This is important,' said Leon. 'If we can get this place

tidy we'll show them. We can do a better job than all their private outsourced greedy Bullingdon Rolodex buddies.'

Daniel lowered his book on futurist architecture. 'I said yes, Leon.'

'Good. Now let's get to work.'

It seemed every tent she called on, someone was missing their significant other. Tommie sometimes shared the brand new upmarket green funnel tent with Tall Paul, but Paul had not seen his bunkmate in days. In any case, he was happy to pick up a rake and pull it through a sea of leaves. Mary and Joe shared a camouflage green pole tent, but she'd gone to visit family. Joe put on his boots.

The wind trap frequently blew rubbish along the wall of the Shac apartments, and behind the mega-marquee. Galway John called it the 'un-compost heap.' Joe scraped a shovel along concrete, picking up cartons, paper, crisp, sweet bags and a pair of tights. Leon poured boiling water into the basin and scrubbed the small plates and the large food tubs from Brown's. On the grass, Daniel found a spray paint can and a solitary rubber glove.

Bob took the first bag to the dumpster, tying a knot in it as he walked. He looked up to the gull proudly ruling over it. With a swing of the arm the scavenger was deposed. He returned to the marquee where Galway was holding a small glass bottle in the air.

'Who leaves an empty jar of pesto just lying around?'

'Oh Christ, not again. Every fucking week without fail,' said Bob.

'Kiera,' Levin testified. 'She says the smell of it is like potpourri.'

Bob took it from John and it landed in the bin bag with a smash. Levin stared at Bob, and opened his mouth to object.

'Fuck recycling,' said Bob.

They collected poster boards, cut six times by storms, and threw them out. Less damaged ones, no use as notices, were stacked in a pile. Later they were redistributed as and doormats and primarily bases for the few tents still on soil. Loose coal was picked up and burned. Galway John brushed rainwater into the drain trench, stopping short so the sticks and stones wouldn't cause a blockage. At the side of the marquee was a wet clump of flyers. Leon was telling Tall Paul to put them in the green bin, when Tommie reappeared. His guarded expression put her on edge.

'Hey, Tommie. Sorry about missing your teach-in. Time just got away from us,' she said.

He nodded, stoically.

'Cat feels awful. She wants to know if you'll do it another time.'

'I dunno,' said Tommie.

Bob called his name. 'Come to help out? Good man,' he said.

Galway John called out for the shovel. Tommie shrugged and picked it up.

The Love Shack wobbled. Padraig unzipped the front, and stuck his head outside. He saw Bob drape an industrial sized plastic sheet over the buckets of coal and firewood. The kettle boiled over the fire but Leon was near it, chalking *'Day 41'* up on the blackboard. Sure that there was work happening and that no one had seen him, Padraig put his head back inside.

Joe was working his way around the marquee tents, threading slack rope through holes and tightening the joins. Tall Paul wiped down chairs. Leon and Levin worked together remounting placards onto the railings while talking about the expansion of the fracking operation in Fermanagh and bitching about the lack of interest in the campaign during the previous night's meeting.

Joe watched the others finish their tasks, as he strengthened a knotted rope to the marquee, and when he was done he announced his conquest. 'Finally!' he called out.

'It better stay like that,' said Bob.

'Oh, we're not quite done yet,' said Galway John sagely.

Levin looked up from studying the seven different

stains on his clothes. He rolled his eyes.

Bob sighed in disbelief, then bitterly he asked, 'What is it?'

John laughed. 'No. You'll like this one. Come with me.'

As soon as they passed Padraig's tent he clambered outside. Padraig took the kettle off the boil and made himself the first cup of tea from the freshly boiled water. He spooned out the teabag and set it on the wall. Levin cursed. He asked Joe if there was a bucket for them to wash Padraig down.

Galway returned with a six foot cut of pine tree over his shoulders. Bob carried a bag of Christmas decorations. Levin suggested planting the tree in a bucket of coal but Tommie pointed out they had nothing so deep.

Instead it was strung up, upside down, from the tree in the centre of the campsite. Joe demonstrated his skill climbing onto the branches and tightening the knots so it wouldn't, as Padraig put it, 'fall and fuck somebody up for life.' Leon liked the idea of an upside down Christmas tree. It symbolised 'the inversion of the celebration of consumerism.' The tree hung close enough to the ground for tinsel to be weaved around it. They were finishing up when Bronagh arrived and admired it: green, gold and red, wobbling in the wind like jelly.

'That brings some colour to the place,' she said. 'Right. Are you all ready to go?'

Bronagh's home was typical of terrace housing, small with two bedrooms. Padraig said it was like the Tardis: bigger on the inside. The wallpaper in her living room was cream, patterned with musical bars and flourishes of gold clefs. Padraig and Leon sat on the reddish-pink three-piece sofa, finishing the cups of tea Bronagh had made them. Two single-seaters close by were occupied by Tommie and Bob. A sixty-five inch black plasma screen was mounted to the wall opposite the sofa, tuned to the re-branded Ulster Television news programme, *UTV Live*.

'Don't mention the occupation. Not on *Unreported Tele-*

cast Views,' snarked Leon.

'Fuckin' look at Cameron. And Clegg! They look like they're wearing masks with photos of themselves on. Mwah-ha-hahaha!'

'They should get... ach, what's his name... the over-the-top gay fella... he should be reading the news,' said Tommie.

'Julian Simmons,' said Leon.

'Thank you. *Julian Simmons!*' declared Tommie.

Padraig took this as his cue to go camp it up to the max. 'But now on UTV, heavens to daisies, our cousins over the border have their selves a wee pickle. Those bold students have occupied the Fine Gael office in Kildare. When they come in to work on Monday morn them politicos are going to be hot and bothered!'

The smell of freshly cooked chicken followed Bronagh from the kitchen at the back. She passed the dining table and rested her hands on the back of the seat by Bob's head. 'Right, washing machine is on. Oven is on. Who's for more tea? Tea? Tea?'

Padraig nodded and lifted a cup off the wood floor. Bob strained as he reached to the glass coffee table.

'Sure bring the pot in and we can help ourselves,' said Tommie.

'Smart thinking Batman,' she quipped, and returned to the kitchen.

Bronagh's fiancée, Brian, could be heard sorting boxes in the spare room above. Bob got up and walked around the fluffy white mat, to the window. He pulled back the autumnal patterned curtains and peeked through the blinds to the grimy row houses.

'Something's in the air,' he said gravely.

'*The Met Office has issued a warning of severe snowfall within the next few days. Forecasters expect...*'

Bronagh called out from the other room. 'Turn it up!'

'*...it to come early on Sunday morning, with west south-westerly winds, more frost, and a drop in temperature to one de-*

gree centigrade.'

Tommie craned his neck to look at Bob. 'You must have developed a sixth sense about these things,' he said.

Padraig yawned to the top of the sofa and laid back into the bottom of it. 'No way I'm going down there in that.'

'There's another thing you were right about: Padraig admitting defeat,' said Leon with some superiority.

Tommie laughed and ran his hands from his brow to the back of his skull.

'Well if you mean defeat as smoking spliffs and playing *Call of Duty* with the heating blasting in every room, it's a funny word to use. I'll be thinking of you, mind. It's just a pity you'll be dead from hypothermia by Monday. Mwah-ha-hahaha! Mwah-ha-hahaha!'

Bronagh set the teapot on the dining table. 'Padraig, you mind your tongue.'

'Oh I'm used to it, Bronagh,' said Bob as he took his seat again. 'I expected him to show his yellow streak sooner or later.'

'That'll be your body pissing itself after it's shut down: a yellow streak in the snow.'

'Padraig, I am not going to tell you again. Last warning. Leon, no harm to you girl but after dinner go upstairs and take a shower. There's plenty of fresh towels in the hot press.'

'Thanks, Bronagh.'

'I might do too if you don't mind, Bronagh. Do you want a hand with any of that?' asked Bob.

Brian came quickly down the stairs and entered the room, two folding chairs in his hands.

'No need. I just have to pop the casserole tray in the oven and its done,' said Bronagh.

'You said that fifteen minutes ago love,' said Brian.

With six of them sat around the table it was a squeeze. Bronagh laid down vegetables and garlic potato cubes and on her second trip brought out a chicken and pasta bake with creamy mushroom sauce and toasted breadcrumbs. Brian, a tall man with cropped grey hair and old cheeks, inhaled the steam coming off his plate.

'So, how are our campers?' he asked.

'Coping, Brian. Nothing else for it,' said Bob, 'I tell you, we could do with a meal like this every day. No offence, Tommie.'

'I'm sick of looking at noodles and rice myself, Bob.'

'Don't be shy. It's stretch or starve in this household!' said Bronagh boisterously.

'I didn't get a wink of sleep last night. Someone was up chopping wood at 3am,' said Padraig, and he shifted his beady eyes in Bob's direction.

'That was 3pm,' he replied bitterly, 'when you should have been helping us tidy the camp.'

'Karma, Padraig. It sounds like you've been punished by karma,' remarked Bronagh.

Leon swallowed and let out a moan of ecstatic bliss. 'Oh, nom! Nom! You've these mushrooms just right!'

Bronagh smiled. 'Glad you like 'em. They're sautéed in butter.'

Brian looked at Tommie's empty teacup. 'Can I get yous beers?' he asked.

'Oh yes please, Brian,' said Padraig.

Bronagh laughed. 'You're plenty polite when you want something.'

Leon and Tommie said they'd have one too. Bob declined. Brian said he had some malt scotch whiskey nearby, and Bob relented.

'Just a tipple.'

'Who's on night shift?' asked Bronagh.

'Muggins here,' said Bob.

'I'll make you a warm broth to take with you. Everyone ready for the Carnival tomorrow?'

'Working,' said Tommie.

'Haven't a clue what we're protesting this time,' said

Leon, 'but I'll be there.'

'What about you, Padraig?'

'I'll be demonstrating my resilience on night watch by campaigning against Russian Ultranationalist forces.'

Leon sighed. 'He means *Call of Duty*.'

'Mwah-ha-hahaha!'

Brian dropped off Padraig first, as he lived closest. He got inside quickly and caught Fred red-handed on his third bag of *Tayto* crisps. From their bitten ripped black couch they played *Street Fighter* and *Mario Kart* as the morning crept up on them. Fred fell asleep in front of the screen. Padraig staggered to his room and dressed down to his tee-shirt and boxers. The bed was luxurious, the duvet heavy and warm; the sleep, divine perfection. He wondered how he could ever have left this.

22

Padraig slept through most of Saturday. He staggered downstairs in his bare feet and fired up the PlayStation before remembering there was a full load to go into the washing machine. His legs ached but he limped to the kitchen and made coffee. The fridge was empty. There was found coffee whitener at the back of the cupboard, found easily because there was no food there either. Thankfully Fred had been out to the shop and returned with roadkill burgers, sandwiches, and crisps. Padraig limped back to the kitchen and put the buns in the toaster, and microwave-boiled the burgers.

'See the photos on the Facebook page?' said Fred.

He was on the sofa with the laptop on his knees. Padraig sat beside him with the plate of burgers in front of him and picked mucus from his eye.

'Are you kidding? I never want to see that camp again,' said Padraig.

Fred tilted the laptop round and he clicked through the photographs of the Saturday event at the camp: Eoghan and Jack making speeches; Anonymous modelling finger-less gloves; Glenn Bean at his guitar; Daniel with tea; parents hurrying prams through a gale with glistening umbrellas; glum Bob at the Christmas tree surrounded by children showing off.

'Mwah-ha-hahaha! Look at the gub on him!'
'Full on candid that one,' said Fred.
'Is that a letter for us?' said Padraig.
'I must have walked it in,' said Fred.

It was a note from a lawyer, dated two weeks back. Their building was under new ownership and they had until December 31st to vacate the property. Padraig got mad with Fred that he was only seeing this now. Fred said it wasn't his fault. Clearly Leon hadn't checked her mail either, unless she hid the news from them, which was unlikely. They had twenty-seven days to find somewhere. If the worst came to the worst, they could live in the tent.

To soothe their nerves they had a toke and watched telly. It was *Q.I.* and *Red Dwarf*, and they felt much better. Fred channel surfed all the way to an over-acting model gyrating in her lingerie, voices muted as she answered a peak-rate call. Padraig tried to match her lip movements with a boisterous Ian Paisley impression.

'Oh Mr. McGuinness. You have been naughty. I think you deserve a good spanking.'

Fred put his hand up and focused on the woman's mouth. 'As a Republican spokesman I am willing to, *oh. Oh hello, ohh…*'

'Yes Martin. In the name of God. *Oh God!*'

'Let's break the taboos. Break all the taboos! Take me Ian. Let us make sweet legacies.'

'Ulster says yes, *God Yes! Yes!*'

They marathoned *Call of Duty* until daybreak. Padraig yawned so hard that pain shot through his jaw. He decided rest was a good cure and went up to bed.

When he awoke it was dark, but early morning dark. He noticed the ache had gone and the sleep had cleared his head. Padraig showered and dressed and found his wayward glasses before walking back downstairs. Fred lay on the couch reading a comic. There were none of the pre-packed sandwiches left so Padraig contented himself with *Tayto Onion Rings* for breakfast.

'We're nearly out of baccy too. Hey, did you ever hear back from the Jobcentre?'

'What about?' Padraig asked.

'The weed?'

Padraig generally filled in his *Looking for Work* book at the last moment. The entries were contrived notes tenuously linked to job searches. A few days before they set up camp in Writer's Square he'd been under a stoned haze and mistakenly copied his cannabis order into the booklet. The gruff clerk was suspicious but she seemed to let it go. Fred had told him to use a new book next time he signed on but he forgot.

'Sure I told them I was applying for a job in a fast food place,' said Padraig.

Fred smirked. 'Tell me again,' he said.

'I said 'ten deal' meant the snack box. And a 'quarter' was a quarter pounder. I think she bought it.'

'So the Social Security don't have my weed?' said Fred.

'That's the Christmas bonus. Mwah-ha-hahaha!'

The hunt for Vladamir Marakov in *Modern Warfare 3* pitted them against waves of soldiers. They shot back, with bullet and fire, and looted the corpses for weapons upgrades. The terrorists fought tactically to pin them down and the split screen blossomed with grey and orange glows. Padraig paused the game and took stubs from the ashtray. Fred tutted.

'Hey, don't blame me! This is your fault,' Padraig replied.

'How is it my fault? What? Am I supposed to be your tobacco taxi service? Bite the hand that feeds you much?'

'Hey, relax. I'm making you one,' said Padraig.

He peeled out tufts of part-burned tobacco from the stubs and planted them in fresh papers, enough for a recycled rollie each. Then it was back to the game and calling on ground support so mass destruction fell upon their pixelated foes. Padraig crept towards the installation and planted a bomb while Fred took down an automated drone. The ashtray was empty, meaning either a hand stuck in the kitchen bin for seedier damp stubs or a trip to the all-night garage. It was four in the morning. On the rare occasion when they ran out of tobacco after midnight, tradition stated they both had to walk the distance.

Padraig put on his coat and opened the front door. A splat of white ice flake hit his lenses and pelted cold on his cheeks. Then another and another. It covered the tufts of his hair and blotted his black jacket.

'Better wrap up,' he called out.

They clumped through snow deep on the pavement, past white-sheeted parked cars, crossing the road which tyre marks made look like an X-ray of a ribcage. The thick blizzard masked the snowball that smacked Fred on the chin. He bent down for a parcel of ammo, his hands pink and white to the knuckles. Padraig ducked it easily. He'd brought gloves, but the weather clung to the wool, and he grew bored of their war. Their journey on the quiet main road was downhill and steep. They made shows of sliding on the ice until the ice slid too much under them. The cold seeped through the holes in Padraig's trainers, drenching his feet. At the all-night garage they stamped it off their boots. It splattered like rice on the unblemished forecourt.

The camp was five minutes from there; an easier walk. The white lay as a virgin field on the pavilion. It lined the branches of the trees over the tents, falling in intervals. In the middle the upside down Christmas tree delayed the ascent and swayed precariously, laden with its stock falling like a drip feed. Snow gathered in the spaces between the tents, and coated most tents. In front of one doorway a black shoe heel stuck out of the drift. There was snow on the railings, the signs and the edge of the super-marquee too. The fire kept its head down. Padraig and Fred stayed low with their missiles while advancing on Joe and Tommie. Suddenly Fred stopped, and put his hand on Padraig's arm.

'Here, I've a better idea. Walk softly,' he whispered.

He put his finger over his lip and rose up, as prominently as he could. He wagged his left finger and then pointed to his sealed lips, until he was sure the night watch understood not to announce them. Joe rolled his eyes. Fred signalled four with his fingers, and pointed towards the pavilion. Tommie was puzzled and wondered if Fred was asking him to fight people.

Behind the camp, Fred whispered his pitch. They would build a snowman. It was important they do it quietly for this was a special snowman. The others were reluctant but they liked the idea. Joe and Tommie began in front of the steps with two shovels and worked their way forward two hundred metres. Padraig didn't go as far and took the hard brush to the middle of the square. Under the south-west blizzard, Fred took the soft brush to the two feet high wall. He swept the underside too, harvesting enough to begin the second sphere. They couldn't risk shovelling beyond the edge of the pavilion so rolling the three foot high boulder required a combined effort. It was ten metres to place it in front of the ridge tent just beyond the marquee. Tommie took the plastic sheet off the coal and they gathered the snowman's head there, carrying it the rest of the way. The operation was performed with maximum stealth until Fred sneezed. It was a high pitched girly sneeze, and sent Joe into fits of laughter, which in turn set Padraig off.

'Mwah-ha-hahaha!'

With the head in position, they built the face: coal for eyes and woodchip for nose and a cardboard cigarette in the mouth hole. Cutlery was used to sculpt its fearsome expressions. Tommie slung the hi-vis jacket around its shoulders. They retired to the marquee and laid back, admiring the six foot monolith facing Bob's tent.

Winds had blown clods from the Christmas tree onto Cat's tent. The noise of the men outside was the decisive nudge to wake her up with a shiver. She put on another layer and let out a tremendous yawn. Although the light beyond her thin tarpaulin was different she'd no idea it'd been snowing until she heard Padraig talk.

'That is a very angry snowman. *Frosty the git.*'

'There's an aul bit of cardboard in the back that will do

for his hat,' said Tommie.

Cat opened her eyes as she saw the snow lined up at her door, stretching back to everywhere. She didn't want to be alone in that and sat with the lads for a cigarette. They'd done a good job, but there was something missing. She went back into the rear of the marquee with a torch and found the marker pens. In short order they had a placard strung around the thing reading, *'Bob the Scare-Snow: Defender of This Camp'.*

Most everyone except Bob, who had been on the early night shift, was awake by about half seven. Some unzipped their doors and looked around and went back inside, slapping snowflakes off their tents as they did so. The excitement wore off quickly.

'Achoo!'
'Bless you!'
'Achoo!'
'Achoo! Achoo! Achoo!'
'Sneeze level: multiple orgasm achieved!'

Padraig told Leon about the eviction notice. She said she hadn't checked the mail but wasn't that bothered: she'd just move her few possessions to the camp. A road sweeper motored along one pavement and down the next but not the square, leaving it as a lone white island. Eoghan brushed the path, respectfully working around Snow Bob, immovable and defiant.

At a quarter to ten Levin and Leon set off for Donegall Square West. They caught the number 23, east along derelict Albertbridge, up fancy Holywood Road and right onto posh Belmont. They were on their way to the Stormont parliament for the debate on fracking. Condensation dribbled down the window from the porthole Levin had made with his arm. The road widened at the roundabout and he pointed to a set of gates tucked in from the road, thick with overgrown plants.

'I grew up around here. That's the entrance to Campbell

College.'

'Isn't that a private school?'

'A boarding school. My mates and I would sneak past the boarders every Saturday. We'd go in through a hole in the hedge with our beer and cider. Behind those trees is Netherleigh Lake. Covered with lilies. Bit of a swamp actually. But we'd sit on a great fallen tree trunk, and leave our cans to be chilled in the lake.'

'Yeah, sounds great,' Leon said, with nonchalance. She looked out at Massey Avenue with its high fence houses conjuring images of wealthy bankers and high court judges. 'This is all money,' she said. 'My God. You're the bourgeoisie, aren't you?'

'Oh you think so? Did I ever tell you how I squatted in a flat in Oxford? I'm no slouch. I've a few tricks up my sleeve, Leon.'

'What like?'

'Well... keep this to yourself for the time being, but...'

Leon was thoroughly excited by the time they got off the bus outside Stormont. It left them within a minute of the classic Greek styled building, off-white and fronted by steep steps and doric columns. They stopped to look down the long rolling hill and the road with cast-iron lamps separating a snow-stepped public park.

'This better not be another protest with only two people showing up,' said Leon.

'They must have gone inside. Here! I'd forgotten what a great view this is. You can see most of the city.'

'Pity that statue of Edward Carson blocks it.'

'True. It looks like he's giving us all the finger,' said Levin.

'Homophobic sectarian-aiding fuck.'

'Now, now. His own brother was gay. Actually, hang on. No, you're right. He took the case to prosecute Wilde in part because his brother was gay. Carson's brother died in exile too if I remember correctly.'

'What a dick,' said Leon.

'Little known fact about the Ulster Unionist leader. Carson said the speeches of Orangemen reminded him of the unrolling of a mummy. *All old bones and rotten rags* was how he put it.'

At ten minutes to ten, Bronagh's people carrier mounted the pavement outside the camp. She busied herself assessing the damage caused by the snow, and made a list. They'd need blankets, towels, new sleeping bags and more. She told everyone she was going shopping, and that Daniel was going with her.

So Bronagh drove east, chatting incessantly, and Daniel listened. On Albertbridge she slowed down for the number 23 bus. They were stuck behind it all the way to the Holywood Road, as far as Belmont. Snow lay in the front gardens of middle class homes in the suburbs and deep on the pitches around Ashfield. Its traces on the dual carriageway were barely a whisper. She turned left into the Holywood Exchange, which was a long strip of road hosting large retail sites.

It was Daniel's first time at Belfast IKEA. The windows of the second floor cafe overlooked the runway of City Airport. There was a service area beyond the till with sachets of coffee and sugar, and Bronagh had Daniel pocket a half dozen of each. She took some more for good measure. She'd gotten each of them a fry and they sat in a cubicle with a good view of the airstrip. Parents screamed each time a plane took off. They spread their arms, making vrooming noises and jumped up in the air; and the children tried to calm them down.

Below the cafe was the labyrinthian shop. The stock was piled high and cleverly displayed but wide corrugated metal pipes hung over every sector of the basement. Daniel walked slowly through the factory of bargains. Bronagh said that if they wanted to survive they had to keep moving. She pointed to the map, and the short-cuts between zones, and pushed through the nearest warehouse doors.

A gust of warm air hit in Stormont's lobby. Leon wrote her name in the Visitors' Book as Phyllis Lutts. They were admitted into the Great Hall where Kaiser Wilhelm II's golden chandelier hung under a green and red ceiling. Deirdre and a few others were watching a plasma screen which broadcasted the debate from the chamber.

'Oh. Levin. Leon. Glad you made it. I'm not long ahead of you. I had a bus on my tail the whole way here,' she said.

'What are they saying?' asked Leon.

'Well I heard Steven Agnew presented a three thousand strong petition highlighting the associated dangers of pollution. That's gone to the *DETI*. Then Edwin Poots-in-Boots, Arlene Foster and Stephen Moutray were on about healthcare. Typical DUP circle jerk it seems. Oh wait, there's Anna Lo. Thank God! Shall we go in?'

The public gallery overlooked the Assembly Chamber which was much like any other centrepiece of parliament: brown wooden walls and rows of seats; two sides, with the deep blue carpet most prominent in the broad square between them. The three occupiers sat down as Anna Lo, the Alliance MP, made her proposal. Lo asked for a moratorium on hydraulic fracking and talked about similar bans in Europe and Africa.

'Given the experience of some US citizens regarding the flammability of home water supplies in the vicinity of fracking sites, I call for a full investigation into the impact that fracking could have on not only aquatic ecology but on our water supply.'

From the aisle seat Levin watched her with optimism. He knew Lo was a socialist with a strong track record on human rights and she spoke firmly about matters. Leon moved around on the seat beside him, distracted and uncomfortable. She looked down on the politicians as they slept, or mocked Lo, who kept her head in her papers and continued reading.

'Dr Theo Colborn was quoted as saying that the contamination of water from fracking could have negative health implications, including dizziness; headaches; and even irreversible brain damage, on human beings.'

'I get that every night at camp,' whispered Levin.

'I've heard tremors,' said Leon.

'Bring your remarks to a close,' said the Speaker.

'In Fermanagh and South Tyrone, the Minister's constituency, it would be hard to argue in favour of fracking for economic reasons, given the potential negative impact on Lough Erne.'

'Time,' said the Speaker.

Lo carried on. 'With a licensed commercial scale —'

'I call Members to order. The Member is over her time. We now move to the next Member to speak.'

'Thank you, Mr Principal Deputy Speaker.'

Leon whispered back to Levin. 'For fuck's sake. Who's this?'

Deirdre whispered back. 'Stephen Moutray: DUP. Free Presbyterian.'

'I am slightly bemused by the motion before us this morning. The motion has been proposed by those --'

Deirdre whispered, 'He ran up fifty thousand on expenses over the last six months.'

'He's got a face like a melted otter,' said Levin.

'The motion has been proposed by those who keep reminding us of the need to identify and utilise alternative sources of energy, and yet they seem to be paranoid about any effort that is made to find solutions to our energy needs —'

Suddenly Leon was on her feet. 'Occupy Belfast calls for an immediate end to fracking!'

A security officer ran down the steps towards them.

'You must stop at once! We are the 99%,' she yelled.

The officer pushed past Levin and took her arm. Leon struggled. The man almost fell onto Levin's lap. There was a second officer behind him.

'We will not be dictated to by liars and thieves! You're

going to be sorry --'

They lifted her out to the aisle and she kicked Levin as she went. A third officer put his hand on Levin's arm and brought him out too. All the while Leon was still yelling.

'We've big things planned! We are the 99%!'

'Order! The sitting is suspended.'

'We are the 99%!'

Daniel sat at the back of the tent cross-legged, taking deep meditative breaths. Bronagh sat inside the flap with her legs outside.

'Plenty of wind cover at this spot. And it stood up against the elements,' said Daniel.

'So, we have a new location for the camp after all. What do you think?'

Daniel looked up to the ridge poles, and the sun shining through. He said, 'It's quiet for daytime. I'm surprised they left the tents up with the snowfall.'

Bronagh shuffled outside, screaming in pain as she stood up. 'Fuck. Me knees!'

She looked over the tents, tents as far as the eye could see, all the way to the front door of the camping shop. Her phone began to ring. 'Yeah. Hello...'

For a minute she was quiet. Disturbed by her uncharacteristic turn, Daniel clambered out and waited.

'I'm with Daniel at the Holywood Exchange. We can be at Strandtown in fifteen minutes. Just sit and wait for us, Levin.'

Bob awoke shortly after midday to find the snowman staring down at him. He didn't scowl, or even say anything. It was as if it wasn't there. He just had his tea and got straight to chopping wood. The snow dropped again over the campsite. Tender flakes spun, like slivers of magic. Then it became a denser flurry. Visitors brought blankets; sleeping bags; more bags of firewood and an extra large flask. Miriam arrived for her meeting with Eoghan to co-ordinate for the student demo at the end of the week. Padraig, Fred and Tall Paul joined them around the campfire.

A squirrel scampered over the branches of the ash trees. Everyone was busy with preparations. Mary was washing the dishes and tossing soap bubbles at Joe. Cat was sorting out her tent, and squeezing every damp thing. The snowman had become damaged and Kiera and Shay were re-building it.

'Go on, Red. Say the words,' said Shay.

She put her hand on her hips and declared, 'You know nothing, Bob Snow!'

While they chuckled, Bob kept his eye on the landscape. When he saw Bronagh's people carrier pull up he set down his axe and began clapping. Leon stepped out of the car and Levin right after.

'Yeeeee-owwwwwwww!' yelled Padraig.

Everyone was clapping and boisterous. Shay wolf-whistled.

'Go on ye girl ye!' shouted Cat.

'Up the revolution!' cried Fred.

'You fuckers,' said Leon, though she was all smiles.

'Stars of the six o'clock news here,' said Bronagh dryly.

'Aye, right,' said Levin. He rolled his eyes and ducked down into his tent.

Eoghan shouted out, 'Levin! Give us an interview!' but he'd zipped the tent up behind him.

'Thankfully they weren't arrested,' said Bronagh.

The group crowded around Leon with questions. She smiled, shrugged and held out her arms.

'Thank you. Thank you. I like to think an important milestone has been reached today. I stood up and told the truth to a cabal of yes-men. And they couldn't handle the truth!'

'Goodness sake,' said Eoghan.

'You were telling a different story at the station,' said Bronagh.

'They'll forever remember your name,' said Daniel.

23

It was Wednesday – two days after Leon's removal from Stormont – when Bart arrived. He was a fast-moving brightly coloured young Polish lad of excitable highs and lows. On the rare occasions he sat still, he was observed wearing a padded navy and gold anorak over a blue tracksuit. He was slim and short, with clear skin, and as a consequence of his hyper-animated movements, his brown hair was spiked in all directions. He was with Tommie for the night shift, and Fred, who was amused by his broken English and unconstrained enthusiasm.

There was little ice on the ground that morning. The snow had cleared, but for a hard, dirty clump that remained of the snowman. Bart was asking where they got their tents. Tommie, as he warmed his hands by the fire, said that people brought them with them, or donated them. Bart wished he had one. Tommie said Bart could have at least a space in one of theirs as long as he needed it. He was so surprised he nearly fell off his seat.

'Are you serious? That is great. That is great. I would rather be here than in the shelter. It is crap. I only am here because I met Daniel. He seem alright. And Shay. Shay is the first person I meet, but then he leave me here. It really is cold and raining all the time.'

'They're talking about more snow tomorrow,' said Fred.

'Hopefully it'll clear up for the carnival on Saturday,' said Tommie.

'*Whaaat? A carnival?* With clowns and acrobats? Is Shay doing his skateboard tricks? I wanted a go on his board but I cannot ride that thing like Shay can.'

Tommie tried to explain the carnival. Fred stood up, laughing again, and pulled back the divider between the marquee tents. Bart got to his feet too and began jogging up and down. Then he sat back down on a different chair.

'*Ach!* Why is it any time I go to sit down it's wet? Why don't we camp inside? Some man was talking about it. A squat. I do not think the government will let him do that.'

'Are you coming along to the marches? There's a student demo on Friday and a human rights thing on Saturday,' said Tommie.

'Bart doesn't want to get arrested,' said Bart.

Fred emerged from the back wearing his Anonymous mask, flapping the divider like a cape behind him.

'This is a very serious business,' said Fred, very seriously.

'I have always wanted one of those,' exclaimed Bart.

Fred took the mask off. 'You can wear it,' he said.

Bart was ecstatic. '*What*, really?'

'You understand that wearing this mask is a contract. The things you are told are told in absolute secrecy,' said Fred.

Tommie shook his head. 'Fred…'

'Absolute secrecy,' said Bart.

'You are entering into a sacred covenant to be Anonymous.'

'What?'

Fred stretched the elastic around Bart's head and told him, 'Your face will never change. This strap binds you to the revolutionary order. Repeat after me. From this moment forth I am everywhere. I am legion.'

'From this moment forth I am everywhere. I am legion.'

'Now, you have to bring five sacrifices.'

'What do you mean?'

'Five blood sacrifices.'

'Is this a joke?'

Tommie stopped laughing. 'Alright Fred, that's enough.'

Bart removed the mask, catching his wrists in the band. 'The person I most want to meet is Leon! She is famous! I hear she is on the teevee and everything!'

When he got excited his voice carried. Four times Tommie had reminded Bart that people were trying to sleep.

He took the lad with him to the art college. Night security buzzed them inside. Tommie introduced them to Bart and showed him where the toilets were. They had water cannisters with them and outside, they filled up from the tap on the wall by Buoy Park. Tommie's shoes were soaked in the process and they squelched on his walk back to camp.

While Tommie looked in his tent for fresh socks and a dry cloth for his shoes, Bart talked to Fred at the rate of a mile a minute. He said his surname was Symanski. He said the upside down Christmas tree was swaying and might fall and kill someone. He said the only plant pot big enough for it was the fire bin. He said a lot of things.

'A man named John at the housing shelter told me about camp. He smelled like shit but I thinks why not go and see them? Am on a waiting list for housing accommodation. I don't know what will happen.'

He rocked back and forth as he spoke. Fred checked the time on his phone: almost two o' clock. He had grown tired of Bart, and sat silently with his head down.

'It is good here. You can think about things at night, it is so quiet,' said Bart.

'*Whaassk all this aburt?*'

Fred looked up to see a wiry man in a tee-shirt with a shock of white unkempt hair staggering towards them.

'This is the Occupy,' said Bart, beaming with pride.

White-Hair sat down and rested his elbow on his knee. He didn't look homeless but he stank of alcohol. He swayed and then balanced himself on the chair beside Bart, giving the lad a long, unflinching stare.

'What?' said White-Hair.

'It is the Occupy camp. We are here to protest,' said Bart.

'We're camping out to protest bankers' bail-outs. Careful there,' said Fred, noticing the man's lopsidedness.

'Protest fucking who?' he growled.

'The banks. And we stay out all night and all day. You can stay but there is no drinking,' said Bart.

White-Hair flashed a crooked smile, and there was a glint in his eye. Then his face contorted and he was full of hate. He raised his middle finger at Bart.

'Fuck off... wasters.'

'No you fuck off,' said Bart, quite upset.

White-Hair raised a pair of limp fists, swaying comically. His smile returned.

Bart told him, 'If you go to try hit me I'll hit you and you'll go to sleep.'

'Oy!' said Fred.

Bart looked away from White-Hair to Fred. 'I do not like this,' he admitted.

White-Hair reached out and tugged Bart's sleeve. The lad sprung to his feet, poised for a fight. White-Hair tried to follow and nearly fell through the back of the chair.

'Take it easy,' cautioned Fred.

'You're going to hurt yourself,' said Bart.

The man stood up, pulled the chair with him and tipped it over. Tommie came running up the path.

Bart fumed. 'Come on fucking try it.'

'Bart, sit down!'

'I didn't start it Tommie!'

White-Hair was already wandering off, his head swaying to the rhythm of the upside down Christmas tree.

'Polish wanker,' he muttered.

'You are the wanker,' yelled Bart. 'Shit-wanker!'

Tommie snapped back. 'Hey. What did I say? I said leave it. *We don't need trouble.*'

'He's lucky I don't go after him. Why am I getting the blame?'

'I never said you were to blame. Now sit down, Bart.'

Tommie looked sharply to Fred, who was bent over laughing.

'Oh for fuck's sake. What use are you?'

The temperature made them brittle that morning. Around six, an hour after Bart went to bed and when the sky was sure he was sleeping, snow fell again. The first celestial fluttering lit the darkness turning over and over like blinking white fairy lights. The flakes danced around one another as if refusing to land, before disappearing in the wet of the paving. It came nearer and faster and sounded like rain as it caught the tents and trees.

It melted quickly on the path though remained on the grass and atop the planter and pavilion walls. From time to time the wind shook the upside down tree and shed its dandruff. Eoghan and others were securing the tents. Kiera, Cat and Levin watched them from the marquee. Leon sat beside them. In the days since the calling out of Stormont she'd spent much time on the phone.

'I wonder is she going through her contacts alphabetically?' wondered Cat.

'The phone hasn't stopped ringing. Oh, I know darling, I know. I'm going to have to get an agent. Kevin Trojan called me but I had to turn him down.'

Kiera laughed. 'The lying cow! Has she heard herself?'

Levin rolled his eyes and shook his head.

He was sat next to Leon and close enough to hear the person on the other end of the call.

'What did you mean when you said, *you're going to be sorry, we've got big things planned?*'

Leon laughed. She was about to confess all when she caught Levin scrutinising her and baring his teeth. It was only the second time she'd seen him angry. Her own expression flipped from unrestrained ego to reticent and bashful.

'Oh that, that was *nothing*. Well not nothing. We're

doing things. We've demos on Friday, and Saturday. And let me tell you all about this fundraiser.'

She jumped up, knocking Shay's CD Walkman off the seat beside her, and she sauntered off to the pavilion.

Out on the white grass Eoghan tightened the guy rope on his tent. Tommie was telling him and Shay about the incident with Bart and the drunk.

'It's a matter of harnessing his enthusiasm into something positive,' said Eoghan.

'Aye. Wire his mouth up to a dynamo,' said Tommie, pressing a peg hard into the soil with the flat of his hand.

'We were talking about trying something like that with Padraig,' said Shay. 'Levin thought with that mad laugh of his we could walk him around the block so the sound would drive people in toward the camp.'

Eoghan laughed. 'I'm pretty sure that's called kettling,' he said.

Shay walked around the side of the green ridge tent to the Christmas tree. It had been tied in closer to the tree to stop it brushing against Cat's tent, but was still loose enough to appear unstable, shaking in a wind. A length of gold tinsel fell onto his arm and he set it up onto the branches again.

Levin joined them then. 'I wanted a word with you about scoping out a place to squat,' he said.

Eoghan nodded. 'I'm surprised Bronagh didn't put you off. It would be good to have cover so people don't have to sleep in the streets. Handy for office space and the like too.'

'Well, we have a few candidates,' Levin informed him.

Suddenly a ball of white whizzed past Eoghan's head and shook the tarpaulin.

'The fuck?'

'Oops,' said Kiera.

Eoghan bent down and balled up tan brown snow in his hands. He flung it past the marquee. Kiera jumped away and it shattered on the path behind her.

'Oops,' said Eoghan.

Shay watched Kiera gather up another. He pressed together a sphere of snow, in bright salmon hands. Without warning, a snowball gently clipped Shay's ear, from Eoghan.

'Fucker! I'm on your side!'

Levin jumped inside his tent. Kiera's snowball struck Shay on the left arm of his patchwork duffel-coat. She and Eoghan were ready to take him down. He did the only thing he could do. He turned around and took aim at Tommie.

Tommie hobbled to the marquee leaving them to their tent warfare, his black jacket and jeans polka-dot with impact marks. He brushed himself down in front of the weak coal fire, where he felt the chill and shook. Cat sat behind him, wrapped in a thick beige throw. Tommie walked to the wall by the marquee, unscrewed the water keg and filled the kettle.

'Mad weather this,' she said.

He took grate and kettle and set them atop the smoking fire bin. 'Yeah.'

'I'm really sorry about your teach-in. We were re-organising, and there was the strike, and Leon's mess. It got easier to put off talking to you…'

He took a seat beside her. 'You forgot.'

Her blue hair fell over her face as she looked down to her knees. 'It all got too much for me. You were one of my best friends here. I hate it that I've fucked things up. We barely speak.'

Cat sniffled and Tommie reached into his jacket pocket and took out a sodden pack of tissues. She blew her nose, a sound like a foghorn.

'I was hurt,' said Tommie. 'It was my big opportunity. Instead you're all in the pub talking about… Jesus… uprooting the camp over-night.'

'It was a load of shit,' Cat admitted.

'I wanted to do something other than be the guy who brings food and flexes his muscles.'

'Those things are important.'

'Yeah sure. It's not who I am though. Just what I have to do sometimes.'

'I wish things were how they were between us.'

'I guess I'll have to spend my time with Padraig and Leon then.'

Cat laughed.

'Let bygones be bygones?' said Tommie.

She put out her hand and they shook on it.

Padraig ascended the winding stairwell of the Shac building, looking out over each window at the campsite below. He struggled to keep up with the Englishman, Nige, who bounded up the steps. Nige was large and muscular with a bald head and a voice that carried. He'd invited him up for a cuppa in that persistent manner which was hard to say no to. The fourth floor hall was clean but narrow and cold with a worn blue carpet. They passed twelve doors on the way. As Nige fidgeted with the lock he assured Padraig he could call by for a cuppa anytime.

The living room had an intercom phone by the door and table and chairs. There was an easy beige sofa in front of a television which Nige implored Padraig to switch on. Padraig looked through the small unwashed window to an impressive view of the roofs of the Cathedral Quarter. Nige offered him a tour. The kitchen was only big enough for one person and the bedroom and bathroom were tiny as well.

'How do you cover the rent on this place? It's not a bad spot,' said Padraig.

'No rent. The benefits cover it. I was on a waiting list for ages, mind. You should put in for one. You never know.'

'Naah. I'll find somewhere. I'll start looking the morrow.'

Nige handed him a mug of tea, and walked over to the window. 'So what do you do down there? Asides from marching. And sitting around picking your arses.'

Padraig shrugged. 'I help out on the media team.'

'I fucking hate the media. Fucking bastards every one of

them.'

Padraig laughed nervously. 'Aye. They hardly print anything we send them. That's what I do. Just sending out emails and posting on Facebook.'

'Facebook's great isn't it? Sure, send me a friend request so we can keep in touch. You say a team? Who's in this team?'

'Leon. You know Leon? The girl with the beret?'

'Oh she's a fucking weirdo. Is she a dyke too?'

'I dunno. She —'

'I see a wee twinkle in your eye, mate. You'll get your fingers burned. But your secret's safe with me.'

'Mwah-ha-hahaha! Mwah-ha-hahaha! No interest, Nige.'

'Oh aye? Oh aye? Here, who's the fit bird, always on a downer when I see her, you know. With the dyed hair...'

'Oh that's Cat. She's on the media team too.'

'I'd give her one. Bang her sideways. Is she on Facebook?'

'I think she just uses the camp's account.'

Eoghan was drying the plates off the rack ahead of Leon and Tommie returning from *Brown's* with dinner. Shay was growing impatient and jogging up and down on the spot to keep warm.

'I'm fucking freezing. Starving too. Staaarving.'

'Awww. We'll get Bob Geldof out to you,' said Eoghan.

Shay rubbed his hands over the fire. 'If I had my way we'd nationalise KFC. Yeah, let's do that. Let's occupy a KFC and run it our way.'

Levin laughed. 'How would you do that now?'

Shay thought for a moment. 'Tommie can work a fryer, so he's the boss. You're brainy so you can do the books. Daniel makes the best coffees. Sorry, Eoghan. Sure Eoghan and I will be in charge of the milk-shakes and ice creams. Cat and Kiera can handle the redesign. We'll put our placards in the front window and the Christmas tree too.'

'Seasonal promotion,' said Cat.

'We'll have it up all year round.'

'Shay, what are you going to do when HQ discover we've taken over one of their shops?' said Kiera.

'There'll be no more chicken,' warned Cat.

Levin played devil's advocate. 'Ah we don't need them. Think of what we could do. Fill the burgers with falafel. Add some Jamaican spices. Serve organic kefir in the dessert menu!'

'And if they try and shut us down we'll start disrupting their supply lines. Bob and Leon could deal with that,' said Shay.

Daniel raised an eyebrow.

Shay continued. 'No more battery farming. We can get some Anonymous into the back office to set a DDOS attack on their suppliers: close down any shops still doing it.'

'What if people see it's run by a bunch of anarchist crusties and just decide not to go to our KFC?' Eoghan asked.

'Then we could take over the other shops. They wouldn't see it coming! Mary and Joe could run one. And you, Cat, and Bronagh too: you've both got good management skills.'

Cat replied, 'You could have Padraig as your mascot. He'd frighten the children, just like Ronald McDonald does.'

Shay felt inspired. 'Think of all the jobs we could create!'

'There's about a dozen KFCs in Belfast,' said Levin.

Daniel, in his understated tones, said, 'We'd be choking a lot of chickens.'

The rains fell and washed the once fierce snowman to the drains. Thursday night turned into Friday morning. The Christmas tree swayed over the tents like some extra-terrestrial craft or Kaiju. Bob sat under a black and red sky watching what he referred to as 'the dregs' emptying out of *The John Hewitt*. Eoghan came through from the partitioned rear marquee with a mug of cocoa in each hand.

'Thanks,' said Bob.

'Spirits will have been lifted at Dame Street tonight.

They had Christy Moore playing there. Here, do you know who I've not seen about in a few weeks? Shelby.'

'The quietest one of the lot of you,' muttered Bob. He inhaled the hot chocolate before setting it on the concrete to cool. 'Dogs are loyal. Labrastaffs particularly. He'll be back. Probably up to some mischief somewhere.'

'Shay's a bit worried about him.'

'I'd say that dog hasn't always been a stray.'

Eoghan set down his cocoa too. 'Aye. Shay knew him before the camp. He said he would sit out on the streets with him. A few days or a few hours. Granted, he said months would go by when he didn't hear from him. By the way, did Gary tell you? I'm going to take three or four days out. Figured I'd go and visit the camp in Cork.'

'Them the ones that taught schoolkids maths in the lobby of a bank?' asked Bob.

'Aye. There's clearly a lot to learn from them. Figure I'll bus down after Human Rights Day,' said Eoghan.

'Oh aye?'

'Yeah. It'll be a bit of craic,' said Eoghan.

'I wouldn't mind that. Sure count me in,' said Bob.

'Are you serious?'

'Sure.'

'Me *and you?*'

'Do you think I like being stuck *here, with these nutters?*'

'*On a road trip?*'

'You're always on at me to take a holiday. But if you'd rather I didn't —'

'No, no. I'm just surprised, that's all. I'll be glad for the company.'

They heard a woman, laughing deliriously. Bob saw her across the street and became distracted. He thought she was just some floozie at first, but then he recognised Cat's laughter. As she came closer he saw she was wearing a long striped dress, one borrowed from Jack's wardrobe. The men either side of her had thrown him too, for they were neatly turned out: Levin in a tie and pressed trousers and Tommie with his shirt-tails tucked in.

Bob checked his wristwatch and widened his eyes. 'Who are these toffs you're gallivanting with, Catriona Kennedy? Keeping you up to this hour. Goodness sake. You've a demo in the morning!'

'Sorry, Mr. Barr,' said Tommie.

'Sorry, Mr. Barr. Won't happen again,' said Levin.

She kissed each of them on the cheek and sauntered off to her tent.

Bob shook his head. 'I'd suggest you boys get some beauty sleep but it wouldn't help.' He sighed.

'Red sky at night, drunkard's delight,' quipped Eoghan.

'Aye,' said Bob. 'Students in the morning, a shepherd's warning.'

24

It was a blinding bright windy day, and Royal Avenue was at a stand-still again. Several hundred marchers were packed together shuffling a few steps at a time with youngsters stepping on the backs of shoes. The chorus of *'cut-back/fight-back'* rang out. *'Protest Against Tuition Fees'* was emblazoned on the red banner which rosy-cheeked Kiera struggled to keep a grip on. Jack synchronised her footsteps with Kiera, Bart walked beside them playing Shay's tin whistle off-key. City Hall came into sight and marchers streamed onto the pavement. The police ordered them back onto the road. Constable Corbett met Bob's gaze and doffed his cap. Bob returned the gesture. The occupiers made sure to be near the front of the crowd but they were bunched tighter in the bottleneck before Royal Avenue met Donegall Square. Cat and Fred waved their placards which read, *'Save EMA.'*

'We march today in defiance!'
'We march today in defiance!'
'Of cuts to the Educational Maintenance Allowance!'

The police had cordoned off Donegall Square and Chichester Street and officers lined the partitions. The measure made no difference to the drivers of the black cabs in the rank on the other side of the cordon. Some honked their horns. Others just smoked and watched, intermittently spitting on the pavement. There were two police cruisers there and two more on the other side of City Hall. There were three large land-rovers as well and some forty officers wearing bulky jackets, radios and hand-guns. Leon eyed them up with suspicion. Mary and Joe eyed up Leon with suspicion. A small raised platform had been positioned in front of the main gates where Gary spoke into a megaphone.

'It's vital we oppose the cuts to student access. Westminster has told us it will carve up tuition fees depriving the poorest of higher education. We're going to hear from a few speakers today…'

Over Writer's Square swallows chased one another. Punctuated splashes of rain water fell off the top of the marquee and Tall Paul watched the cars go by. Dewey-eyed, he looked into his cold tea. Padraig's head was bundled up in his coat. He let out a four beat snore. Galway John looked up from the book he read to the Christmas tree, wondering if he should take it down in case it fell and damaged someone. It was more bother than worth to tinker with right now, and he continued flipping through Daniel's tome on designed agricultural ecosystems. A pigeon grunted as it stared at the ground outside the orange dome tent.

At City Hall Miriam, wiry, with mousy brown curls, stepped onto the platform. She looked over the thousands of demonstrators and held onto the megaphone, tightly, to balance her nerves.

'This week *Queens' Students Union* are to meet with the European Commissioner for Human Rights. They will discuss how the proposed cuts are going to affect children and young people. In scrapping the Educational Maintenance Allowance in England, the coalition government has threatened a whole generation eager to learn.'

Miriam's voice had become hoarse and she coughed to clear her throat before continuing.

'Abolishing the EMA will make young students here vulnerable to homelessness. It will put them at risk to mental and physical illness. Thank you for coming here today to signal your opposition to it.'

The crowd applauded as Miriam stepped off the podium. She exchanged a few words with Gary before he took up the megaphone.

'Thank you, Miriam. Please talk to Miriam and your other student representatives if you're concerned about this. It is not a done deal. The devolved Welsh and Scottish governments are continuing the scheme. We need Stormont to finish their review and follow suit. Make your voices heard. Call or write to your MP. There are members of Occupy Belfast here with information and sign-up sheets to keep you updated. So talk to them after, or at the camp or the SU. Thank you all and have a safe journey home.'

Hands clapped and mouths cheered and then another round of chanting before the police let a few at a time out of the bottleneck. Cat and Fred had brought the sign-up sheets Gary mentioned and realised they ought to get closer to the front. Fred apologised as he squeezed between the bodies.

'Pardon me, thanking you, excuse moi, coming through.'

Officers broke up Gary's conversation with Miriam and Shay as a tide of people moved in, keen to get out. Levin held Eoghan's placard as he searched his pockets for a pen and his own sign-up sheets.

'You all need to move back,' yelled an officer. 'You and your party need to be elsewhere.'

'Everyone back!' said Gary.

Sergeant Barker was beside one of the police land-rovers and Gary called over to him. 'We need some room! Everyone back!'

Inspector Tarbard made strides towards Gary. 'I need you back from the railings,' he scowled.

Eoghan looked at the other protesters stuffed together with nowhere to go. 'Fucks sake.'

Gary raised his hands to signal people to spread out. A few officers moved into the crowd. Miriam and Shay were backed towards the van.

'I've asked you three times now,' said Tarbard. 'If you won't comply --'

'There's nowhere to go,' shouted Kiera.

'Maybe you all should move,' yelled Cat.

Someone fell. Two officers lunged at Gary. An arm tightly grabbed his. Constable Louse put his arm under Gary's, and pulled. He let his body go limp. They began to drag him with his shirt and jacket pulled above his stomach. Kiera ran forward and grabbed Gary's leg.

'Shame on you,' yelled Jack.

'Let him go,' yelled Cat.

His left shoe came off. Cat grabbed Gary's leg. Joe went in to help Kiera. Gary was swinging like a hammock in a storm. His other trainer had come off. Kiera was screaming.

Daniel pushed past Eoghan, towards Leon and away from the scuffle.

Levin pressed forward in time to see Inspector Tarbard enter the tug-of-war over Gary.

'I am arresting you under the Public Disturbances Act and --'

'Bastards,' someone yelled.

'Stop it!'

'-- And the charge of resisting arrest.'

'Ah ballix,' snarled Sergeant Barker.

Barker and two other officers rounded on Cat and Kiera, pulling them off Gary.

Barker reached out to Cat. 'That's enough. You'll have to come with me,' he said.

She saw another officer drag Kiera away. She jerked her arm away from Barker. His colleague grabbed Cat roughly. She went limp.

The crowd booed.

Tarbard put Gary's arms behind his back and cuffed him. 'On your feet, Mr. Carell,' he said.

Gary's shoe flew over the crowd and struck Tarbard on the ear. The crowd erupted.

'Yeeeeee-ohhhhh!'

Tarbard looked to the sea of possible perpetrators while Louse led Gary to the van. Kiera and Cat were being led inside too. People were screaming.

'You say cut back,' yelled Levin.

'We say fight back!'

'You say cut back!'

'Disperse at once!' yelled Tarbard.

'We say fight back!'

'Pigs! Where are you taking them?' yelled Bart.

'They'll be formally charged at Musgrave Station,' said Barker.

'Do you want to join him, sonny?' said Tarbard.

'No sir, I don't wanna,' said Bart.

'Musgrave,' yelled Levin.

'Musgrave,' yelled Eoghan.

Fred took up the fallen megaphone. 'To Musgrave!'

Under the slow drips off the front and rear marquees, Galway John leafed through a newspaper. Each photograph had a beard drawn on it. Tall Paul looked down at his feet and listened to the few passing cars. Padraig set the kettle on the grate over the fire bin. The sticks and firelighters inside glowed but did not crackle or flame.

'How come my coffee's always cold five minutes after I make it?'

'Must be the temperature, Padraig,' said Tall Paul.

Galway John rose and went into the back. He returned to his chair with the radio in his hand.

'Right. Let's get some dance tunes going!' said Padraig.

Galway switched on in the middle of the BBC news.

'In the illegal trade in confidential information, private detective Whittamore admitted to having three hundred journalists as clients.'

Padraig danced, jerking his muscles, body-popping. 'Rupert Murdoch's going down. *Down, down, down.*'

'Other news now. A woman in Dorset has trained the ducks in her local park to ask rabbits out on dates. The rabbits which also live in the park, typically only show intimacy with other rabbits. However Mrs. Pebblewobble's work is far from conclusive.'

Seventy plus protesters chanted as they marched to the bottom of Chichester Street. Others made the five minute walk through back streets. They crossed over busy Victoria Street, turning left before the garden plaza at the law courts, and met upon a thin slither of pavement. The wall rounded Musgrave: eight feet of grimy white and above that twenty feet of diagonal bars of black, red, silver and grey. There was a window covered with a grille built into the wall but no-one was there. Levin and Fred counted off the names and faces to figure out who was being held. The land-rovers arrived five minutes after the protesters, having followed the one-way system all around the city. They parted to let their vehicles through the opening gate, booing and cursing. When those shutters finally closed over, Mary and Jack banged on them a few times. Bob called for them to stop. It wouldn't do any good. Corbett appeared at the window soon after.

Eoghan pressed his face against the grille. 'I want to report a bunch of unlawful arrests.'

'You need to step back and get off the road,' explained Corbett.

'The ones arrested on the student march have a right to have witnesses present,' said Levin.

'Only one person has been charged at this time,' said Corbett.

'Are you aware you've lifted a minor?' yelled Mary.

'Disgrace how you handled them,' shouted Leon.

'Please,' said Corbett. 'Stand back from the entrance and clear the foot-way.'

'Oh fuck off!' bellowed Leon.

On the pavement opposite, Bronagh's jeep screeched to a halt. Padraig and Tommie got out. They waited for the traffic to ease and crossed over.

'What happened?' asked Padraig.

Mary yelled at Corbett. 'Shame on you!'

'Free the students,' yelled Leon.

'Free the students wrongfully arrested!'

'Free the students!'

Timid Corbett backed away. Levin rapped on the grille but it was no use. Corbett was gone from the window.

The police land-rovers were known in local slang as 'meat wagons' and weren't so much road vehicles as small mobile jails. This one was colder than the camp. Time crawled even though the siren blared overhead. It was partitioned into little cells so they couldn't see each other. They heard Gary comforting them, and someone sniffing.

Inside the yard, Cat counted ten of them. Miriam, Shay and Gary were all handcuffed. Kiera and others were not. They were led into a building at the back, one at a time through a turnstile, and through metal detectors. Their pockets were turned out and the contents stored in clip bags.

Cat was taken first, down a hall to a room with a small window. Underneath there was a desk, like an old school desk, two chairs, and a four-drawer file cabinet. The constable was a woman in her forties with a bony nose, but the rest of her face was soft and full.

'Could I have your name, age and address?'

'I already told the front desk.'

'Okay. Can you verify you are Catriona Kennedy, born 19th August, 1989, residing at 216 Falls Road?'

Cat nodded.

'Can you verify you were involved in an altercation leading to an arrest at City Hall, just after 3pm today?'

She looked down at the greasy floor and said nothing.

'You're not under arrest, Ms. Kennedy. This is only a caution.'

'If you've already made your mind up, I don't see why

I'm here.'

'Your statement will help us to establish what transpired... Why were you there, Ms. Kennedy?'

She looked at the officer, her pencil poised on the lined page. Cat took a deep breath.

'I was there to demonstrate my allegiance to the social movement actively opposed to crippling educational funding by twenty-five per cent. As a student in higher education my livelihood and life choices are affected by the economical theft of the corrupt ruling classes at Westminster and Stormont.'

The officer sighed as she wrote.

'Did you obstruct the officers during the protest?' asked the constable.

'I don't believe I did obstruct them, rather, that I altered the flow of a draconian physical assault upon a community leader who sought to inform people about the right to an education without being bankrupted.'

Cat smiled inwardly, and waited for the constable to catch up.

'During the abduction and assault on the person of Mr. Carell, who was exercising his strict code of non-violence, I intervened, seeking to ensure the aforementioned community leader would not come to physical harm as he was man-handled by members of the Police Service of Northern Ireland, and to re-attach his shoes and socks to restore some degree of dignity.'

The officer put down the pencil and handed the statement to Cat.

'Sign there please,' she said.

Cat was taken to a holding room where she was reunited with the others. Kiera was coughing and wheezing. Before Cat could hug her, she was called out for an interview. Kiera shrugged. Her face was pale behind the curls which had none of their red flash in the greasy amber light. The door closed behind her.

'They had me reviewing their version of events,'

moaned Cat.

'They questioned me too. Same crap,' said Joe.

The room reminded Cat of the old bath-houses: a blue band along a white wall with no more to it than a jutting out thin steel bench. She sat beside Shay, who rocked compulsively and looked to the floor. She put her arm round him. He was freezing.

'Hey, hey. There's no need for that,' she said.

'Love, I'm tripping balls, and it's not good. Oh fuck. Oh fuck.'

Cat looked around the room. The students, Sadie and Miriam, were furious. Anonymous Michael was just bored. There were two kids she didn't know and they looked scared out of their wits.

'There's nothing to worry about,' said Joe.

'I've got priors. They're gonna find out and, fuck, I'm done,' confessed Shay.

'Tell them you're homeless and you're sleeping at the camp. They might not make the connections,' said Cat.

Shay pressed his hands, as if in prayer, tight against his temple. 'Am fucking done. What did they ask you? Tell me.'

'They just wanted to know what I saw there,' explained Joe.

'Same here,' said Cat.

'Am done, am done. Oh, Christ.'

'It's not an interrogation. They just want a witness statement,' said Joe.

'You can handle this,' said Cat.

'Just tell them there were a load of people and you couldn't see anything.'

'That's exactly what happened,' said Miriam. 'They snatched us up without any warning.'

'Right, right,' said Shay nervously.

'We didn't do anything wrong,' confirmed Miriam.

'See? Just tell them the truth,' said Cat.

Shay pondered on this, and added, 'Gary's been gone a

long time.'

There was an icy silence and then the door opened.

'Seamus Berry.'

Shay let go of Cat's hand and stood up.

The station wall stretched around the corner to Ann Street. The pavement widened there, and there was a clearer view into the yard. Most remained by the gates on Victoria Street, close to the traffic. The light had gone and it was approaching rush hour. Cars muscled by or stopped in congestion with their fumes stinking out.

'You want a justice movement?'

'Hurry up and free the students!'

'We don't need no litigation!'

'We just want an education!'

Some of them honked their horns on seeing people lined in double file with placards. One guy, when he was sure the congestion was easing, wound down his window and called them communists.

'What are yous protesting about anyway?'

Mary banged on the grille in an un-characteristic fit of temper, screaming for them to let her Joe out. Tommie had to calm her down. Reporters set up across the road with their tripods and boom mics, not yet daring to venture closer. The number of protesters dwindled. Bob complained about the sciatica in his knees so Bronagh drove him back to the camp. Tommie tried to see in through the grilled window but it was black and empty. He turned around and faced Eoghan who looked weathered and brittle.

'I tell you what I do know, Eoghan. If those cunts hold them without trial the whole of Belfast will be down here. I'll be storming the fucking gates myself.'

Deirdre put herself between them. 'Okay. It's been little over an hour. Just wait. Maybe Levin will have got some answers,' she replied.

A few minutes later the side gate opened. Kiera and

Levin exited. People cheered. Leon gave Kiera an almighty hug. She didn't speak. Padraig, Mary and others drew as close to Levin as they could.

'What's going on?' Deirdre asked.

'Good news and bad news. They're releasing the others but Gary has been formally charged.'

'They fine him?' Padraig asked.

'They're holding him overnight,' said Levin.

25

The moon and sun hung side-by-side against creeping ethereal clouds above Musgrave. Eoghan sent the call-out for eight o'clock for the Saturday morning vigil. Over a dozen protestors showed up. They had *'Free Gary Carell!'* marked on paper glued to placards. Eoghan held his wearily. Fred paced back and forth with his. It was mostly campers although Bronagh was there and Martine Mallory too.

'This is a fucking scandal. Free Gary Carell! Excuse me, excuse me. This march today. It's to City Hall?' said Martine.

'That's right love,' said Bronagh.

'I don't see why we should stop there. We should go over the fucking railings!' said Martine.

Padraig yelled. 'Yeeeee-ohhhhh!'

Leon looked at Martine. 'Where were you yesterday?' she said.

Martine ignored her and yelled at the grilled window. 'You'll not brutalise my people further!'

Leon stared. 'Your people? You've been at the camp, what, three times?'

Martine carried on shouting at the gate. 'You black bastards!'

'That's enough. Just leave it,' insisted Leon.

'No I won't. Prosecution without trial is internment. He wasn't violent! Or resisting!'

Mary and Joe rolled their eyes. Martine pushed through them to Constable Corbett at the window. He shook at the sight of her.

'YOU struck out at a peaceful protest. The people of Belfast will remember what happened and heaven help yous!'

'Same thing with her, every time,' muttered Eoghan.

'*MARTINE,*' said Leon.

'WHAT?' she roared.

Leon sighed, shook her head and said nothing. Martine turned away from the grille, waving Corbett away. Fred stepped into the space.

'Look. If you wanna arrest her you'd be doing us a favour,' he said.

'What did you say, you misogynistic little man?'

A steel bolt rolled back. A plated door opened and Gary stepped through. He had tired rings underneath his eyes which were lacking their sparkle. His broad chin seemed to droop. Kiera rush-hugged him. Behind her he saw Cat, Shay and Eoghan and colour came back to his face.

The rhythmic shower of cars passed by as gentle rain patted drenched flysheets. Wet grass and mud in the space between homed a constellation of hazel leaves. A pigeon picked on the path. Tommie stood over a sizzling frying pan on the smoking grill. They clapped as the party from Musgrave returned. Gary crossed the marquee line of wet to dry and took a seat inside. Levin put a scalding cup of tea in his hands. He rested it on the concrete. Tommie put a fry-up in his hands.

'Aw, you shouldn't have. Thank you.'

'Systemic discrimination is what it is,' said Martine.

'I'll run you up home once you've that into you,' said Bronagh.

'I would appreciate it.'

'You'll want to get your head down,' said Shay.

The wind cried and muffled their words.

'I'm fine. A change of clothes and a shower, and once more into the breach,' he said, attempting to lighten the mood.

'Mwah-ha-hahaha! Right. Gandhi Carell here.'

'Were you thinking of going to the march?' asked Kiera.

'Why shouldn't he?' said Martine.

Gary chewed on a sausage and nodded.

'We understand if you wanna take a break. We'll survive. Take a day or two off,' said Eoghan.

'I agree,' said Bronagh. 'You need to –'

'I'm fine. I got some kip. I just want to get back into it.'

'Screw The Man!' announced Leon.

'Gary's unstoppable,' said Jack.

'THEY don't get to win,' exclaimed Martine.

'Right well look, I was thinking, I'm not going to Cork. I can spend time here. We can all pitch in,' said Eoghan.

'Oh come on. Please don't cancel your trip,' said Gary.

'I'm serious. This thing's going to court, right?'

'It might be a week or two, or a month away. It's not tonight for goodness sake.'

Gary lifted his egg onto the soda farl, cutting them so the yolk spilled into the bread.

'Right enough. It's not going to be anytime soon. You'd get Housing Executive accommodation sooner,' said Levin.

'Bastards,' said Martine.

'The people at Cork would appreciate the two of you being there,' said Gary.

'Who are you going with?' Padraig asked.

Twenty seconds later, Padraig's laughter again echoed across the pavilion.

He was cackling again at midday though it was drowned out by the sound of hundreds gathered there, and in Buoy Park. It was International Human Rights Day. They marched with drums and whistles and danced in brown pullovers and skipped in skirts of olive green. Over their heads they held notices, large and small:

'Trade Unionists for Human Rights Against Discrimination'
'If You're Against Abortion Don't Have One'
'While Poverty Persists, There Is No True Freedom'

'Women's Rights Are Human Rights'
'Gay Pride'
'Decriminalise Abortion'
'It is better to light a candle than to curse the darkness'

The latter message was plastered on a banner held at the chests of six people, stretching the width of Royal Avenue. Families and lovers walked together with the pissing rain barely scratching their optimism. Deirdre and others cycled alongside them. Minutes later the sun was out, blazing. Babies cried during the speeches at City Hall and few minded all that much. Eoghan left early for his bus from the Europa station. The wind hammered the new season home as the rally made its way back to the camp at Writer's Square. Some whistled and many chanted.

'LGBT Rights Now! LGBT Rights Now!'
'My Body, My Choice! My Body, My Choice!'

The Carnival of Resistance was the usual swirl of prams, guitars and donations: tuna; pesto; doughnuts; chickpeas; jam. Water pooled in the cracks on the pavement as Levin laid out his theory that *Star Trek* was a first-person propaganda film, and Padraig and Shay tucked into their *Cornettos*. Among the donations was a travel chess board and Daniel tried to explain to Tall Paul how the game was played. Leon made a speech and called Gary up so they could all applaud him. She wanted Gary to update the chalk-board but he said he'd hardly camped lately and someone else should do it. It was left up to Cat and the crowd parted as she walked to the marquee where Padraig presented her with the ceremonial chalk. She wrote, '*50 Days Occupied. 1 Day Since Last Arrest.*'

Miriam held a teach-in on sexual reproductive rights and it was well received. Bart told anyone who'd listen he was proud to be one of the campers. Anonymous Martine posed on Shay's skateboard for photographs. Deirdre managed to get Kiera to sign up for a subscription to Amnesty International. The afternoon was blown out in a gust. Someone said if Bob could see the beaten state of the Christmas tree he would tear it down. Leon disagreed, said it looked miserable so he'd approve. The more miserable the better as that was indicative of their cause. It looked like a heart. Random raindrops fell on canvas: rip, rip, rip, rip, rip. Fred took himself off to the college for a shower while Bronagh and Jack handed out tea and coffee. Mary tucked away her baggie of tobacco as the Englishman Nige joined them. Joe kept a close eye on him. Nige wasn't bright. He mainly indulged in small talk. His efforts were clumsy and awkward.

'Are you a Protestant or a Catholic?' asked Nige.

Joe shrugged.

Levin said, 'I stayed out of all that. As soon as I learned Martin Luther was a lying anti-semite who said divorce was worse than bigamy.'

'Oh. Right,' said Nige.

Filipe was Polish, six foot and then some; bony, with a wiry black goatee and he wore army surplus slacks from a second-hand shop. Levin showed him the water tap at the top of the pavilion and soon discovered he was about as talkative as Daniel. Filipe took a shot of the occupiers under the marquee with the photo-bombing Anonymi before Levin left for the evening. Padraig introduced Filipe to Tommie at *Brown's* and they returned with tubs of egg fried rice and spring rolls buried deep within. They ate around the sleeping fire and rain fell onto their plates of crimson sauce, boiled noodles and chicken strips.

The General Assembly was short in deference to Gary and his long day. Bronagh proposed a campaign around rising utility costs, targeting *Phoenix Gas*. The utility regulator was based in Queen Street and taking action was quickly agreed upon. Cat told how Levin had organised two teach-ins: one on land reform and the other to be led by a representative from *Positive Money*: they'd talk about research, policies and how to influence decision makers locally.

Afterwards Bronagh drove Daniel to her and Brian's

home for a spot of respite. He'd stay in her spare room as Shay and Bob had done the previous weeks. Cat, Shay and Miriam were folding up chairs when Cat mentioned to Miriam she hadn't seen her since her teach-in ended. Miriam said she'd been tired and Jack had offered her use of her tent for a lie down. Shay was all smiles.

'She let me stay there a few nights when she was away. Now that is something,' he said.

'Matching pillowcases and duvet. Firm inflatable airbed...'

'That big cosy blanket with the gold feathers on it. Completely dry too, while the rest of the camp is soaking,' said Shay.

'Pot-pourri everywhere, and those lilies in the corner were the perfect touch,' said Miriam.

Jack was in the rear of the marquee, she and Filipe lighting candles set into glass lanterns. Just inside the tarp flap was a tower unit: plates and bowls were stacked on an upper shelf; and then the cutlery tray; a ledge of tea lights, torches and spare pegs; at the bottom, the great pot and the great pan. In the corner lay a dozen placards like a crop in need of baling. Cat, Shay and Miriam joined them, bringing in the chairs for the sub-committee meeting.

'Okay. First order of business is this fundraising party,' said Cat, squinting into her notes.

Bart peeled back the tent flap. 'What's going on?'

'We're having a meeting of the outreach team,' said Jack.

'Oh great! Can I be on it? I've been talking to everyone!'

'Sorry Bart. We're full up,' said Cat.

'Okay,' he said, and let the flap go.

Shay said he looked disappointed, and that they could maybe use him if Jack was going to London the following weekend. On learning this, Miriam said she was jealous. Jack's travel was booked as a *Rail and Sail*, which meant Miriam could easily join her.

Miriam beamed 'I will then. That's a done deal!'

Cat screwed up her face. 'That's the weekend of the

fundraiser.'

'Yeah. Bronagh went to lengths to book the Printer's Cafe…' Shay's voice trailed off.

Cat was not impressed. 'It's a bit short notice. Christ. But if you want to tell Bronagh that?'

'Settle, petal,' said Shay.

'I know a few poets I could hook you up with before I go,' said Miriam.

'Shay, you're in touch with most of the musicians who come by the carnival, aren't you?' said Jack.

'Yep. They've got their own speakers too.'

'I have a friend who can lend us disco lights,' said Filipe.

'I suppose we'll manage,' said Cat.

'Outreach team: Shay part-ay!'

Jack suggested, 'Part of the proceeds could go to Gary's legal fees.'

Cat thought on this while listening to Tommie moan to Kiera about work on the other side of the tent. She was thinking both Tommie and Kiera were on the fundraising team. Cat was looking at Shay: both of them were on the fundraising *and* the outreach team.

'Can we all go out to the front a minute?' Cat got up and drew back the partition. 'Kiera, Tommie, the outreach team need help planning next week's party.'

'What sort of help?' asked Tommie.

'Everything.'

'Well, I could do the doors,' he said.

'That'd help,' said Jack.

'Anyone can do the doors. What about giving me and Filipe a hand with sound and lighting?' Shay asked.

'Don't see why not.'

'Galway John will have plug adaptors. And I can get you one of those rubber stamps,' said Kiera.

Miriam took a seat beside the fire. 'We'll need to make up a change float. You know, pounds and pennies.'

'Is it not free?' asked Leon as she put the last wet dish in the drying rack.

Kiera tutted and stared daggers at her. 'Leon, why do you think it's called a fundraiser?'

'I'm a full-timer. We're raising funds for us, right? If you let us in for free, you're saving money!'

Bart returned from the bins. 'Are you done with your outreaches meeting? That was quick! You did not have much to discuss.'

'They wanted to consult me and Tommie as we're on the fundraising team,' said Kiera.

'Fundraising? But I thought – oh! This is a super-super-meeting! I should join the fundraisers. I have loads of ideas on spending!'

'Eoghan's on fundraising too. Is he not around?' asked Miriam.

'The two of them are on their way to Cork,' said Cat.

In the time it took to reply, Cat's expression turned from pessimism to joy. The corners of her mouth sparkled.

'Oh? Who's gone with him?' Filipe wondered aloud.

Jack began to laugh, then Shay, and then they were all at it, but for Filipe and Miriam.

'What's so funny?'

'Bob. Bob and Eoghan! Cork's so far they'll probably be there most of the week. Them two, stuck together! They're going to kill each other!' Cat screamed hysterically, and buckled over, howling with laughter.

The coach made its way along the M2 with sleet bearing down. Inside tinted, dirty glass, all the lights – strip, lamp bulbs and LEDs – were turned on. Eoghan was sat in the back corner kitted out in marine green threads.

'I was hoping Levin or Joe would step up,' he said. 'But no. Because no-one chopped firewood Tommie's having to do it right there in the middle of the Media meeting. Next thing he gets a splinter and Mary's got the tweezers out. Padraig's saying she's giving him a handy and laughing his balls off. Hee haw hee haw.'

'Do I look like I give a fuck?' asked Bob.

'Fine then. I was only saying.'

'Well don't. I'm very tired.'

'Lighten up. We've to spend the next three days together. What's that look for?'

Bob straightened up his bag up on the seat between them, reaffirming the partition.

'Are we going to sit in silence?'

'Yeah,' said Bob.

Eoghan sang, *'We're not going to live in silence, we're not gonna --'*

'How long's this take? To Cork?'

'Two hours to Dublin, a bit of waiting around, and another two and a half to the rebel city.'

'But we left ages ago! That clock!'

'Those are always broken.'

'Right. Look. Eoghan –'

'When we get there we should introduce ourselves.'

'Right,' said Bob.

'Tell them their Northern comrades stand as one with them.'

'Right. How long does this take?'

26

The cold front had begun right after the strike. Now they were suffering through their eleventh day of it. Sunday's temperature was around freezing point. It was chilling in the daytime but rarely so bitter. Some campers dressed in four layers, some five as sleeping bags and blankets were common features at the campfire. Daniel and Shay often sat on night watch and were looking increasingly afraid. They knew the sensations: feeling wet all over, hacking coughs, sniffing and sneezing and hawking out phlegm. Shay said he knew his nose had a cold, icy bone but he couldn't shake the feeling it was dripping and would fall off at any moment. Others volunteered to take over watch early Monday morning. No one wanted to sleep alone those weeks and Daniel and Shay shared a tent, nestling in fetal positions.

Around midday on Monday the temperature began to rise again. Clouds passed over the sun. A south-western wind rocked the banners and smacked the tents around. Shay passed by Bart's tent and heard a scream. He'd been startled by a squirrel which quickly sprung from the side of the tent and up the ash tree. When Shay had watched it go he examined the upside down Christmas tree, It seemed ready to come off its moorings and had cast tinsel and shed needles onto tents below. Bart went to the college for a shower. Shay joined the marqueestas.

'Fucking freezing this morning. Hey, spare us a fag, would ya?'

Leon flipped over her pouch and read the instructions. '*Smoking Kills. Quit Now. Oh gawsh! I wish I'd knowed dat before I smoked dem.'*

'Maybe you can get your money back,' said Daniel.

Cat laughed. 'What you want to do is collect the set. There's one where a baby's smoking a fag through his dummy. That's my favourite. Here! Do you remember back we were talked about no drink, no drugs, and Martine wanted to ban cigarettes too?'

Daniel smiled and gave Shay his cigarette.

'She was passionate, I'll give her that,' said Shay.

'We need to stock up on coal,' said Cat.

Suddenly the morning light was blocked out by Bronagh. She stood before them, hands on her hips, with a sour expression on her gub.

'What's this about a meeting of the fundraising team on Saturday night, and why was I not notified?'

'The outreach team wanted to talk about the party,' said Leon.

Shay lit his smoke and waved it around like a magic wand. 'Party's happening!' He pointed it at a bobbing pigeon on the tiles. 'Rock pigeon!'

'And what did you learn? What's our budget?' enquired Bronagh.

Cat got up, showing off the grass stains on her trousers, and went into the rear marquee. 'Just a minute,' she called out. She came back with the camp diary and flipped through the pages. 'Last count is… six pounds, one penny and two… Kunas? What's a Kuna?'

'We'll have to go down to the currency exchange and find out then. We're going to need balloons; raffle prizes; *M&Ms* for the performers. I don't know how far a Kuna goes. I think the pound shops are our best bet,' said Shay.

'We'll need flyers and we'll need posters with some good graphic design.'

'Knock yourself out Bronagh. Oh, I found the camp diary by the way. The *Phoenix Gas* protest is on the same day as the *Vodafone* protest. That's gonna work out lovely,' griped Cat.

Shay flicked back his flowing locks. 'Isn't Kiera taking care of Vodafone? Cat, love, don't fret. I'm gonna take care of organising this fundraiser. Give you a break.'

'Shay's in charge?' said Bronagh with a smile. 'God save us! Fine.'

'Sorted love. Party, party, happening.'

Bronagh turned around to see Gary walking down the path. She recognised his expression. Her face fell.

'What's the matter?' said Leon.

Over two hundred miles away Bob opened the door to a bright furnished room. There were two beds and it was decorated with pin-ups of models and soccer posters; a television on a ledge and a bookshelf. He took off his heavy boots and Eoghan pulled the curtains. After two nights sleeping on the ground with the Occupy camp in the heart of Cork's busy city centre, Bob laid his bald head down upon a dry pillow. The room was tidy and warm and the darkness soothed him.

'We'll get the bus back on Wednesday or Thursday sure,' said Eoghan.

'Oh,' said Bob, every ache in his body being absorbed by the king mattress. 'Ohhhhh...'

'Wow. Incredible,' said Eoghan.

'Ohhhhhhh,' sighed Bob in ecstasy.

'I haven't slept in a bed like this since... ahhhhhh.'

From Bob's bed there was a hum; the low snore of a man at peace. Its cadence multiplied. Within minutes it took on a quiet nasal tone. Ten minutes in it was louder, and in twenty it verged on a rumbling. Eoghan's gentle snores overlapped with these, drifting out to a higher plane like a rowing boat across a sea of dreams, oars chopping in the water, powering up to a deeper rumble, a motor-boat surfing on the waves through to morning.

The wind picked up around noon on Tuesday and the air was humid. Levin examined a plant pot, which was delivered after a wish list was posted on Facebook but it was much too small for the Christmas tree. Galway John called him over. The men – most of them from the construction team – lined up with the marquee behind them and the sun in their eyes. Their expressions were stern and serious, all except for Bart who couldn't stand still. Galway John walked the line. Though his tone was friendly it was all business. He pointed each man to various fixtures around the camp and the work which needed to be done. When he'd said his piece the band of volunteers fell out. Tommie walked inside the marquee and folded up a chair. He raised it to the over-hanging water-logged roof and pushed. Fred brushed the spillage over to the drain. Tall Paul was picking up litter among the wet grass by Levin, who was tightening the guy ropes. Daniel lifted stray mugs from under the seats. Galway John took two mugs off him, looked into them and looked away in horror.

'That's disgusting. Who left that?'

'As long as there's no blue or green it'll be okay,' said Tommie.

'Some mug's used it as an ashtray,' spat Galway.

'You English-Irish take strange tea,' said Bart. He clapped the side of the tent that Fred was straightening, and the one beside it. 'This all looks fine to me,' he exclaimed.

'It's not,' said Fred.

'Are we going to use the spare palettes for decking in the rear of the marquee?'

'No, no, no. Too much to lose to clutter underneath, Levin,' said Galway.

'Shouldn't we be looking at each tent?' asked Tommie.

Galway John nodded. 'Good idea, lad. Full site inspection it is.'

'For goodness sake, they is all fine,' announced Bart.

'Bob said to be thorough,' said Tall Paul in earnest.

'Camp construction is a priority. We don't want mud and rainwater seeping through,' said Galway artfully.

'Hold on. Bart's right. Most people secure their tents

every couple of days. We don't need to worry about that,' said Levin.

'You are all too serious.'

'It's a serious job, young Bart. People will ask what the construction team have been doing.'

Fred agreed. 'Bob wants us doing this right. It's gotta look the part.'

'Sure as nails. He made us do the face,' said Tommie.

'*The face?*' Levin asked.

'Right, yeah. He wanted us to look above question. It's a construction group thing,' said Fred.

'You've been indoctornated,' said Bart.

Levin laughed. Daniel raised an eyebrow.

'Indoctrinated,' said Levin.

'That attitude has served us well so far,' said Galway.

'I thought this was because of Gary and to show him that we are coping,' said Bart.

'What's that about Gary?' asked Galway, after having done the mental arithmetic and still not sure of Bart's meaning.

'His summons came in. The hearing's on Thursday morning,' said Levin.

'It is bad. But they can't do anything to him, can they?' said Bart.

'That's certainly a surprise. They don't usually move so quickly. I expect they're hoping to catch him unprepared. What time's the hearing?'

'Ten thirty. There's little we can do about it but show up and lend him our support,' said Levin.

'Right. And for now, I think we ought to get a move on,' said Galway soberly.

'We can clean up so Gary and Bob and Eoghan have a nice place to come back to. Let's do it!' yelled Bart.

Cat stepped under the shadow of the bridge and away from the sun rays. She pushed through the high winds and pushed open the door of the art college. Kiera dug into the pockets of her heavy satchel and found her ID card. The glass barrier had closed after Cat entered and she put her own bar-code on the scanner. The gate jerked open. Students entered and exited as they walked towards the busy staircase in the broad hallway.

'Did you do the assignment?' asked Kiera.

'God, no.'

'Me neither. We're going to have to cram for this. Maybe an all-nighter at the camp?'

'Good idea, but Bob will never go for it. Sure it'll be no big deal,' said Cat, pragmatically. 'How many flyers did she give you?'

Kiera made sure they were out of security's eye-line. They passed the steps and she opened her satchel just wide enough for Cat to see.

Cat gasped. 'Eighty? A hundred? I've told Eoghan and Bronagh a million times not to get more flyers than we going to need!'

'We've one flyer for each time you told them.'

They kept walking to a large noticeboard with six layers of announcements. Kiera pulled out a few of their flyers, adorned with a graphic of a smashing fist.

'Where are we expected to put these? They'll have to build a new wing. The School of Cork-boards,' said Cat.

'Eoghan should have taken them to… *CORK!*'

Cat groaned. Many flyers on the board were for past dates. A few were from 2010. Cat shook her head and took down a half dozen, replanting the pins in a cluster. Kiera hid the folded remnants in her bag and gave an Occupy Belfast flyer to Cat, who reached up to the top of the board with it. They mounted two more of their flyers for good measure. Kiera led the way along the hall, past the bathrooms, to the next board.

'When does it end? Gary's hearing tomorrow. These on Friday. Saturday: demo, carnival and fundraiser?' Cat groaned.

'Right. And when are we cramming in course-work?'

asked Kiera.

'Probably before Bob gets back. You know what he's like. *No wee girls on night shift.*'

The second board was splattered upon less densely:

'Elect Sue Fischel as your SU Official'
'Blood Wanted: we'll pay, see Dr. Acula'
'Get first hand job experience: Become a trained professor overnight!!!'

Cat took a flyer from Kiera and found a spare pin. She jammed their notice hard into the centre of the board:

'PROTEST PHOENIX GAS. OPPOSE AUSTERITY. MARCH TO QUEEN'S HOUSE. MEET WRITER'S SQUARE, FRIDAY 16TH, 10AM.
PROTEST VODAFONE. DEMAND THEY PAY UK TAX. MEET CORNMARKET STORE, FRIDAY 16TH, 2PM.'

Laganside Courts sat off Donegall Quay in the garden plaza behind Musgrave and opposite the Royal Courts of Justice. The five storey building was less than a decade old with a facade of reconstructed stone panels and glass. In front of the tall black railings surrounding the building and spacious pavilion, smokers squeezed in their last puffs.

The Magistrate's Court was on level two, room six. Leon slapped the fake plants as she walked the pristine white stone hallway. Padraig and Fred walked quickly along the hall after her. Joe was ahead and he sneezed four times before entering the public gallery. Below them in the gallery were spotless brown pine walls and tables with microphones. Everything was new, but for the worn blue carpet. There was a hard light over the gallery where Gary's supporters were packed together over three rows.

Gary had three charges against him: committing a provocative act, resisting arrest, and obstructing lawful activity in a public place. The prosecutor showed that Gary appeared as one of the signatories on the Parades Commission Form 11/1. The notice of intent marked him out as the organiser. The form hadn't been submitted within the required thirty days. He drew attention to this as part of a pattern of habit, of behaviour going back months, and said Carell could be a disruptive influence in the future.

Inspector Barnabas Tarbard was called to speak. 'The late notice was a direct cause of the Police Service arriving unprepared. Hundreds were pushing and shoving in a fracas of which Mr. Carell was at the centre.'

'Achoo!' screamed Galway, and four others in the gallery took this as their cue to sound off with irritated coughs.

'He was the ringleader of a group of thousands which brought the city centre to a standstill. Mr. Carell brought the crowd together, with a megaphone, instigating circumstances which led to missiles being deployed on the scene. Police units were under threat from further hostilities,' said Tarbard.

The prosecutor and judge confirmed they had looked at the police video footage from the day in question. It was confirmed the missile which struck Inspector Tarbard was Gary's shoe, but that of course, he could not have thrown it.

Padraig sniffed and whispered, 'I wouldn't mind seeing that. I bet Harry Hill on *You've Been Framed* would pay us for it.'

'We can get it through the Freedom of Information Act. We'll cut Gary in for a slice of the pie,' replied Leon.

The prosecutor said, 'You can clearly make out Mr. Carell's words on the recording. *'We say fight back.'* And these words were repeated by the crowd upon his urging.'

Gary's counsel presented his case.

'Student Union heads at *Queen's* and the *University of Ulster* each turned in copies of Form 11/1 for this demonstration. Together they underestimated the number of people in attendance. However, they do show the police could hardly have been *unaware* of the scale of the event. This is backed up by the number of officers present before the incident began.'

The defender posited that Gary was an innocent victim

in a peaceful protest. He held up a copy of the *Belfast Telegraph*, where a front page photo showed the tug-of-war at City Hall.

'My client didn't resist arrest. Rather, Mr. Carell was caught between the heavy-handed actions of PSNI officers and over-zealous protesters. My client has no criminal record. He has previously held good relations with the police and the local council. Mr. Carell holds a reputation as a much valued community leader among residents of West Belfast.'

The judge said he was satisfied there was no way Gary Carell could have been resisting arrest and dismissed the prosecution's claim that he was obstructing lawful activity.

'Nonetheless, trouble did break out, and Mr. Carell served as a magnet for the trouble which did break out. Given how these marches are of a provocative nature and the evidence shows his use of provocative language, he bears some responsibility for this. I feel obliged to deliver a sentence of guilty on the charge of committing a provocative act.'

Bronagh's jaw dropped and her eyebrows vaulted. Levin sniffed and shook his head in disbelief.

'The ruling of this court is that Mr. Carell be prohibited from taking part in similar activities...'

Cat turned red, and bared her teeth.

'...within the highly trafficked city centre area for a period of one year. The Department of Public Prosecutions will mark up the areas Mr. Carell is to be restricted from and send those over. Court adjourned.'

'*What in the fucking heavens?*' said Galway.

Hours later on Kinsale Road, three kilometres south of Cork city centre, there was a meeting. Kinsale was largely an industrial centre though with plenty of commercial properties around. Inside a community centre with peach painted walls fifty to sixty people were in the grip of anxious chatter. A middle-aged woman with beads and scarves walked the aisle between two rows of chairs. The noise settled and she began to address the audience.

'This afternoon thirty-two workers at the *Vita Cortex* plant are to be made redundant. Redundant without pay and with immediate effect. Those affected have given most of their working lives to Vita Cortex. Seán Kelleher worked at Vita Cortex for forty-seven years.'

Her audience were seated except for two of the newcomers. They stood to the right by the tables clothed with clean plates of triangle sandwiches, iced buns, chocolate and digestive biscuits and tea and coffee. The cups had saucers. Bob rubbed his hands together and lifted up a plate. A long smirk stretched out to his red rosy cheeks as he set to stacking it high.

'Vita Cortex and *Veda bread*,' he said.

'Together they are owed €1.22 million in redundancy payments. Now, the talk on the ground is the workers will sit-in at the plant until they are properly compensated. Cork will support them. We at the *Feminist Real Action Cork Collective Network* will give the workers all the support we can.'

'Feminists,' muttered Bob.

'Fracking,' said Eoghan.

'What's that?' murmured Bob.

'The group's abbreviation. It's *fracking*.'

Bob let out a hearty laugh.

'Shush, this is serious,' said Eoghan.

'You started it.'

'We've got posters and info-sheets to give out to the Press and visitors at the front gate. There's also been discussion of closing off the roads every day until the workers' demands are met.'

'S'cuse me. Would you not be pissing off other people by doing that?' said Bob.

'I'm sorry? Pardon? You at the back!'

'Not here,' murmured Eoghan through gritted teeth.

'It's just I noticed there were a lot of other businesses in the area. Forget it. It was just a thought,' said Bob.

'She's talking about a show of strength. Sending a message,' said Eoghan.

Bob lowered his voice and said to Eoghan, 'I was just saying they want to make sure the message isn't *feck the lot of you.*'

Bob's deep voice inevitably carried. The audience gasped. Bob shrugged.

'What my friend meant to say is… is… sorry. I don't have a clue what…?'

'Yeah, he's clueless. I can speak for myself. You don't want to turn the city against you.'

A man in the centre of the room stood up. 'Maybe another form of direction action would be better?' he said.

'If you've something to say Terry, let's hear it,' said someone.

'Well, I…'

'*You're wrong.* That's your answer to everything,' Eoghan told Bob.

'No different from you. Except I don't mask it in some airy-fairy Marxist dream. You're a good deal more authoritarian than you let on, Eoghan.'

A man in the centre stood up. 'You can close off the road around the factory without it impacting other businesses.'

Folk talked over one another, rising in pitch to make themselves heard.

'I'm authoritarian? That's rich coming from you. Why are you always so abrasive? If it was up to you the fight for rights would be only one person in one wee quiet corner,' said Eoghan.

Beside him, old Mrs. Costello rose from her aisle seat. 'What's the point if it's not inconveniencing anyone?'

'Eoghan, do you ever hear what you sound like?'

Across the room another man shouted, 'It's one rule for us and one rule for Mr. Jack Ronan and those other greedy men who'd leave us all in the cold!'

'Fuck the rich,' shouted Eoghan, and a cheer went up.

'I'm having a sit down protest right now. My knees are killing me,' said Bob.

'That's right,' shouted Mrs. Costello. These young ones need to be thinking more about the elderly!'

Bob sat down beside her and began work on his piled high plate of sandwiches.

That evening Daniel wiped the chalkboard clean and wondered if it was Day 56. He marked up *Day 55* to be on the safe side. He rubbed his arms together, breathing out thick steam. He'd gotten three hours of sleep despite the night before being one degree below freezing. The night watch were working a three-shift rotation because temperatures, though not as bad as Thursday morning, were still generally quite low.

The rainwater bulge fell off the sides of the marquees in two constant streams. They shivered and sneezed and Cat wrapped herself in the thick beige throw. It was nine hours since Gary's trial and emotions were still raw. He was gone. The court had ruled Gary Carell could no longer be part of their protest. There had been talk of an appeal afterwards but it didn't stop Leon getting teary-eyed. There were too many chairs at the general assembly. The assembly had provided some catharsis, particularly the news of the sit-in at the Vita Cortex plant in Cork. Enthusiastic speculations circulated on the extent of Eoghan and Bob's involvement. However, the GA ended earlier than usual. People were worn out. Leon had motioned for the sub-committee meeting to be held in the front marquee for the sake of transparency. Levin was too tired to argue. He was also mildly annoyed with her about the letter which had come to camp earlier in the day, but it was the wrong time to say anything. Levin felt obliged to include Bart in the direct action team meeting. This came upon hearing he'd tried and failed to join the outreach team, the fundraising team, the legal team, the admin team, and the construction team.

'I'm so excited about tomorrow. It is still one of my first, I think my third demo.'

'You'll get sick of them soon enough. Believe me,' said

Leon.

'Are you kidding? We should have a protest everyday!'

Leon glared at him.

Cat rubbed dry mucus from her right eye. 'Sounds like a certain someone I know.'

Leon shrugged it off but managed a smile. The coal smoke from the fire can swelled out toward Cat and Fred and Fred waved at it with a heavy hand. Levin swept back his brown hair, moist with silver beads.

Fred screamed. *'ACHOO!'*

'Bless you. Has anyone been near Facebook lately?' Levin asked.

'Yes. I saw that,' Deirdre replied sourly.

Levin continued, his words dulled by speaking with a blocked up nose. 'Sixteen posts up linking to Axel America's *Truth Live*. Right, so that stuff about Murdoch being told about the phone hacking years ago? Good.'

'ACHOO! ACHOO! ACHOO!'

'Bless you.'

'Bless you. My point is, there's stuff coming out of our account: about first amendment rights. Hardly local. Then we get onto the posts about the New World Order. *Apparently, they're gearing up for kiddie sacrifices on New Year's Eve*,' said Levin.

'And you know that anti-vaccination shit or Jewish conspiracy theory is only clicks away,' said Leon.

'That is not good. It is definitely not good,' said Bart.

'Who's doing it?' murmured Daniel.

'Was it you Fred?' asked Leon.

'Fuck off.'

'Padraig's my guess,' said Cat.

'Most definitely Padraig,' said Leon.

'Fred, will you have a word with him?' enquired Levin.

'I've no control over him!'

Levin's sneeze nearly blew his face off. *'ACHOO! ACHOO!* Sorry about that. Was there anything on Facebook about Saturday's fundraiser?'

'Way at the bottom. With the demo announcements just underneath that,' said Leon.

'Tomorrow's demos? Christ almighty,' said Cat.

'There's little we can do about it right now,' said Deirdre.

'We can delete all that shit,' said Leon firmly. *'ACHOO!'*

'Blesh you,' said Fred.

'Bad enough that we've got those anonymous trolls on there,' said Cat.

'I saw that. Anonymoose; and Ginty fucking McGinty,' he replied.

'Yer man Sneaky Weasel's pretty funny,' said Levin.

'Who's actually on the media team?' Deirdre wondered.

Leon said, 'There's myself, Eoghan, Mary and Joe… they've not been that active; Gary, Padraig…'

'Tch! Padraig!' exclaimed Bart.

In wind, rain and darkness, before moon fall or sunrise, Eoghan climbed onto the bus at Cork station. Bob raised his ticket to the driver and followed the lad to the back of the bus.

'We should do something like that for Christmas. A headline protest,' said Eoghan.

'Come on, I'm taking the window,' grunted Bob.

He shuffled into the rear and put his bag on the seat next to him. Eoghan struggled to put his in the overhead. The bus driver moved before he was ready. Bob looked out through the window for the River Lee, though the condensation would be his only view of it. Eoghan climbed into the seat in front and sat with his back against the window.

'What's your problem?' said Eoghan.

'You! For one: can you not tell when you're hitting on a lesbian?'

'She was bi.'

'She was nearly getting a harassment order on you.'

'That's bullshit,' said Eoghan coolly.

'Figure of speech.'

'Apologise.'

Bob continued looking out the window.

'Fine. What about you and that one with the dye in her hair? *Oh missus, I like a good piece of cake. Is there any sugar?*'

'Dunno what you mean. I don't talk like that.'

'*It was so wet outside. Sniff-Sniff. I like your dress. The bed was very comfortable.*'

'Of course it was. You know what? So's your ma's.'

'Senile oul' git.'

'Naive wee vegan.'

'I'm not a vegan!'

27

It was a grey, misty Friday morning with only the tall flames giving any light. Levin woke up for a pish and a wash, coughs over coffee and in time for the 9am news over sweeping, shifting traffic. The news-reader talked about thirty-two workers who had begun a sit-in at the *Vita Cortex* plant in Cork. Bronagh and Fred made a racket bringing out the placards and Levin turned the radio up. The workers were planning to stay over-night until the with-held redundancy package was paid. Galway John brushed white firelighter flakes off his trousers and handed Levin his copy of *The Irish Times*.

'There's more detail on the Vita Cortex thing in there. I haven't had a chance to look at it. Perhaps it'll mention Bob or Eoghan, though I very much doubt it.'

Deirdre cycled onto the path, braking just in front of Fred as he set down more placards. Bronagh loudly cursed the Christmas tree as a health hazard and then walked to the front of The Love Shack and bent over so her head was under the flysheet.

'*Padraig!* You asked us to shout when it was nine o'clock!'

A sickly whisper came back. 'I might give it a miss. Bit tired, Bronagh.'

Cat was securing a tent nearby. 'He was up half the night. I *knew* he wouldn't make the gas protest. Anyway, Padraig's a major supplier, aren't you?'

There was only a short muffled whimper.

'Don't you dare miss the Vodafone one,' said Kiera, crawling out backwards from their tent.

Under the marquee, Levin's pink hands gripped the newspaper. 'It says here, *the thirty two Vita Cortex workers have a combined service of eight-hundred and forty seven years between them.*'

'I saw that,' remarked Bronagh.

'*Mr. Ronan's assets include retail parks, a soil fertility business, luxury apartments, a stud farm and an investment property group.*'

'The courage of those poor men. Well good on them for taking a stand,' said Galway, and he rubbed his gloved hands together.

'Fuck the bosses,' said Leon.

'The spirit of Occupy,' said Cat. 'Any word from Eoghan?'

'Last I heard was yesterday: a text about a big important meeting,' said Levin.

'Interesting. Remember that shit Bob pulled on *The Trojan Show*? Man's a wild card,' said Leon.

'Right place, right time,' said Deirdre.

'There's no way they wouldn't have been involved in that. Eoghan's impulsive and they're both always sticking their noses in,' said Fred.

Galway laughed. 'That *is* true.'

Bronagh nodded.

And then through the mist and red spitting flames, Eoghan and Bob walked towards them, rucksacks on shoulders. Eoghan stopped so Bob almost collided with him and then stood legs apart and arms outstretched out like a ringmaster. Two pigeons flew off the ground.

'*Good morning comrades! Fresh from their show-stopping appearance at Occupy Cork I give you... the ambassadors of anarchy!*'

'Nine hours of that, God save me.' Bob pointed at the tent nearest to him. 'Those guy-ropes are loose.'

When he looked back to the others they were smiling, each and every one.

'I'll stick the kettle on,' said Fred.

'Sure let me take your bag, Bob,' said Galway.

'Legends in our time,' said Leon.

'Welcome back,' said Cat.

'The whole camp's been talking about you two,' said Bronagh.

'Well done,' said Deirdre.

The men were taken aback. Eoghan tried to speak.

'Uh...'

Then Bart was on the scene, running round them. 'Welcome back Eoghan and Bob! Tell us what happened. I want to know everything.'

'Well, Bart. They were in Cork for five days and suddenly there's a major sit-in announced. I'm already hearing thousands are going out on the street in support of the workers. Isn't that amazing?' said Leon.

Eoghan smiled cautiously.

'I'm kicking myself I wasn't there,' said Deirdre.

'It's not going to look good for Jack Ronan this happening almost a week before Christmas,' said Levin.

'His corporate empire: brought to a stand-still!' announced Leon.

'There'll be no asset stripping while they occupy the plant,' said Galway John.

Bob breathed in deeply. His expression didn't change but the gears in his head were turning.

'Ronan's powerless. The people have the power. Three cheers for Bob and Eoghan,' exclaimed Leon.

'Hurray!'

'Hurray!'

Many of the occupiers raised their arms and clapped. Joe and Shay put their heads out and clapped too. Eoghan smiled sheepishly. Bob took his hat off and rubbed the back of his head. He weakly parted his lips to set them straight when Bart interjected.

'This is brilliant. Really brilliant!'

'Cork's loss is our gain,' said Galway John.

'I want to hear all the details,' said Cat.

Eoghan stretched out his arms out and yawned. 'Actually, I thought I might hit the hay.'

'Me too,' said Bob.

'Aw come on Bob,' pleaded Deirdre.

'There really wasn't much to see,' he said.

'Aww,' said Bart.

Levin shrugged. 'I guess, sleep well then.'

Eoghan zipped open his tent and crawled inside, sealing it as soon as he'd ripped off his shoes. The wind was warring with itself and the slim polyester tent was caught in the middle. Eoghan moved Levin's clothes and sleeping bag off his own and found a folded envelope. It was addressed to Occupy Belfast and had been opened. He tossed it to one side. He wasn't in the mood to hear from anyone for a while.

Queen's Street was lined with bus stops for services starting their journeys to the North and West of the city. The shops there were medium sized, moderately affordable and most locally run. There were several art galleries and art supplies stores. It was the proximity to City Hall that made for its busy character. Half-way down, between a cafe and hair salon, signage hung over the street: *Queens House* in royal blue with silver-plated serifs. The building had a covered, open hallway to a front door. A wall sign there read that the utility regulator was on floors two through five. Thirteen protestors gathered on the street. Subdued Tall Paul had accompanied them and Bronagh was smothering him with mothering.

'Don't you worry. We'll have all the trimmings of a real Christmas dinner. I'll make sure there's a full, hot meal in front of you. Shay! *Shay!* This party tomorrow. Have you been getting the word around?'

'Some people weren't sure about it, after the arrests. On the other hand there's ones are keener to be a part of it because of them,' said Shay.

'Good. And have the bands confirmed?' said Bronagh.

'Yes,' said Shay.

'Are you sure? Okay. And you've talked to the venue?'

'Yes.'

'After lunch we'll go through a list of what needs done,' said Bronagh.

'Yes, Bronagh.'

Fred was filming the gathering on his mobile phone. The Anonymi were intent on getting in shot, and posed like hip-hop rappers under the winter sun. A few of them held placards. A new batch had been marked up by hand for the demo.

'Hold Phoenix Gas Accountable.'
'End Gas Hikes.'
'This Is No Laughing Gas!'
'Frack off!'

'Don't you love the smell of activism in the morning?' exclaimed Leon.

'You don't tire of saying that, do you? This afternoon's the main feature,' said Kiera.

Leon studied the young girl. There was a curious certainty there. 'Hey. Did I hear you're volunteering to run the Secret Santa?'

'That's right.'

'I need a favour. I need you to pair me with someone.' Leon's voice was down to a whisper and they couldn't help but hear Levin talking with others behind them. His voice was raised.

'Padraig's done what now?'

'You ought to have seen the length of it this morning,' said Mary.

'I saw. A real pile-on of comments. In your face stuff,' said Joe.

'Padraig's a real fucker,' said Anonymous Norris.

That afternoon Bob was out on Royal Avenue, looking at the items hanging from a rack: earphones; chargers; plug adaptors.

A line manager stood in the middle of the phone store, dressed in slacks and a red pullover. Shay was looking at the latest releases of megapixel smartphones and the high price tags. Kiera walked towards him, holding a sheet of paper in her hand.

'Ready to go,' he murmured.

She smiled, turned away, and with curls of red hair falling down her back she approached Fred.

'Mic check,' she said.

He took his phone out of his pocket. 'Mic check,' he said.

'Mic check,' said Mary and Bart.

Kiera raised her voice. 'We are Occupy Belfast!'

Cat and Leon were lined up by the rack of SIM cards, and they called out, 'WE ARE OCCUPY BELFAST!'

Kiera walked the width of the store. 'We would like to state this is not against the workers of Vodafone.'

Bronagh and Levin called out with them, from the front of the store. 'WE WOULD LIKE TO STATE THAT THIS IS NOT AGAINST THE WORKERS OF VODAFONE.'

'Today we are targeting Vodafone to demand that they pay their tax,' said Kiera.

Eoghan and Padraig at the back of the store called out, 'TODAY WE ARE TARGETING VODAFONE TO DEMAND THAT THEY PAY THEIR TAX.'

A dozen others called back from all around the store, amplifying Kiera's words. 'WE DEMAND THAT THE TAX LOOPHOLES...'

Kiera said, 'That allow the mega-rich corporations...'

A sour-faced line manager stood at the till, watching.

Joe, Ryan and Steph followed Kiera speaking out another wave of their chorus. 'THAT ALLOW THE MEGA-RICH CORPORATIONS...'

'To dodge their tax duties are closed.'

'TO DODGE THEIR TAX DUTIES ARE CLOSED.'

She walked the width of the store again, reading aloud. The red-shirted line manager approached and tapped her page. She walked away from him towards Fred, who was filming everything on his phone.

'CURRENTLY 133 BILLION POUNDS'

'Worth of corporation taxes,' said Kiera.

Cat brought a sign out of her shopping bag. It had a Vodafone logo on it, and read, 'Pay Your Tax'.

'WORTH OF CORPORATION TAXES'

'Are legally avoided,' said Kiera.

Kiera paused to breathe in a draw from her inhaler.

Bart crossed the line manager's route to Kiera, slowing him down. The manager put his hand on his back. Bart joined in on the chorus as they walked.

'VODAFONE HAS DODGED SIX BILLION IN TAX MONEY!'

'Public money for public services!' said Eoghan at the back of the store.

'Public money for public services!' said Bronagh at the front of the store.

'Public money for public services'! said Bart, now out on Royal Avenue.

Inside the two-man olive green ridge tent, Levin read Chomsky. He had sleeping bags draped over his knees and a pillow under his bum. A boot nudged the front of the tent.

'Knock, knock,' said Eoghan.

'It's your tent. You don't have to knock.'

'I've got my hands full.'

Levin set down his book and climbed forward to the door-flap. He took Eoghan's mug of tea from him and held it still.

'Fucking hell. Some change around here while we were away.'

'You heard then?' said Levin.

'Aye. It had to happen to one of us sooner or later. Just a shame it was Gary.' Eoghan steadied himself with a fist on the ground as he shuffled his bum into the pile of clothes. He put his lips to his mug, and drew away from the heat. 'I bet he was targeted. The cops probably wanted payback after Leon pulled that stunt in Stormont. What the hell happened?'

'They had that twisted cop giving evidence and the judge wasn't much better. His bullshit detector did throw two of the charges out right away, I'll give him that. The evidence for provocation was all nonsense.'

'And what about this fucking nuts sentence? How can they ban him from protesting, even with the charge?'

'I don't know. I don't know. They said it's only in certain parts of Belfast. We're waiting for more information. Anyway, Gary's lawyer is going to appeal.'

'I'll give him a call later on,' said Eoghan.

'I think he'd appreciate that.'

'God. What a nightmare. We'll have to cope as best as we can without him here.'

A fly had snuck into the tent with Eoghan and was buzzing around his head, him swatting at it furiously. 'Hey. Did Wee Kiera throw that Vodafone protest together?'

'All her idea. I gave her a hand with the script but she took the lead with it,' said Levin.

'Gives you hope for the future.'

'Aye.' He laughed. 'Did you see Shay running round the shop, all slippery like?'

'I saw Bart go back in,' said Eoghan with a smile.

'He's getting schooled.'

'And how's things for the morrow night?'

'Dunno. No clue. I'm going home for a spell. I've been working like a dog here. We've got some —' The wind slapped the tent against Levin's head and he slapped it back. 'We've got some interesting teach-ins lined up.'

'Actually I wanted to ask you about this idea of occupying a building. You've Leon all fired up about it. Transport House? The Union building?'

'You found the letter,' said Levin.

Eoghan picked up the damp envelope from the side of the tent.

'Nothing to do with me. Guy from *Unite* gave it to me after Gary's trial. I wanted to think on it before I spoke to her.'

Eoghan swatted the fly away again. 'I only skim-read it. Read it aloud.'

'*Dear Leon McCallum. Re: Occupy Belfast. Thank you for your letter earlier this month. Unfortunately we have no interest in providing Transport House as a site for habitation. We have the greatest respect for your efforts to oppose austerity. However, I must point out that any attempts to occupy Transport House would be illegal. Yours in solidarity…*'

Eoghan was laughing. 'Jesus. What drugs was she on?' he said, unknowingly.

28

The wind whipped the tents amid the screams of the Saturday Carnival of Resistance. A video blogger interviewed Levin about their plans for Christmas Day and he delighted telling him about the meal they were having, though admitted sadness he couldn't be there himself. The vlogger filmed Bob strapping the Christmas tree tighter to the trunk of the ash with a twisted nylon rope. Someone had donated a suitable planter for it but a prior GA debate had decided it would be left in place.

Tommie shuffled to the door of his tent, his black leather jacket trailing behind him. Eoghan and Shay stood outside facing three ministers gathered below the steps of *St. Anne's*.

'What's up?' asked Tommie as he pulled his shoes on.

'Just keeping an eye on the clergy. What are they doing?' said Shay.

'The one in the middle is the Vice-Dean. He sits out there every year the week before Christmas, collecting money for charity,' explained Eoghan.

'Right, right. Yeah, I saw him set up about half nine. What is it he calls himself?' said Tommie.

'The Black Santa. I'd have thought Krampus was the black Santa,' said Eoghan.

Tommie got to his feet and followed their gaze to the cathedral. The Vice-Dean stood on the kerb clothed in cap and cape, all in black. Well-wishers slotted coins and notes into the three foot tall whiskey barrel beside them.

'He seems to be doing okay for himself,' noted Tommie.

Eoghan gave his glasses a rub against his pullover. 'I'm sure he's been picking up some of our footfall.'

'Maybe some of his ones will come over to us,' said Shay optimistically.

'I suppose,' murmured Eoghan.

Tommie rubbed his thin head of hair. 'You're not sure though. And I don't blame you. Them ones standing there talking about bonds between us and God. And all the while not payin' any taxes.'

'Aye but what about that get-up? The cloak. All in black. They've pretty swish threads. Like Batman,' said Shay.

Tommie laughed.

'Do you not fancy it? Being a man of the cloth? Father Tommie!'

Eoghan laughed. 'Father Tommie!'

Shay pulled one side of Tommie's black jacket away and tried to get it over his shoulder.

'What are you doing? Oy! It's really nippy!'

'*Work with me, dah-ling!*' Shay took the jacket off him, turned it around and fed the sleeves back up through his arms so the collar was up to his neck. 'There you are. Father Tommie!'

Tommie smiled and raised one of his arms. 'By the power vested in me I bless this camp.'

Under the marquee, Bob, Daniel and Padraig were listening to the three o'clock news when Levin joined them, fresh from his afternoon shower.

'Kim Jong-Il's dead. Seventy years of age,' said Bob.

'No way. He only looked twenty-three,' quipped Levin.

'*The final US troops withdrew from Iraq today, twelve days ahead of deadline,*' said the newsreader.

'In their place, sixteen branches of McDonalds, and eleven Starbucks,' said Padraig.

'*However not everyone is happy. Country-wide insurrections followed…*'

'*However not everyone is happy.* What the fuck kind of

framing is that?' asked Levin.

'Maybe if you kept your gob shut I could hear.'

'The Reverend Doctor Ian Paisley gave his final sermon yesterday...'

Padraig launched himself out of his chair and punched the sky. 'Yes! YES!'

'No,' said Levin.

'He told his congregation, 'Thank God I'm nearer home, nearer Sweet Jesus, nearer the great Apostles, nearer all our blood-washed friends.' Paisley dismissed rumours that he is unwell.'

Levin said, 'That's his trailer for the Edinburgh Fringe. Daniel, do you know who Paisley is?'

'I heard him all the way from Alicante.'

'King Dox,' said Padraig.

Helen Hazlett came by the marquees with a heavy bag of groceries. She'd gloves, tins, and chocolate. Levin offered her a cuppa. Bob got up from his seat, but she declined, and he sat back down again. It was a week until Christmas and there were presents to buy. There'd be a cup of tea there for her on the way back. She was barely gone when Ricky Phelan passed her with more supplies for the occupiers. Then Ali Knipe: fifty, curly-haired and moustached, he brought two bulging grocery bags to them. Inside were a couple of blankets, a pillow, pillowcases and a few tins.

'I couldn't fit any more in,' said Ali.

'Oh this is just what we need to keep the cold from the door,' said Levin.

'Fair play to yous,' said Ricky. 'There's not a lot who'd sit out in this.'

Ali asked about their Christmas. They talked about Bronagh bringing down a Christmas meal and how Kiera was running a Secret Santa. Tommie offered Ali and Ricky a cuppa but they declined. Bart came by and asked if he could have a banana. Padraig pushed in front of him and took two.

'Thanks guys. You can see they appreciate it. Can I get you a cuppa?' wondered Levin.

'Oh no. No thanks. I best be on my way,' said Ricky.

'Me too,' said Ali.

Mary marched towards them, shouting, 'Padraig, I'm gonna string you up!'

'Mwah-ha-hahaha! Kinky! Mwah-ha-hahaha!'

Joe was right behind her and as angry, his toe catching a lump of coal which skittered across the path. 'Didn't you get our messages?'

Ali backed away. Ricky didn't know where to look, but found himself facing Bob, who nodded and smiled.

'Thank you for the donation,' said Bob.

'That crap on Facebook. We asked you to let it be,' said Mary.

'There were a few people talking shit online and I gave them a smack-down. That's all that happened,' insisted Padraig.

'Some of them our own members,' said Joe.

'Friendly fire! And it wasn't like anyone else stepped up,' said Padraig.

'You just made things worse!' complained Mary.

'Excuse me,' said Bob. 'How about yous ones take it somewhere else? Ali and Ricky don't want to hear this. I don't want to hear this.'

'Sorry,' said Joe.

'A thank you might have been in order,' said Padraig as he walked away.

'Sorry Ali, sorry Ricky,' said Mary.

That night the rain pelted lightly on the marquee. The wind blew cool and hard. Moths swanned around the flaming fire, Padraig bound to a spit on top of it. Or so some wished.

'When the online stuff starts spilling over into the camp, I'm not having that,' said Bob.

'We'd a half dozen events to promote and *his* answer was to start a flame war,' said Joe.

'*A flame war!* That's just nonsense.' retorted Padraig.

'You should have just left it,' said Bronagh.

'Bob.'

'Yes, Kiera?'

'Cat and I have final coursework to cram for. We need to work in the peace and quiet.'

'No. No. No.'

Cat said, 'It's not like we'd be doing night shift on our own.'

'I don't want you sitting up the whole night talking. The rest of the camp has to sleep.'

'What about this matter with Padraig?' asked Galway.

'There's no fucking matter! Why am I getting the blame for this?'

Bob found a greenfly crawling on his hand and smacked it dead.

'This is Padraig using his own account, right? I mean, mostly? There's a difference between that and the camp account,' said Eoghan.

'It wasn't just me. Levin, Fred and Jack were at it too.'

'Tout,' said Fred.

'Bollocks,' said Levin.

Bronagh threw her head back and puffed up. 'Now hang on a moment. There's plenty of troublemakers on that Facebook page and Padraig's by far the least of them. This Ginty McGinty one who keeps mouthing off...'

'I'm pretty sure that's a bar in Glasgow,' said Galway.

'Could you not ban him first?' Bronagh said it less as a question than an order.

Eoghan looked confused. 'How are Levin, Fred and Jack connected?'

Cat said, 'It all started over some randomer. The usual *'go get a job'* knob. And then someone, I think it was Leon, said there are no jobs because of austerity.'

Bronagh stuck her neck out and folded her arms. 'Everybody was chipping in!'

Jack had the page open on her phone.

'Here it is, he's called Jason Greaves. *I know you don't agree with the coalition government but you must respect the democratically elected will of the people.* And Levin's response: *Oh. I do declare we shall enact the mandate spiffingly so all class of man may go to the ball.*'

'Mwah-ha-hahaha!'

A few others laughed too.

Jack put her phone away. 'It would have been just us having a laugh, until people start citing stuff from the guy's page.'

'What like? Personal stuff?' asked Shay.

She nodded. 'Sneaky Weasel or Anonymouser or one of those writing under a psuedonym saw Jason Greaves was from Castlereagh. From that they deduced the man lives in a castle.'

Fred fell into a giggling fit. 'Half of Castlereagh's a dump, right?'

'I live in Castlereagh,' said Kiera.

'Sometimes its better to let sleeping dogs lie,' said Bronagh.

Kiera admitted, 'Actually Castlereagh is kind of a dump.'

Bob snorted, unimpressed. He got up and stoked the fire.

'Did you have to challenge the guy to a fight, Padraig?' said Mary.

'You did what?' demanded Bronagh.

'He said the cops were right to ban Gary. So I said, mwah-ha-hahaha, I said he was looking slapped around the one-way system. Mwah-ha-ha!'

'None of this is that important. I'm more concerned with this shit I'm hearing about Zionist conspiracy videos,' said Eoghan.

'*There were no fucking Zionist conspiracy videos! Jesus. Give us a break. Fucking Zionist conspiracy videos!* I do more work on that page than most of you. As much as Eoghan and Cat. I even went to all the bother of uploading Fred's video of the Vodafone protest. It took bloody ages.'

Cat was raging. *'What the fuck Padraig?'*

Eoghan fumed. 'It might have been a good idea to bring it here, to the GA, first.'

'God's sake! What's the issue?' snarled Padraig.

'I had my face covered up. I don't want to be on a Facebook video,' said Cat.

'YOU HAVE BLUE HAIR!' he screamed.

Leon didn't have many possessions, which she felt was the best way to be in case someday she got to see the world. Her Saturday evening was spent packing up her belongings. She arrived at the camp with the first box at half nine. The two older men were doing their usual *Statler and Waldorf* in the marquee.

'Bob, would you not take yourself off to the party for a while?'

'Don't be daft, John. It's kids. Anyway, what good can come from a political party?'

Leon set the box beside her condensation soaked pillow. She licked her finger and wiped it against a discolouration on her grey shirt. After waving goodbye to the hecklers she walked into a heavy cloud of deodorant moving over the front of The Love Shack. She began to cough. Padraig shuffled out of the tent.

'We were just going over to the fundraiser,' he said.

'Did anyone say anything about me at the GA? Levin or anyone?' asked Leon.

Padraig got to his feet and Fred began crawling out after him.

'It was me they tried to boot out,' said Padraig.

'What? What about?'

'I put a few things on Facebook that weren't *'approved.'* Freedom of speech my arse. Course, there was fuck all they could do once they realised all those comments were on the post that was advertising the gig.'

'Wider audience reach for sure,' Fred acknowledged.

The party was at *The Printer's Cafe*, a minute up

Donegall Street and bordering on a narrow arched alley: Exchange Place. The alley was filled with sounds of guitars, drums and screaming revellers. Leon passed the stylistic black and white paintwork and pushed on the red door, which barely opened. There were about fifteen people in the cafe all packed in tight to one another. Folk sat at tables with coloured drinks and snacks. Leon looked back at the boys as she entered.

'Have you got to clearing out of your place yet?'

'What?' Fred shouted. 'It's really loud!'

'What?' Padraig shouted.

'Three pounds Leon,' shouted Bronagh, rising from a table just inside the door.

'What?'

Padraig ducked the tax for the alley-way, where Cat and Eoghan were dancing to beats piped through small subwoofers. Exchange Place was about ten foot wide, and packed. A small crowd gathered around Shay. He was showing off his break-dancing moves on the cobblestones. Tommie twirled Jack in his arms.

Fred made his way through the loud bacchanal, found Padraig, and raised his voice to a shout. 'Bronagh made me pay. I just paid tent rent! Hey! Is Bart jumping on the spot?'

A large figure crossed by them and shouted out, 'Fuck you Fred Poke!'

'Who was that?' shouted Padraig.

'No idea! I've never seen him before!' shouted Fred.

'Hey! Look who it is!' shouted Padraig.

Fred looked past Leon to the top of the alley and a familiar silhouette. There were screams. Kiera pushed through. Leon was already running towards him. Bronagh had just come outside and saw him too.

'*GARY!*'

Leon and Kiera hugged him with such speed and firmness he could have fallen over, but for Bronagh hugging him from the rear. Then Cat piled on.

'What are you doing here?' said Joe.

'Who cares? Gimme some!'

'Oy! Mary!'

Eoghan laughed. 'Let the man breathe!'

Leon and Kiera relented. Gary was gasping.

Eoghan hugged him. 'We didn't expect to see you here.'

'The court said I couldn't attend any protests. They didn't say anything about socials.'

'It's bullshit,' said Leon.

'Everybody's missed you,' said Fred.

Gary laughed. 'It's only been a few days, guys.'

Earnestly Padraig said, 'Aye but even so...'

The music faded out and Shay's voice boomed through a microphone. His skater friends were chanting.

'*Shay! Shay! Shay! Shay! Shay!*'

'If I could have your attention? Thank you all for coming to the Occupy fundraiser for Occupy, like. Bronagh has asked I remind you raffle tickets are on sale at the door. Quick announcement: *I'll drink anything!*'

'Yeeee-owwww!! *Shay! Shay! Shay! Shay! Shay!*'

'We have a star in the crowd tonight. All the way from his sofa on the Falls Road. Give it up for Occupy Belfast's first arrest, for speaking truth to power: the one, the only Gary Carell!'

Tommie, Eoghan and Padraig lifted him up in their arms. His head brushed the top of the archway.

'Aw come on. Don't!' pleaded Gary, his face a bright red.

'*Gary! Gary! Gary! Gary! Gary! Gary!*'

'And before we get back to the band, one last announcement. And even I don't know what this is.'

Shay handed the mic over to Mary.

'Welcome back Gary,' she said. 'Joe, would you let him be and get over here? Gods save us!'

The audience laughed.

'I'm so glad you could be here. We have big news.'

She grabbed Joe's hand and pulled him closer to her and up to the mic. They looked at one another and smiled.

'Mary and I are getting married.'

She raised her left hand for the shine from the ring to catch the spotlight. The crowd went wild.

From grey Sunday morning silence on the desolate street cathedral bells rang out over the camp. A slim gloss of rain lay upon the orange dome tent Gary had brought that first afternoon. For the time being it had been left to Eoghan to look after. Mary and Joe walked by and greeted Eoghan when he put his head out and flinched in the too-vivid daylight.

'Best. Fundraiser. Ever,' he said.

Kiera and Bob were sat under the marquee, synchronised smoking. Eoghan walked through to the rear marquee and made himself a bowl of cereal. Cat was further down the path, zipping up the orange dome tent. Eoghan sat down, a few chairs away from Bob. Cat took a chair next to Kiera.

'Someone had a few too many cokes last night,' said Kiera knowingly.

'Cokes and smiles,' said Bob, and he added a few playful tuts for good measure.

Eoghan looked at Cat and back to Bob. He puffed out air turning to steam. 'We'd be grateful if yous would keep this between yourselves. Please?'

Bob laughed. 'Around here secrets don't keep, you should know that.'

Kiera remarked, 'Yous were a bit loud.'

Cat blushed and shifted about anxiously.

'Cat, isn't there something you want to ask Bob?' said Kiera.

'Fuck's sake. What?'

'You know.'

'Kiera, I don't know.'

Kiera sighed. 'Cat and I have to study and --'

'A hundred times, final time, no,' said Bob.

'You don't even know what I was going to say!'

'Yes I do. You were going to ask if you could do your

schoolwork here on an all-nighter.'

Cat reclined, now relaxed; happy; no regrets. She brushed her fingers through her hair. 'Oh. I remember now. *Girls don't do night shifts.* Unaccompanied, yeah. Eoghan, will you sit up with us?'

'We've been over this,' said Bob. 'No more people up all night talking. Besides, Eoghan's lazy, and he snores.'

A smile spread over Cat's face. 'He talks in his sleep too, Bob.'

Eoghan's face fell. 'I told you that in confidence.'

'Told her what?' wondered Kiera.

'What happened in Cork,' said Cat boldly.

Bob looked over the three of them and back again. 'If you're trying to blackmail me think again,' he said coolly.

Whatever he was referring to, Kiera was incensed by the accusation. 'Woah. Back up!'

Cat's eyes met Kiera's as she rose on her way to the water kegs at the wall.

Kiera held back her fury, at least in tone. 'I get that it's been a tough week for security. A fight nearly breaking out at the carnival. A known felon wandering around near the camp.'

Bob's jaw dropped. 'What? No-one's been telling me any of this!'

'Well now you know. So don't throw around accusations of blackmail.'

Cat slammed the kettle down on the fire grate.

Bob raised that suspicious eyebrow. 'A known felon? Do you mean Gary?'

'Of course I mean Gary!'

Bob paused for a moment, his mental faculties ruffled. 'There's mind games going on here. Haven't you girls got homes were you can sit up all night?'

'Aye, our parents would love that,' said Kiera. 'So what's this gossip then? About Cork?'

Padraig marched in with his phone in his hand, and plonked himself down in the middle of them. 'I'm going to prove to you fuckers I was right to put this online.' He held the phone in front of them and pressed play on a video. It was Fred's footage from the Vodafone protest.

'THERE IS UNWILLINGNESS IN STORMONT...'

'To represent the people,' said Kiera there, and they re-watched the line manager putting his hands on her left arm. Then he'd his hand on her right arm, and tried to lead her from the store with his hand on her back.

'Don't touch me, please don't touch me, or I'll get the police on it,' said Kiera.

'RATHER THAN CALLING FOR A REDUCTION...'

They watched the manager step forward and take the line manager's arm and send him away.

'... IN CORPORATION TAX...'

The manager had drawn in close to Kiera and decided to go around the other side of her. At the exact same time she had moved away from him.

Watching it back Kiera told Cat it did look good. She agreed. The camera panned across the shop to Mary and Joe.

'See?' said Padraig, feeling vindicated. 'A video scrapbook of fine memories for the newly engaged couple.'

'THE PARTIES AT STORMONT SHOULD BE...'

They could barely see the face of the manager though he'd come over close to the camera.

'I haven't called the police but I will,' he said.

'... CALLING FOR THE RETURN OF PUBLIC MONEY.'

'You are all on CCTV, just to make you aware of it,' said the manager.

From behind the camera they heard Fred reply, 'Aye. Well you're on YouTube, mate!'

'We are the 99%!'

'WE ARE THE 99%!'

'WE ARE THE 99%!'

The video ended and Padraig lowered the phone. The others were nodding, genuinely pleased with the results.

'You see. I was right, I was right. We look bloody great.'

29

Monday's humid rain splatted upon the chalked notice. 59 days occupied. Padraig was still showing around the video of the Vodafone protest. Tall Paul seemed traumatised by the viewing. Bob, as he wiped his coal stained fingers on his jeans, told Fred he was no David Attenborough. Levin said it reminded him of *The Blair Witch Project*, but he was only having a laugh. A car door slammed announcing Bronagh. *The Black Santa* and the other clergy almost jumped out of their cloaks. She ventured through the sleet carrying a bin bag in each hand and set them under the marquee.

'There you go. Latest pile of laundry, care of your Auntie Bronagh. Washed and dried and folded. One at a time, Padraig!'

Daniel and Bob were the first to thank her.

'I'm happy to do washes for people who need them.'

'Anything for me in there?' said Fred.

'You didn't give me anything. Yours are in there too, Paul, when these gulls have finished.'

Levin made eye contact with her. 'Coffee, Bronagh?'

'Tea please. Thanks, love. Shay, your CD player is in there. Don't ask me how. I didn't wash it.'

The CD player rattled as he pulled it out, *The Best of Bob Marley* broken into six slices. Bronagh said that was exactly how she found it. Levin confessed, reluctantly, that he'd seen Leon get excited and knock it to the ground a few weeks before. Shay took the broken player and his clothes to his tent.

'Maybe it still works,' he said.

'Probably not,' said Fred.

'Wee bitch. She'll have hidden it in there to blame on me. And ten to one that incident at Stormont led to Gary getting arrested.'

Levin took in the remark and shrugged. Bronagh asked him for a cigarette and he pulled out his transparent bag of tobacco.

'Not that I think she intended it, mind you. It's just that some people are all about themselves,' said Bronagh.

Padraig returned after chucking his clean clothes into his tent.

Bronagh huffed and puffed. 'There's too many people talking about one another around here and who did what. They're probably saying all sorts about me. Anyway, I'm thick-skinned and I'm no pushover.'

'What do people say about me?' said Fred.

'That you're short, and you smell bad. And you don't care about the politics,' said Padraig.

'That's a little harsh,' said Levin.

'It's true. And I knew you'd say that. You don't like to rock the boat,' Padraig replied.

Levin half-laughed. *'What?'*

'That's how people see you. As impartial.'

'You're sensible. You don't take risks,' said Fred.

'Bollocks!'

Bronagh agreed. 'It's true. You're a safe pair of hands. Daniel, how would you describe Levin?'

'Practical,' said Daniel.

'See? Boring. But in a good way,' Padraig assured him.

'Oh come on! I'm not --'

'Levin and I were signing on the other day. You know they have that plasma screen on the wall at the dole? All I said was, *I bet we could unscrew it and take it home,* and he's whispering, *Fred, come and sit down.*'

Bronagh pretended not to hear that. 'It's a good thing, Levin. It means you're dependable.'

'Dependable? Oh, come on!'

Though it was midnight there was a warmth in the air. Eoghan pondered the street lamps against the black sky. He found them almost romantic, up until Leon pointed out a freakishly flapping mutant moth. Eoghan aimed a cigarette butt at the bin.

'He shoots, he scores!'

Candle and solar lanterns let Cat and Kiera read over one another's essays in the rear marquee, drinking champagne from lemonade bottles. They took a break when Jack and Miriam arrived and began to show off their photos from London.

'These are great!' exclaimed Eoghan.

'There were a thousand people at Occupy St. Paul's and easily twice that on the Saturday,' said Jack.

There were photos of a massive gathering at the second camp in Finsbury Park.

'We couldn't count the tents at St. Paul's. There must have been seventy at the Finsbury Park site.'

'That's it! I'm booking the next flight out,' declared Leon.

'Did you know the pigs wrote to businesses around St. Paul's saying they were part of a potential terrorist threat?'

'Everybody was really friendly to us,' said Miriam.

'Let me see.' Cat gripped the phone with delighted envy. 'It seems like you got the real London tour.'

'Oh you bet,' said Jack. 'Wait 'til you come to the ones --'

Suddenly Levin came thundering up the path. When he sat down he was sweating and panting. He waved at Jack, weakly, before throwing his head down.

'Where were you?' asked Eoghan.

Cat recoiled. 'Is that paint on your sleeve?'

There was a splat of purple on the cuffs of Levin's brown jacket. He tried to cover it up and was still too out of breath to speak. Kiera was looking at Jack's phone, with some confusion.

'Where's this?'

'That's the occupied bank building in Hackney,' she replied.

Leon moved Kiera's hand and the phone closer to her. *'The Bank of Ideas?'*

'See that room? Last week Thom Yorke and the man from *Massive Attack* gigged there,' said Jack.

'*3D*, Robert Del Naja,' said Miriam.

'Is Padraig back yet?' asked Levin, with a little panic in his voice.

Eoghan shook his head.

'The Hackney building is quite organised: a manned reception; offices; a massive lecture room,' said Jack.

Miriam elaborated. 'We went to a talk on systemic resistance to social change. It's running all week. The quality was easily as good as at *Queen's*. They've got a plasma screen on the wall too. They're teaching Philosophy, Economics, Physics, Yoga, all sorts.'

'Sounds really positive,' said Levin.

He'd tried to wipe the paint off his jacket. Now there were two purple smudges on his left hand. Eoghan asked him point-blank what had happened.

'I did something really stupid,' he admitted. 'Padraig got hold of some paint, and we splashed it over the front of *HSBC*.'

No one spoke for a moment. Then Jack began to laugh and Cat and Kiera. Eoghan couldn't quite find the words.

'You and Padraig?' said Eoghan.

Jack facepalmed. 'How long were we gone?'

'Well done,' said Leon, approving and slyly mocking.

'No. It wasn't good. Half the paint ended up over Padraig and we tripped the alarm.'

Again they roared with laughter. Two pieces of gold tinsel hit Levin in the face. He looked over at the Christmas tree, twelve metres away. The tinsel on the tree was shaped like a mouth, laughing at him too, as it rocked from side to side. They laughed until they heard a yell from Bob's tent.

'Fuck up!'

'What got into you?' whispered Eoghan.

'2012 is just around the corner. I think he has end times

madness,' said Kiera.

'I swear I'm never doing something like this ever, ever again.'

They talked some more about London, and then Leon's plan to move permanently to Writer's Square when her tenancy was up. Eoghan gave her all the advice he could: on storage, laundry, health and well-being, and taking time away. She wasn't worried. Fears for Padraig's safety grew over the hour. Then he emerged from the pavilion wearing only his boxer shorts, with paint-stained clothes and shoes bundled up in front of him.

'Final warning,' yelled Bob.

When Bronagh was at camp with no sole purpose she cleaned the kitchen area in the rear marquee. It was done as noisily as possible. She called it, 'clatter for clutter.' On Tuesday afternoon Levin stacked the pots, and she chased him out of there.

'Let me fix it, Levin! You can help Daniel by taking tea over to the clergy. I don't want you getting paint everywhere!'

Out front, Padraig and Leon reached for the cups of tea coming towards them, and missed the chance to intercept.

'There he goes. *Paintball Assassin*,' noted Leon.

'Leave no man behind,' said Padraig.

'You wouldn't steal a cup of tea,' said Leon.

'You wouldn't steal a lamp-post,' said Padraig.

'You wouldn't steal a cathedral,' said Leon.

'Video piracy is MURDER!' boomed Padraig.

'The Stop Online Piracy Act. Because ACTA only invades your privacy so far.'

'Coo, coo,' said a pigeon crossing in front of them.

Then it took off with the sound of an an almighty crash from the rear marquee. They looked at one another, shrugged, and flipped cigarette ash onto the paving.

'Sure America was built on piracy and moving counterfeits. Fake fucks,' said Padraig.

'Right. And now it's all, *oh no, piracy is so wrong.* Boo-hoo.'

'Yanks, fucking yanks.'

'If Obama gave a shit about stopping piracy he'd make the drone codes open source,' remarked Leon.

'We should do something. A protest.'

'The Australians and EU are signing up to ACTA too. The last desperate vomit of capitalism.'

Padraig took a puff on his fag and hurled it towards the fire. 'Why the fuck aren't we doing anything about this, Leon?'

'Brand it. Brand it all,' she said despondently.

Padraig stared at her. 'Jesus. This is about you.'

'What?'

'Two weeks ago you got cautioned. Leon Luther King. But now Gary's taken your crown.'

Leon laughed. 'You're a cock.'

'*Ra, ra. End poverty. Ra, ra. Stop the bad banks.* It would be great if we tried something instead of just sitting here.'

'What do you have in mind?'

With Bronagh on the other side of the partition Padraig lowered his voice. 'Tackle this shit head on. They need a focus for Saturday's protest. We've nearly a dozen Anonymous we can call in. We can use the internet to fight... the anti-internet!'

'Right, right. Put the hackers on the street. Show The Man. Let's go to the direct action committee with this.'

'Aye. All I'm getting from them is shit. Like fuck they'll go for it.'

'The revolution is inevitable either way,' said Leon, and she cast her cigarette into the fire bin.

Cat and Kiera spent Tuesday afternoon scanning documents at the art college. They brought back news, via Twitter, that Occupy London had taken an abandoned magistrates' court in Shoreditch. Even while the City of London prosecuted the activists there was irony to be had. At six o'clock Levin and Tommie prised open the food tanks of egg fried rice mixed with orange chicken. The gales blew cold as they ate, and some shivered, their rice falling onto the paving below.

Cat informed Levin, 'You dropped something on the paint-ment.'

'What's purple and smells like red paint?' asked Bob.

Padraig avoided looking at him.

Levin smiled. 'I dunno. Is it purple paint?'

'Are you okay? You sound a bit monotone,' said Shay.

'You took a while to get the food,' remarked Daniel casually. 'I was worried you'd gotten marooned.'

There was sniggering and chuckling. Mary couldn't keep her food in her mouth. Tommie was clutching his sides.

'*What's love got to do, got to do with it?*' sang Eoghan. '*What's love but a second hand emulsion?*'

Padraig gurned, 'Is nothing private round here?'

Levin knew their attentions would soon be elsewhere. He had already arranged for Tommie to reprise his teach-in on security, and Tommie had asked Bob to help him with it.

'Will this teach-in help me get a job?'

'Nothing would, Fred. You may as well leave now,' said Bob.

'In twos, look at the person next to you. From the left,' said Tommie.

Padraig looked at Fred and Eoghan looked at Bronagh. Tommie instructed them to look at the space around each other.

'How likely are they to smack you?' said Bob.

'Do we have to do this?' said Bronagh.

'What are the obstacles between you?' asked Tommie.

'This teach-in,' quipped Joe.

Bob said the first tool in security was the eyes. Eyes ascertained the threat level. Eyes supplied information. He said eyes so many times Levin and Leon struggled to keep a straight face. He pointed to the pigeons, one bobbing on the path by the tents, another at the wall of the Shac building. Pigeons could see up to twenty-five miles away. Tommie said their spatial awareness was something to emulate.

Shay asked how they'd take down a potential attacker:

for example, if someone broke your CD Walkman. Tommie put his thumb inside a fist, and grabbed Fred by the head.

'See, if I was to come at the little man with my fist like this...'

'Get off!'

'Bam! I've broken my thumb. My knuckles are skinned and bloody. But if I hit him with the palm of my hand, around the bone, maximum damage to my opponent and no harm to me.'

'Just so you know, you scare me sometimes,' said Eoghan.

Tommie said it was just role play. Shay asked how they'd deal with a time travelling killer robot from the future. Tommie got Shay to stand up and to pretend he was the robot. He backed Shay into the corner of the marquee where heavier drops of rain fell on his head. Bob told Shay it was a test of endurance, and to stand his ground. Tommie put a light finger on the canopy and more water rolled down Shay's neck.

'Jesus, man!'

'The water will damage your robot's internals rendering it... what's the technical term, Tommie?'

'Fucked, Bob. The robot's fucked.'

The following afternoon, a Wednesday, Padraig and Levin walked around the city taking count of vacant buildings including a residential by *The Gasworks.* There was also a derelict church in *The Holylands,* near to Levin's flat, which they stopped off at to use the toilet. Almost returned to the camp, Padraig suggested the abandoned Bank of Ireland building on Royal Avenue. Levin said they'd be far too conspicuous looking at it in broad daylight.

The main reason for their walk was to find homeless people to invite to the camp for Christmas dinner. So far they'd only talked to two men and Padraig needed to get back to the camp for a meeting. The campsite had twenty-four tents now. They were packed in tight from the kerb to the ash trees, the Christmas tree with its tip brushing the ground, right up to the marquees. There were new placards too: *'JUSTICE FOR GARY CARELL'*, *'WE OCCUPY IN SUPPORT OF THE VITA CORTEX WORKERS'*, and halfway up the lamp-post, *'WE ARE NOT MERCHANDISE IN THE HANDS OF POLITICIANS AND BANKERS.'*

'Shay, stick the kettle on!' said Padraig.

'I can't believe we only talked to two men,' said Levin.

'We'll tell Bronagh we looked everywhere.'

'There must have been loads of places we could have tried.'

'The homeless are at a premium this time of year.'

'Did you try the shelters?' asked Tall Paul.

Levin stopped short of slapping his head. Just then, Padraig spotted a woman in full combat gear on the path. She was glaring at the clergy across the road. The air vibrated irregularly around her and she let out a lion's growl. The clergymen hid behind their casket. The woman carried on up the path towards them.

'I've some business here, sure yous go on,' said Padraig.

'Is that Martine?' asked Shay.

'I think I'll go for a lie down,' said Tall Paul, remembering the impression Martine had made on the morning of Gary's release.

Daniel got up too. Shay offered to take Levin to one of the homeless shelters, preferably, right away. They walked down the path, avoiding Martine, and Padraig called out after them.

'Don't forget to spread the word. The GA proposal to oppose ACTA is tonight!'

'We'll warn everyone in the shelter about ACTA!' said Levin sarcastically but in a sincere tone.

Padraig looked for Martine but he couldn't see her. Then she was just there, beside him, looking him up and down. He struggled to find his breath. Martine gave a twitch of her nose.

'Padraig.'

'You're early,' he said.

'I think if you are going to have a revolution it should be early.'

'Mwah-ha-ha-ha. Well you've come to the right place.'

'I've been saying this since day one. The internet must be reclaimed. We've neglected the web so it has become a vulnerable space in the capitalist terror axis of armoured markets.'

'Right. Right on. Yeah. This is going to be great. We're putting action against ACTA front and centre,' he said.

'How do you propose to do that?'

'Me and Leon are on the committees to make this happen. There she is now. Hey, Leon! I got hold of Martine.'

Leon was frozen to the spot ten metres away. The wind howled and flapped the tents as they faced off. The sun fell behind the clouds. Padraig was reminded of a classic Sergio Leone showdown.

Leon walked slowly towards them. 'Fuck's sake!'

'Bitch,' said Martine.

'What's she doing here?' Leon asked.

'I'm not leaving.'

'Heh. Well… it's not as if you're not on speaking terms,' said Padraig.

'The revolution is bigger than you,' sniped Martine.

'Bigger than you,' Leon sniped back.

Even in the buffer afforded by narrow Gordon Street the wind blew bitterly. Levin's shoulders were hunched up to his ears and Shay was mostly hoodie. They passed the brightly coloured murals of the *Oh Yeah! Music Centre*. Levin made out the *Salvation Army* shelter, *Centenary House*, across the busy road in front.

'The weather's supposed to get worse. I'd not mind spending the night in one of their beds,' remarked Levin.

'Aye. But it's just like fancier jail cells, sleeping in rooms with strangers and bars over the windows.'

'Can't be nice.'

'We joke we get the same weather all year round. But the summer? I've sat in doorways with the blinding sun in me eyes. Just draining my energy it was,' said Shay.

'Yeesh.'

Three wide lanes of cars sped along the A2 leaving the city centre for the north and west and on the other side moved inward or to the east. They waited by the kerb for a gap in the traffic to let them cross.

'Once you've a few days of stubble, looking at all the legs going past, you become certain there's nowhere to go,' said Shay.

'Right. So it's just as much about the state of mind.'

'You feel cold inside, man.'

The lads got across the road as smartly as their wits could take them. Centenary House stretched around the bend from Victoria Street to Queen's Square. The front was covered with all the grime of the A2. They climbed the steps and Shay hit the bell. A burly man in his thirties came to the window, and on recognising Shay, he buzzed them inside.

There were thirty men in the common room: talking with tea, or quiet by the television; a few of them were at the snooker tables. Some were ex-prisoners, some ex-inpatients, some were both. The hostile and alien of them lightened up when Shay was greeted by some like a long lost sibling. He introduced Levin as his home-boy. Levin recognised Shitty John among them, and shook his hand.

'We've missed you around at the camp.'

'Yous are round at them political tents,' said one of the men.

'That's right, Kenny,' said Shay.

'Ya need yer heads examined!'

'Protesting the church for something,' said Ade.

Levin was shaken. 'We're not protesting the church.'

'Are yis terrorists?' asked Bez.

Levin spluttered.

Shay laughed. 'Bez is winding him up! Oh mate!'

Levin took a moment to process it. 'We came to invite you to Christmas dinner in the square: turkey, stuffing, mash, parsnips. All the trimmings.'

'Now?' asked Kenny.

'He means the twenty-fifth. Christmas day. Will there be profiteroles?' said Ade.

'Maybe, maybe,' said Levin.

'No I'm serious. The *Welcome Centre* in Millfield has profiteroles,' said Ade.

'They're bringing them here too,' said Kenny.

Levin thought about this a moment. 'We could get profiteroles.'

Shay whispered to him. 'Now you just sound desperate.'

Ade said, 'I'm booked into the *Simon Community* meal after here. Gotta store it up for winter. Hey Charlie. You've got a vacancy on Christmas day, haven't you?'

An older fella in a red bobble hat joined them. 'I'm free in the evening.'

'Or come round anytime. We usually get noodles and chicken in around six,' said Levin.

'Any chips?' asked Charlie.

Two hours later they ate together, steaming noodles and chips and spring rolls, wood smoke from the fire can watering their eyes. There was no shortage of conversation. Bart had learned he'd been accepted for a flat at the *Shac* building and would move into it in early January. When he heard Fred still had no place to move to, he said he could sleep on his sofa. The art students had submitted their coursework: Cat was sure she'd fail though Kiera was optimistic.

She told Cat to share what she'd read about the *Vita Cortex* sit-in. The Mayor of Cork had announced a solidarity visit to the occupying workers. Kiera said he'd be on the factory floor, right where Eoghan and Bob had been. Both men nodded. They suspected Cat had told Kiera the truth but were grateful to her for covering their tracks. Daniel said being there at the beginning of the sit-down must have been pretty exciting. They didn't realise he was humouring them, because Kiera had told Daniel and Tommie and Jack and Bronagh, who clamped down on her smirk and took their empty plates over to the basin.

'Mary, maybe we could stop off at the plant tomorrow. We're going to give my parents the good news when we visit them in Baltimore.'

'You are taking a plane to Baltimore in America?' exclaimed Bart.

'This Baltimore's in Cork. The southern most tip,' said Mary.

'You don't have an Irish accent,' said Fred.

'My parents moved to Cork in 2005. I decided to remain here in Belfast,' replied Joe.

'Oh cool. If you're visiting Vita Cortex give them our regards,' said Fred.

'I'm not sure we have time to stop off,' said Mary. She had also been told about Eoghan and Bob and was keen not to overplay her hand. 'Where's Padraig and Leon? It's not like them to miss dinner.'

A pigeon crept under her chair looking for scraps. 'Coup, coup.'

'Maybe they're looking for a place to live,' said Eoghan. 'They were here this morning. We were explaining that living at the camp is a lot different from having a place of your own to go back to.'

'We tried. I think we were wasting our breath,' said Bob.

Daniel nodded, Tall Paul too.

Bronagh rounded up the rest of the finished plates and dropped them into the basin Just then three members of Anonymous appeared beside her. They came from the pavilion, with three more behind them. Then there were another four. The unit lined up in front of the marquee. When they spoke they spoke – mostly – in unison.

'WE ARE ANONYMOUS. WE ARE MANY/LEGION.'

Applying distinct elocution Jack said, 'Pardon me? Only that you look like twats.'

'Remember what Tommie told you,' said Bob. 'Smack them with the bone in the palm of your hand.'

'We're not here to cause harm,' said Anonymous Wallace but the others spoke over him, together, almost.

'WE DEMAND/OCCUPY/OCCUPY BELFAST/ TAKE/ IMMEDIATE/URGENT ACTION TO PROTEST ACTA...'

'...The Anti-Counterfeiting Trade Agreement,' said two further out of synchronicity from the others.

Eoghan raised his hand. 'The General Assemblies are at seven. You know that, Leon.'

Anonymous Maurice spoke up. 'There is no Leon. There is only Anonymous.'

Bart chimed in. 'That one there is Padraig.'

'Take off those *silly* masks,' said Bronagh.

'Even I think you look dumb,' declared Bart.

Levin laughed. 'All this because you want us to protest ACTA on Saturday? You do know it's on the agenda already?'

'Nobody told us!' yelled Anonymous Martine.

'Well, Martine, perhaps if half of you you actually showed up to a GA you could have proposed the action sooner,' said Eoghan, now quite irate.

'Fine,' she seethed.

Anonymous Padraig shook his head angrily.

'It's half six now. Some of these ones are still eating. Do you know what I feel like for dessert, Bronagh?'

'What's that, Bob?'

'Paint au chocolat.'

30

From the roaring flames against the dark night to the sunlit four degree chill, Bob endured. And when the others awoke he lay down. Though he had a roll mat and a pallet under him he could feel the slither of mud, or ice. No pillow could soothe him. For nine weeks now, it was the same ritual of tuning out the sounds of the street. He heard Monty gurn about being covered in mud stains. Or Eoghan bitching to Levin over their beans and toast about Anonymous's sad coup on the Wednesday. Then there was Bronagh, complaining that all they had to have done was to show up and vote. Greater numbers assembled for the march and the carnival. Leon whispered conspiratorially not five feet away. And Padraig with his cackling, always Padraig with his cackling. Cat was squeezing out her socks on the path. She reminded Kiera it was Christmas Eve and she had to get her stockings ready for her presents. Bob contemplated telling her there was no Santa.

The sky above the marchers was like a grey static curtain, muting the shops and vehicles all around. Christmas shoppers scrambled everywhere on Royal Avenue. Rain pitter-patted off the black and white plastic masks of the Anonymous, which jutted out of dark hoodies. Their eldritch painted features seeming to operate on a different frequency. They marched with their placards: *'STOP ACTA'*, *'NO ACTA'*, *'NO TO ACTA'*, a few with *'ACTA'* crossed out, and one conscientious soul carrying *'STOP INTERNET CENSORSHIP BY ACTA.'*

Levin looked one of the Anonymi up and down. 'Eoghan, is that you?'

'Fuck it. If you can't beat them, join them,' he replied.

A few of the campers were dismayed when the rambunctious Anonymi decided they'd march anywhere they pleased.

'The ACTA agreement threatens all our rights to privacy and security,' screamed Leon through the megaphone.

'We are the 99%!'

'We will not be spied upon by the power elite!'

'We are the 99%!'

'I danno watt they're sayin,' an old woman told her grandchild. 'They're very angry people.'

With them was a big bald man-boy in a boy's blue puffer coat. 'Bloody Shinners,' he shouted.

Padraig decided to use his own style of activist hand signalling. He mimicked fellatio, and slurped.

'Stap ruining Christmas!' Puffer shouted at him.

Cat tapped Kiera on the shoulder. 'This is shit. Wanna go grab a coffee?'

Bart stopped in the street and looked at Puffer, who was just a few metres from him.

'Wait,' said Kiera. 'Bart's going to --'

'No! You are the one who is ruining Christmas by starting fight and mention Sinn Fein! Why are there people like you argumenting on Christmas Eve? It's a time of peace!'

The marchers around Bart applauded.

Kiera smirked from ear to ear. 'We can go now.'

Back at camp she and Tall Paul decorated the tree and draped tinsel around the bust of the Spanish Civil War volunteer. Deirdre arrived with a Christmas hamper on front of her bike. Many visitors bound for Occupy stopped short on seeing the Black Santa vigil opposite. They found extra bags or pockets to conceal half their donations so as to split them between the causes. Parishioners did the same after paying tribute to the men in black cloaks, crossing the road to music and brighter decorations.

Eoghan threw himself into a chair between Fred and Kiera. 'I want to do a direct action on Boxing Day.'

'On Boxing Day?' asked Kiera, horrified.

'I'm working, mate,' said Tommie.

Cat puffed out her cigarette. 'The direct action team meet was on Thursday.'

Levin put his arms behind his head. 'It's Christmas, Eoghan. We're off the clock.'

'Great, great. I'll ask Leon.' He sounded hurt.

'I want to know what Eoghan's idea is,' said Bart.

Levin sighed. 'Okay then. Let's hear it.'

'Guerilla marketing. Every shop for miles will be full of people clamouring for bargains. I was thinking we could get in among them and tape leaflets to fridges, televisions, you name it. Anything with a price tag. Then a few of us gather around one of the 'sale' items and draw a crowd --'

'And everyone's pushing and shoving,' said Cat.

'We'll get separated,' Fred pointed out.

'Sure this lot will still be stuck at home with their hangovers,' said Tommie.

'It is a good idea but you will have to do it without me. I do not want the police to say, *we know you. Your name is Bart Symanski.*'

Eoghan just needed two people from direct action to back him up at the GA. Fred relented under petition. Cat agreed if only to shut him up about the action and on the proviso Eoghan make the next pot of tea.

The gazebo and a table had been set up on the pavilion side of the marquee were a line formed to make donations. Padraig and Shay managed it, each wearing red, festive stocking caps. Three Anonymous dressed in cloaks bowed before them as they presented wrapped gifts. Padraig asked if any of them had a smoke. One produced a box of *Camels*. Another person gifted a tall pillar ivory candle, perhaps meant for the cathedral. As the line diminished, wheels skittered across concrete: three skateboarders, each with a bag of groceries in hand. They drew to a stop in front of Padraig.

'Welcome to the Occupy Christmas Grotto. Let's see what you've brought us? Oh very good. Very good lads.'

'Thanks guys,' said Shay. 'If you like, there's coffee, tea, milk and cookies around the corner.'

'My elf will sort you out. But don't sit on his lap. Mwah-ha-hahaha!'

On the wall of a planter opposite, Bart and Shitty John listened to Fred's sad story about a pal who'd slid into alcoholism. New/Shitty John said it was a terrible thing and a selfish way to be. Bart was surprised to hear this. He genuinely thought John was mute.

Carol singers sang on the pavilion. Cat and Daniel decorated the rails with placards: *'Reclaim Democracy'* and *'No Man Is Above The Law And No Man Below.'* Afterwards came the speeches. Leon addressed them from the steps, exorcising a pent-up need to lecture on the *Daily Express's* obsession with Madeline McCann, the tabloids who'd hacked the PSNI's phones and the PSNI's own targeted oppression of Gary. Deirdre followed her, addressing the issues around the Irish Republic's water tax. She praised the campaign to refuse to pay the €100 household charge, and highlighted ethically disturbing breaches of data protection in *Irish Water's* management.

Under the marquee, Eoghan strummed his guitar:
'In the tents, in the tents,
Which the sun don't ever dry
You would sneeze the whole night through
With mud and stones as your floor
Tell me how could you sleep last night?'

'Very good, very good. Reminds me of the sort of thing you'd hear at the Rotterdam,' remarked Tommie.

'Where's that?' asked Fred.

'It's a really old bar in Sailortown,' said Levin. 'People just show up with guitars and fiddles and start playing. Dogs laying at your feet. Proper working class.'

'My uncle slipped me my first drink at the Rotterdam. Got me my first job too, loading off the docks,' said Tommie.

Eoghan smiled. 'No kidding! My grand-dad used to work there as a loader.'

'Small world. How about that?'

'How about we race through the GA and get to the Rotterdam for a few jars?' said Eoghan.

Levin and Fred were keen.

'I'd love to, but I need an early night. I'm not a young man anymore.'

'Ah go on, Tommie. *Go on, go on, go on.*'

'I said no, Eoghan. Leave it.'

A car horn honked five times. Bronagh waved from the roadside. Levin and Tommie helped her pull boxes from the people carrier, these packed with supplies for the Christmas dinner. Some cutlery hit the concrete and Leon picked it up.

'Sorry I'm late,' said Bronagh. 'I fell down the Facebook hole. I was on the Occupy Dame Street page.'

'Oh? How are our comrades in the South?' asked Leon.

'They had some singer there yesterday. Damien Dempsey. Do you know him?'

Eoghan replied. 'Not personally. He's worked with Sinead O' Connor and Brian Eno.'

Bronagh flashed her eyebrows. 'Very good. Well today they have another singer with them. Glen Hansard?'

'Glen Hansard. He played with *Pearl Jam*,' said Leon.

'Really?' asked Levin.

Eoghan sighed. 'I remember how once upon a time I pretty much had Billy Bragg and Tommy Sands in my tent.'

'Don't we all want Billy Bragg and Tommy Sands in our tent?' asked Leon gleefully.

Many did slumber in their tents as the sun crept up on Christmas Day. Bob, in heavy thermals, poked a stick into the fire can. Through the smoke a wretched figure emerged.

'God, you look terrible son,' he said, as Levin limped towards him.

'I don't remember...' he murmured, his head foggy.

'It's a good thing you're up. There was a road-sweeper here a while back. With a face like yours it'd be back fer another sweep.'

Levin sniffed an armpit and wished he hadn't. He rubbed the thick bush on his head, a sleep-tossed head of Gorgon's snakes. The dawn-lit streets were empty and cold, whipping at his senses.

'I thought you were having a silent night,' mused Bob.

'Aye, that got a bit out of hand. I don't remember much...'

Bob shrugged. The marquee partition shook and slapped, disclosing the darkness from the rear. Then a male voice blew in on the ethereal draught.

'I would have liked us to go over the road for mulled wine, Bob,' said the tortured voice. 'But it'd be tetanus shots by the look of those two bar-flies.'

Bob raised an eyebrow at Levin. A creature pushed at the canvas partition: Tommie, and practically bound to his chest, a basin of dishes and steaming water. Levin stumbled backwards.

'Speak of the devil,' quipped Tommie as he set the basin on the wall. 'You oughta be careful mate. 'Tis the season for drinking folly.'

'Tommie's a good boy,' said Bob sagely. 'Does his work when he's asked.'

There was an almighty groan then and an animalistic roar from behind Levin. Bob pointed out to the tent with his thick leathery finger.

'One drink my arse. Look at the state of this critter! Behold: the beast!'

Eoghan emerged. His hair was misshapen and there was a moustache drawn on his face. But those weren't the most noticeable things about him. It was the pink frilly D-cups braced to his chest. Eoghan felt them, looked at Levin a moment, and went back inside. In the tent he removed the bra, and lifted out a traffic cone. He threw it limply onto the path, although it bounced twice.

'Fuck's sake,' muttered Levin.

'It wasn't enough he force-fed me a bottle of gin! Literally kept me awake half the night singing,' Eoghan complained.

Bob rubbed his fists against his eyes in a crybaby gesture. Levin and Tommie began to laugh.

'Eoghan, you should see the state of you,' said Levin.

'Him? What about you, pretty boy? Tommie, fetch yer man a mirror.'

The cold air grew full with an almighty stench. A dark cloud loomed over Levin's face. Some 'thing' passed him. It was Shitty John and he sat down under the marquee and stared. Tommie returned from the rear tent and put a small circular mirror in Levin's hands.

He saw his face: a palette of chestnut blusher, peppered with amber eyeliner and green eyeshadow. His eyebrows were fluorescent orange and his lips were ruby red and sparkling.

'You are the ghost of Christmas Present,' said Bob. 'Yer a fucking haunting.'

Levin noticed another marking on his chest. He unbuttoned his shirt to a lipstick ring wide around a blue-eyed nipple. He unbuttoned to his other nipple, also made over as an eyeball. A sloping nose in brown marker pen glided down to his belly where a jumbo red *Sharpie* had illustrated a fat set of lady lips.

'Aye, and you did that to yourself,' said Eoghan.

Tommie tapped a water keg. 'If you want we could douse you.'

'Wouldn't waste it on him,' said Bob.

'Must be Christmas, Bob. I've hardly seen you laugh before,' said Tommie.

Levin smelled his own stale whiskey and fags and then

something fouler: the ill wind of an anus.

'*Jesus, John! That stinks!*' he gurned.

'Gods save us,' exclaimed Eoghan.

'That's how you two are going to turn out if you keep this up,' said Bob.

The wind blew forth. Padraig awoke to a piece of tinsel slowly sliding down the side of his tent. Contrast in traffic noise on Donegall Street was almost tangible. Fred opened his eyes to Padraig shuffling out of a sleeping bag. Fred rolled over to the edge of the tent and felt the wet of it sliming down his face. He jolted over onto his other side and cursed. As he unzipped the bag they heard Eoghan and Bob say their goodbyes to Levin, and the sound of foot-steps.

Outside, Tommie was unpacking a box of a dozen eggs and a giant pack of bacon. Eoghan shoved a dessert spoon into a tub of drinking chocolate.

'You don't want to bother with that. It tastes like gravel,' said Padraig.

'It's damp alright,' Tommie confirmed.

'Sure, how about a wee Christmas drink?' suggested Padraig.

'No drink,' said Bob and he rose from the chair. 'I'm gonna get a few hours' kip.'

'You're not having breakfast?' Tommie asked.

Bob shook his head. 'Sure use that lot up. Wake us around midday.'

'Right you are,' said Eoghan. 'Sweet dreams.'

Tommie oiled the large pan and set it over the fire grate.

The cathedral bells petitioned with a strike tone in a low pitch. Keeping time, Leon and Tall Paul chinked their spoons against milky cornflakes.

Tommie, Padraig and Fred got into the service just as it began. They sat in the back row miming the hymns. The sermon echoed in the hollows of the church. Ornate depictions of suffering and tradition were muted in the light, the coloured glass providing a neon-like effect. It was a different kind of cold. Tommie watched the pews nearest him for guidance on cues of how to act. He enjoyed watching the children playing with their toys in the aisle and then felt sad. He was missing his own little girl. After the service the Dean shook their hands at the doors to the vestibule and they exchanged smiles.

The sky was grey like evening already and the air was bitter. Some parishioners crossed the road to the camp, having prepared gifts for the occupiers. They chatted about homelessness and Stormont and while they wondered if the Dean would show up they talked about the general assemblies. Eoghan made sure to make everyone aware they should come to these and invited them to the direct action leafleting on Boxing Day. Four pounds and fifty pence went into the donation tin.

Leon returned from her walk around the city. 'All the shops are shut! We did it! We won!'

'Can we get our Secret Santas already?' Cat asked.

'Bob's still asleep,' said Eoghan.

'I'm getting up!'

'What about Bart?' said Shay.

'Away and wake him,' said Kiera. 'God. My ma's texting me every ten minutes.'

Padraig turned to Fred and told him, 'Bart won't get any sleep when you two move in together, what with all the wanking you do. Mwah-ha-hahaha!'

Cat pleaded with him. 'Padraig, please. It's Christmas.'

'Jealousy's a terrible thing,' said Fred. 'Have *you* got anywhere to live yet?'

Padraig said nothing.

Tommie said, 'Would you not move in with your ma and me?'

Cat buckled over laughing and hit him a slap.

'I did find somewhere, aye. I've got my own gaff,' said Padraig and Fred eyed him suspiciously.

Bob stuck his feet outside the blue ridge tent. The funnel tent where Bart slept began to wobble upon Shay's urging. Kiera went into the rear marquee and brought out a black bin bag full of gifts. Leon began to rummage. She pulled out a knotted white plastic bag with a sticker bearing a name in black ink. Shay returned and Leon thrust the damp bag into his hands.

'Cheers!'

'You know Secret Santa's meant to be secret?' said Eoghan.

'Some kind of box... *a CD player! Cracker!* Thanks!'

'There's batteries in it too. It's the same model as the one that got smashed. They don't make them any-more. I found this one on eBay.'

'Hurray for capitalism!' he sang.

'Very good,' said Bob.

'Well I guess we may as well go ahead now. Kiera, why don't you pick them out?' said Cat.

Leon's was next, wrapped in gold and green paper. It was a box of mint chocolate *Matchmakers.* She nodded approvingly.

Padraig tore his way through silver wrapping to a copy of *Resident Evil 4.* 'Yeee-Ohhh!' He slapped the box and flipped it around, momentarily entranced by the back cover. 'Was this you?'

Fred sealed his lips in a smile and shrugged.

'Well we're going to have a few games of this when I move into the new gaff. Thanks.'

Fred's gift was a book in a sellotaped brown paper bag. It was Mark Thomas's *Belching out the Devil: Global Adventures with Coca-Cola.*

'Cool,' said Bart as he slid mucus out of his right eye.

'I'll let you read it after me. Thanks, whoever got me this.'

Kiera said, 'Next one's for you, Bart.'

'Oh! I am so excited! *What? What is it, a harmonica?* This is a thoughtful gift. But I have never played the harmonica. Do I just start it up?'

'Just start it up,' said Shay.

Cat got a large spiral bound hard-cover notebook. The front was pastels, and in italicised cursive were the words, *'Proceed as if success is inevitable.'*

Tommie un-knotted a big Poundland bag. Inside was a remote control car. 'Not what I was expecting,' he said.

'Bart, just put it to your lips and blow,' said Shay. He set his CD player on the chair and brought his tin whistle out. 'Go on. I'll accompany you.'

Kiera's eyes lit up unwrapping a set of dip-colour pencils. Eoghan got a pack of guitar strings. Padraig looked over Bob's shoulder as he took apart neatly tucked wrapping paper. Inside there was packing paper around a tub of cocoa and a gift box with a bottle of *Jameson's* whiskey and a shot glass. Bob said nothing, because he'd no words. It was the happiest they'd seen him.

Padraig reached out and tugged on the gift box. 'Okay Bob. No drink at camp!'

Eoghan, Cat, Kiera and Fred left for dinner with parents and siblings soon afterwards. Bearded Charlie came from *Centenary House*, wearing his red bobble hat, and a few others from the shelter arrived too. While they waited they opened the Christmas crackers which Bronagh had left the day before. Bez and Kenny laughed as they tugged on each end. Daniel gave up much too easily and Bob caught his paper whistle before it hit the ground.

'Welcome to the Occupy Belfast band,' said Shay, while fixing his orange crepe paper crown.

'There's a low bar for entry,' said Bob.

'My dog has no nose. How does it smell?' asked Shay.

Bart announced, 'I got a plastic comb! It must be for when I grow my moustache. Okay. *What kind of motorcycle does Santa ride?* Give up? The answer is a *Holly* Davidson.'

Tommie shared a red cracker with Leon, lowering his arm and tilting it towards him and pulling firmly with both hands. A bang and the tube of rewards smoked in his hand. Leon felt it should have been hers. Padraig offered to pull one with her and smugly wrested it from her. He didn't like that his party hat was pink and he put it on Bob's head. Padraig almost got chinned.

Tommie read out his joke. *'My dog has no nose, How does it –'*

'Oh, come on! That is same as mine!' said Bart. 'What did you get as your joke, Bob?'

'What's purple and smells like red paint?'

Padraig retorted, 'My joke's just one word: Bob.'

'You should not be mean,' said Bart.

'What's purple and smells like red paint? Purple paint. Really. That's what it says,' said Bob and he rolled it up and tossed it into the fire.

At two o' clock they were joined by Bronagh, her fiancée Brian and Daniel, who had stayed in their spare room. Brian brought a tray of turkey in foil into the marquee to a round of applause. Daniel carried a large pot to the hot plate, which Galway John had left for them.

The partition between the marquees buzzed with activity. Fred and Tommie erected the three fold-out IKEA tables. People weaved between one another carrying pots, plates, and twenty-two chairs, laying out cutlery, tumblers and mugs. Crepe paper hats fell to the ground. While they waited in their seats more crackers were pulled.

'Breast or wing?' shouted Bronagh.

A dozen sets of eyes looked at Padraig.

'What?? I wasn't going to say anything!!'

The chicken was succulent, going down easily. There was a plate of sliced ham and bowls of veg and potatoes; a porcelain boat of cheese and white wine sauce; gravy, still hot and rich; peppered stuffing; green mash with spring onions, with a creamy texture. The crisp roast potatoes disappeared quickly.

Padraig refused the Brussels sprouts. 'Brussels sprouts

are behind the growth of the EU.'

'That's a fallacy!'

'I think Padraig is only joking, Leon. This is all really great. Thank you Bronagh,' said Bart.

They all raised their soft drinks to her and she said she was glad to be spending the day with them. A few flies buzzed around. Bronagh had brought coloured flyswatters, one at each end of the table. Mostly the pests were swept away before landing.

'I really like what you've done with the chips,' said Shay.

Bronagh laughed. 'Chips? Do you mean the roasted parsnips?'

'Are they? I thought I hated parsnips. Are there any more?'

'Leon, you'll be disappointed we're missing the Queen's Speech,' said Brian.

'Absolutely gutted... actually I don't know if I've ever heard it.'

'Doesn't she talk about her doggies?' said bobble-hatted Charlie, his tone warm and meek.

'Dunno. She's an oul bitch,' snarled Ade.

Bart put his head down, unsure of his place. Bez, who'd also come from the shelter, hummed the mournful *God Save the Queen*.

Leon sang, *'She ain't no human being!'*

Bart and Charlie joined Bez on the national anthem, with higher pitched humming, all over the top.

'She talks about family and the commonwealth,' said Bob.

'What common wealth?' asked Leon.

'Mwah-ha-hahaha! I saw it a few years ago. It's got clips in with the dukes and princes. They all get dressed up with big hats and tops and tails. You know how lizards have tails? Mwah-ha-hahaha! And there's bits repeated. Like flashbacks.'

'What is it?' asked Polish Filipe.

'Her speech? Ah just like we should do this and that.'

'Sturdy confidence; duty; stiff upper lip,' said Monty.

'Yes sah, Sergeant Major, sah,' barked Kenny, one of the older men from the hostel.

'That's about right. Always praising the soldiers, and Jesus of Nazareth. And what Padraig said: telling us all what to do,' said Bronagh.

'I get it. It is like the Queen is a life coach,' said Bart.

Tommie threw his head back and tried to remember what Jack had taught him about elocution. 'We are gathered on this special occasion to re-evaluate our goals, and with God's help to draw up a new plan, based around identifying strategies to steer HMS Britain around her obstacles.'

'Pretty much,' said Bob.

Bez fell asleep at the table and began snoring. Charlie put his hand on his shoulder and gave him a shake.

'Don't feel the need to sit here. People can get up and stretch their legs if they want,' said Bronagh. 'There's plenty more for anyone who wants more.'

'I'll make a start on the dishes,' said Tommie.

'Don't be daft. I'll take them home and throw them in the dishwasher.' Bronagh leaned back and sparked up a cigarette, which was the all-clear signal for others wanting to do the same.

'I'll get this and then pack the leftovers.'

When she'd had her smoke Brian touched her arm. 'We should get the dessert out before the cream melts. Who's for profiteroles?' he asked.

Shay slapped Ade on the back. 'See? Profiteroles!'

As the sun set Leon took out the plug for the hot plate and put on a string of fairy lights which Bob had draped over a pole of the marquee. The bright coloured lights were pretty in the shifting wind. Tall Paul was happy with his woollen gloves and amused with the collection of hand-made badges inside: '*I heart Belfast*', '*Bout Ye*', and '*Yer Ma.*'

Cat came by. At home she'd dyed her hair orange. People

were surprised and Shay told her it was cute. Cat was keen to pull a few people out to the pub with her. Instead she wound up joining Tommie and Shay as they played with Tommie's remote control car. It was not as fast as the pigeon, but fast enough. The car sailed backwards and forwards, with graceful lefts and veers to the right, around the concrete pavilion. Accelerating too fast it smashed into the stone archway's pillar. After that, the car lunged forward drunkenly of its own accord.

Bronagh got to unwrapping her gift: a luxury soap called *Sea Vegetable*. She inhaled the scent, attracted to it so that her eyes widened. She told Leon her head was going to explode with happiness today. Bronagh passed the soap around for a few of them to smell.

'Have you found somewhere to live yet?' she asked Leon.

'Nope. But I'm fairly sure I can survive this place until I have somewhere. I'm all packed up and ready to go.'

Padraig asked, 'Where are you going to put your stuff? I can't figure that bit out. I need storage for a week or so. There's no room here.'

'Sure you can put it in my flat,' said Bart.

Daniel carefully took apart wrapping paper around a thermal hat, not a cheap brand either. 'The old one's seen better days. Thank you, whoever got this for me.'

Bronagh looked behind her to the round with the pavilion and announced mockingly, 'Oh would you look who it is? Public enemy number one!'

'Known felon,' added Cat.

And there was Gary: clear-eyed and with a smile that melted hearts, stood beside them in a clean blue sweater and navy jacket. 'Hello Padraig. Hiya Cat. Bronagh. Leon. Bob. God there's a lot of you.'

Many of them hugged him, again. Bronagh tried to force a small plate onto him. He made his best effort to talk to everyone and helped Tall Paul to fit his badges onto his jacket. Gary picked up his present: a fine pen and a small leatherbound notebook. He was delighted with it. The pot was freshly brewed and they enjoyed a cup of tea together.

'What's your favourite Christmas movie?' said Cat.

'*Duhhh!* Die Hard,' said Padraig.

'Star Wars. Star Wars is absolutely a Christmas movie,' said Leon.

'All those lights. Everyone cheering and kissing,' said Tommie.

'Here, Bob. Have you ever been kissed under yer mucus toe?' said Padraig.

'You're skating on thin ice, sunshine.'

'I think Padraig has eyes for Leon,' said Daniel.

Laughter rang out from Bronagh in the rear marquee. Leon shuddered. Cat gasped and Gary flexed his eyebrows.

Daniel elaborated. 'He fell asleep on her shoulder on the way back from Dublin.'

'No I didn't!'

'Right enough: they've been hanging out, and plotting together,' said Cat. 'Do you remember our first day here when they hated each others guts?'

'I wouldn't look at him if he was the last man on Earth.'

'You two *have* been cosying up,' said Fred.

Gary smiled. 'You've changed too, Fred.'

'True,' said Bob. 'From a wee toe-rag showing up once a week and now he barely leaves. He's all grown-up. Almost.'

'No way! There's nothing going on between me and Leon!'

'As if,' she sneered.

'Right that's all packed away. Now you can go to the pub,' said Bronagh.

31

It was Boxing Day and chattering classes were busy with bargains inside *Curry's* electrical superstore. Eoghan drew in close to Tall Paul. He whispered for Paul to stay fixed to the spot. Eoghan moved behind him out of view of the security guard. All around them – or more specifically, the fridge freezers and washing machines – Boxing Day shoppers swarmed. If Eoghan did any flyering now he would draw the guard's attention.

A few aisles over, Padraig was lingering by the televisions. They met one another's gaze. Eoghan discreetly waved him away. Padraig squinted. Eoghan pointed to the top of the store. Padraig craned his neck forward and began to walk towards them. Eoghan looked away and rolled his eyes.

The shoppers moved from the rear of the shop so Eoghan went there, to the kettles. He took a roll of sticky tape from his trouser pocket and bit off a piece, which he hung on the inside lining of his jacket.

'What is it? What's the matter?' asked Padraig loudly.

Eoghan had a strip of tape hanging from his mouth when he turned to face him. Tall Paul joined them in the corner.

'Eoghan, the man at the door was looking at me,' said Paul.

Padraig took a few of the flyers out of his pocket.

'Jesus, hide those will you! Also, it's not helping that we're stood plotting in a huddle,' he added, before biting into the tape again.

'Right enough, we don't want to get pegged as shoplifters,' said Padraig. His voice drew down to a rushed whisper. 'Shit! Here comes security!'

'Fan out! Fan out!' whispered Eoghan.

Padraig replied, 'They don't sell fans. Oh. Oh. I see. Come on Paul.'

A strip of tape stuck to Eoghan's fingernails. He fought to straighten it but it stuck to his palms, grubby with fingerprints. He rolled it into a ball.

Surrounded by shoppers on the other side of the store, Padraig ripped out his sticky tape quickly, sounding like a bad dose of flatulence. He pulled one flyer out of the bundle in his jacket, and taped it onto the frame of a 60" Panasonic TV:

STOP AVOIDING TAXES!
Zanussi, Panasonic, Samsung, Hotpoint,
Whirlpool, Russell Hobbs, Siemens
These companies are rated 6/10 or under on human rights
 - Ethical Consumer Magazine

Eoghan was on the run from an unsuspecting but helpful shop assistant. He darted around a family of four and was held up by an obese pensioner. He saw another assistant advance on Padraig and notified him in a loud whisper.

'Bogey at three o'clock!'

'What? Paul, you were supposed to be look-out! Walk towards yer man there!'

'I'm not getting in trouble,' said Paul, in his deep, plodding tones, a little too calm and polite for Padraig's liking.

'It's me he's after!' said Padraig in a hurry.

He weaved his way cautiously through the cluster: a parked child screaming in a pram, a man who might have been the puffer-jacketed yob from the ACTA demo. The televisions were all on a raised platform and he dropped flyers onto them as he walked by.

Meanwhile Eoghan circled back to the aisle of fridge freezers. He got in as close as he could. With pre-prepared strips of tape inside his jacket he hung a flyer on a machine door with pinpoint precision. Then another, and another: five flyers on machine doors in rapid succession. He looked back down the aisle. Only one strip of tape failed to plant, that flyer falling to the carpet underneath the impending boot of the security man. He saw two customers stop to read a notice on the front of a washing machine. The blockage they caused gave Eoghan time: he loaded up another strip of sellotape; pulled out a flyer; pinned it to the shirt of a shop assistant.

'I said, he was expecting more people to turn up,' shouted Padraig, above high winds rattling the marquee.

'I'd no intention of going. We tried to tell him it was a bad idea,' said Levin flatly.

'It was embarrassing. Yer man's shoving Eoghan out the door and he's babbling, saying that Panasonic runs surveillance for the US military.'

'It's true. They're a major tech supplier,' said Leon and then repeated herself shouting above the clanging of a pot falling down behind her.

'I looked into it,' said Daniel in his usual quiet tones. '*Curry's* have a bad record on labelling for energy efficiency. And problems with greenhouse gas emissions.'

Cat held the chalkboard close and marked up day 66.

Shay got up from his chair and raced after a plastic spatula the wind was dragging across the path. The afternoon sky was pale: the sun was peeking from behind clouds; light rain pushing into the marquee from the rising wind which beat, beat, beat on glum tents. Tall Paul sucked his cigarette. Cat drank her coffee. Shay tossed the spatula into the basin and rejoined them, soaked to the skin.

'Was Eoghan angry no-one else showed up?' asked Kiera.

'At first. Then on our way back to the camp he got really quiet,' revealed Padraig.

'Sure he sat here half an hour while we were talking

about how we spent Christmas Day. He didn't say so much as a word,' noted Shay.

'I think that's more terrifying. Mwah-ha-hahaha!'

Levin's brow creased. 'It's not like him.'

'We don't have to talk all the time,' said Cat.

Kiera tried brushing loose tobacco from her damp trousers, but in fact rubbed it into them. 'Oh! That reminds me. My parents and I had a big row on Christmas day.'

'What's strange about that?' said Padraig.

'They want me to spend more time at home. Sorry, Cat. You're on your own for a while. Unless you've someone to keep you warm?'

'Ah. No. No. I'll be fine. You'll leave your sleeping bags and blankets though?'

She nodded.

They sat in silence for a moment, and listened to the roaring wind and the cars rumbling by on the rain pelted concrete. Everyone had already complimented Cat on her orange hair and after the Boxing Day protest autopsy there seemed little more to say.

Eventually Levin spoke. 'Oh, thanks whoever gave me the book token through Secret Santa. I'll put it towards next year's studies.'

They looked down the path to where Eoghan was in a fight to zip up his flapping tent.

'Sociologists write big expensive text-books,' Levin informed them.

Eoghan – wet right through – sat down with them. A fly landed on his beanie hat and stayed there.

'I clean forgot about the *Curry's* thing. Sorry about that,' said Leon.

'That's okay. It's got me thinking.'

'What about?' asked Shay.

'About Anonymous showing up for the GA earlier in the week.'

Leon and Padraig shifted uncomfortably.

'It needed to happen. People felt strongly enough about it to make us take action.'

Levin glanced casually at the two culprits present and back to Eoghan. 'Aye but how they went about it was totally out of line.'

'There's no point trying to force something that no-one wants,' said Cat.

Eoghan nodded. 'Totally.'

Bronagh's car door slammed.

Full of cheer she recounted the events of Christmas Day. She said if the people who'd missed dinner at the camp had seen what they missed, they would wish they hadn't. 'Heaven help us, that weather's terrible,' she boomed. 'So how did this morning's action go?'

'So-so. It was a low key affair,' said Eoghan casually, slowly.

No one else offered a verdict.

'We'll make up for it on the Saturday march,' announced Bronagh

Leon chimed in. 'It's the anti-poverty demo.'

'Can I speak at it?' asked Fred.

Everyone began to laugh, except Eoghan, who remained silent and Fred, who lowered his chin into his chest.

'You?' Padraig balked. 'You're not serious?'

'I don't see what harm it would do,' said Levin.

Bronagh nodded. 'When you put it like that, none I suppose. Now! I need a volunteer to help me get those big tables out to the car.'

'I'll do it,' said Eoghan.

At the kerb Eoghan firmly gripped two folded tables so twenty five mile an hour winds wouldn't push them into the rear of the people carrier. Bronagh opened the boot and set to clearing away the clutter therein.

'I've been meaning to have a word, Bronagh.'

'Oh?' she replied, focussed on taking down the rear seats

to make room.

Eoghan raised his voice to be heard over the noise of the road. 'I know we haven't gotten along in the past. I take my share of the blame.'

She paused, only briefly, and kept her back to him. 'That's big of you to say that, Eoghan.'

'And I'm sorry. I think it might be better if we'd forget our differences.'

Bronagh turned. She didn't make eye contact, just took one of the tables from him. 'Hold that one a moment.'

'You've done a lot for this camp and I think I, and others could do more to involve you in the decision-making.'

When she did look at him, Eoghan had the second table raised. He slid it inside the vehicle, carefully.

'Okay Eoghan,' she said, and slammed down the lid of the boot. 'I respect when someone has the guts to say they were wrong. And absolutely, we could be a lot more efficient working together. Let's make more of an effort.'

He offered his hand and she shook it.

Later, Eoghan and Bronagh worked on compiling a new camp wish-list. It was extensive and more encompassing than any list before. Bronagh read it aloud at the evening assembly.

'... and plates, new roll mats, solar lights, sticky lights, a half dozen pairs of thermal socks, umbrellas, smokeless coal, blankets, rugs, rechargeable batteries and hot water bottles.'

'We already have some of those,' said Cat, her arms wrapped around herself, shivering in the fluctuating gale.

'It's always a good idea to have more. What doesn't come in through donations we can get from the pound store,' said Eoghan.

Fred looked around at the bored faces. 'Well, I think it's a good idea to stock up.'

'The point of reading the list is so we don't have to hear people say they weren't consulted,' said Bronagh and took a swipe at the billowing wood smoke.

They rushed through the agenda together: making arrangements for a substitute printer, organising who would be on night-shifts and how to get new life into the media team.

'I've been on the media a while. It's time I got access to the email account,' said Padraig.

'Uh, no?' said Leon. 'N-O.'

Bronagh asked, 'What's the problem, Leon?'

'Well no offence, Padraig, but you've been a bit of dick on Facebook. If you can't be trusted to speak for us on there, you can't be trusted to manage the emails.'

'No offence, but *you're* a dick on Facebook,' he replied in a squeaky voice, 'If you can't be trusted to speak for us on there, you can't be trusted to --'

'See he's at it again. That's trolling! And have yous forgotten all giving off about him putting up links to conspiracy theories? He doesn't speak for me!'

'You sound delusional,' said Padraig calmly.

'Facebook and email are two quite different things,' said Bart.

A few people nodded sympathetically.

'I'm sorry,' Leon said sarcastically. 'Do you remember last week when he asked someone on Facebook if their penis was too small?'

'I don't know, Leon. What about that incident with Anonymous? It was like yous were staging a coup,' said Bronagh.

'That got out of hand,' said Padraig. 'We didn't mean it that way.'

Bronagh looked to Eoghan for guidance.

'Maybe we can table the discussion for another time.'

'We'll have a think on it and come back to you,' said Bronagh.

Bob's concerns about the lack of space at the camp led to a lengthier talk about squatting.

'We're at the point where we need a permanent space with better facilities,' said Levin.

Leon quickly agreed. 'We've talked around it long

enough, and it's been done by many other groups.'

'I feel where-ever we choose should be prominent and centrally located,' said Eoghan.

'It ought to be accessible, and suitable for meetings and people living in, as well as public events,' said Bronagh.

'Levin has somewhere in mind,' Leon blurted out.

He glared at her. 'Actually I have quite a few places.'

Bronagh asked Cat to note down his suggestions but he already had a list: there was a five-storey block at the end of the street, built as a warehouse for *Eason's* newsagents, which later became a German restaurant; the old art deco *Northern Bank* building which sat on the corner of Waring Street and North Street; the *Nambarrie* building, also on Waring Street, just a few doors from the opulent *Merchant Hotel*; the old *First Trust Bank* on High Street which was a perfect office space; and the *Bank of Ireland* on Royal Avenue which was large and iconic and had lain empty for two decades.

When he was done Leon added, 'Those, and the dozen shops on North Street are just the sites a few minutes walk away.'

'It's a disgrace these places sitting empty with so many homeless,' complained Bronagh.

There was unanimous consensus for a small team to scope out the most suitable sites. Bart was very excited by this. Padraig voiced his thoughts that it would be a bit of a laugh. They agreed Levin would pick a team from the volunteers.

The wind speed dropped considerably by midnight though there was a light rain. Moths flickered around the street lights. Padraig and Leon's tempers had cooled. They were on speaking terms again. Padraig didn't bear a grudge though Leon was despondent. Bob barely said a word to them for a half hour, preferring to bury his head in the paper.

Levin came in off the darkened street, swinging a plastic bag, his face glowing with health.

'Hello my friends, hello,' he sang.

Bob put his head above the newspaper parapet and gave Levin a long, hard stare.

'Oh. I love the art college showers. Warmth flowing through every bone. All the sweat and stink of the city just disappearing.'

Bob dropped his eyes back into the newsprint and said, 'Levin, you don't have to be in such a bad mood all the time.'

Levin sat next to him and grinned. When mischief seized Levin he had the widest grin. Bob found it particularly irritating and Levin knew this. 'Ah, come now, Bob. Tell him Leon. Remind him how we're part of a global movement now rising up against institutional horrors.'

Leon shrugged, and brought out her tobacco. Levin saw her nonchalant expression, but he carried on talking.

'You've got the Spanish fighting off repossessions. Rupert Murdoch taking a bloody nose. American veterans trying to arrest Donald Rumsfeld...'

'Mwah-ha-hahaha! Did you see they raised a pirate flag over the Royal Bank of Scotland. Mwah-ha-hahaha! That was great!'

Bob shrugged.

'And whatever you think of Anonymous, when they hacked five hundred thousand from the accounts of the one per cent? Lockheed Martin, the Defence department... that's gotta sting,' said Levin.

Leon lit her cigarette. 'I don't know. There's bound to be reprisals.'

'You think so?' asked Padraig.

'The elites aren't going to let that go. They just double down. If SOPA or ACTA dies it'll just come back as something else.'

'I suppose,' said Padraig.

'This place might even be crawling with agent provocateurs before too long,' she said.

'Stop gurning,' exclaimed Levin. His grin was lit up by the flames from the fire. 'It's been a great year!'

Padraig nodded. 'These might be the last days, mind. 2012, the Mayan calendar and all that.'

'Still, I'm glad we can stop dicking about with the plan for the squat. When are you gonna tell them?' said Leon.

'Tell us what?' said Bob.

'Nothing. It's not important. But here, let me ask yous something. Did any of you find Bronagh and Eoghan agreeing with each other all through that meeting a little...'

Leon interjected. 'Creepy as fuck? Oh yes. God, yes. Finishing each other's sentences too.'

'It's good they've buried the hatchet,' said Padraig.

'Gives my eardrums a rest,' said Bob.

The side of the marquee flapped, hard, spraying them with rainwater. Levin brushed it off his face and sniffed. He reached into his pocket for a hankie.

Padraig got up to fill the kettle and the tent fold whipped again, and stung his cheek. He took the kettle and keg to the wall. The water glugged. The wind whistled and the temperature seemed to drop. He'd just set the metal grate over the fire when he heard a deep voice spring up out of the darkness.

'Good evening.'

'*Shit!*'

Padraig turned around to see Sergeant Barker and Constable Corbett looming over him.

'You bloody scared me!'

'That's how the wife reacted last time I worked overtime and forgot to tell her,' said Barker.

'There was a full investigation,' said Corbett.

'She made the Leveson Inquiry look like a pub quiz,' said Barker.

'Evening, officers. Everything quiet tonight?'

'Levin, isn't it? Yep. No incidents or accidents. Well... on the West Bank, there was a drive-by shouting,' said Barker.

Levin smiled. '*Half Man Half Biscuit*. You know your music.'

Cat climbed out of her tent with a heavy blanket

wrapped tight around her, looking mournful.

'Good morning. I hope we didn't wake you,' said Corbett meekly.

She walked right by the officers to a damp seat and began rolling a cigarette. Bob looked at the others, all as mystified as he, and looked back at Cat. She kept her stringy orange hair of head down until she'd sparked up, at which point she threw her head back and looked straight in front.

'Hello? Anybody in there?'

'I'm fucked off, Bob.'

'Anything in particular?'

'I'm going to fail my exams. And I'm out here catching pneumonia. God knows why.'

'Why is everyone so cynical all of a sudden?' Levin asked.

'You know you are all making a big difference being out here?' Barker said.

'How?' asked Cat bluntly.

'Crime has been way down in this area since you pitched your tents.'

'Really?' said Padraig.

'Homelessness too,' said Corbett.

Barker went on. 'And you're a damn sight easier on the budget than when it comes to policing the nutter twats.'

'Cat. If you fail the exam you can just take it again,' said Levin.

'I took my policing exam twice. And I've been serving on the force for twenty-five years,' Barker informed her.

Padraig counted out the date on his fingers. 'Nineteen-eighty... six?'

'That's right. I joined when I was eighteen. After seeing Robocop.'

Leon broke her silence. 'So we've made your job easier. Doesn't mean we like you. Not after what happened to Gary.'

'Inspector Tarbard's orders. But I am sorry about that,' replied Barker sincerely.

'Genuinely sorry. I felt awful,' said Corbett.

Padraig got up and went into the rear marquee.

Bob asked, 'When's Gary's appeal again?'

'January fifth,' Corbett answered.

'As the arresting officer, Tarbard is responsible for the paperwork,' said Barker.

'Great. Give him this,' said Padraig, and pushed a filled form 11/1 into Barker's hands.

'Except the bastard doesn't like paperwork,' seethed Corbett.

Bob studied Corbett: it was the first time he'd heard him swear, or seen him angry, and judging by Barker's expression this was a rare case.

'No, Barnabas Tarbard does not like doing it,' said Barker. 'And he should have thought about that before passing his paperwork off to Stan here. Well, good night, ladies and gentlemen.'

'Good night.'

'Be safe.'

'Take care.'

Before leaving, Corbett drew up close to Leon and whispered, 'Fuck the police.'

32

The following morning, Tuesday 27th, the southern winds relented. Regardless they still manically seized the camp and tossed it about. Alone in her tent, Cat shivered. Light rain splashed and streaked the sides and no matter which way she turned she always seemed to be too close to it. Shay was in the next tent over and she could hear him snoring. Beneath that were his earphones piping reggae, then folk, and sweet rhythm and blues.

Shay was dreaming of eating a full Battenburg cake. The magic quartet of colours propelled him to a new astral plane where a rainbow grew from a cloud and the cloud was hashish smoke and on the rainbow was Jimi Hendrix riding a guitar. But suddenly Hendrix was driving in reverse. And the spectrum of colours with him. Shay felt himself falling. He heard the zip in the air around his body and he saw the grey plateau of Writer's Square below him. Then he was in his tent, which was sliding along the top of a palette. Hands reached out for him and Shay curled into a ball.

'Fuck off, fuck off, leave me alone!' he called out.

Cat sat bolt upright. Through the canvas she saw two men lugging Shay outside in his sleeping bag onto the grass.

'Stop that!' shouted Daniel.

Tommie's raised voice, too. 'Oy! Leave him alone!'

'It's only a joke,' said Fred.

'Fucking dicks,' cried Shay.

'That's fucking bang out of order.'

'Mwah-ha-ha-ha, settle down, Tommie!'

'We were gonna put him in a different tent.'

'Aw, the state of his wee face,' said Padraig.

'You two get over here now,' barked Tommie.

Cat doubled up her pillow and pushed her face into it. She wanted to scream. Maybe, she thought, she'd freeze to death out here, and it would all be over.

Galway John thanked Bart for the tea. John had returned to Belfast on the first ferry, which docked at six, and had gone home for four hours sleep before getting out to Writer's Square. It made sense. He'd left his sister's home outside Dumfries at one in the morning to get to Cairnryan port. Fred wanted to know where he could find Dumfries. Galway John explained the Scottish town in terms of proximity to many places, only a few of which Fred knew. Bart didn't know any but made John explain them all. Bob cursed four times. He pulled back the partition and emerged a minute later with Galway John's Secret Santa gift: a box of five fat Hamlet cigars.

'Well here we are,' said Tommie, and he supped his tea. 'In five days time, it'll be 2012.'

'New Year's Eve is gonna be a frigging nightmare around here,' said Bob.

'End of the world, according to the Mayan prophecies.'

'Young Fred. Did I ever tell you about the time I saw a UFO?' asked Galway John.

'Oh here we go.' Bob put his hands in his wet face.

'Bright as day. Actually brighter than the day, for it was shining: amidst the summer blue skyline.' Galway raised his arm to demonstrate. 'We walked toward it, my friend and I, and whoosh! Just like that it crossed what must have been about a mile.'

He raised a cigar and simulated the acceleration.

Levin ducked under the canvas and joined them. 'What are yous talking about?'

'John got an anal probe,' said Fred.

'Ouch,' said Levin.

'Well if you're just going to mock...'

'Sorry, I wasn't making light. It sounds serious,' said Levin.

'Never mind,' said Galway.

'He says he saw a UFO,' said Fred.

'Where did you see a UFO?' said Levin.

'Bangor.'

'Why would a UFO go to Bangor?' asked Bob.

'To get to the other side,' said Levin.

'We watched this... it was a silver disc, in the afternoon sun. It hung there for about three minutes. Then in a blink of an eye, it vanished completely.'

Bronagh arrived at camp soon after, stepping out of the car at the exact moment Eoghan emerged from his tent. She wanted to make best use of her time before the college she worked at opened for a new semester. With help from Fred, Bronagh and Eoghan got cleaning the kitchen area and tidying the rear gazebo. A digital flyer had to be created for Saturday's march and Fred had ideas. Eoghan expressed an interest and the lads went off to the library together.

Bronagh returned about six thirty when the light had gone. The engaged couple had returned from Cork. They were perturbed at the sight of Bronagh and Eoghan, across the crackling fire, laughing and chatting with one another. Levin assured Mary and Joe the familiarity was genuine. He had dubbed the process 'Broghan.'

Mary opened a brown paper bag, a Christmas gift from a local art shop. It was a brooch in the shape of a butterfly with polished silver and red beads on the wings and a copper frame for the antennae. Joe had gotten a *Trocaire* gift card. He found a torch and ran the light over the inscription:

'*Education is the pathway to a better future, but many families cannot afford to send their children to school. Your gift of a school kit will send a child to school, pay for school fees, teachers' salaries and books and pencils too.*'

When he got back from the toilet, Eoghan shooed away a protesting pigeon and called the General Assembly to order. Bronagh, taking the role of the chair, clapped her hands for quiet. Cat shivered in the beige blanket and looked down to the ground. The first order of business was the posters for Saturday's events, which had gone missing.

'I will be happy to look for them,' said Bart.

'No,' said Bronagh. 'No. We'll have to go back to the printers. There's a backlog at the one a few doors down. Tommie, would you mind taking a walk up to Botanic tomorrow with the memory stick? I know it's a distance. Why not take Bart with you?'

Miriam and Jack joined the meeting and apologised for arriving late.

'Mwah-ha-hahaha! What did you two get up to? Some lesbo stuff going on?'

Bronagh rebuked him. 'Don't be rude, Padraig.'

'So? Are yous getting it on?'

Miriam's calm features creased up. 'Can a hot gay girl be friends with a hot straight girl without people assuming they're fucking?'

'You knob-end,' said Leon.

'Oh dear,' said Jack with a level of refinement. 'Prick. Tiny, tiny prick.'

Cat groaned. 'See? It's shit like this has me wanting to jack it all in, no harm to yous.'

'We've all felt like that at one time or another. But if that's what you want to do,' said Eoghan

'No-one will think any less of you,' said Bronagh.

'I understand. It is hard sometimes,' said Bart.

The rain dripped one drop at a time, like seconds on a clock. Bronagh swivelled around to Leon, sat under the soggy rope of the ruffled marquee.

'Now, Leon. Eoghan and I had a talk. We feel you're a bit too...'

'Spontaneous,' said Eoghan.

'You dive right into things without thinking,' she said.

'We felt that energy would be better poured into the legal team. Practical learning that could be useful for everyone,' said Eoghan.

'Right. Okay,' Leon said, barely sure she'd heard them correctly.

Eoghan picked up without missing a beat. 'Good. Now Gary's busier than usual meaning the Media Team is a bit light on bodies. Bronagh and I had some ideas --'

'No, hold on. I'll try to help Legal but I'm not coming off Media,' stressed Leon.

Eoghan thought it over. 'That's... okay? Bronagh?'

'Certainly. Just make sure you give Padraig access to the email account.'

'No! We've been over this!'

A few others raised objections as well, including Cat.

'The mailing list is tied to the email. Do we really want Padraig emailing out to four hundred people?'

Padraig gave a short shake of his head. 'Here we go again.'

Bronagh steeled herself. 'Need I remind you Padraig has been the only person regularly posting on Facebook over the previous fortnight?'

'Fine. Don't listen to me.'

'There's no need to be snippety, Cat. Padraig's been managing very well. Fred, you're good with computers, aren't you?'

'I'm okay. I know my way around.'

'And I hear Eoghan and Levin have been teaching you. Fred and Padraig work very well together. Don't you think?'

Eoghan looked uneasy but confessed, 'They've both attended a lot of the teach-ins. And Mary, Joe and myself are available and on board to keep them right. And Leon, of course.'

They took a vote. Most people felt if Padraig, Fred and Leon were prepared to volunteer for the work they should have the jobs. The motion was carried.

'You can see Leon after about getting email access,' said Bronagh.

Bob always got a migraine on Christmas Day. Usually it was a day-long affair but this year it persisted days later. He'd been asleep for three hours on Wednesday morning when the car doors banged shut and there were footsteps on the path. He heard people yelling and someone slapped the front of his tent hard.

'Do you mind?' bawled Leon.

'Fucking leave me alone,' screamed Cat.

'Piss off!' shouted Joe.

Bob's bones ached as he reached forward and unzipped the door. Daniel had his head outside of his tent too and Bob followed his gaze. Bronagh's people carrier was on the kerb. Fred was struggling with a busted up cardboard box of flyers. Padraig was walking tent-to-tent slapping the front of each one. Bob made eye contact with him.

'It's ten thirty. What's your problem, son?'

'Sorry Bob. Just trying to get volunteers. Go back to sleep. Joe, come on. We need help sorting out the supply tent.'

Joe sneered. 'Well if you want my help you could try not acting like the Stasi.'

From on up the path, Eoghan called out, 'Joe! There's no need for that.'

'Suck my dick,' yelled Mary.

Bob laid back down again. A half hour of on-site noise followed and so pushed him out of hibernation. He was met with the sight of Padraig emptying the black ridge supply tent. The items were laid out on the grass for Bronagh and Fred to sort: boxes and loose tools, a PlayStation, a CD collection and clothing.

'Get those firelighters in off the damp grass!' said Bob.

Bob found Cat in the rear marquee, making a cup of tea. The marquee was disorganised as well.

'What's the plates doing out there?' said Bob.

'I don't know. I didn't leave them out.'

'I didn't ask if you left them out.'

Cat put the teabag in the plastic bag on the railings and took the cup back to her tent. Bob caught sight of Bronagh, making her way to the people carrier. He called her name.

'Sorry Bob, I've got to run,' she called back. 'Padraig will fill you in!'

Bob watched her drive away and turned his attention to the mess outside of the supply tent. Fred was putting a few of the larger items back inside.

'Leave the rest of those!' shouted Padraig. 'We've to get to the library. Priority updates due!'

'In Heaven's Name!' Bob yelled. 'Are you just going to abandon the rest of this?'

'Sorry, Bob,' said Fred.

Padraig called out to Bob. 'It's digital cities. The worldwide movement. All that stuff!'

'You can't just leave this shit lying on the grass.'

'Ah, Filipe or Paul can put it away. What was that other thing, Fred?'

'Eoghan asked if you wouldn't mind chopping up palettes for sign holders? Think global, act local.'

Momentarily, Bob was lost for words. They were halfway over the pavilion when he called out after them.

'If you two are too busy to help, well, you can fuck off and not come back!'

Eoghan had found the missing box of flyers during the first wave of the supply tent purge. Bart and Tommie – at the printer's shop in Botanic – were not impressed when they got the call. When they'd gotten back to Writer's Square, Padraig had returned from the library in time to meet them. He'd assembled a half dozen occupiers to hand out the flyers around town. Cat was not pleased at having been woken from her sleep.

She lifted a pile of seventy flyers out of the box, all stuck together. 'They're fucking soaking?'

'There's about five hundred of them, Just take the wet ones off, mwah-ha-hahaha!!'

'Two hundred, three hundred…'

'The bottom of the box is damp,' said Levin.

Joe put his palm over his face. 'You're kidding me.'

'Jesus, Padraig! They're all soaked!'

'I didn't know! Tommie, you're going to have to go back to Botanic.'

'You what?'

'No!' shouted Bart. 'We walked over an hour there and back already. It is not fair.'

Tommie scowled. 'Waste of my fucking time, sunshine.'

'Don't shoot the messenger. I just assumed because Eoghan and Bronagh okayed it --'

'You just assumed. And none of you bothered to check? This is *some* bullshit,' said Cat, and she walked off to her tent, head held high.

Jack nodded. Mary threw up her hands and looked at Joe. Padraig ignored them and looked at Tommie; Tommie was fuming, so he looked at Bart instead.

'Look, I'm sorry,' said Padraig, 'but we need these flyers for Saturday. You understand that, don't you Bart?'

'I guess so.'

'Go see Fred at the library and tell him what's happened. He wanted to make some changes. Ask him to give you a memory stick with the updated file on it.'

Tommie wasn't having any of it. 'I'm on my feet most fucking days feeding this camp and you want me doing laps around the city on some nonsense. Well listen here Padraig…'

Leon sat in her tent looking out at the fire bin burning wildly and all the palaver around it: Tommie giving Padraig a piece of his mind; Mary and Joe walking away; Tommie storming off. Jack crossed the path and Leon noticed her hair had lost its stylised shape and her mascara was smeared. Bronagh's door slammed. She called to Jack who was ignoring her which was cause enough for one of Bronagh's mini-rants.

Leon heard sobbing from the next tent over.

'Go away, go away, go away.'

Leon whispered urgently. *'Cat! Cat!'*

There was no answer.

She put on her boots, all the while watching Bronagh and Eoghan enter the rear marquee. Padraig's back was turned and Leon scampered outside and around to Cat's tent.

'Cat! Are you okay?'

Again, no answer.

'I'm coming in,' she said.

Cat sat on her bum at the end of the roll mat, washed-out orange hair dangling over pale blue eyes with tired rings around them. Her skin was white and clammy.

'I wasn't spotted,' said Leon.

Cat flinched as Leon sat down beside her. But for that brief instance she didn't move.

'Cat. Come on.'

They sat in silence for a minute. Cat seemed to be somewhere else. Her cheeks were damp from the tears. Leon didn't like seeing her like this.

'Cat?'

'What?'

They'd spent over two months living together but weren't especially close. Leon struggled for something to say.

'We need you out there,' said Leon.

'I'm not,' she said weakly.

Cat shuffled forward, laid down and rolled on her side with her face buried in the pillow.

'Come on. There's new people coming in. Fresh new faces? And you're really good at outreach. Come New Year's nobody will care about any silly little factions which may have formed.'

'I'll just wait it out until then.'

Leon sat with her quietly for another minute. There was only the sound of the wind whistling and clanging outside.

'At least Kiera got out.'

Leon disagreed. 'All this backstabbing and blame games? It happens in any revolution. The only way we're going to get past that is with decisiveness. And we will. We'll seize the initiative and gain momentum. Next week you won't even remember I said this. You'll be in the thick of it.'

Suddenly, Bronagh called their names. Their hearts pounded.

She was at the door of the tent. 'Cat, Leon, could I have you both out here a moment?'

'No,' whimpered Cat.

'I better go and see what she wants. I'll be back to check on you later.'

She crawled towards the door. Cat lay, eyes shut, listening to Leon's long legs trailing through her things, and the opening and closing of the zip.

Leon found Bronagh smiling, her shoulders relaxed. Padraig stood with her, his hands on his hips.

'Eoghan doesn't remember the email login. What is it?' said Bronagh.

Leon brushed back her black hair. Behind them Mary – with two bags of crisps in her hand – crept back inside her tent. Leon pretended not to notice.

'I'm not sure,' she said, bluffing.

'She doesn't trust me.'

'Padraig, let me handle this. Do you think you could find out?' said Bronagh.

Leon laughed. 'You're gonna let him… send out his bullshit to our mailing list?'

'You see! You see how she is!'

'Don't be silly, Leon. This was the decision of the GA. I don't care whether you give it to Eoghan, Padraig or Fred. Please, just find it.'

'Alright! I'll have a look for it,' she said.

'Thank you,' said Bronagh, and she led Padraig back to the marquee.

'The hell I will,' she murmured.

33

Eoghan led the General Assembly dogmatically. The agenda covered the hunt for a squat, though Levin was absent. They addressed Tommie's tantrum, though he was absent too, and the flyer, which hadn't been printed. Cat chose to remain in her tent, putting the onus on Padraig and Fred to put out word about the carnival. To do so they'd need Leon to show them how to manage the mailing list.

'Right, sure,' she murmured, gazing down at the pigeon by her chair and its brittle orange legs. She quickly changed the subject. 'Weren't we going to do something about the troll situation?'

'I've been hoping we'd get around to that,' said Eoghan.

Bronagh explained, 'We're still having this issue with shit stirrers on the Facebook. Anonymoose. Sneaky Weezer, or Weasel, or something. Mr. McGinty.'

'Sneaky Weasel's not really a troll,' said Fred.

Leon nodded. 'Weasel seems to be on our side. It's Ginty McGinty is the problem. He's really out for blood.'

'He said Eoghan is a tinpot dictator and the camp is full of troublemakers,' said Bart.

Eoghan coolly flicked his cigarette ash. 'Let them do their worst.'

A pigeon picked around Padraig's shoes. He lifted a leg and the bird lifted too, before his foot came down noisily on the tile.

Bob was in a stinking mood. 'Can we talk about camp security? It'll be New Years Eve in a few days, and drunks and drug addicts roaming the streets...'

'In a minute, Bob. There's a lot of people missing tonight who should be here,' said Bronagh.

'I haven't seen Shay in a few days,' said Daniel.

'And where is Mary and Joe?' said Bart.

'They're doing a bed-in,' said Leon.

'Like a sex protest? Mwah-ha-hahaha!'

'They're keeping to themselves since that crap this morning. You're pushing them too hard,' said Leon.

'For goodness sake,' said Eoghan.

With bitter sarcasm, Bob said, 'Are you going to launch an investigation?'

'Okay Bob. You've made your point. Let's talk about security,' replied Bronagh.

Bob was concerned about the influx of new people: there was already no space for new tents. Fred suggested pushing all the tents into the middle of the site. Bob told him to leave the tents. Furthermore, the night watch were stretched thin. People sat up to three in the morning but no-one committed to the full stretch. They'd need a doubling up of manpower on New Year's Eve too. Eoghan asked Filipe if he was free, but he was working that night.

'Tommie?'

'Long shift that day. Count me out.'

'Paul? Paul?'

'Yer man's fast asleep, mwah-ha-hahaha!!'

'Maybe he wouldn't be if the GA didn't go on for three bloody hours,' said Leon.

'68 Days Occupied' read the chalkboard. West winds, twenty miles per hour, knocked it over. The bang on the concrete greeted Leon as she stepped into the muggy air and light, humid rain of Thursday morning. Fred's legs were hanging out of the front of the supply tent. Padraig stood above him tapping a clipboard and Daniel next to him, looking annoyed. The boxes were out on the moist grass again. Leon recognised them as her belongings from home.

'That's my bloody stuff! Could you not?'

Daniel said, 'I told them. Bob will have a fit too.'

'Don't get your knickers in a knot! It's going back in,' exclaimed Padraig.

Inside the marquee Bronagh was on a phone call. Eoghan was sipping a hot cup of tea. Leon asked if he'd seen Levin. Eoghan thought maybe he was looking at potential buildings. Bronagh finished her call, which Leon took as her signal to leave.

'That was Tommie. The printers have come through and we can pick the flyers up this afternoon. Would you like to come along for the ride, Eoghan?'

'Sure. Wait, there's Jack. *Jack!* Can you come here a moment?'

Jack had her muddied string laundry bag over her shoulders. When they tried to enlist her help she said she wouldn't have time to give out flyers on Royal Avenue with them that afternoon. She was on her way to the laundrette.

'Bronagh just put in a fresh load of laundry this morning,' said Eoghan.

'All you had to do was ask,' said Bronagh.

Jack kept walking.

Tommie and Bart's dirty laundry were among the pile collected by Bronagh earlier that morning when she sweet-talked them into returning to the printers. It helped that she gave them a ride there, but had called to say they'd have to make their own way back. They returned around eleven, and Tommie dumped the memory stick in Eoghan's palm. He told Eoghan his feet were aching, and he was due to begin his shift at *Brown's* at noon. He went for a brief lie down, not affording Padraig so much as a glance.

Bronagh stirred the pot of beans over the smoky fire. Bart was talking in her ear ceaselessly until Eoghan told him to 'put a sock in it.' There was enough noise around the camp and it would help if he wasn't obsessed with talking. Fred was shocked, even Padraig was a little surprised, but neither said anything. They ate lunch in silence until Levin and Leon returned.

'How goes the squat hunt?' asked Fred.

'Not so good,' Levin replied. 'I thought we might get into the *Northern Bank* building around the corner but someone's been in and closed the window.'

'Well, it was too exposed anyway,' said Bronagh.

'We do not need no trouble. You do not want to bring the cops down on us,' said Bart.

'Except for that blonde one. I wouldn't mind her going down on me. Mwah-ha-hahaha! Mwah-ha-hahaha!'

Leon got snarky. 'We're not idiots. And we're not shouting about it to every Tom, Dick and Harry.'

Levin opened his mouth to speak but Eoghan cut him off. 'We need somewhere that'll make a political statement.'

'But no breaking and entering. If you cause any damage, it's not legal,' said Bronagh.

Bronagh and Eoghan folded their beans into their toast at the same time.

'Well, there's still a few places to look at,' said Levin.

Bob woke up a few hours later and drank his tea. The marquee was unusually quiet: just himself and Fred, who was insistent about his idea to solve the overcrowding problem.

'I seriously think we need some of the tents moved around, Bob.'

'I heard you the first time. It's not happening until it goes through the GA. And last time, the GA told you to fuck up.'

'Hey! I'm only passing on what Eoghan said!'

Bob left his tea unfinished and picked up the axe and a palette. Ripples of a rising northern wind rolled over the camp, accentuating the weary cacophony of axe on wood. Leon and Bart arrived back, lugging ten litre kegs of water.

The door of Filipe's tent was open as he cut his toenails.

'This one will need fumigating,' said Padraig, making a note on his clipboard.

'Can I help you?'

'Filipe, isn't it? I'm just going around the tents. Are you in here on your own?'

'At the moment.'

'That's great. Whoa, pongs a bit. What it is, is I need to put one of the new people in with you.'

Filipe laughed. 'It's my tent!'

'I'll try to put you further down the list. No promises.'

'What is this? Bedroom tax?'

'Mwah-ha-ha-ha!'

Filipe pushed the trimmers down on a toenail. Padraig had escaped before the nail ricocheted to the door.

From the marquee, Leon watched as Padraig surveyed occupants tent-to-tent. She left the marquee and walked to Cat's tent.

'Cat, it's me.'

'Go away, Leon.'

She unzipped the front and crawled inside. Cat laid on her side, in the same position Leon had left her in the day before. Leon zipped up the door again and sat cross legged beside it.

'You know people are calling them *Broghan*? Eoghan and Bronagh? *Broghan, and the deputy dogs.* You know, because they're both easily distracted.'

'I don't really care.'

'We can't let them win! *Listen to me.* I near enough lived with Padraig and Fred. I know how domineering they can get. But they're also lazy shites. They're stretching themselves too thin.'

Cat rolled over and looked up at her. She'd been crying again.

'Padraig has an ego. His hubris will topple him. We need to stand up to him. And Fred? Well he just does what Padraig does. He doesn't even care about the politics. Not really.'

'Bronagh never liked me. I don't really care. But Eoghan? I thought he was my mate. He's not been by once to see if I'm okay.'

'Maybe he didn't want to bother you.'

'I can hear everything that's been going on. He's up his own arse lately.'

'Yeah, well…'

'Tell them I'm sorry. I really don't feel like going to the GA tonight.'

The blackness of charred wood smog hid in that night sky. Flies buzzed around the bin bag on the rails. Dishes soaked starch, eggy rice and meat bits in the basin. Something stank. A slimy snail crawled up the wall of the marquee. There were less people at the meeting that night.

Daniel vigorously rubbed a wet tissue against his shirt. 'We're running out of coal.'

Eoghan cut him off. 'Excuse me? Are you forgetting something?'

Daniel looked puzzled.

'We have a protocol. If you want to say something put it on the agenda or raise your hand.'

Daniel opened his mouth to laugh. Eoghan was serious.

'Eoghan's right, Daniel. These procedures are there for a reason,' said Bronagh.

'We can't afford to make exceptions.'

'Okay but —'

Eoghan raised his fingers in a triangle. 'Point of order. Or wiggle your hands with your thumbs down.'

'Mwah-ha-hahaha! Mwah-ha-hahaha!'

'This is daft!' exclaimed Leon.

'Are we being serious here?' asked Levin.

Fred pulled his tobacco baggie out and sat down.

'Come on,' said Eoghan. 'There's been plenty of meetings were people have been talking over one another and no consideration for another person's viewpoints.'

'Just don't do it again,' said Bronagh and she gave Daniel a large smile.

Padraig pointed two fingers to his two eyes to indicate he was watching him.

Bart was counting. '...seven, eight, nine. *There's nine people here!*'

'Where is everyone tonight?' Bronagh boomed. 'I'm fed up with it. Eoghan and I went to all the trouble of picking up the flyers and not one person has volunteered to hand them out.'

Eoghan nodded. 'There'll have to be changes.'

'I'm taking Bart to pick up his keys tomorrow and driving Padraig and Fred home to pick up their stuff. I expect everyone present to help Eoghan give out the flyers.'

'We all need to pull together. The anti-poverty march is less than forty hours away,' said Eoghan.

'Where are Mary and Joe?' asked Fred, innocently.

Eoghan grunted. 'I'm getting really fed up with those two refusing to make an effort. And Leon? Would you at least try to work with the new media team?'

'I gave them the password.'

'She did,' said Fred.

'No problem then,' said Levin.

'What about the mailing list?' said Eoghan.

Bronagh shot a glare at Leon. 'Most of Padraig's stuff is already moved. He can take a half an hour tomorrow and you can show him how it works.'

'I'm good with that,' said Padraig.

Leon scowled. 'Fine. Half three tomorrow. If it'll get the monkey off my back.'

Around eleven, Eoghan put his bum in the door of the tent he shared with Levin. Levin rolled around in his bag as Eoghan pulled his sweaty shoes away. He tossed his black jacket over the shoes at the foot of his roll mat and laid down.

'Bob just gets grumpier by the day,' said Eoghan. 'Did

you hear him? I don't think he'll be round to Bronagh's house any time soon.'

'I think I liked it better when you and Bronagh were at each other's throats.'

He seemed to be joking but Eoghan wasn't sure. 'Everyone around here has gotten so paranoid. Why can't they just get over themselves and work together? Ach, fuck 'em.'

'Oh… kay.'

'I'm not mad at you. You're the only one who's stuck by me.'

Levin laughed. 'That's not true.'

They were interrupted by Joe's yelling, a few tents away. *'Oh yes!'*

'Sweet fucking love!' yelled Mary.

Eoghan yelled back. *'Would you two pipe down?'*

'Easy, Eoghan. I think Padraig was joking when he said they were protest shagging.'

Eoghan wriggled into his sleeping bag. 'You'd think we were in the same tent. *Some of us are trying to get some FUCKING sleep!'*

Mary yelled back. *'You're a dickhead!'*

Eoghan whipped the bag back down his chest. 'Right, that's it. I'm going over there.'

Levin reached out his hand and put it on Eoghan's arm. 'If they see you're not bothered they'll shut up.'

'I guess so.' Eoghan laid back down.

'Could you not maybe dial it back some?'

'What do you mean?'

'Stop telling people what to do. You're only pissing them off.'

'GREAT. Leon's poisoned you against me,' said Eoghan bluntly.

'Calm down. There's no conspiracy. People have complained, but look at that as a good thing. They felt strongly enough to voice an opinion and that they could talk to you about it.'

'You want me to take Leon's side. Mary and Joe are right, is that it?'

'It's not about sides, just don't choose sides! Leon shouldn't be told she's alone to prove what she says against Padraig. And no-one wants to be speaking their grievance and not be taken seriously."

'I don't need this.'

'Just take a step back is all I'm saying.'

'Uh-huh. I don't want to have this conversation now. I'm knackered with all the work I've been putting in. Good night.'

'They didn't even go inside the factory grounds!' exclaimed Mary.

The following afternoon Leon begrudgingly accompanied Padraig to the computer suite in Central Library. She explained to him what a database was, where the information was stored and how to export it to *MailChimp*. The librarian came by twice to shut down Padraig's excited chattering. Leon got through the tutorial as quickly as she could and told him she was done. She moved to the next terminal and sat with her back to him, surfing the web for updates on the Vita Cortex sit-in. She checked in on the group in Cork. On Christmas day an anonymous donor had left the city's Occupy camp the keys to a six-storey vacant office block. It had previously been used by the National Asset Management Agency. Suddenly, Padraig cursed and lashed out at the keyboard. Leon kept her eyes on her screen. Padraig quickly got over whatever his issue was, reading and typing casually over the next twenty minutes. Leon was almost grinding her teeth when he got up and walked out. He'd gone to the toilet, she assumed. Leon glanced over to see he'd left his screen on, logged into Facebook. She put on her beret and jacket and stood over Padraig's terminal, wondering where to begin taking retribution. Her eyebrows climbed and then circled down, paying close attention to what was already on the screen.

Meanwhile gloom coloured the campsite and dull whacking thuds echoed on the path. Bob continued to work out his aggression with the axe, exploding palette after palette.

Daniel spoke to Levin with his usual calm and innocuous pitch. 'I could do without Eoghan. Leon would be useless. Kiera's too young and naive. Bart and Padraig are both noisy. Padraig would attract predators.'

Levin was annoyed. '*The idea of the game* is to say which of them you could live on a desert island with. *Not who you couldn't.*'

'That's what I'm saying. Bart's consistently noisy. Having him around might get us rescued.'

'It's a desert island. The point *isn't* to get rescued.'

Jack sat between Daniel and Tall Paul. 'It's not? That changes my choices completely.' She gave a loud sigh.

'I don't have to choose between Bronagh and Eoghan, correct?' asked Daniel.

'I'd take along neither,' said Jack.

Just then Tommie returned, a giant bag of coal on his back. A hole in the base spread shards upon the damp path. He slammed it to the ground in front of the marquee.

'I AM FUCKED OFF! *Carry ten kilo of coal, Tommie? Would you walk four miles to the printers and back for the sake of it? Oh you should have asked someone for bus fare from the kitty!* Fuck lot of use after the fact! And who cares if I'm on two warnings from work for doing all this?'

Slow-talking Tall Paul answered 'They're helping Fred move. It's not their fault.'

Daniel nodded. 'I sympathise. It's getting so someone is constantly telling you what to do and what not to do.'

'I agree. It's gone too far,' said Jack.

They heard a clatter of metal on concrete. Hulking Bob left a dropped axe and began to sway towards them. He bore his teeth. 'I spent an hour, an hour, the other night, arguing to leave the camp layout the way it is. This morning I hear from Fred they don't care what I say?'

He was ready to erupt when he was cut short by a shout from across the street, a track-suited baseball-capped man passing by. 'Here, what are yous protesting about anyway?'

Bob, Jack and Tommie turned, yelled as one, *'FUCK OFF!'*

Levin lowered his arms. 'Can we just remain calm?'

Tall Paul beside him looked sad. The rest looked at one another, too focussed on rage to see Leon cross the pavilion.

'Hey! Hey!' she cried out. There was a massive smile on her face.

'Where did you get to?' asked Levin.

'What is this? A police state?' said Tommie.

Leon replied, 'Back up, Tommie, back up. I was at the library with Padraig. And I found something very interesting.'

'I very much doubt that,' said Jack.

'At the library,' she said. '*Wait for it!* Padraig was logged into Facebook as... Ginty... McGinty. *Dun dun dunnn!*'

'Are you sure?' asked Daniel.

'I double checked when he was at the toilet.'

'I don't understand,' said Tall Paul.

Bob seethed. 'Padraig did what at the toilet?'

'He hacked into the site?' asked Tommie.

Leon tried explaining. 'He trolled us. Like what Bob does but without the charm. And using a fake name.'

'Padraig's been trolling us.' Levin threw up his arms. 'I guess if it had to be any one of us, it would be Padraig.'

Bob tried to wrap his head around it. 'Let me get this straight. Padraig's been telling these people on the internet we're wasters.'

'Yes, Bob. He's said we're all in little cliques, and fighting among ourselves,' said Leon.

Tommie shrugged. 'Well that bit's right.'

Noting Tall Paul's confusion Levin explained. 'Over the last few weeks Ginty McGinty aka Padraig has been mouthing off about us.' Levin looked around to Bob and Tommie. 'He's been having a spat with another troll called Sneaky Weasel, that's were a lot of this has come out. He's been saying things such as we're not doing anything useful here. I wonder, did this start as a joke? What the fuck? I honestly don't know.'

There was burning heat in Daniel's calm tones. 'Bronagh and Eoghan won't take too kindly to this.'

'Right. McGinty, Padraig, mentioned them by name,' said Jack.

'It'll not ruffle them. Padraig's practically their firstborn,' declared Tommie.

Jack shook her head. 'By name. He had a go at them, *by name.*'

A loud dull lurch and a thud on the kerb made Tall Paul jump. Bronagh's people carrier had climbed the pavement. Levin's heart pounded. They were still barely a moment, when Bob clapped his hands together.

'Right. Let's grass him up,' he said with relish.

'Hang on,' said Jack. 'It's not just Padraig who's at fault here. He wouldn't have been let to run riot if not for...'

Leon seethed. *'Broghan.'*

'This is new information,' said Levin. 'Let's think a while about how to deal with this. *Together.*'

'What, like a conspiracy?' asked Leon.

Levin hesitated. 'Yeah, okay. Something like that.'

Leon straightened her beret and her voice dropped to a whisper. 'Okay. Here's what we're going to do.'

Boxes in hand, Bart led Bronagh and Fred straight to the front door of *Shac.* They climbed the stairs to the third floor. The main room was similar to Nige's: a kitchen with table and beyond, a sofa by the window. They laid down their boxes and Bronagh threw herself on the sofa. Fred felt the upholstery. The sofa might be his bed for the coming months, better than a night in the rain. Bart put the kettle on. Fred had one more box to come up. Bronagh handed him the keys and he bounced into the hall and down the stairs.

He pushed open the swing door of Shac onto Donegall Street in time to see Levin, Tommie, Jack and Daniel shuffle into *The John Hewitt.* He called out to Levin, who briefly looked back. Fred looked at Bob and Leon under the marquee, shrugged and walked towards the people carrier.

The two-man tent blew around and above Joe as he read *Manufacturing Consent.* More footsteps passed their tent. Mary looked up from her medical journal as the zip at the door moved. A rolled up slip of paper fell to the floor.

Sat in her shaking light green dome, Cat blew a ball of snot into her tissue. She took another tissue from her bag, wrapped the first tissue in it, and dried her nose. When she looked up a curled shop receipt poked through the zip of her tent. She unravelled the paper. The message was scrawled in purple felt tip: 'Pub – Now.'

Fred closed the lid of the boot, locked the car, and took the box off the roof. Bob called his name, in a tone which made all Fred's hairs straighten up. The old man's razor sharp gaze was upon him and a fist was clenched.

'Leon's away working on one of your computery things and I'm not sitting. I'm going for a pint. Stay here with Paul and watch the camp.'

Fred looked at Paul: silent, subdued, more worn than usual. 'Sure. I just need to take this last box up.'

Bob watched him leave, and unclenched his fist, revealing a slip of paper with a message in purple ink.

'She could have just told me,' he muttered to Paul as he threw it into the fire.

Cat gathered the will to leave the tent and walk into the crowded bar. The evening diners were in. There were nine occupiers plotting in the bar's alcove. She pulled up an extra chair from the smaller table. Levin slid her over a half filled bottle of cider.

'Thanks. Who sent the messages?' she asked.

Leon gracefully raised her hand and Bob pointed his

thumb towards her. 'Underground resistance over there,' he said.

'I think we should invite Padraig over,' said Daniel.

'Why?' asked Mary. 'Are we blackmailing him?'

'I doubt he can explain himself,' said Tommie.

'We don't want to do this in public,' said Levin.

They listened a moment to the background chatter of the bar and the music. Bob recognised it as the title theme from *The Big Country:* a fast-moving orchestral score accelerating from quiet hope to energy and expanse. It didn't draw them away from tensely pondering the confrontation to come.

Soberly Joe said, 'There's the possibility Padraig is a long-term plant: working with MI5 to sow discontent.'

A minute later they were still laughing. Cat laughed so hard tears rolled down her cheeks.

'God, I needed that.'

'He's just thick enough for them to hire him,' said Leon.

Daniel slid his finger down his glass of water. 'Levin's right though. If you have a go at Padraig at the GA, then you'll put Eoghan and Bronagh on the defensive.'

'Right,' said Bob. 'Then everyone's at each other's throats.'

'Maybe they'll turn on each other. That'd put a stop to it,' said Mary.

Tommie grimaced. 'Fuck them. I'm sick and tired of them throwing their weight around. What do you reckon, Bob?'

'I'm looking forward to seeing that wee shit squirm.'

Leon put her hand up. 'Here's the simple answer: we boycott the GA. For tonight, at least.'

'General Ass-embly,' said Joe.

'I don't mean to be a stickler, but how can we resolve this if it doesn't go through the GA?' asked Jack.

Leon contended, 'It's already been established they won't listen to what the majority wants.'

'They have to know how upsetting it is,' said Daniel.

'I'm with Leon. Occupy The John Hewitt,' said Mary.

Elmer Bernstein's rousing *Magnificent Seven* theme filled the air.

The idea of boycotting the GA gained traction over the next ten minutes. Kiera joined the plotters then. She'd gotten a text from Leon to come straight to the pub. They brought her up to date.

'On your way here who was at the site?' asked Bob.

'The team who were giving out the flyers…'

Leon had been paying attention to the comings and goings that Thursday. 'That's Eoghan, Galway John, Deirdre, Filipe and Miriam.' She found Bob examining her, impressed with her recall.

'They're in the middle of dinner: Bart, Bronagh, Padraig, Fred, Paul and a few others. Everything seems calm enough,' said Kiera. 'So are we really not going to the GA?'

Levin sighed. 'I have to admit. I'm really not keen on going back there until these problems are sorted.'

'There should be a time limit on those meetings,' said Tommie.

'Christ, yes,' said Cat.

'There should be a safe word,' muttered Joe. 'Anyway, I'm going to the bar.'

A few gave him cash to fetch drinks.

'Here,' said Kiera. 'I'd go myself but I've no ID with me.'

'That's okay. Me and Mary can manage.'

Leon got snarky again. 'I expected this from Padraig. And Fred. Bell-ends.'

'Now Fred's okay,' said Levin. 'He's a good lad. But Eoghan's changed.'

'So has Bronagh,' said Bob.

'I think too much talking about people behind their backs is just going to add to the problem.'

'You were there, Daniel,' said Jack candidly.

Leon counted out the issues on the fingers of her right hand. 'Bossing people around about moving the tents; the mess with the storage tent; the mess with the printers; the dishes; the email...' Leon switched to the fingers on her left hand and continued. 'The mailing list; the wood pile; the coal pile...'

'That nonsense about moving the tents,' said Bob.

'Moving the tents...'

Fred entered the alcove. Everyone else fell silent. The music stopped playing. His eyes were wide, theirs were narrow, and they were all around him. The music began to play: Ennio Morricone's theme from *The Good, the Bad and the Ugly*.

'I was, uh, sent over to see if you're all coming to the GA. There's something important they need to discuss.'

'We're not moving the tents,' said Bob.

Fred scratched the back of his head. 'There's that and...'

'Spit it out,' said Tommie.

'I heard there was talk of action against Mary and Joe,' Fred confessed.

'For what?' asked Cat.

'Eoghan says they've not been helping the media team and they've been antagonistic? I think there's going to be a decision on whether they're allowed to stay.'

Cat's jaw dropped. 'Expulsion?'

'Not my idea. I'm totally against it,' insisted Fred.

'You must be fucking joking me,' bellowed Tommie.

Levin shook his head. 'Wait, Eoghan said this?'

'I can't remember who I heard it from. It might be just a rumour.'

Tommie pushed his hands into his temple. *'I'm going mad, I swear I'm going mad.'*

'Is Padraig over there now?' asked Bob.

'Aye, he's over at the GA with the rest of them,' Fred replied.

'He's a sneaky weasel,' said Bob.

The colour drained from Fred's face. 'A-a what?'

'I said he's a sneaky weasel,' said Bob casually.

'Puh-Padraig's Sneaky Weasel?' asked Fred.

'Bob, Sneaky Weasel's the other one. You've got them confused,' explained Cat.

'Sneaky Weasel's the one that trolls Ginty McGinty,' added Levin.

'Aye. Aye. Sneaky Weasel's the good guy. Always sticking up for us.' Fred tugged on his collar, feeling the heat of the crowded room, and the glare from Bob on red alert. His innocent mistake had flagged something.

'Padraig's been trolling us under a fake name,' said Jack.

'Padraig's a troll? God. That *is* a surprise,' said Fred.

'I'll bet,' said Leon sarcastically.

'Hang on. I think there's a few sneaky weasels around here.'

Levin looked at Bob and back to Fred. 'You mean...? *Fuck me.*'

Leon saw it too and pointed accusingly. 'Weasel.'

All eyes tightened on Fred. He was sweating profusely. He looked behind him to Mary and Joe standing right there.

'Just you take a seat, son. We're going to have a nice long chat,' said Bob.

34

'Bronagh, you had better sit down,' said Bob.

Eoghan lurched forward. Joe sat down, but not beside him. The other pub occupiers – there were eleven in all – took seats too. Fred sat, penned in by Tommie and Bob.

Bronagh shook her head and looked disappointed. 'If you're here for the GA it ended a few minutes ago.'

Joe glared at her. 'What was the decision then? Are you expelling Mary and me?'

Bronagh laughed. 'Nobody said anything of the sort!'

Galway John gasped. 'Who put this idea in your head?'

'Fred heard it from Padraig,' said Bob.

Padraig nervously pleaded. 'I didn't mean seriously! I just said people *might* have been thinking it!'

Fred gave Padraig a look like he wanted to punch him.

Bronagh whined. 'I'd never do anything of the sort! Are yous mad?'

Eoghan pressed his fingers together into a steeple and shot accusing looks at Bob, Leon and Cat. 'So you've all been plotting against us over... shit you think we *may* have said. That's your evidence: Padraig's imagination.'

Leon shot back. 'What do you expect when you act like a pair of slave-drivers? Putting these two arseholes in charge of communications?'

'Sounds very much to me like Padraig's not the one with the problem,' said Bronagh. 'Maybe if you'd actually come to the meeting...'

'Padraig's the troll,' said Leon.

'What?' said Eoghan.
'I'm not any fucking troll,' cried Padraig.
'I saw you with my own eyes,' said Leon.
'You're lying,' he said.
'I don't think she is,' Levin remarked.
'Ginty McGinty,' said Cat resolutely.
'This is bullshit!'
'Padraig, if you've done nothing wrong you'll sit right where you are,' Bronagh said.

Bob looked her in the eye. 'Fred has something to tell you too.'

The howling west wind, which had seemed to be blowing half the Cathedral Quarter into the camp, lulled just then – and a hush fell over the marquee.

Fred looked sorrowfully at the drizzled pavement. 'I was posting on Facebook as Sneaky Weasel.'

'Jesus,' said Eoghan.

'I didn't like all the shit we were getting from people like McGinty... him.'

'Wait a minute. You're telling me... let me get this straight in my head... Padraig is this McGinty fella? Padraig, is what they are saying true?' asked Bronagh.

'I was only having a laugh. Like a straw man. There's people on there have said far worse!'

Through gritted teeth Mary asked, 'Do you see anybody laughing?'

'You were laughing at me plenty, and you all treat me like shit!'

Bronagh seemed to leap out of her skin. 'Excuse me, excuse me. Who brought you to their house for dinner? Did your laundry? Helped you move?'

'I didn't mean you, Bronagh. It just got out of hand.'

'Why would you do this?'

'Nobody was taking me seriously. Taking the piss all the time. Sure I had to throw my weight around to get the ACTA protest happening.' His pleas did not alter the aggression of their body language. 'And there was all that dicking about in the lead up to the strike. And the mess with the Trojan interview!'

Eoghan was raging. 'Fred, you knew about this and didn't tell us?'

'I didn't know! Leon and the others told me!'

Bart chimed in. 'So, wait. Padraig and Fred were arguing online with fake names, and they didn't know they were arguing with each other?' He began to laugh and Kiera and Miriam joined in.

Tommie did not. 'Maybe you two would have noticed if you weren't so occupied sending me back and forward to the printers!'

Bronagh folded her arms. 'I already apologised for that.'

Tommie craned his neck. 'I'm disappointed. We're all disappointed, and fucked off with it to tell the truth, Bronagh.'

'Now, now,' said Galway John. 'Cool heads prevail.'

'You haven't been here for most of it,' said Cat.

'They've been carrying on as if everyone has to fall in line behind them,' said Leon.

Eoghan put his hands up and called for calm. 'I think everyone's thinking a little too negatively. Let's take a step back.'

'Nobody's saying what Padraig and Fred did was right,' said Bronagh.

Levin made eye contact with her. 'We talked this over. The consensus is we don't want these two on the media team. They can't be trusted to represent Occupy Belfast.'

Levin's remark cut and kept Fred awake on Bart's sofa for a few hours. He got up and looked out the window once or twice, down to the marquee were Galway John and Daniel sat on night watch. Padraig stayed in his tent: he wasn't willing to be subjected to their contempt. He drank, with the front open when he wanted a smoke. He could hear Eoghan talking to Levin, already blaming Bronagh for their decisions. It was bloody freezing. Padraig thought about going back to the flat but the meter was empty and the beds had been stripped bare. He mulled over using his phone to change the passwords on the media accounts.

Around three he went out for a walk: a lap through Corn Market to City Hall and back via Royal Avenue. Mary, Joe and Filipe had taken the second watch. He didn't acknowledge them. The walk didn't improve his mood much but it did help him sleep, eventually.

Levin got up around eight. Tommie had already relieved the night owls and Bob was unpacking cans from the standing shelf in the rear marquee: red kidney beans; tuna; value boiled potatoes and spaghetti. Levin joined him, hunting through supplies.

'Last day of 2011,' said Levin.

Tommie sighed. 'Thank fuck.'

'Where's the cereal?'

'You won't find any. Christmas foods all gone too. I'm making dog's bollocks,' said Bob.

'Huh?'

'Dog's bollocks. Cooking the scraps and odds and ends.'

Tommie – seeing Galway emerge from his tent – added, 'Or in Galway John's case, it's called an unidentified frying object.'

'New Year's Eve: the time of the crazies,' muttered Levin.

Galway greeted them with his usual unabashed cheer. 'Good morning, everyone. God, that's a miserable cloudy auld morning. Actually it's not good at all.'

'Wind's the same as last night. Just blowing the other way,' said Tommie.

'It'll be blowing both ways if we eat this shit,' said Levin dryly. 'Value boiled potatoes, from a can?'

'If it tastes wrong, this was John's idea,' Bob grunted.

'Ah. you're making Bubble and Squeak!' Galway exclaimed. 'Just how I showed you. Yes. Those potatoes are horrible. The magic is to cut them into small cubes and then they absorb the taste of whatever they're cooked with. Like tofu.'

'Levin, make yourself useful and chop up that garlic,' said Bob.

The fire smoke swirled into Tommie's lungs as he looked over the oscillating grey and green tents. Rain drops blobbed from the ash trees onto them. Eoghan's bum left his tent and then the rest of him. Tommie got out his tobacco. There was a nip left, tucked into the corner of the transparent bag.

'Good morning,' said Eoghan, muted; non-committal.

'Did you sleep okay?' asked Galway.

'No. Not really.' He pulled out his own tobacco. When he'd rolled his cigarette he turned to Tommie. 'I still think yous should have come to me and we'd have dealt with Padraig and Fred quietly.'

'You're missing the point, Eoghan. We didn't feel we could.'

'Well I've learned my lesson. Once the movement starts getting into petty factions that's when it all falls apart.'

Galway piped up. 'There's your New Year's resolution then. No more bickering.'

'That's all well and good John, except that's how this all started. It wasn't easy for me either you know: working with Bronagh.'

A few metres away the front door of Shac slammed shut. Bob put the frying pan on the grill as Bart approached with a spring in his step and waving the smoke away with his arms. Fred was behind him: hair a mess and eyes barely open. Bob began dumping the contents of the tins on the pan.

'Hey, everyone! How did you all sleep? Fred and I slept very well but he is a terrible snorer! What is that, Bob? I do not know if I want to eat that.'

Tommie scowled. 'Fred, where's my tobacco?'

'I'll go see my guy later. Soon as I get a shower,' he said.

'It is so nice to have hot water in my own place,' said Bart.

Levin added the garlic to the pan. 'Fred, would you pick me up some tobacco as well?' He brought a fiver out of his pocket.

Bob dumped more cans into the mix.

Meanwhile, Cat and Kiera were rising. Or trying to. The light green canvas punched Cat repeatedly as she crawled forward. The tent hammered blows on Kiera's head. Cat unzipped the front and punched their way out. When they got to the fire they found Bob stood over the pan with a bottle of oregano in one hand and cumin in the other. Levin sprinkled on paprika and ground black pepper. A big fly buzzed around it and flew to the far side of the pavilion as fast as it could.

Kiera screwed up her face. 'Looks disgusting.'

'Beg pardon, your grace,' said Bob.

'One star on *Trip Advisor*,' said Cat.

They took a seat beside Galway. 'Don't knock it until you try it, girls. Come on. Where's your sense of adventure?'

Cat sniffed. 'Accident and Emergency.'

'I'm really sorry about this last week and not being there for you,' Eoghan confessed. 'I shouldn't have listened to Bronagh so much.'

Bob ground the pan mix with a masher, and smacked the handle off the edge of the pan to shake the food mess loose. 'Levin, would you keep stirring that? Oh wait, here comes Padraig. He's good at stirring.'

Eoghan continued. 'In my defence, I didn't want to bother you with more work.'

'Same here, Cat. On the bright side all the info about the demo is already up on Facebook. That's done and dusted,' said Fred.

Cat nodded silently. Padraig took a seat next to Fred, who avoided making eye contact.

'I got a few posts up about it before you all ganged up on me,' said Padraig.

'You've only yourself to blame,' said Tommie bitterly.

'I don't even know why you're still here,' Cat told him.

'Please! Can we not start this again?' pleaded Galway.

Padraig put his hands in his pockets. 'Well you got what you wanted. Best of luck managing Facebook without me.'

Fred got to his feet. 'I'll take that shower now, Bart.'

Bart volunteered to boil his kettle, what with the pan taking up all of the grate. They left Padraig watching Bob crush used tin cans with his boot.

'What's with all the cans, Bob? Are we not hoarding them for 2012?'

'That's right. Midnight tonight and the Illuminati unleash their planet killer,' Levin quipped.

'Good. I'm looking forward to the coming apocalypse,' said Bob.

Eoghan began to relax. 'We'll all be eating brains.'

'That mess in the pan looks like you cracked open a few brains already, mwah-ha-hahaha! Mwah-ha-hahaha!'

The mix had fried into a hot, stodgy sauce. Levin volunteered to try it first. He poured a ladle's worth into a bowl, sniffed it, and had second thoughts.

Galway urged him on. 'That's survival food at its best.'

'Get the grub down your gub,' said Bob.

'A bit spicy. Mmm, not bad actually.'

Eoghan watched as Bob spooned out some for a taste. 'Well? Is it Hugh Fearnley Wittingstall or huge for yer shitting-stool?'

Bob pushed his bowl into Eoghan's hands. He threw his head away and coughed and coughed.

He got up and spat a mouthful of it at the fire bin. 'I'm okay! I'm okay!' he protested, but the coughing began again.

Galway got to his feet. 'I'll get you a glass of water.'

That afternoon, between forty and fifty people marched on Royal Avenue. The sun shone on the plastic covers of the baby buggies and the shivering activists were wrapped in hoods and scarves.

'Bring an end to Austerity!'

'No more people trapped in poverty!'

Fred made his way through the union reps and teachers. Shay had reappeared and he was in conversation with Levin, Tommie and Billy, the worker from the Salvation Army shelter.

'You want to stay away from that shit,' Tommie told Shay.

'People were worried about you,' said Levin.

Fred greeted them. 'Shay, good to see you again. Here's your tobacco, lads.'

'Thanks,' said Tommie coolly.

Fred weaved on through the crowd and reached Bronagh and Eoghan.

'Don't take that tone with me, Eoghan. I've spent the last few days helping those ones move house. I'm up to here with worry over Brian's job. I don't need this!'

'Stop over-reacting! All I was saying was you spent more time with Padraig than anyone!'

Fred inserted himself between them. 'Sorry I'm late. Who else is going to be speaking?'

'Miriam, though she's only just found out,' said Eoghan.

Bronagh turned her head. 'You really screwed us over Fred. All that Sneaky Weasel nonsense. I don't know if I can trust you and Padraig again. Is that Shay back there?'

At the gates of City Hall Eoghan used the loudhailer to rattle off poverty statistics in percentages. Miriam and Fred stood in front of him, looking back to the crowd: Leon, Bronagh, Cat, Kiera, Daniel, Filipe, the half a dozen Anonymi. Fred suspected Padraig was hiding among them.

'That's a total of seventy-nine percent in nine months. They said no more price hikes and made a big show of a thirty-seven percent reduction!'

'Eoghan's butchering it,' murmured Fred.

'I'm not going to do any better,' said Miriam. 'I've nothing prepared. I don't want to do this, to be honest.'

'Never mind that they'd been milking it at a forty-seven percent raise since the start of the 2008 crisis!' cried Eoghan.

Fred told Miriam. 'You can wing it, or not bother. Three speakers or two speakers, it doesn't matter.' He pulled his index cards out of his coat pocket.

'Wait. You're going up?' asked Miriam.

'That's what we decided.'

'They only asked me because they wanted me to fill in!'

Eoghan finished. The crowd applauded. Fred stepped forward and took the megaphone. The sudden move surprised Eoghan who wasn't sure where to look.

'What's he doing?' asked Leon.

Bronagh cried out. 'FRED!'

Fred put his finger on the trigger, and spoke. 'We're here today to talk about fuel poverty. The BBC put the gas rise at a cost to the average household of £580 more a year. That supposes the average household will be there to pay that.'

Leon was momentarily fascinated, as if unaware it was Fred speaking.

'No wonder the Consumer Council issued a warning. A thirty-nine percent price hike on gas. Thirty-nine percent! That's the same number as those in North Belfast *already* living in fuel poverty,' announced Fred. 'Last month the Department of Social Development said an extra fourteen thousand Northern Irish children were living in poverty in 2011.'

Galway's jaw had dropped. 'I didn't think he had it in him,' he murmured.

'Child tax credits, cut. Working tax credits, frozen. A three year housing market collapse and no new social housing planned. How long before these utilities companies push their own workers out on the streets? They say cut back?'

'We say fight back!'

'They say cut back?' yelled Fred.

'He's come a long way,' said Levin proudly.

'We say fight back!'

35

An hour later Writer's Square was hosting the year's last Carnival of Resistance. Though the campers were wrapped up and padded with insulating clothing, a ghoulish air blew through their veins. Cat and Kiera opened the supply tent to retrieve the packed away gazebo. Bob came off his seat and swatted them away from it.

'No you don't. Not after all the fiascos last week.'

'We need the gazebo,' insisted Cat. 'For painting the kid's faces?'

Kiera pushed forwards. 'We'll have it up in no time,' she said confidently.

Bob blocked her. 'I'm bloody sure you'll not. I'll set it up. Properly.'

He pulled the bag and poles out to the pavilion. When he was gone from view, Kiera raised her hand and Cat gave her a high five.

Cat adopted a superior air. 'No heavy lifting for us.'

In five minutes the gazebo was standing. Under the weak sun, light rain popped on the gazebo roof. Kiera laid out the pens and paints on the table and began painting the first child. Cat called in to the marquee and asked someone to make up a jug of orange juice.

'Sure. But I'll go shortly. I want to search for buildings while there's still daylight,' said Levin.

'I'd help but I have to get on my bike,' said Deirdre.

'Where are you going?' said Padraig.

'I have to get away through the green-way to discuss

mortality with Amy from Amnesty. A great woman with a plan. She's come up from Strabane.'

'Ah, right,' Padraig replied. 'Well happy New Year!'

Padraig joined Levin in the rear marquee, items rattling as they searched for the juice jug.

Cat returned. 'Is the juice ready yet?'

Padraig pulled back the partition and pushed a stick of chalk into her hands. 'Day seventy at Occupy Belfast,' he said.

By the Spanish volunteer bust, Bart hunkered down outside Shay's tent. Shay wasn't in the mood to join the festivities. Bart played his new harmonica: caterwauling at first and then more clearly a version of *When the Saints go Marching In*. Shay was eventually lured out, bringing his tin whistle with him.

At the planters facing the marquee, people congratulated Fred on his speech.

Leon was enthusiastic. 'I guess I underestimated you. You did really well.'

'I thought you were going to get up there and slag us all off but what you did was magnificent,' said Eoghan. 'I think we should be getting you back on the media team. How about it, in a week or two when the dust clears?'

Fred was happy with that and they shook hands.

'You lads, get over here!' yelled Bob.

Eoghan and Fred crossed to the wall of the Shac flats where Bob had assembled Filipe, Tommie, Joe and Galway John, all shoulder-to-shoulder in a line.

Leon, now in the marquee, yelled, 'I know they misbehave but the firing squad's a bit much!'

Bob ordered them to, 'Listen up! It's New Year's Eve so we're doubling the night watch. I want yous scrutinising every detail tonight. Eyes on the tents and the road at all times. A stray firework could have this entire camp up in flames.'

'If you can't see round corners you'll be busted down in rank!' Mary heckled.

Two pigeons circled one another by the edge of the pavilion. On the pavilion wall, Padraig found himself blowing up balloons.

Jack said, 'All that hot air has to be good for something.'

Bronagh was sitting further along the wall, chatting to one of the parents, when a black shape accelerated towards her. The dog threw it's sixty pounds of weight into her arms.

'Goodness gracious, where have you been? Aw yes, you remember your Auntie Bronagh, don't you? Don't you?'

Shelby pawed at her knees, and got a foothold with which to lick her face. She ran her hand over his head and rubbed behind his ears. Bronagh pushed him away.

'Sit! SIT! Tommie, look who's here! Sit!'

Tommie had seen him coming and knew exactly where to find the green rubber ball Shelby loved. He held it high and Shelby jumped up excitedly. Minutes later, Shelby ran back across the pavilion into the welcome of a family of three. He dropped the ball at their feet and a young lad picked it up. Shelby left with them.

'They grow up so fast,' said Tommie.

Fluctuating wind pushed into the metal bin, billowing smoke into the night air. It turned direction, forcing smoke into the lungs of random new victims. There was a strong turn-out at the general assembly: twenty-seven people, coats wrapped stiffly round them. Cat officially welcomed a new camper, Petrus, and he got a round of applause. There was consensus the march and carnival had run smoothly.

'Perhaps now we can put yesterday's ugliness behind us,' said Bronagh.

Leon put her hand up and Bronagh sighed.

'The New York camp are planning on re-taking Zucotti Park at midnight.'

'I saw that. We'll want to get a message of support out,' said Eoghan.

'Kiera, that's my rollie,' said Shay.

'I rolled this. Yours is on the ground.'

'I'll tell you what's worrying me,' said Bob. 'Take a look over there. We're at capacity. You couldn't get another tent in that patch of grass if you tried.'

'Well, we might see a drop off in the winter: more space becoming available as people leave us,' said Galway.

'Maybe people can double up,' suggested Bronagh. 'Off the top of my head? Padraig, Shay, Leon and Filipe all have space.'

'I've half my house in there!' said Padraig.

Leon nodded no. 'I'm not keen on on sharing with a stranger.'

Shay shrugged. 'I don't mind.'

'What about the supply tent?' asked Bronagh.

'Absolutely not. No way,' said Bob.

Tommie was sat beside him. 'We don't want to be putting people we don't know in with the supplies.'

Bronagh's voice raised in pitch. 'Well I'm not taking them. I'm not a half-way house!'

'You're always going on about who you're bringing home to look after,' said Eoghan.

'Who I have in my home is entirely my business.'

'Yes. And we all know who's welcome and who's not.'

Cat threw up her arms. 'Everyone, please. Let's give it a rest.'

'No, Cat. I want to hear this. What exactly are you saying, Eoghan?'

Kent Street was more of an alley than a street, mangy and mostly bricked up. There was a street light illuminating the grille gate, and the sliding handle which opened it with ease. The concrete path was eight metres to the door, darkening under the metal stairs of the fire escape. Levin slid his fingertips along the edge of the door. He worried someone had locked up after his visit four weeks before, but the door came open.

He looked back quickly to the dimly lit street, and then stepped inside. With the door closed behind him Levin took out his phone to illuminate the cold, dark basement.

The branches of the ash tree jerked nervously in the rough wind and rain pounced upon the marquee. Galway John held his hands up and appealed for calm.

'Now, come on! We can discuss this calmly. If we're to solve the problem of space, we should hear from the construction team.'

Bronagh cut him off. 'No, John. I'm not going to let this go. I've done more for this camp than him, more than a lot of people.'

Eoghan shot back. 'I've been here since day one. A lot of us have. Yet you just swan in, taking charge. But to hell with what other people have done!'

Bronagh fumed. 'I'm not gonna sit here and take this.'

Cat screamed. *'I'm sick of this: playing favourites; turning people against one another! Stop it!'*

'It's not going to fly Eoghan.'

'You, Bronagh! I'm talking about you,' yelled Cat.

Bronagh got to her feet. 'After all I've done. Washing and cooking. Cleaning. Giving people a break. You forget about all that, didn't you, the pair of you!'

Galway John got up too and put his hand on Bronagh's shoulder.

'Get off me, John.'

'This is silly,' he said.

'I think people should calm down,' said Bart.

'Agreed,' said Daniel.

'Sure, 2012, we're preparing for reptile rule and the new world order. Mwah-ha-hahaha! What does it matter anyway?'

'Your laugh is very annoying,' said Bart.

Bronagh clawed at her handbag. 'I don't need this. I'm going to the pub and anyone else who's sick of this is welcome to come with me.'

Leon was furious. 'Oh, here we go again. Oh, the poor victim!'

Padraig glared at her. 'Leon, fuck up. All you ever do is stir the shit, and it's me gets the blame for it.'

Tommie groaned. 'This is ridiculous.'

'Sickening,' said Bob.

Padraig got to his feet too. 'Yeah. I call bullshit. Are you coming, Fred?'

'I'm staying right here.'

Bronagh seethed. 'Eoghan, you claim to speak for all of us like butter wouldn't melt in your mouth. Now I see you've poisoned Leon and Fred against me: they're young and vulnerable enough not to know any better.'

'Aye, I'm the great puppet master. What about Shay? He was so sick of your carry on he went to the homeless shelter!'

'Leave me out of it,' said Shay.

He got up and walked back to his tent.

Levin passed an old empty lift shaft full of exposed wires and rubble. He began to climb the stairs, increasingly aware he was alone in this quiet, opulent building. A step cracked under his weight. He instinctively took hold of the hand-rail, which wobbled as if it would come loose. He kept the torch trained on the steps in case of more surprises. On the first floor there was a large raised concrete platform to the right. The brick and flooring were cracked and the air dusty and dirty. He backed up and made his way to the front of the building. Four pillars were spread across the bay room, lit in gold from the street lights on Royal Avenue. Though sure he'd not be seen at this height, he navigated the edge of the room carefully. Turning right on the second floor he found a back corridor were the air was chilly. It led to a few smaller rooms with open doors, perhaps managers' offices.

Bronagh and Padraig were on their feet and Eoghan and Tommie as well, with Galway John stood between them.

Joe lurched forward in his seat. 'Would you all stop shouting and calm down?'

'Bronagh, stay. Please. We've lots to get through,' said Miriam as diplomatically as she could.

Tall Paul's eyes watered. 'What's going on?'

'I don't understand,' pleaded Bart. He was hurt and seemed to be taking the argument personally. 'What has this got to do with me?'

'Are yis done yet? You selfish bastards. Bronagh, will ya sit down?' said Bob.

'You're acting like infants,' said Kiera.

Bronagh rounded on her. 'What would you know? You're only seventeen. When you reach my age perhaps you'll be wiser.'

'You're old enough to know better,' said Fred.

'Seventeen? And you had me buy you drinks and lied to my face about it?' said Bob.

Kiera made more of it than she should have. '*Oh, lighten up!* How exactly did you think everyone got released from Musgrave? They were interviewing a minor without permission. See if that doesn't come up in Gary's appeal! And we all know you weren't at Vita Cortex.'

Wood fire smoke flared around Bronagh's nostrils. 'And you, Leon. Eoghan told me all about your letter to Unite about occupying Transport House!'

'We were off our faces!'

'Who was off their faces?' said Tommie.

'Me and Shay. We thought it'd be a good idea,' said Leon.

Bob exploded. 'Drugs? You brought drugs into my camp?'

'Breathe Bob, just breathe,' said Mary.

'That's it. If she's staying, I'm leaving,' said Eoghan

Tommie shook a finger at him. 'Oy! Wise up!'

'Oh come on! This is my home,' said Daniel.

Bronagh zipped up her jacket. 'If you got rid of Eoghan you'd all be better off! Think about that.'

'Aye, Bronagh, aye. Maybe when you're at the pub you can plan an anti-eviction campaign,' said Cat.

Leon laughed. Eoghan began laughing too. Bronagh lunged toward him. Galway reached out and caught her arm, Bronagh's back-hand accidentally smacked his face. It stung but he didn't flinch. Unaware of what she'd done, Bronagh wrestled her arm loose. She faced the marquee, tears running down her cheeks.

'John, you're wasting your time. Eoghan and Cat and Leon, they only care about themselves. Bugger everyone else!'

'Dickheads,' said Padraig.

She turned away and Padraig put his arm on her shoulders as they walked down the path. Bob, Daniel and Tommie got up and followed them.

Tommie looked back at Eoghan and Leon with a scowl. 'Real classy.'

'Ach, what next?' asked Fred.

Fireworks lit up the grey canvas of the tent. There were boots, always people walking by, but they sounded louder now. The occupier turned over in bed, still wearing a coat and thermal cap, too close to the cold ground not far below. Car horns blasted out short tunes. Drunks were fighting. The camper forced their way to sleep amid the flashes and bangs. The mind swirled with paranoia and the smell of damp and smoke. They heard their own low snore and felt the absolution of rest, daring to dream of a better future. Then there was a sharp kick to the tent. The camper lurched forward, the mat sliding under them as they did so. The whole of the tent shook: their clothes, towel, and shoes. The roof overhead spun and seemed to collapse.

Levin lingered at the front bay area. This room needed a big brush and shovels and a few days of people painting. The bays were over fifteen metres long and almost ten metres wide: each large enough for an event holding up to two hundred people. He thought about how one bay room could sleep as many as were at the camp site. He followed the steps down into the basement and opened the door into the yard. New Year's celebrations afforded him the cover to pass the front of the building on Royal Avenue unchallenged. *'Bank of Ireland'* was engraved above the three ornate green metal-framed windows and again on the corner steps at the junction with North Street. Levin had read the four-storey art deco structure was built at the end of the twenties and modelled on the Empire State building. He knew already, before he stepped back, and studied the limestone carvings, the rising tower and the clock set to six. He knew time had come, time to occupy.

ABOUT THE AUTHOR

Andy Luke is a multi-disciplinary artist based in Belfast, Northern Ireland. He holds a B.A. (Hons) in Education, Media and Social Sciences from Oxford Brookes and is a former member of the Occupy Belfast camp. His work in comics includes the critically successful 'Gran', the UnLtd Award winning autobiography 'Absence: a comic about epilepsy' and 'Bottomley' from the Eisner nominated 'To End All Wars' by Soaring Penguin Press. He hosted and co-produced Northern Visions TV's acclaimed documentary on the history of Northern Irish comic strips, 'The Invisible Artist'. His prose works include 'Axel America and the US Election Race', 'Spide: The Lost Tribes' and the Patreon exclusive, 'Thor's Day in Juno'. His poetry appears in 'Chaos Magic: Collected Poems 2011-2020' with a second compilation forthcoming. He produces audio essays in the form of 'The Drew and Look Podcast', one of four monthly 'things' at his micro-subscriber platform, https://patreon.com/andyluke

Acknowledgements

So, you occupied this long book: well done! No Pasaran! Stick with me for a few more pages while I tannoy tribute to some of our other comrades. Editing is the bulk of writing so Claire Burn can be considered a co-author as well as a first reader of this tale. Her DNA is all over this book. Claire's diligent input made it into this novel in every way from corrections to courses of our cast. Her notes made me think, wise up, laugh and steal. This book's for you, bud. I'm extremely grateful. A less difficult and less lonely journey because of you.

Our weekly writing group reviewed, edited and discussed chapters 4-10. They critically savaged it and so made it much better. As with Claire, their feedback made for incisiveness, suggested extended scenes and greater coherency. I'd like to thank prolific Peter Drysdale, our Greg Davidson, Bruce Logan and Mr. Chris McCoy, who played a key role in the decision to include a glossary. Thanks also to part-timer Heather Alexander for 'playing Leon' in workshopping the difficult scene with Bob in chapter 8. Thanks also to Kate Rizzo at Greene & Heaton literary agency for reading earlier drafts of chapters 1-3 and for the detailed discussion that followed. Their encouragement was felt.

Occupied's origins sprang from our first writer's room around that smoky fire bin in 2011. Scenes and lines of dialogue survived from our imaginings then. I am indebted to former members of Occupy Belfast who – after I began writing in 2014 – agreed to be interviewed about their memories of the time: Monty, Kevin McNicholl, Eoghan Ward and John Wright shared valuable insights and tales, many of which made it into the book. Thanks also to Joel Auld for answering questions later in the process. Indispensable. Thanks to St. Anne's Cathedral, Belfast for answering my queries over Facebook. The cathedral doesn't actually have bells. Unless in your head canon they do.

The book's cover designer is Katarina N. Katarina delivered on time, to description and the addition of the Belfast skyline in the backdrop was all hers. You can see more of her work at https://www.fiverr.com/nskvsky

This wouldn't have been possible without the monthly support of my patrons: the inestimable Artemiy Kondratiev, my Leo – Arsalan Haider Ali, Michael 'NinjaBear' Daly, Ian 'Layin Down The' Lawther, Benjamin Benchilada Stone, James Gumble of XPand, 'Dancing with Lunacy' Linda Harley, Peter Duncan of 'Splank!', the cerebral letterer John Robbins, Andrew Bolster, gentleman David Annette, Michael Duckett, Richard Huang, Mr. Phil Weir of Flax & Teal, Neill Stringer, Johnny Porter, The Alan Rowell, Bob McCullough, Claire Burn, magical Aoibhinn Nic Aoidh, Dave Cromie, Silas Rallings, Zoe Gadon-Thompson, Ljerka Jemric, Richard Barr and Jessica Odell. Patreon is how I put food on the table and all these people are responsible for my opportunity to be an author of fiction and making that a viable thing. That's https://patreon.com/andyluke

To everyone who supported us at Occupy Belfast during our year-long campaign, I thank you. You kept us supplied with blankets, food, chat and love. Thanks to other members of the Belfast movement I didn't mention yet, many who patiently answered my queries: Terry Williams, Kelly, Steph and Ryan Barnes, Sadie Fulton, Gerry Carroll, Claire Heaney, Hanita Dadswell, Katie Jones, Katrina McKee, Bart Karpinski and Cara Dixon. Dedications to our dear Barry, Dee and Michelle, those no longer on this plane and greatly missed. And to Mick, our camp's security man: paternal, grumpy, funny and wise. These people aren't those depicted here but times spent with them - and those whose names I can't recall - made for the love put into this. Some of their names are listed in chapters 18 and 24. Thank you to those who were part of groups all around the world, and to the community, 'Support the Vita Cortex Workers.'

Gratitude to my personal assistant Kateryna Kyselova for help sorting my trafficked brain into a coherent schedule. Kateryna also mock interviewed me for practice in promoting the book and for realsies for an episode of The Drew and Look podcast. Her judgement and friendship proved valuable.

The plot's framework structure was sourced from global news down to local group events. These are largely accurate in the chronology. A notable exception are the arrests depicted in chapter 24. These occurred on 9th December 2010. The court sentenced ban of Gerry Carroll's rights to protest in the city centre occurred 2010-2011 and not 2011-2012 as suggested in the fate of Gary Carell. For shedding light on this chapter, thanks to Sadie Fulton for her personal perspective on the arrests and Claire McNeilly of the Belfast Telegraph in her interview with Gerry Carroll in October 2017.

Chapter 18 contains extracts from the live broadcast of Country Céilí, a radio show on Downtown Radio transmitted late November, 2011. These appear with permission and blessing of host Tommy Sands and courtesy of Downtown Radio and producer Stuart Robinson. Thanks to Tommy for his kind words and encouragement regarding the book.

The Stormont Parliament fracking debate in chapter 22 uses the Official Report (Hansard) for Tuesday 6th December 2011 and contains Parliamentary information licensed under the Open Parliament Licence v3.0.

Snippets and named tracks of the playlist: "A Hard Rain's A-Gonna Fall" by Bob Dylan (Columbia), "Milkman of Human Kindness", "Help Save the Youth of America", "There is Power in a Union" by Billy Bragg, (Elektra/Rhino) and "Never Buy The Sun" (Bragg Central Ltd), "Roll Over Beethoven" by Chuck Berry (Chess Records), "Ghostbusters" by Ray Parker Jr. (Arista), "Oops!...I Did It Again" by Britney Spears (Zomba), "E.T." by Katy Perry ft. Kanye West (Capitol/EMI), "19" by Paul Hardcastle (Chrysalis), "Faith" by George Michael (Columbia/Epic), "The Stripper" by Daniel Rose (MGM), "House of the Rising Sun" by The Animals (Columbia/MGM), "There Were Roses" by Tommy Sands (AMIGA), "Behind the Barricades" by David Rovics (AK Press), "We Will Love or We Will Perish" by Pete Seeger (Appleseed), "Your Daughters and Your Sons" by Dick Gaughan (Rounder), "You're the Voice" by John Farnham (Sony BMG), "Dancing Queen" by Abba (Polar Music and Universal/Union Songs), "Breaking News" by Half Man Half Biscuit (Probe Plus) and "Where did you sleep last night?" by Leadbelly (EMI). These are acknowledgements and any extracts appear briefly under fair use without copyright infringement.

For their encouragement along the way my friends who I've not mentioned: parents John and Marilyn Luke for keeping me afloat in rocky times, Belfast blogger supreme Alan Meban, gallery curator Frankie Quinn, Bronagh Lawson for helping me shine, the artist Suzanna Raymond, Dave Cromie at Nerdgeist, Valerie Moss, Dr. Chris McAuley for his counsel and of course Dundas Keating for pizza, jobs and boisterous rebellion. Thanks to everyone at Farset Labs makerspace for letting me get my work done. To Andrew Gallagher, the editor on Axel America, who trained me up to a solid foundation in the art of editing. To Paul Maddern at the great River Mill for writing retreats, and Mary Smyth and Angela in Limavady for space to edit. Those who were there when I was down and out: Hitesh – my Boone, and Jeremy, Damian and Arsalan.

A lot of time thought and effort went into publishing this text. My thanks to all those who 'pay it forward' by helping make the book go further by leaving a review anywhere it'll be seen.

¡No pasarán!

Andy Luke
Belfast, Late 2021.

Printed in Great Britain
by Amazon